About the Authors

Kim Lawrence was encouraged by her husband to write when the unsocial hours of nursing didn't look attractive! He told her she could do anything she set her mind to, so Kim tried her hand at writing. Always a keen Mills & Boon reader, it seemed natural for her to write a romance novel – now she can't imagine doing anything else. She is a keen gardener and cook and enjoys running on the beach with her Jack Russell. Kim lives in Wales.

Amanda Cinelli was born into a large Irish-Italian family and raised in the leafy green suburbs of County Dublin, Ireland. After dabbling in a few different career paths, she finally found her calling as an author after winning an online writing competition with her first finished novel. With three small daughters at home, her days are usually spent doing school runs, changing nappys and writing romance. She still considers herself unbelievably lucky to be able to call this her day-job.

Brenda Jackson is a *New York Times* bestselling author of more than one hundred romance titles. Brenda lives in Jacksonville, Florida, and divides her time between family, writing and travelling. Email Brenda at authorbrendajackson@gmail.com or visit her on her website at brendajackson.net

Passionate Encounters

Passionate Encounters
Risking It All

KIM LAWRENCE

AMANDA CINELLI

BRENDA JACKSON

MILLS & BOON

First Published in Great Britain 2022
by Mills & Boon, an imprint of HarperCollins*Publishers* Ltd,
1 London Bridge Street, London, SE1 9GF

www.harpercollins.co.uk

HarperCollins*Publishers*
1st Floor, Watermarque Building,
Ringsend Road, Dublin 4, Ireland

PASSIONATE ENCOUNTERS: RISKING IT ALL © 2022 Harlequin Enterprises ULC.

A Passionate Night with the Greek © 2019 Kim Lawrence
One Night with the Forbidden Princess © 2018 Amanda Cinelli
Possessed by Passion © 2016 Brenda Streater Jackson

ISBN: 978-0-263-30485-5

MIX
Paper from
responsible sources
FSC **FSC® C007454**
www.fsc.org

A PASSIONATE NIGHT WITH THE GREEK

KIM LAWRENCE

CHAPTER ONE

ZACH HAD RECEIVED the message he had been waiting for while he was stuck in traffic. Sometimes a first-hand knowledge of the back streets of Athens, combined with a flexible attitude to rules, came in useful.

Zach possessed both.

For some of his formative years he had lived by his wits on those streets, finding it infinitely preferable to living with the grandmother who had resented having her daughter's bastard foisted on her, and the drunken uncle who had perfected bullying into an art form.

It took him just under half an hour and a few probable speeding fines to reach the hospital. He remained oblivious to the covetous stares that followed his long-legged progress from his car and through the building. It took him three more minutes to reach the intensive care unit where Alekis Azaria had spent three days in a medically induced coma after being successfully resuscitated following his last cardiac arrest.

Zach, as the closest thing the older man had to either friend or family, had been there the previous day when they'd brought him out of the coma. Despite the warnings that he had chosen not to hear, he had fully anticipated that Alekis would simply open his eyes.

The consultant had explained this sometimes happened but admitted there was a possibility that Alekis might never wake up.

Given the fact that the Greek shipping tycoon's presence here was on a strict need-to-know basis, it was no surprise that the same consultant who had issued this gloomy prognosis was waiting for him now, at the entrance to the intensive care unit.

The medic, used to being a figure of respect and authority, found himself straightening up and taking a deep steadying breath when the younger, tall, athletically built figure approached.

Zach didn't respond to the older man's greeting; instead, head tilted at a questioning angle, he arched a thick dark brow and waited, jaw clenched, to hear what was coming.

'He has woken and is breathing independently.'

Impatient with the drip-feed delivery Zach could sense coming, he cut across the other man, impatience edging his deep voice.

'Look, just give it to me straight.'

Straight had never been a problem for Zach. His ability to compartmentalise meant personal issues did not affect his professional ability.

'There seems to be no problem with Mr Azaria's cognitive abilities.'

A flicker of relief flashed in Zach's dark eyes. Intellectual impairment would have been Alekis's worst nightmare; for that matter it would have been his own.

'Always supposing that he was fairly...*demanding* previously?' the doctor tacked on drily.

Zach gave a rare smile that softened the austere lines of his chiselled, handsome features, causing a passing pretty nurse to walk into a door.

'He is accustomed to being in charge. I can see him...?'

The cardiologist nodded. 'He is stable, but you do understand this is early days?' he cautioned.

'Understood.'

'This way.'

Alekis had been moved from a cubicle in the intensive care unit to a private suite of rooms. Zach found him propped up on a pile of pillows. The events of the last week had gouged deep lines in the leathered skin of his face and hollowed out his cheeks, but his voice still sounded pretty robust!

Zach stood in the doorway for a moment, listening, a smile playing gently across his firm lips.

'Have you never heard of human rights? I'll have your job. I want my damned phone!'

The nurse, recovering her professional poise that had slipped when she'd seen Zach appear, lifted a hand to her flushed cheek and twitched a pillow, but looked calm in the face of the peevish demand and stream of belligerent threats.

'Oh, it's way above my pay grade to make a decision like that, Mr Azaria.'

'Then get me someone who can make a decision—' Alekis broke off as he registered Zach's presence. 'Good, give me *your* phone, and a brandy wouldn't come amiss.'

'I must have mislaid it.' Zach's response earned him a look of approval from the flush-faced nurse.

Alekis snorted. 'It's a conspiracy!' he grumbled. 'So, what are you waiting for? Take a seat, then. Don't stand there towering over me.'

Zach did as he was bade, lowering his immaculately clad, long and lean, six-foot-five athletic frame into one of the room's easy chairs. Stretching his legs out in front of him, he crossed one ankle over the other.

'You look—'

'I look like a dying man,' came the impatient response. 'But not yet—I have things to do and so do you. I assume you do actually have your phone?'

Zach's relief at the business-as-usual attitude was cancelled out by his concern at the shaking of the blue-veined hand extended to him.

He hid his concern beneath a layer of irony as he scrolled down the screen to find the best of the requested snapshots he'd taken several days earlier for Alekis.

'So how long before the news that I'm in here surfaces and the sharks start circling?'

Zach selected the best of the head shots he had taken and glanced up. 'Who knows?'

'Damage limitation is the order of the day, then.'

Zach nodded and extended the phone. 'I suppose if you're going to have another heart attack, you're in the right place. I'm assuming that you will tell me at some point why you sent me to a graveyard in London to stalk some woman.'

'Not stalk, take a photo...'

Zach's half-smile held irony as he responded to the

correction. 'All the difference in the world. I'm curi-ous—did it ever occur to you I'd say no?'

Zach had been due to address a prestigious interna-tional conference in London as guest speaker to an au-dience consisting of the cream of the financial world when Alekis had rung him with his bizarre demand, thinly disguised as a request.

Should he ever start believing his own press he could always rely on Alekis to keep his ego in check, Zach mused with wry affection as the short conversation of several days before flickered through his head.

'You want me to go *where* and do *what*?'

'You heard me. Just give the address of the church to your driver—the cemetery is opposite—then take a photo of the woman who arrives at four-thirty.'

'Try not to let it give you a heart attack this time,' Zach advised now, placing his phone into the older man's waiting hand.

'Waiting for you to deliver this picture didn't give me a heart attack. Seventy-five years of over-indulgence did, according to the doctors who tell me I should have been six feet under years ago. They also said that if I want to last even another week I should deprive myself of everything that gives life meaning.'

'I'm sure they were much more tactful.'

'I have no use for tact.'

Greedy floated into Zach's head as he watched the older man stare at the phone.

'She's beautiful, isn't she?'

Zach deemed a response unnecessary. There was no question mark over the haunting beauty of the woman captured by his phone. What he *had* questioned was not

Alekis's interest, but his own fascination, bordering on obsession, with the face he couldn't stop thinking about. Until, that was, he had realised it wasn't the face, it was the puzzle of her identity, the mystery of the affair, that had tweaked his imagination, not those golden eyes.

'I'm always willing to lend a hand to a friend in need. I assume that you have lost all your fortune and no longer have access to your own personal team of private investigators in order to have needed me? How did you know she'd be there at four-thirty?'

'I have had her followed for the past two weeks.' He looked bemused that Zach would ask such an obvious question. 'And hardly a team was required... Actually I had reasons for not wanting to use in-house expertise. I was employing someone who proved to be an idiot...'

'The same person you had following her?'

'And he can whistle for his money. He was utterly inept, took any number of photographs, mostly of her back or lamp posts. And as for *covert*? She noticed him and threatened to report him for stalking... Took *his* photo, then hit him with her shopping bag. Did she see you?'

'No, I'm thinking of taking up espionage as my second career. I had no idea I was signing up for such a dangerous task. So, who is this scary lady?'

'My granddaughter.'

A quiver of surprise widened Zach's dark eyes as his ebony lashes lifted off the angle of his cheekbones. He really hadn't seen that one coming!

'Her mother was beautiful too...' The older man seemed oblivious to Zach's reaction as he considered the photograph, his fingers shaking as he held it up. 'I think she has a look of Mia, around the mouth.' His hooded gaze lifted. 'You knew I had a daughter?'

Zach tipped his head in acknowledgement. He had of course heard the stories of the wild-child daughter. There was talk of drugs and men, but no one knew if Alekis had seen her since she'd married against his wishes, and so the story went that she'd been disinherited. This was the first time Zach had heard mention of a granddaughter, or, for that matter, heard Alekis speak of his family at all; though a portrait of his long-dead wife hung in the hallway of his palatial home on the island he owned.

'She married some loser, Parvati, threw herself away on him—to spite me, I think,' the older man brooded darkly. 'I was right. He was a useless waster, but would she listen? No, he left her when she got pregnant. All she had to do was ask and I'd have…' He shook his head, looking tired in the aftermath of emotional outburst. 'No matter, she always was as stubborn and…' His voice trailed away until he sat there, eyes half closed.

Zach began to wonder if he had fallen asleep. 'Sounds like the apple didn't fall far from the tree.'

To Zach's relief, the older man opened his eyes and directed a scowl up at Zach, which slowly faded. The smile that replaced it held a hint of pride. 'Mia was a fiery one. Like her mother to look at but…' His voice trailed away again.

If the likeness in the painting he had seen was accurate, Alekis's wife had been beautiful, though not in the same style as the granddaughter with the glowing amber eyes. Zach could see no similarity between the two. The portrait was of a beautiful woman with a beautiful face but not a face to haunt a man. Unlike the face of the woman with the golden eyes. She was Alekis's granddaughter—he was still struggling to get his head around that.

Alekis's lack of family had been something they'd had in common, part of their unlikely bond that had grown through the years. Now it turned out that there was family and he was assuming Alekis wanted to be reunited. If the older man had asked his advice, Zach would have told him it was a bad idea. But Alekis wouldn't ask or listen any more than Zach would have if someone had told him beforehand that reconnecting with his own past would leave him with memories that would offer no answers and no comfort.

'I suppose I could have made the first move. I was just waiting but she never...' He wiped a hand across his eyes and when it fell away Zach pretended not to see the moisture on the old man's cheeks.

The truth was, he was finding it uncomfortable to see the man he had always considered self-contained and unsentimental and way past being a victim of his emotions show such vulnerability. But then maybe that was what a reminder of his own mortality did to a man?

'I suppose everyone has regrets.'

'Do you?'

Zach raised his brows at the question and considered it. 'We all make mistakes,' he said, thinking of his grandmother staring out of the window with blank eyes on his last visit to the home. 'But never the same one twice.' Twice made you a fool or in love—in his eyes the latter made you the former.

He could not imagine ever allowing his heart, or at

least his hormones, to rule his head. Not that he was
a monk; sex was healthy and necessary but he never
mixed it with sentiment, which had given him a reputation for being heartless, but he could live with that.
Living with the same woman for the rest of his life?
Less so!

'I regret…but it's too late for that.' Alekis's voice
firmed. 'I want to make amends. I intend to leave her
everything. Sorry if you thought you were getting it.'

'I don't need your money.'

'You and your damned pride! If you'd let me help
you'd have got to the top a lot quicker, or at least with
a lot less effort.'

'Where would be the fun in that? And you did help.
You gave me an education and your advice.' Zach spoke
lightly but he knew how much he owed to Alekis, and
so did the shipping magnate.

'A gift beyond price, wouldn't you say?'

Zach's lips quivered into an appreciative smile. 'You
really are feeling more yourself, but the moral blackmail
is unnecessary, Alekis.' He spoke without heat. 'What
do you want me to do?'

'Bring her to me.'

The face with the golden eyes floated into his head
and Zach felt some nameless emotion flare inside him
at the idea of seeing that face again.

The older man was staring again at the image on
the screen.

'Will you?'

Zach's thickly defined sable brows lifted. 'Bring,
as in…?' He shook his head, adding in an attempt to
lighten the rather intense atmosphere that couldn't be

doing Alekis's heart any good, 'I'm assuming we are not talking kidnap here.'

'It shouldn't come to that.'

'That wasn't actually an offer.'

The older man didn't appear to hear him.

'Does she have a name?' Zach asked, pretending not to see the moisture the older man wiped from the corners of his eyes.

'Katina.' Alekis's lips tightened. 'Greek only in name, she was born in England. Her history is...'

Zach was amazed to see a look close to shame wash over the older man's face.

'She has been alone for a long time. She thinks she still is. I intend to make it up to her, but I'm concerned that the shock will...'

'I'm sure she'll cope,' Zach soothed, repressing the cynical retort on the tip of his tongue. Discovering you were set to become wealthy beyond anyone's wildest dreams was the sort of shock most people recovered from quite quickly.

'It will be a culture shock. She's about to become an heiress and the target of vicious tongues and gold-diggers. She'll need to be protected...'

'From what you say she seems pretty well able to protect herself,' Zach inserted drily.

'Oh, she's clearly got spirit, but it takes more than spirit. She needs to be taught how things operate,' her grandfather continued. 'And I'm stuck in here, which is why I'm—'

Zach, who had listened with growing unease at the direction of this, cut in quickly. 'I'd love to help but that sounds pretty much like a full-time job to me.'

His mentor gave a deep sigh that made Zach's teeth clench; the smile that accompanied it was a nice blend of understanding and sadness. 'And you have every right to refuse.' Another sigh. 'You owe me nothing. Please don't run away with the idea I'm calling in a debt. I will discharge myself and—'

Zach lowered his shoulders. He knew when he was beaten.

'You know, sometimes I forget it was *me* that saved *your* life.'

The first lesson you learnt on the streets was to look after number one, the second was walk, or preferably run, away from trouble. Zach's problem was bullies. He hated them, and seeing those knife-wielding thugs surrounding the foolish old guy who was refusing to hand over his wallet had produced a red-mist moment that had led him to run towards danger and not away from it.

Zach believed nothing positive could be achieved by reflecting on the past, but if he had, his objective view would have been that there hadn't been anything remotely brave about his actions. Though stupid had flashed through his head at the first cut that had slipped between his ribs.

He might have saved the older man's life, but Alekis had given him a life and until this point asked for very little in return.

He watched, an expression of wry resignation twisting his lips, as the man's air of weary defeat melted away in a beat of his damaged heart.

The elderly Greek's smile oozed smug satisfaction. 'If you're sure?'

'Don't push it,' Zach growled out, torn between ex-asperation that he had been so expertly manipulated and amusement.

'It is important to control the flow of information when the news does leak. I know I can rely on you for that. The media will be all over her like a rash. We must be ready; she *must* be ready. *Go away!*'

The loud addition was directed to an unwary nurse who, to give her her due, stood her ground.

'I'll leave him to you. Good luck,' Zach added as he rose to his feet. 'You can email me the necessary,' he added before the exhausted-looking patient could react to his intention. 'Just give me her details and I'll do the rest, and in the meantime you get some rest.'

Kat danced around her small office and punched the air in triumph, before controlling the fizz of excitement still bubbling in her veins enough to retrieve the let-ter that she had tossed in the air after she had read it.

She read it again now, anxious that she hadn't mis-interpreted it. That really *would* be awful. The tension that had slipped into her shoulders fell away as she came to the end.

It really did say what she'd thought, but what puck-ered her smooth brow into a slight frown was what it *didn't* say. There was a time she was expected to be there, at the address of the law firm, but no clue as to *who* was looking forward to meeting her.

She shrugged. Presumably a representative of one of the individuals or businesses known for their phi-lanthropy to whom she had pitched her appeal—or *wasted her time with,* as some of her less optimistic-minded colleagues and volunteers had put it. Fighting against the negativity, she'd pointed out that she wasn't expecting any one person or organisation to step into the breach, but if she could persuade a handful to make some sort of donation it could mean a stay of execution for the refuge once the local authority funding was pulled the coming month.

Who knew? This could be the first of many.

There was a short tap on the door before Sue, with her nose stud, stuck her orange-streaked head around the door. 'Oh, God!' She sighed when she saw Kat's face. 'I know that look.'

'What look?'

The older woman stepped inside the room and, after closing the door, said, 'Your "campaign for a good cause" face.'

Kat blinked. 'Do I have a…?'

'Oh, you sure do, and I love—we *all* love—that you're a fighter, but there comes a time…' She sighed again, her skinny shoulders lifting before they fell. 'You've got to be a realist, love,' she told Kat earnestly. 'This place…' Her expansive gesture took in the small office with its cardboard-box system of filing—there always seemed to be something better to spend the limited resources on than office furniture. 'It's a lost cause. I've got an interview Monday. Just giving you the heads-up that I'll need the morning off.'

Kat was unable to hide her shock; her face fell. 'You're looking for another job?' If Sue, who was as upbeat as she was hard-working, had already given in… *Am I the only one who hasn't?*

'Too right I am, and I suggest you do too. There's always bills to pay and in my case mouths to feed. I care about this place too, you know, Kat.'

Kat felt a stab of contrition that her reaction might be read as judgement. 'I know that.' But the point was she didn't know what it was to be like Sue, a single parent bringing up five children and holding down two jobs.

On the brink of sharing the good news, she pulled back and moderated her response. She didn't want to raise hopes if nothing came of this.

'I know you think I'm mad, but I *really* think there's a realistic prospect someone out there cares.'

The other woman grinned. 'I know you do, and I really hope life never knocks that starry-eyed optimism out of you.'

'It hasn't so far,' Kat retorted. 'And Monday's fine. I'll cover… Good luck.'

She waited until the other woman had left before she sat down at her desk—actually, it was a table with one wobbly leg—and thought about who she might be meeting. Whoever it was didn't hang around. The meeting was scheduled for the following morning and the letter had been sent recorded delivery.

Well, she could cross the two off her list who had already sent a sympathetic but negative response, so who did that leave?

But then, did the identity of the potential donor actually matter? What mattered was that someone out there was interested enough for a meeting. So there was no beacon of light at the end of a tunnel but there was a definite flicker. Her small chin lifted in an attitude of determination. Whoever it turned out to be, she would sell her cause to them. Because the alternative was not something she wanted to contemplate—failure.

So for the rest of the day she resisted the temptation to share her news with the rest of her gloomy-looking colleagues. Not until she knew what was on offer, or maybe she just didn't want to have anyone dampen her enthusiasm with a bucket of cold-water realism? Either way there was no one to turn to for advice when she searched her wardrobe for something appropriate that evening.

There wasn't a lot to search. Her wardrobe was what designers called capsule, though maybe capsule was being generous.

It wasn't that she didn't love clothes and fashion, it was just that her budget was tight and in the past used up by impulse *bargain* buys, which inevitably sat in her wardrobe untouched and were eventually donated to a charity chop.

After a mega charity shop clear-out at the beginning of the summer and an unseasonal resolution to avoid sale racks, she had adopted a pared-down wardrobe. There had been the *one* slip. She looked at it now, hanging beside the eminently practical items. She rubbed the deep midnight-blue soft cashmere silk fabric between her fingers and gave a tiny nod; it was perfect for tomorrow's 'dress to impress'.

Smiling because her moment of weakness had been vindicated, she extracted the dress that stood out among the white shirts, T-shirts, black trousers and jeans, and hung it on the hook at the back of the bedroom door. Smoothing down the fabric, she checked it for creases, but everything about the dress managed to combine fluid draping with classic tailoring and the look screamed designer. The only fault she'd been able to find that had caused it to be downgraded to a second was the belt loop that needed a few stitches.

It had fitted so perfectly when she'd tried it on and had been marked down so much that, even though her practical head had told her there would never be an occasion in her life where the beautifully cut dress would come into it, she had bought it.

If she'd believed in fate—well, actually she did; the problem, in her experience, was not always recognising the door left ajar by fate as a golden opportunity.

It took her a little longer to dig out the heels buried among the piles in the back of the wardrobe, and she was ready. All she needed now was to go through her plan of attack. If she wanted to sell her case, make it stand out amongst the many deserving cases, she needed facts at her fingertips and a winning smile and someone with a heart to direct it at. The smile that flashed out was genuine as she caught sight of her face in the mirror…her eyes narrowed and her forehead creased in a frown of fierce determination.

So her winning smile could do with some work!

CHAPTER TWO

ZACH WAS EXPECTED. The moment he strode into the foyer
his reception committee materialised. He was shown
up to the empty boardroom by the senior partner—the
only Asquith left in the law firm of Asquith, Lowe and
Urquhart—and three underlings of the senior variety.

If Zach had thought about it—which he hadn't, because he'd had other things on his mind—he would have
expected no less, considering that the amount of business Alekis sent this firm's way had to be worth enough
to keep the Englishman's Caribbean tan topped up for
the next millennium and then some, not to mention add
a few more inches to his expanding girth.

'I will bring Miss Parvati up when she arrives. How
is Mr Alekis? There have been rumours…'

Zach responded to this carefully casual addition with
a fluid shrug of his broad shoulders. 'There are always
rumours.'

The older man tilted his head and gave a *can't blame
a man for trying* nod as he backed towards the door, an
action mirrored by the three underlings, who had tagged
along at a respectful distance.

Zach unfastened the button on his tailored grey

jacket and, smoothing his silk tie, called after the other man before he exited the room. 'Inform me when she arrives. I'll let you know when to show her up.'

'Of course. Shall I have coffee brought in?'

His gesture took in the long table, empty but for the water and glasses at the end where Zach had pulled out a chair. Watching him, the older man found himself, hand on his ample middle, breathing in. The sharp intake of stomach-fluttering breath came with an unaccustomed pang of wistful envy that he recognised as totally irrational—you couldn't be wistful about something you had never had, and he had never had the sort of lean, hard, toned physique this man possessed. His own physical presence had a lot more to do with expensive tailoring, which permitted him to indulge his love of good food and fine wine.

'The water will be fine.' Zach reached for one of the iced bottles of designer water to illustrate the point and tipped it into a glass before he took his seat.

The door closed, and Zach glanced around the room without much interest. The room had a gentlemen's club vibe with high ceilings and dark wooden panelled walls—not really his usual sort of environment. He had never been in a position to utilise the old-school-tie network, but he had never been intimidated by it and, more importantly, not *belonging* to this world had not ultimately hindered his progress. If he was viewed in some quarters as an outsider, it didn't keep him awake nights, and even if it had he could function pretty well on four hours' sleep.

He opened his tablet and scrolled onto the file that Alekis's office had forwarded. It was not lengthy, presumably an edited version of the full warts and all document. Zach had no problem with that; he didn't need the dirt to make a judgement. The details he did have were sufficient to give him a pretty good idea of the sort of childhood the young woman he was about to meet had had.

The fact that, like him, she had not had an easy childhood did not make him feel any *connection*, any more than he would have felt connected to someone who shared a physical characteristic with him. But he did feel it gave him an insight others might lack, the same way he knew that the innocence that had seemed to shine out from her eyes in the snapshot had been an illusion. Innocence was one of the first casualties of the sort of childhood she had had.

She had been abandoned and passed through the care system; he could see why Alekis thought he had a lot to make up for—he did. Zach was not shocked by what the mother had done—he was rarely shocked by the depths to which humans could sink—but he was mildly surprised that Alekis, who presumably had had ways of keeping tabs on his estranged daughter, had not chosen to intervene, a decision he was clearly trying to make up for now.

While many might say never too late, Zach would not. He believed there was definitely too late to undo the damage. He supposed in this instance it depended on how *much* damage had been done. What was not in question was the fact that the woman he was about to meet would know how to look after herself.

She was a survivor, he could admire that, but he was a realist. He knew you didn't survive the sort of childhood she'd had without learning how to put your own interests first, and he should know.

The indent between his dark brows deepened. It concerned him that Alekis, who would normally have been the first to realise this, seemed to be in denial. The grandfather in him was putting sentiment ahead of facts, and the fact was anyone who had experienced what this woman had was never going to fit into her grandfather's world without being a magnet for scandal.

As Zach knew, you didn't escape your past; you carried it with you and learnt to look after number one. When had *he* last put someone else's needs ahead of his own?

There was no occasion to remember.

The acknowledgement didn't cause him any qualms of conscience. You didn't get to be one of life's survivors by *not* prioritising your own interests.

And Zach was a survivor. In his book it was preferable to be considered selfish than a victim, and rather than feel bitter about his past he was in some ways grateful for it and the mental toughness it had gifted him, without which he would not have enjoyed the success he had today.

He responded to the message on his phone, his fingers flying as he texted back. He looked down at the screen of his tablet. The vividness of the woman's golden eyes, even more intense against the rest of the picture that seemed washed of colour, stared out at him before he closed it with a decisive click.

Maybe he was painting a bleaker picture. He might be pleasantly surprised—unless Alekis had deliberately hidden them, it seemed the granddaughter hadn't had any brushes with the law. Of course, that might simply mean she had stayed under the radar of the authorities, but she did seem to hold down a steady job. Perhaps the best thing the mother had ever done for her child was to abandon her.

There was the lightest of taps on the door before Asquith stepped inside the room, his hand hovering in a paternal way an inch away from the small of the back of the woman who walked in beside him.

This wasn't the fey creature from the misty graveyard, neither was it a woman prematurely hardened by life and experience.

Theos! This was possibly the most beautiful creature he had ever laid eyes on.

For a full ten seconds after she walked in, Zach's entire nervous system went into shutdown and when it flickered back into life, he had no control over the heat that scorched through his body. The sexual afterglow of the blast leaving his every nerve ending taut.

He studied her, his eyes shielded by his half-lowered eyelids and the veil of his sooty eyelashes. He felt himself resenting that it was a struggle to access even a fraction of the objectivity he took for granted as he studied her. He expected his self-control to be his for the asking, irrespective of a bloodstream with hormone levels that were off the scale.

He forced the tension from his spine, only to have it settle in his jaw, finding release in the ticing muscle that clenched and unclenched spasmodically as he studied her. She was wearing heels, which made her almost as tall as the lawyer, who was just under six feet. She was dressed with the sort of simplicity that didn't come cheap, but to be fair the long, supple lines of her slim body would have looked just as good dressed in generic jeans and a T-shirt.

He categorised the immediate impression she projected as elegance, poise and sex…

Her attention was on the man speaking to her, so Zach had the opportunity to prolong his study of her. She stood sideways on, presenting him with her profile as she nodded gravely at something the other man was saying, eyelashes that made him think of butterfly wings fluttering against her soft, rounded, slightly flushed cheeks. It was a pretty whimsical analogy for him.

Stick to the facts, Zach, suggested the voice in his head.

He did, silently describing what he saw.

Her profile was clear cut, almost delicate. There was the suggestion of a tilt on the end of her nose, her brow high and wide. The fey creature in the snapshot had a face framed by a cloud of ebony hair; this elegant young woman's hair was drawn smoothly back into a ponytail at the nape of her neck to fall like a slither of silk between her shoulder blades almost to waist level. Dark and cloud-like in the photos, in real life it was a rich warm brown, interspersed with warm toffee streaks.

The slight tilt of her head emphasised the slender length of her swan-like dancer's neck; the same grace was echoed in her slim curves and long limbs, beautifully framed by the simplicity of the figure-skimming calf-length dress. The length of her shapely legs was further emphasised by a pair of high, spiky heels.

'I'll leave you.'

'Leave?' Kat echoed.

Zach registered the soft musicality of her voice as her feathery brows lifted in enquiry, then, the moment he had been anticipating, she turned her head. Yes, her eyes really *were* that impossible colour, a rich deep amber, the tilt at the corners creating an exotic slant and lending her beautiful face a memorable quality.

Kat had been aware of the man in the periphery of her vision, sitting at the head of the long table. Up to that point, good manners had prevented her from responding to her curiosity and looking while her escort was speaking.

She did so now, just as the figure was rising to his feet.

The first thing she had noticed about her escort was his expensive tailoring, his plummy accent and old-school tie. This man was equally perfectly tailored—minus the old-school tie. His was silk and narrow, dark against the pale of his shirt. But what he wore was irrelevant alongside the impression of raw male power that hit her with the force of a sledgehammer.

She actually swayed!

He made the massive room suddenly seem a lot smaller; in fact, she experienced a wave of claustrophobia along with a cowardly impulse to beg her escort to wait for her.

You're not a wimp, Kat, or a quitter. Appearances and first impressions, she reminded herself, were invariably misleading. She'd found the first man's air of sleek, well-tailored affluence and accent off-putting initially, and yet now, a few floors up, he appeared cosy and benevolent. In a few minutes this dark stranger might seem cosy too. Her dark-lashed gaze moved in an assessing covert sweep from his feet to the top of his sleek dark head. Or *maybe not*!

Unless you considered large sleek predators *cosy*, and there was something of the jungle cat about him, in the way he moved with the fluid grace, the restless vitality you sensed beneath the stillness that a feral creature might feel in an enclosed space.

Aware she was in danger of overreacting and allowing her imagination to run riot, she huffed out a steadying breath between her stiff lips.

'Good morning.' She gave her best businesslike smile, aiming for a blend of warm but impersonal.

Easier said than done, when there were so many conflicting emotions jostling for supremacy in her head. Not to mention the fluttery pit of her stomach. She had no idea what she had been expecting, but it hadn't been this, or him!

She never rushed to judgement. She prided herself on her ability not to judge by appearances, so the rush of antagonism she had felt the moment his dark eyes had locked on hers was bewildering—and it hadn't gone away.

Her heart was racing, and it wasn't the only thing that had sped up. Everything had, including her perceptions, which were heightened to an extraordinary, almost painful degree, though they were focused less on the room with its background scent of leather and wood and more on the man who dominated with such effortless ease.

She had taken in everything about him in that first stunned ten seconds. The man stood several inches over six feet, and inside the elegant suit his build was lean yet athletic, with broad shoulders that were balanced perfectly by long, long legs. The strong column of his neck was the same deep shade of gold as his face, the warm and vibrant colour of his skin emphasised by the contrasting paleness of his shirt.

He was sinfully good-looking, if your taste ran to perfect. Such uncompromising masculinity attached to perfect symmetry, hard angles and carved planes, a wide mouth that was disturbingly sensual and the dark-as-night eyes framed by incredible jet lashes set under dark, strongly delineated brows.

There was no reaction to the smile she somehow kept pasted in place. She told herself to keep it together as she struggled to make the mental adjustments required.

'Oh, God!' It wasn't the pain in her knee when she hit the chair leg that made her cry out, it was the sight of the carefully arranged contents of the folder she carried sliding to the floor. 'Sorry,' she muttered as she bent to pick up the scattered papers, jamming them haphazardly into the folder.

Walk, think and string two syllables together, Kat. It's not exactly multitasking! It's all on your phone so it's not a disaster!

Cheeks hot, she straightened up. Forget old-school tie, *this* was who she was dealing with. *Fine.* Except, of course, it *wasn't* fine; she *was* making an impression, but not the intended one. Having gathered the papers, she promptly dropped them again. She bit her tongue literally to stop herself blurting a very unladylike curse.

Zach watched her silky hair fall over one shoulder as she fumbled for the scattered papers. The action drew attention to the curve of her behind, and as the soft, silky dark material of her dress stretched tight so did his nerve endings.

He could not recall the last time he had needed to fight his way through a fog of blind lust. If Alekis had had a window into his mind at that moment he might have doubted casting him in the role of protector and mentor. Or maybe not. There was some sense in it. Who better to guard the fluffy chick than a fox? Always supposing the fox in question could keep his own baser instincts in check.

Not that this creature was fluffy, she was more silky-smooth. *Smooth all over?*

Calming down this illicit line of distracting speculation, he let the silence stretch. It was amazing how many people felt the need to fill a silence, saying things that revealed more than a myriad searching questions.

Unfortunately, and uncomfortably on this occasion, in a moment of role reversal his own mind felt the need to fill the silence.

Alekis trusted him. The question was, did he trust himself?

The moment of self-doubt passed; even taking the trust issue with Alekis out of the equation, the logic of keeping the personal and professional separate remained inescapable.

'Won't you take a seat?'

She responded to the offer with relief; her knees were literally shaking. 'Thank you.' At least the table between them meant she was not obliged to offer her hand. Instead, she tipped her head and smiled. 'I'm Kat.'

'Take a seat, Katina.' He watched the surprise flare

in her amazing eyes and slide into wariness before she brought her lashes down enough to veil her expression momentarily.

The use of her *full* name, which no one ever used, threw her slightly. Well, actually, more than slightly.

He couldn't know it, but the last person to call her that had been her mother.

For many years Kat had believed that while she could hear her mother's voice in her head, her mother was not gone...she was coming back. Nowadays the childhood conviction was gone and so was her mother's voice. The memory might be lost but she did know that her name on her mother's lips had not sounded anything like it did when this man rolled his tongue around the syllables.

'Th-thank you,' she stuttered. Recovering from the shaky moment, she gathered her poise around herself, protective-blanket style. 'Just Kat is fine,' she added finally, taking the seat he had gestured towards and reflecting that it wasn't at all fine.

Though she was normally all for informality, she would have been much happier with a formal, distant *Miss*...or *Ms* or maybe even, *hey, you*. It wasn't just her physical distance she felt the need to keep from this man. His dark gaze seemed able to penetrate her very soul.

She forced herself to forget his disturbing mouth, equally disturbing eyes, the almost explosive quality he projected, and move past the weird inexplicable antagonism. She was here to make a pitch, and save the precious resource that the community was in danger of losing. This was not about her—she just had to stay focused on the prize.

All great advice in theory, but in reality, with those eyes drilling into her like lasers... Were lasers cold? She pushed away the thought and tried to dampen the stream of random thoughts that kept popping into her head down to a slow trickle.

Reminding herself that a lot of people were relying on her helped; the fact she was distracted by the muscle that was clenching and unclenching in his lean cheek did not.

'Water?'

Repressing the impulse to ask him if he had anything stronger, she shook her head.

'I'm fine,' she said, thinking, *If only!*

Nervous was actually how she was feeling and this man was probably wondering why the hell she was here.

She cleared her throat. 'I'm sure you have a lot of questions?'

His dark brows lifted; there was nothing feigned about his surprised reaction. 'I would have thought *you'd* have a lot of questions.'

True, she did. She gave voice to the first one that popped into her head. 'What do I call you?'

It wasn't really a change of expression, but his heavy eyelids flickered and left her with the distinct impression this wasn't the sort of question he had anticipated. She took a deep breath and tried again.

'It really doesn't matter to us *who* you represent— when I say it doesn't matter I don't mean... We would never accept anything from a...an...illegitimate source—obviously.'

'Obviously,' Zach said, realising for the first time

that she wasn't wondering why she was there, because she thought she knew.

He was intrigued.

His eyes slid to her plump lips. Intrigued had a much better ring to it than fascinated.

'Not that you look like a criminal or anything,' she hastened to assure him.

His lips twitched. 'Would you like to see character references…?'

She chose to ignore the sarcasm while observing that even when his mouth smiled his eyes remained as expressionless and hard as black glass. There was no warmth there at all. She found herself wondering what warmed that chill, and then gathered her wandering thoughts back to the moment and her reason for being here, which wasn't thinking about his eyes, or, for that matter, any other part of his dauntingly perfect body.

'We are just grateful that you are willing to consider contributing.'

'*We?*'

She flushed and refused to be put off by his sardonic tone. 'This *we*…' Kat pulled the folder from her bag and pointed to the logo on the cover. 'The Hinsdale project and family refuge. *Dame* Laura…' she put a gentle emphasis on the title; it was hard to tell sometimes but some people were impressed by such things, not that she had to pretend pride or enthusiasm as she told him '…began it back in the sixties when there was just the one house, a mid-terrace, a two-up two-down. It was all a bit basic.'

'And now?'

'We have extended into the houses both sides, the

entire row, and can take thirty-five women at any one time, depending, obviously, on the number of children. In the eighties the chapel across the road came up for sale and we bought it. Now it houses the nursery and crèche, which is available for women when they have moved out. It also contains a drop-in centre, which provides legal help and so forth. Dame Laura was personally involved, right up to her death.'

Had her own mother found Hinsdale, or a similar place, both their lives might have been very different.

Zach watched the wave of sadness flicker across her expressive face. Letting this interview play out a little longer might be on shaky ground morally, but practically it would provide a swifter insight into this woman whom he was meant to be *babysitting*.

'And what is your role?' Zach was experiencing a strange reluctance to abandon his mental image of a person so damaged they never looked at anything other than their own self-interest—a person, in short, much like himself.

The frown that came with the unbidden flicker of self-awareness faded as he watched her beautiful face light up with a glow of conviction and resolution as she leaned forward in her seat, losing the nervousness as she answered proudly.

'I run the refuge, along with a great team, many of whom are volunteers, as was I initially. I began by volunteering at the crèche when I was at school, and after I left I was offered a salaried position. I like to think Dame Laura would have been proud of what we have achieved.' Kat had met the redoubtable lady once; she had been frail but as sharp as a tack and totally inspirational. 'Her legacy lives on.' Embarrassed, Kat swallowed the emotional lump in her throat and reminded herself that there was a fine line between enthusiasm and looking a little unhinged. 'We have a dedicated staff and, as I said, so many volunteers. We are part of the community and don't turn anyone away.'

'That must make forward planning difficult.'

'We build in flexibility—'

He felt a twinge of admiration that, despite the starry-eyed enthusiasm, she was not so naive that she didn't know how to sidestep a difficult answer.

'Is that possible fiscally?'

'Obviously in the present financial climate—'

'How much do you need?'

The hard note of cold cynicism in his interruption made her blink, then rush to reassure. 'Oh, please, don't think for one moment we are expecting you to cover the total shortfall.'

'As negotiating tactics go, that, *Kat*...' the way he drawled her name made the fine hairs on the nape of her neck stand on end '...was not good—it was bad. It was abysmal.'

Her expression stiffened and grew defensive. 'I came here under the impression that you *wanted* to contribute to the refuge.' She struggled to contain the antagonism that sparkled in her eyes as she planted her hands on the table and leaned in. 'Look, if this is about me... There are other people who could do my job. The important thing is the work.'

'Do you think everything is about you?'

Kat felt her face flush. 'Of course not, it just felt... feels as if you find me...'

'So you are saying you'd sacrifice yourself to save this place?'

She swallowed, wondering if that was what it was going to take. Obviously it was a price she would be willing to pay, but only as a last resort. *Crawl and grovel if that's what he wants, Kat.* She heaved a deep sigh and managed an *almost* smile.

'You don't like me, fine.' *Because I really don't like you.*

Zach watched the internal struggle reflected on her face. This was a woman who should never play poker. As a born risk-taker, he enjoyed that form of relaxation.

She left a space for him to deny the claim.

He didn't.

'But, please,' she begged, 'don't allow that to influence your decision. I am one person easy to replace, but there is a dedicated staff who work incredibly hard.' Breathing hard, she waited for a response, the slightest hint of softening, but there was none.

Her chin went up; she was in nothing-to-lose territory.

She flicked to the first page of the thin folder, except the first page was now somewhere in the middle so it took her a few moments to locate it. 'I have the facts and figures; the average stay of a client is...' With a sigh she turned the page of figures over. It wasn't the right one. 'The average doesn't matter. Everyone who comes is different and we try to cater to their individual needs. The woman who is my deputy first arrived as a client. She was in an abusive relationship...'

A nerve along his jaw quivered. 'Her partner hit her?'

The hairs on the nape of her neck lifted in response

to the danger in his deceptively soft question. Underneath the beautiful tailoring she sensed something dangerous, almost feral, about this man. A shiver traced a sticky path up her spine as she struggled to break contact with his dark eyes.

'No, he didn't.' He hadn't needed to. He had isolated Sue from her family and friends and had controlled every aspect of her life before she'd finally left. Even her thoughts had not been her own. 'It's not always about violence. Sometimes the abuse is emotional,' she said quietly. 'But she now works for us full-time, is a fantastic mum and was voted onto the local council. The refuge has helped so many and it will again in future, the cash-flow situation is—'

Her own earnest flow was stemmed by his upheld hand. 'I am sure your cause is very worthy, but that is not why you were invited here.'

'I don't understand...'

'I had never heard of your refuge, or your Dame Laura.'

As his words sank in, the throb of anger in her head got louder; her voice became correspondingly softer. 'Then why the hell am I here?'

It was an indulgence, but he took a moment to enjoy the flashing amber eyes that viewed him with utter contempt.

'I am here to represent Alekis Azaria.'

The name seemed vaguely familiar to Kat but she had no idea why. She leaned forward, arching a questioning brow. *'Greek...?'*

He nodded. He had seen several reactions to Ale-

kis's name before, ranging from awe to fear, but hers
was a first. She clearly didn't have a clue who he was.

'Like you.'

She frowned, then realised his mistake. 'Oh, not really. The name, you mean? Oh, I suppose I must have
some Greek blood, but I've never been there. Are
you…?' she asked, searching for some sort of explanation, some sort of connection to explain him and this
interview.

'I am Greek, like Alekis.'

'So why did this man who I have never heard of invite me here?' The entire thing made no sense to her.
'Who is he?'

CHAPTER THREE

'HE'S YOUR GRANDFATHER.'

He watched as the bemused confusion drawn on her face froze and congealed. As her wide eyes flickered wide in shock.

It took a conscious effort for Zach to hold on to his objectivity as she gasped like a drowning person searching for air. She sucked in a succession of deep breaths.

'I have no family.' Her voice was flat, her expression empty of the animation that had previously lit it. 'I have no one, so I can't have a grandfather.'

He pushed away an intrusive sliver of compassion and the squeeze of his heart and hardened his voice as he fell back on facts, always more reliable than sentiment.

'We all have two grandfathers, even me.'

Another time she might have questioned the significance of the *even me* but Kat was in shock. The sheer unexpectedness of what he had said had felt like walking…no, *running* full pelt into a brick wall that had suddenly appeared in the middle of a flower-filled meadow.

'I don't even know who my *father* is, other than a

name on a birth certificate.' It had never crossed her mind to track down the man who had abandoned her pregnant mother. The decision to search for her mother had not been one she had taken lightly, though, as it turned out, she had already been five years too late. 'Why should I want any contact with his family?'

Zach narrowed his eyes, recalling the one line in the file on the man Alekis's daughter had married in defiance of her father's wishes. 'He might have a family, but I don't have that information.'

'I don't understand…'

'It is your mother's family, or rather her father, that I am representing.'

She listened to his cold, dispassionate explanation before sitting there in silence for several moments, allowing her disjointed thoughts to coalesce.

'She had a family…' She faltered, remembering bedtime stories, the tall tales of a sun-drenched childhood. Was even a *tiny* part of that fantasy based on reality? The thought made her ache for her mother, far away from home and rejected.

'Your grandfather is reaching out to you.'

Shaking her head, Kat rose to her feet, then subsided abruptly as her shaking legs felt too insubstantial to support her.

'Reaching…' She shook her head and the slither of silk down her back rippled, making Zach wonder what it would look like loose and spread against her pale gold skin. 'I don't want *anyone* reaching out to me.' Her angry amber eyes came to rest accusingly on his handsome face. She knew there was a reason she had never trusted too-good-looking men besides prejudice and the fact the man who had spiked her drink all those years ago had been the one all the girls in the nightclub had been drooling over. 'Is this some sort of joke?'

'It is real.' As real as the colour of those pain-filled, angry, magnificent eyes.

'He's rich?'

Her words did make it sound as though a yes would be a good thing. This was not avarice speaking, he realised, but anger. The former would have made his life a lot easier.

'He is not poor.'

Her trembling lips clamped tight, the pressure blanching the colour from her skin as she fought visibly for composure.

'My mum was… She was poor, you see…*very* poor.' She eyed him with contempt, not even bothering to attempt to describe the abject hand-to-mouth existence that had driven her mother to drugs and the men who supplied them. A man who looked like him, dressed like him and oozed the confidence that came from success and affluence could not even begin to understand that life and the events that trapped people in the living hell of degradation.

'Yes.'

One of the reasons she rarely mentioned her early years was the way people reacted. She mentally filed them into two camps: the ones that looked at her with pity and those that felt uneasy and embarrassed.

His monosyllabic response held none of the above, just a statement of fact. Ironic, really, that a response she would normally have welcomed only added another layer to the antagonism that swirled inside her head as she looked at him. By the second he was becoming the personification of everything she disliked most in a person. Someone born to privilege and power without any seeming moral compass.

Ignoring the voice in her head that told her she was guilty of making the exact sort of rush or, in this case, more a *stampede* to judgement that she'd be the first to condemn, she sucked in a deep sustaining breath through flared nostrils.

Despite her best efforts, her voice quivered with emotion that this man would *definitely* see as a weakness. '*He* didn't reach out to her…'

'No.'

Her even white teeth clenched. 'Where was *he* when his daughter needed him? If he makes the same sort of grandfather as he made father, why would I want to know him?'

'I don't know…' He arched a satiric brow and pretended to consider the answer. 'He's rich?'

Her chin lifted to the defiant angle he was getting very familiar with. It was a long time since Zach had been regarded with such open contempt.

Better than indifference!

The knee-jerk reaction of his inner voice brought a brief frown to his brow before he turned his critical attention to the play of expression across her flawless features. He had never encountered anyone who broadcast every thought in their heads quite so obviously before.

The concept of a professional guard would be alien to her. Though in her defence, this *wasn't* professional to her—it was very personal. He was getting the idea that everything with this woman might be.

For someone who compartmentalised every aspect of his life, the emotional blurring was something that appalled him.

'So you're of the "everyone has a price" school of thought,' she sneered.

'They do.'

His man-of-few-words act was really starting to get under her skin.

'I don't. I'm not interested in money and…and… *things*!'

He arched a satiric brow. 'That might be a more impressive statement if you hadn't come here with a begging bowl.'

She fought off the angry flush she could feel rising up her neck. 'That is *not* the same.'

He dragged his eyes up from the blue-veined pulse that was beating like a trapped wild bird at the base of her slender throat. This might be the moment he told himself to remember that the untouched, fragile look had never been a draw for him. He had no protective instincts to arouse.

'If you say so.'

His sceptical drawl was an insult in itself.

'I am *not* begging. This isn't for me.'

He cut her off with a bored, 'I know, it is for the greater good. So consider that for the moment—consider how much you could help the *greater good* if you had access to the sort of funds that your grandfather has.'

He allowed himself the indulgence of watching the expressions flicker across her face for several seconds before speaking.

'You see, everyone *does* have a price—even you.'

'There is no *even me*. And I'm not suggesting I'm a better person than anyone else!' she fired back.

Zach watched her bite her lip before lifting her chin and found himself regretting his taunt. As exasperating as her attitude was, she had just received news that was the verbal equivalent of a gut punch.

And she had come out fighting.

'If you say so.'

She blinked hard, not prepared to let it go. 'I *do* say so, and,' she choked out, 'I really don't want to know the sort of person who would abandon his daughter.'

'Maybe she abandoned him?'

The suggestion drew a ferocious glare. On one level he registered how magnificent she looked furious, on another he realised that he was now in uncharted territory—he was playing it by ear. Zach trusted his instincts; his confidence was justified but, in this instance, it had turned out to be massively misplaced.

The unorthodox role assigned to him had been unwelcome, but he had approached it as he would anything. He'd thought that he had factored in all the possibilities…had considered every reaction and how to counter them to bring about the desired outcome with the least effort on his part.

Pity she didn't read the same script, Zach!

In his own defence, it hadn't seemed unreasonable to assume that the idea of being wealthy beyond any person's wildest dreams would swiftly negate any anger the heiress might feel towards the absentee grandparent.

He had never found it particularly admirable when people were willing to disadvantage themselves for a point of principle. He found it even less so now, when those so-called principles were making his own life hard work.

Not that it crossed his mind that in the long run she would reject the fortune. She'd find a way to trick herself eventually into believing she wasn't betraying her principles. He just had to help her get to that point a little quicker.

'He was the parent,' she quivered out. 'Parents care for their children.'

'In a perfect world, yes.' But, as she of all people should well know, the world was not perfect. It took a very stubborn idealist to retain a belief system like hers in light of her personal experiences.

She gritted her teeth. 'It's got nothing to do with a perfect world. It's called unconditional love. Not that I'd expect someone like you to know anything about that.'

'You'd be right, I don't,' he lied, pushing away the image that had materialised without warning in his head. His mother's thin, tired face, her work-worn hands. The memory was irrevocably linked with pain, which was why he didn't think about it, *ever*. 'Do you?'

The sudden attack threw her on the defensive. 'I see women willing to lay down their lives for their children every day of my working life.'

'Does that make up for your own mother abandoning you?'

He ignored the kick to his conscience when she flinched as though he had struck her. The illusion of fragility vanished as her chin lifted and she looked at him with angry eyes.

'None of this is about my mother.'

'Are you trying to tell me you're not angry with her for dumping you? My mother left me because she died…and for a long time I hated her for it.' They were words he'd never even thought, let alone voiced before, and they came with a massive slug of guilt and anger that her attitude had dredged up memories he had consigned to history. 'And you expect me to believe that you were never angry that you got dumped on a doorstep somewhere?' Maybe she genuinely didn't remember and that was why she was able to continue to lie to herself.

'It was a car park of a doctor's surgery. She knew that someone would help me, that I'd be safe.'

Safe… He closed his eyes, trying to banish the poignant image in his head of a dark-haired child standing there waiting for a mother who never came back.

'Some people should not have children,' Zach condemned. He had decided long ago that he was one of them. It was too easy for a bad parent to scar their children, so why take the risk?

'She needed help, she had nowhere to go—'

'I find your determination to see this woman as some innocent victim slightly perverse. She was the one who walked away from your grandfather. And she was an adult, not a child.'

Unable to argue with the facts the way he presented them, she snapped back. 'If this so-called grandfather of mine is so anxious to make contact, why isn't he here? Why send you?'

'He's in intensive care.'

It was a slight exaggeration; according to his latest update, Alekis had been downgraded from high dependency to whatever the medical equivalent was. He was the next step up…the walking wounded, maybe?

Her reaction was everything he had expected from someone who seemed to have *bleeding heart* stamped into her DNA. Like a pricked balloon, her anger deflated with an almost audible hiss.

Her eyes slid from his. 'Well, I'm sorry about that,' she mumbled stiffly. 'But I have no room in my life for someone I despise—' She broke off as he suddenly leaned back in his leather seat and laughed.

'That's it, of course!'

'What's *it*?'

'It's just I've been wondering who you remind me of.'

The suspicion in her eyes deepened. 'What are you talking about?'

'Someone who doesn't understand the word *compromise*, who can't forgive anyone who lets them down—in fact, anyone, even family, no, es*pecially* family, who doesn't live up to their idea of what is right…' He arched a dark brow. 'Sounding familiar?'

It took her a few seconds to divine his meaning. Her horrified reaction was instantaneous. 'I am *nothing* like my grandfather.'

'Well, that's an improvement. You admit you have one now. I've never put much faith in the whole gene thing. I might have to rethink it—you've never met the man and yet in your own way you are as stubborn and self-righteous as Alekis.'

'How dare you?'

'Easily.' He dismissed her outrage with a click of his long fingers. 'Your grandfather couldn't forgive your mother so he lost her. You can't forgive him and you're willing to reject him when he makes the first move.'

'A move that was twenty-four years coming!'

'Granted.'

Kat's head had sunk forward, her chin almost on her chest, so that her expression was hidden from him as she muttered, 'I'm nothing like him.'

'Prove it.'

She lifted her head in response to the soft challenge, making herself look at him, mainly because once their eyes were connected it was difficult to break that connection, she observed angrily.

'You are a very manipulative man.'

He gave what she considered a heartless laugh, which sadly didn't make it any the less attractive.

'I'm impressed. It takes most people much longer to figure that one out.'

'And by then it's too late,' she said bitterly as she realised it already was for her. Like it or not, she had been put in a position where she had to prove that the future of the refuge was more important than…what? She realised that it hadn't been spelt out yet what her side of any bargain would be.

'What does he expect from me?'

'Alekis?' His broad shoulders lifted in a negligent shrug. 'You should ask him that.'

She squeezed her eyes closed, then opened them wide. 'Do I have any other family?' The sudden possibility that she had an entire family out there, aunts, uncles, cousins, felt strange…and yet exciting.

'Not that I am aware of,' he said, feeling quite irrationally guilty when the spark faded from her eyes.

Another emotion broke through his defences that Zach couldn't put a name to, didn't even try. It took seconds for him to douse it, but the memory of that nameless feeling remained like a discordant echo as he responded to the question with evasion that came easily.

'But again, I suggest you should ask the man himself. I am not privy to all his secrets.'

She nodded. 'And if I do…see him…how does that work?'

Before he could congratulate himself on a job well done she gave a fractured little sigh and added, 'Does he have any *idea* what sort of life she led? The places, the men…?'

Without warning an image of the little girl she had once been flashed into his head again, along with a compulsion to ask, 'Do you remember?'

'She used to tell me stories.' Without warning her eyes filled with tears; the stories were true. 'Does he live on an island?' she asked, remembering the wistful quality in her mother's voice when she told those stories. 'He didn't want us and now I—I don't have a grandfather. I don't have anybody.'

He clenched his jaw as the plaintive cry from the heart threatened the professional distance he needed to retain. 'I know this has been a shock.'

She gave a bitter little laugh. *'You think?'*

Shock? Was that what you called making someone question everything she'd thought she knew about her life?

'Look, I have no vested interest in this. I am simply the messenger boy. You make your decision and I'll relay it.'

She took a deep sustaining breath and looked him straight in the eye. 'I'll do it.' *Oh, God, what am I doing?* 'So, what happens now? If I agree to see him, I'm assuming he can't come here…unless that was a lie?'

'He is ill.'

'So that is real?'

He actually took some comfort from the fact that she was not *quite* as naive as she appeared, though even if she turned out to be half as naive it would be cause for serious concern.

'I wasn't lying. Alekis is seriously ill.'

'Is he in pain?'

'Not that I know of. Do you want him to be?'

Her eyes flew wide in comic-book shock-horror fashion. 'What sort of person do you think I am?'

'I think you're—'

The driven quality in his unfinished words made her shake her head in puzzled confusion.

'You want to know what happens next?'

Diverted, she nodded.

'The plan is for me to take you to Tackyntha via Athens, where you will meet your grandfather before his next surgery.' The doctors had agreed with the utmost reluctance to Alekis's plan to meet them at the airport, and then only after he had agreed to have a full medical team with him.

She shook her head. 'Tackyntha?'

'It is your grandfather's home, an island.'

'Where my mother lived.'

'I presume so.'

'So, you want me to go to the hospital.'

The obvious solution, but Alekis was determined that when he met his granddaughter he would not be lying in a hospital bed. 'At the airport.'

'And what if I say no?'

'I'd say fair enough, though it's a shame because your cause sounded pretty deserving.'

'Do you work for him?'

His lips twitched. 'He did offer, but, no, I do not work for Alekis.'

'Does he think you can buy love? Buy me?' Her words had an angry, forlorn sound.

'That is not in my field of expertise.'

'What *is* your area of expertise?'

'Well, it's *not* babysitting reluctant heiresses.'

She responded to the barely concealed disdain in his observation with an equally snooty glare of her own. 'I do not require a babysitter, thank you.'

'Let me rephrase it. You need to learn the rules of the society you're about to enter.'

She pounced angrily on the refined definition. 'So that I don't embarrass my grandfather, you mean! Oh, to hell with this. My home is here. I'm needed here.'

'Really? You already told me that you are not irreplaceable. That you have a talented second-in-command whose task, I think, would be a lot easier if your refuge had financial security. Besides, being an heiress does not make you rich in the present, but you will be a target for shady gold-diggers and tabloid journalists, which is where I come in.'

'So, what are you—a bodyguard or a babysitter?'

'I am a man at the end of his patience,' he intoned grimly. 'Look, the options are you flounce off or give me the details so that I can arrange a bank transfer into your refuge's accounts.'

'And what do I have to do?'

'Come and say hello to a dying old man.' For starters, he added silently, before reminding himself that her future and her happiness were not his business.

Who said be careful what you wished for? Maybe, she reflected grimly, someone who had dreamt of finding a family only to have it feel... How *did* she feel?

Unravelling the confused tangle of emotions she was struggling with, Kat knew that a dream come true wasn't meant to feel this way. 'So, who would he have left his money to if he hadn't decided to make up for a quarter of a century and look for me?'

'Me, I would imagine. However, you can relax. I don't need it.'

Which explained the arrogant manner and the air of self-importance.

'If I do come with you to Greece, I will need some guarantees. Firstly, I need to know that the future of the refuge is guaranteed.'

'My word is not enough for you?'

Her eyes narrowed at the hauteur in his manner. 'In writing, for my lawyer to check over.' Her expression dared him to challenge the fact she had a lawyer. Well, Mike *was* a lawyer, though not hers, but lawyer sounded so much more impressive and businesslike than her friend from her baking class who'd like to be more.

'Agreed,' he said calmly. 'You can have the papers by the end of the day.'

'And I need to know that I can leave whenever I like.'

The idea that he or Alekis had any control over her

movements was something he allowed to pass. 'Two months.'

'What?'

'You will give your grandfather two months to get to know you. That only seems fair, wouldn't you say?'

Nothing about this seemed *fair* to Kat, who nodded. 'Two months.' She started to get to her feet and stopped. 'I don't know your name.'

'Enter the name Zach Gavros into your search engine and you'll find out all you need to know about me. Some of it might even be true.'

CHAPTER FOUR

SOMEONE FILLED KAT'S glass with the wine from the party-sized box that she was pretty sure Zach Gavros would have turned his autocratic nose up at. It was still in her hand as she slipped out of the room, where the mood was definitely party, and into the relative quiet of the office. Though no longer *her* office.

She had said goodbye to everyone earlier, fighting the emotional lump in her throat, reminding herself that she was the only one, barring Sue, who knew that this was a permanent parting. The goodbye was of the 'for ever' variety.

Maybe she would come back after two months, but it didn't seem fair for her to ask Sue to step down when or if she returned, so she was making a clean break. Which had left her with no real option but to tell Sue, considering she was relying on her deputy to step into her shoes, the task that wasn't as easy as she had hoped. While she had been convincing a sceptical Sue how perfect she was for the job and how smooth the transition would be, Kat realised just how true it was. She supposed everyone liked to think they were indispensable, that they would leave a hole, be missed, but it was depressing to realise that she was so easy to replace.

'You should go back to the party,' she said to Sue, who she had seen slip away a few minutes earlier. The older woman, who was bent over a carboard box of files, straightened up and nodded.

'I will, but I couldn't let you go without a last hug.'

Feeling the tears press against her eyelids, Kat blinked and turned her head, putting her half-full glass down next to a pile of books on a cabinet. 'Nice photos,' she said, her glance taking in the framed photos of her children that Sue had already arranged on what was now *her* desk.

Sue looked anxious. 'I hope you don't mind?'

'Of course not,' Kat responded, feeling guilty because she had minded—just a bit.

'So, when do you want me to tell the others that you're not coming back from the *management course*?' Sue asked, framing the words with inverted commas. She had made no secret that she was mystified by Kat's determination to keep the truth under wraps, and Kat hadn't really known how to explain it herself. It was hard to tell other people about something that still seemed unreal to her. Besides, they might look at her the way Sue had initially, as though she'd changed or she were a different person.

Well, she wasn't, and she didn't intend to be. Kat was determined that, whatever happened, she would hang on to her own identity. If her grandfather or Zach Gavros thought they could mould her into something she wasn't, they would soon learn otherwise.

Of course, she had searched for his name. There was

plenty of information there to give her an insight into the man her grandfather had chosen to tutor her in how the super-rich behaved, and also a few significant gaps.

His past seemed something of a mystery, which had sparked a thousand conspiracy theories. A favourite being that he had underworld connections. Another that he was Alekis's bastard son, which would make him her… No, that *couldn't* be right, she decided, sure that there could be no blood connection between them.

There were almost as many stories of his financial genius and ruthless dedication to amassing wealth as there were to the sleek cars he drove, and the even sleeker women who lined up to have their hearts broken by him.

And to be fair, in a number of cases their public profiles and careers had been enhanced by their association with the man. Kat didn't feel it was fair, though, as an image floated into her head of her mother's grave as it had been when she'd finally found it. Overgrown, untended…lonely. Her mother's heart had not been as resilient as the women whose names had been associated with Zach Gavros, but she liked to think that her mother had finally found a man worthy of her love. The beautiful gravestone in the cemetery gave her hope.

Kat pushed away the intruding thoughts with a firm little shake of her head. She smiled at Sue.

'That's up to you. You're the boss.' A sudden whoop from the other room, where the party was still in full swing, made her turn her head. When she looked back, Sue was looking at her suitcase.

'That is one very small case for a new life.'

'Just what I was thinking.'

Both women turned to the owner of the pleasant voice—*pleasant* was a good description of the man who was standing in the doorway. A little above average height, he was fairish and good-looking. Mike's newly acquired and carefully tended beard made him look less boyish and gave him, according to him, the maturity his clients expected of a solicitor earmarked for partner in a successful practice.

'I did knock but nobody heard. Am I too early?'

'Perfect timing, and I always travel light,' Kat told them both truthfully, seeing no need to explain that it was a hangover from her childhood, when for years she had been utterly certain that the mother who had left her sitting on the car-park wall of a health centre would come back to her. Her faith had been absolute; she had kept her small suitcase stowed neatly under her bed, packed, ready for the day her mum would come to claim her. Which was probably why none of the early foster placements had ever stuck, and the couple who had been interested in adopting her had backed out. *Polite,* she'd heard them tell her case worker, but unable to respond to love. They hadn't understood that Kat didn't need a family, she already had one, though seeing as they had said she was a polite child she hadn't wanted to upset them by explaining this.

In the end she'd found her way into a long-term foster home. A mad, hectic household with a rare and marvellous couple who didn't expect love, they just gave it, and they never mentioned her case under the bed.

Kat still had a packed case under her bed that she didn't have to explain, because Kat didn't share her bed or her history with anyone.

'You know everyone is going to be gutted they didn't get to say goodbye properly.'

Kat smiled. For a day or two, a week maybe, they might miss her. Might even say some affectionate *remember when* things about her in the future, but people forgot and that, she reminded herself before she slipped into a self-pitying spiral, was the way it should be. She would be in a position now to help them more from a distance than she ever could have here.

'What shall I tell them when you don't come back?'

'That's up to you. Like I keep saying, you'll be the boss, you'll do things your way. Oh, sorry!' She straightened the photo her elbow had nudged. 'This one of Sara is so cute. She looks just like you.'

'So everyone keeps telling me.'

Kat placed it carefully back down. The photo was the reason why Sue would always be missed, never forgotten. She had family. Shrugging off the wave of sadness tinged with envy that threatened to envelop her, Kat picked up her case and reminded herself that she travelled light, something that Sue, with all her responsibilities, couldn't do. She was lucky.

'This is your office—you might even splurge on that new desk I never got around to getting. Nobody suspects, do they?' She nodded towards the door, behind which there was the gentle hum of laughter.

'Not a thing.'

'I must be a much better liar than I thought.'

No one had had any problem accepting that a philanthropist who wanted to remain nameless had appeared, and that he was willing to not only fund the shortfall, but very generously fund the expansion of an annex and playground they had always dreamt of, and send Kat on a management course. And why shouldn't they? Everyone loved a happy ending.

Sue's reaction to the full story had made her realise that in most people's eyes she had her own happy ending. She was an heiress; she was living the dream. The dream of so many children living in care.

Not hers. Maybe she just didn't dream big. She had never thought of castles...just somewhere small, enough money to pay the bills and a mum. Her little fantasies had never contained any male figures; her own father, she knew, had walked out before she was born, and the men in her mother's life afterwards, well, the moments of peace she remembered coincided with their absences.

The only male figure who had been a reassuring presence in her life had been her foster father, but when he had died completely unexpectedly she had seen first-hand how devastated his wife, Nell, had been.

So the options, it seemed to Kat, were between being involved with a man who turned out to a bastard who abused or deserted you, or a man who, to quote dear Nell, you 'loved so much you became half a person after you lost them'. Those heartbroken words had stayed with Kat, as had the haunted, empty look in her foster mum's eyes.

Neither of the above seemed an option anyone with half a brain would voluntarily choose, though maybe falling in love removed the choice?

She was open-minded about the power of love, but it was a power she had never felt and she didn't feel deprived. Actually, she'd started to wonder, if you *had* to have a relationship—and the world did seem to be constructed for pairs—a relationship without love might be the way to go?

A choice made for common-sense reasons with someone you knew was nice and dependable—like Mike?

It was ironic that lately she'd even been contemplating saying yes, the next time he asked her out. Though that wasn't going to happen now.

Mike picked up her case. 'You sure about this?' he asked, his expression concerned.

'Of course she is—it's like a fairy tale and she's the princess. Aren't you excited? Your life is going to change.'

Fighting the impulse to yell, *I liked my old life,* she lifted her shoulders in a delicate shrug, smiling to take the edge off her words.

'I quite liked the old one. I'm still a bit in shock,' she added, feeling she had to defend her lack of enthusiasm as she returned Sue's hug and gave a sniff. 'Stop that,' she begged the weeping Sue. 'I said I was not going to cry.'

She did, a little, and Mike, being tactful, didn't comment on her sniffles as they drove along. Instead, he kept up a desultory anecdotal conversation that required nothing from her but the occasional nod and smile until they reached the private airfield.

A barrier lifted as they approached, and they were waved through to a parking area that appeared empty apart from two limousines parked at the far end.

Mike lifted her case from the boot and turned to where she stood waiting, her slender shoulders hunched against a chill autumnal breeze. 'I've done some research, and your grandfather, Kat, he's mega wealthy.'

Kat nodded. She too had looked up her grandfather's name and seen the results that spilled out. Knowing that her mother had lived the life afforded by such unimaginable wealth and privilege and then been reduced to such a miserable, degrading existence somehow made her fate worse, and intensified the anger Kat felt towards the man who had refused, up to this point, to acknowledge he even had a granddaughter.

'So, I suppose we're never going to have that movie and take-away night.' Underneath the lightness of his words she glimpsed a genuine sadness that made Kat experience a pang of guilt, acknowledging her own selfishness.

She'd turned to Mike for help, knowing that he wanted to be more than a friend, and had not spared a thought for his feelings. Maybe Zach had been right: she *was* like her grandfather.

Horror at the thought made her respond with more warmth than she might have otherwise shown as she threw her arms around him in a spontaneous bear hug.

'We can keep in touch.'

Zach emerged from the limo to see the embrace. He tensed, his teeth grating together in a white unsmiling barrier as the pressure of outrage building in his chest increased. Waving away the driver and his bags, he kept his eyes trained on the couple, ignoring the whisper in the corner of his brain that suggested his reaction to Katina having a lover was a bit OTT.

The soft sound of her laughter reached his ears, low and *intimate*, he silently translated, feeling the rush of another nameless emotion that pushed him into action, and strode across the concrete. It was nothing to him if she had a lover or a string of them, but the information, he told himself, might have been useful. It wasn't like Alekis to leave out such a detail, so presumably he didn't know about this man either.

He did not doubt that Alekis would manage to separate them, but he found he could see a quicker and more efficient way to facilitate this.

'Good afternoon.'

Furious with herself for jumping guiltily away from Mike at the sound of Zach's voice, she laid a hand on Mike's arm.

'Hello.'

The warmth lacking in her eyes as she had acknowledged the tall Greek's presence was there as she turned back to her friend. 'Mike, this is Zach Gavros. I told you about him.'

She had actually told him very little of what she had learnt online, because, like Sue, Mike's recognition of the name had been instantaneous, though, unlike Sue, Mike's depth of knowledge was more focused on Zach's apparent financial genius than the number of hearts he'd broken. And he hadn't shown the same degree of interest in what the Greek would look like without his shirt as Sue.

Kat, whose Internet trawl had been extensive, and had thrown up pictures of Zach and his ribbed, golden torso on a private beach with a model wearing nothing but a pair of minuscule bikini bottoms, already knew the answer. As she looked at him standing there, in a dark suit topped by a long overcoat, open to reveal his snowy white shirt, she realised that the knowledge of what he looked like minus the tailoring made her cheeks heat.

'This is my friend, Mike Ross.' She tore her eyes from the sensual curve of Zach's mouth and focused on his cleanly shaven jaw while she caught her breath, as Mike stepped forward, hand extended, and for a horrible moment she thought Zach was not going to take it.

'Friend and lawyer. I hope everything was in order, Mr Ross.'

She wasn't surprised that Mike didn't respond. Zach Gavros sounded coldly aloof and slightly bored, and he was already looking over the other man's fair head to a uniformed figure who came across and took Kat's case.

Kat's temper fizzed. The man was rude! To compensate, she bent in and kissed Mike's bearded cheek, her voice huskily emotional as she spoke.

'I'll be in touch.' The warmth faded from her voice as she tilted her head up to the tall, hovering figure. 'Given his form, I needed to know that the money for the refuge is ring-fenced should my *grandfather* decide to chuck *me* out too.'

Zach's eyes narrowed on the beautiful face turned up to him. She was spoiling for a fight but he had no intention of obliging. 'Not the time or place for this conversation, I think—Mr Ross.' The nod was curt as he took her elbow.

She had little choice but to respond to the hand under her elbow. It was either that or be dragged along the concrete. She skipped a little to keep up with his long-legged stride before taking advantage of a slight drop in his pace to snatch her arm away.

Panting, she lifted both hands in an 'enough is

enough' gesture as she shook her head. 'Will you slow down? I can't breathe!'

Zach swore under his breath as she started to back away. In seconds she was going to provide the paparazzo he had so far shielded her from with a full-face shot if the two members of his security team zeroing in on the guy, who he knew from experience had the tenacity of a terrier without the charm, didn't reach him in time.

It was a risk Zach was not prepared to take.

He acted on instinct; the question was, *what* instincts?

He moved with speed that bewildered Kat, certainly gave her no opportunity to react as he dragged her with casual ease into his body.

There were no shallows in the kiss. It was hard, deep and possessive. Above the paralyzing shock, on one level she registered the taste of his mouth, the skill of his lips, the hardness of the body so close to her own, but those factors were drowned out by the level that was all shuddering pleasure and heat.

It ended as abruptly as it had begun.

Rocking back on her heels like a sapling in a storm, Kat opened her mouth and no words came. There was a disconnect between her brain and her vocal chords.

'Let's take the "how dare you?" outrage as read,' he drawled, sounding bored and smoothing back his dark hair with a hand that might have held the slightest of tremors as his head turned towards the shouts of protest being issued by the paparazzo as he was escorted away.

Kat followed the line of Zach's gaze, comprehension dawning. The colour rushed to her pale cheeks.

It wasn't as if you thought he'd been overcome by lust for your body, Kat.

'A shot of me kissing a woman is not worth much.'

'The market being saturated.'

'Whereas the face of a mystery woman fighting me off would be, and that guy may be scum, but he's not stupid,' Zach conceded. 'He has a nose for a story and there were some shots of me leaving the hospital after visiting Alekis. If he had made the link...'

Kat barely heard anything he said after his initial comment. 'I wasn't *fighting* you!'

'Never allow the truth to get in the way of a good headline,' he told her with a cynical smile. 'It's all about perception, trust me, and don't worry, the boyfriend didn't see.'

'He's not my boyfriend, and even if he was that would be none of your business.'

He clicked his long brown fingers. 'In that case, no problem.'

Actually there was, and it was a problem of his own making. His strategy had been effective but it came with a price tag.

His gaze sank to her lush lips.

The price was the frustration of starting something he couldn't finish, and finishing was obviously a non-starter. It would be a massive betrayal of the trust Alekis had put in him.

His expression concealed by hooded eyelids, he watched as she angrily tapped one foot clad in a spiky little ankle boot. There was an element of compulsion in the slow sweep of his eyes as they travelled up the long smooth curve of her calves covered in dark tights.

Not being able to see the outline of her thighs through the kicky little woollen skirt she wore somehow made it more sexy. Imagination was a powerful aphrodisiac.

'Plenty of problems,' she rebutted grimly.

Zach found himself agreeing.

'I do not appreciate being mauled by you whatever the reason.'

'You have a novel way of showing your lack of appreciation.' The memory of how soft and yielding she had felt, how well her curves had fitted into his angles, created a fresh crackle of heat that settled in his groin.

If she had needed a warning that he was dangerous, the slow, predatory half-smile that left his eyes cold would have provided it.

The gesture was casual, his hand did not even make contact with the skin of her cheek, but it was close enough for her to feel the warmth. She swayed away from it but, warning or not, she had no facility to prevent the image that surfaced in her head. It was a very specific image, sensory in its strength, long brown fingers moving over pale… She escaped the images in her head before she fell over, her breath leaving her parted lips in a raspy gush.

Well, that couldn't be good, could it?

Shame rushed through her as she lifted her chin. There was no way she was going to add herself to the long list of women who had made fools of themselves over Zach Gavros. For starters, she had too much self-respect, and secondly, a much too strongly developed sense of self-preservation.

History would *not* be repeating itself. That was not an option, she told herself, as an image of the sad, overgrown grave flashed into her head. It was an image that represented a life wasted. She was not her mother; *her* hormones were not in charge. If that meant staying a tight, buttoned-up, but safe virgin, it was a price she was happy to pay.

Kat might not know a lot about heart-racing excitement, but she did know she didn't need it and this man was the living embodiment of heart-racing.

His hand dropped; useless to deny this situation was eating into his reserves of self-control. It was going to get very tiring if he had to remind himself every five minutes that she was Alekis's granddaughter, and as such totally off-limits—a matter not just of respect but practicality.

He needed a distraction, not to mention a release for all the sexual frustration that was clawing low and painfully in his belly, threatening the legendary cool he had long taken for granted. And he knew just the distraction. Andrea Latkis, a very talented and ambitious lawyer on Alekis's Athens-based legal team. Not coy, she had made her desire to sleep with him clear. It was an invitation that he had always intended to accept, but they both had busy lives and their calendars had never been in sync.

It would never have occurred to Andrea to make adjustments to her calendar. He liked that about her, because neither would he, but then maybe drastic situations, or at least uncomfortable ones, required him to make some concessions.

Having come to this conclusion, he was able to experience the rush of heat he endured when Kat removed a glossy strand of hair from her plump lips with something that approached acceptance.

His problem was not Alekis's granddaughter, it was the fact that he had not scheduled a sexual outlet into his life for too long—hence this reaction to having a beautiful woman forcibly thrown into his orbit.

He could relax, though not too much, he cautioned, remembering how he had felt as she'd smiled at the boyfriend. At least there was one interpretation of that moment he could delete—he did not do jealousy.

'Your grandfather is looking forward to meeting you.'

Like ice cream in a heatwave, the antagonism and defiance in her face melted, leaving wide-eyed deer-in-the-headlights fear. He ignored the tightening in his chest that was perilously close to sympathy and looked around.

'Where's the rest of your luggage?'

'I just brought the essentials.'

'For an overnight trip? No matter, we can take your wardrobe in hand when we arrive, and I can arrange to have your belongings shipped over.'

She adopted a calm, no-compromise attitude as she explained, 'No. I intend to keep my London flat on.'

'Alekis has several properties in London. Your things can be moved into whichever you prefer.'

Clearly he had trouble recognising no compromise. 'I prefer my own place, and what do you mean by *take my wardrobe in hand*?' She stopped. She was talking to empty space. Zach had turned and was striding off, his elegant long-legged figure drawing glances to which he seemed utterly oblivious.

She had to trot to catch up with him. 'In hand?' she echoed in a dangerous voice before tacking on breathlessly, 'Will you slow down? We're not all giraffes,' she told him, thinking that a panther was probably a better animal kingdom analogy. His legs might be long but they were in perfect proportion to the rest of his lean, square-shouldered, narrow-hipped frame.

His mouth quirked as he angled a glance down at her lightly flushed face. 'Sorry, I'm not used to—'

She paused as a thoughtful expression flickered across his saturnine features.

'Used to what?'

'Considering anyone else.'

There was nothing even faintly apologetic about his admission. *'Never...?'* Was anyone really that selfish? Kat struggled with the concept.

'You sound shocked.'

'That there are selfish people in the world?' She shook her head. 'I'm not that naive. It's just mostly people try to hide it.'

It wasn't as if he had never been criticised—he'd actually been called a lot worse than selfish—but this was the first time he had ever experienced an inexplicable impulse to defend himself. It wasn't as though her approval meant anything to him—it was an impulse that he firmly crushed as he pushed out coldly, 'There are also virtue-signalling martyrs in the world who, in my experience, rarely try and hide it.'

He heard her sharp intake of breath as she came to an abrupt halt. He took a couple of strides before he stopped and swung back. She was standing there, hands fixed on her hips, her head thrown back as she stared up at him through narrowed amber eyes.

'Are you calling me a martyr?' Her eyelids fluttered as her eyes widened with astonished indignation.

He arched a sardonic brow and heard the sound of her even white teeth grating.

'If you can't take a little constructive criticism, Katina—'

She recognised he was baiting her but not before a strangled *'Constructive!'* had escaped her clenched lips; then she managed a smile of jaw-clenching insincerity. 'Then I suppose I should say thank you, and I promise you that any further *constructive* comments from you on my behaviour will be treated with the same degree of appreciation that I'm feeling now!'

His low, quite impossibly sexy rumble of appreciation—was it possible for a laugh to make you tingle?—had her tumbling from sarcastic superiority back to tingling sexual awareness.

She looked away quickly, embarrassed and confused by her reaction to a laugh, and took a moment before she trusted herself to look up again. When she did the mockery she had come to expect had faded from his lean face, replaced not by sympathy but something that came close to it.

Zach had not got to where he was without possessing an ability to read feelings, so recognising the fear underlying her tough stance was nothing more than he would have expected. What he didn't expect was the surge of irrational guilt attached to the surfacing need to offer her some sort of reassurance.

'I know this must feel frightening, being plunged into an alien environment, but you know, it does us all good to step outside our comfort zone once in a while.' He stopped, his expression closing as he realised how far outside his own comfort zone he was straying. There was a very good reason he didn't wander around emoting. In the financial world, empathy had a way of revealing your own weaknesses.

In his private world it had never been an issue. His relationships, if you chose to call them that, were about sex, not establishing an emotional connection.

The unexpected softening of his tone hit Kat in a weak spot she hadn't even known she had. If he had opened his arms she'd have walked into them wanting...*what*?

When did I turn into the sort of girl who needed a big strong man to turn to?

She let her breath out in a slow, slow hiss, tilted her chin and gave a cool smile. She hadn't turned into that girl and she never would.

'Please don't insult my intelligence by pretending you care,' she snapped back, ignoring the voice in her head that said she was using him as a scapegoat.

The weakness might be hers, but he had exposed it.

'Or do you even know how to spell empathy?'

'Well, if I need to borrow some, I'll know where to come.'

'Meaning?'

'You really are the original bleeding heart. How many men have figured out the way into your bed is by being weak and needy and...*damaged*?' he sneered.

She sucked in an outraged breath through flared nostrils and stalked past him, tossing over her shoulder, 'You are worse than disgusting!'

The sardonic arrogance stamped on his features

faded as she walked across the tarmac, her angry posture as graceful as a ballroom dancer's, chin up, her long neck extended, narrow shoulder blades drawn back. He might arguably have won the brief war of words, but the triumph felt hollow. Something possibly to do with the fact his body, reacting independently of his brain, was sending painful slug after slug of raw hunger in response to the movement of her slim body.

Theos, but this woman was killing him, or rather the lusting after her was.

He might consider her out of bounds but there were plenty that wouldn't. His task was getting less enviable with each passing moment.

CHAPTER FIVE

ANY OF THE pleasure Kat might have felt at the sheer
novelty value of the travelling style of the rich and famous was ruined for her by the thought of what lay
ahead when they landed.

Every time she thought of the man who had left his
only daughter to suffer a life a step from the gutter,
icy anger rose up in her like a tide. She was not used
to such feelings and they made her feel physically sick.

What did he want from her? Forgiveness? A second
chance? Kat did not feel she had either in her.

The emotions surging and churning inside her must
have shown on her face because at one point during the
flight an attendant came and discreetly pointed out the
bathroom facilities.

Happy to play along with the assumption she was a
poor flyer, Kat vanished in the restroom for a few minutes of solitude she didn't really want—it left too much
time for her dark thoughts.

Trailing her hand under the water and looking at
herself in the illuminated mirror, she found it easy to
understand the attendant's assumption she was about
to throw up. She looked terrible, the emotional tussle

in her head reflected on her face. She felt bad enough to wish for a foolish split second that Zach, who had fallen into conversation with one of the pilots as they'd boarded and vanished with him, was actually there to distract her—and that was pretty bad!

Nothing as dramatic as the kiss, of course. That had definitely been a step too far, she decided, a dreamy expression drifting into her eyes that she had no control over as she trailed her fingers across the outline of her lips, before snatching them away a moment later with a self-conscious grimace as she realised what she was doing.

When she retook her seat, despite her assuring the attendant she was feeling much better, the woman suggested she should alert Mr Gavros to the situation.

Kat hastily assured her that the only situation was her need to catch up on some sleep.

The attendant reluctantly complied, leaving Kat alone with her own thoughts and her rising sense of panic and trepidation for the rest of the flight. Zach didn't reappear until after they had landed; actually she didn't see him first, she *felt* his presence.

Even though she hadn't looked around she knew the *exact* moment he had appeared. It made her fumble as she released her seat belt and got to her feet, smoothing down her hair and straightening the row of pearly buttons on the square-necked sweater she wore tucked into the belt that emphasised her narrow waist, then stopped because her hands were shaking. The amount of adrenaline circulating in her bloodstream was having a dizzying effect. A situation not improved when she lifted her chin and was no longer able to delay the moment she looked at him.

He had lost the coat and jacket and was standing there, looking elegant and as relaxed as someone as driven as him could. Also, overpoweringly sexy. She blamed the enclosed space and the slight tingle left on her lips from that kiss.

'Where… How…?' She stopped, hating the breathy delivery, and ran a tongue across her dry lips and lifted her chin and husked out, 'Is he…my…*grandfather* here?'

The toughness she had adopted was paper thin; something about the way she stood there looking as vulnerable as hell and too proud to show it awoke something in a tiny, previously dead corner of Zach's heart. He tensed as some nameless emotion clutched at him, making his voice abrupt when he finally responded.

'He's waiting in a hotel next door to the terminal, but don't worry, it'll be private.' Alekis had taken over the penthouse floor to ensure privacy for the meeting, and presumably space for the specialist team on hand with defibrillators.

Zach just hoped this meeting was not going to be memorable for all the wrong reasons.

Her lips tightened. 'I hope he doesn't expect me to pretend, because I won't. I'll tell him what I think of him.'

Her words jolted loose a memory. He remembered saying as much to himself before he'd walked back into the seedy apartment that for seven years had been what some would laughingly call his home. His nostrils flared now as he remembered the sour stale stench that had hit him as he had opened the door.

He was a realist; he hadn't anticipated any sort of

an apology or even regret, just an acknowledgement of what they had done. It had become obvious very quickly that he wasn't going to get even that. He'd found his grandmother in her bed, hair matted, unwashed; her eyes had had a vacant look as she'd stared at him without recognition.

Of his uncle there had been no sign. Clearly when free bed and board was not worth the effort of living with a woman with what the doctors had diagnosed as advanced dementia, he had vanished. Later, Zach had discovered he had not got far. It seemed he'd picked a fight with the wrong solitary, weak-looking person, who, it had turned out, had not been alone. His uncle had died of his head injuries three days later—a sordid end to a sordid life.

He pushed away the memory and simultaneously dampened an uncharacteristic need to say something comforting, and almost definitely untrue, to soothe the conflict he could see in those golden eyes.

He couldn't see this meeting being comfortable.

'You mean you can pretend?' He had rarely encountered honesty of the variety she possessed in a world where it was rare for people to speak the truth. She stood out. His eyes slid down her body. She stood out for a lot of reasons.

'He is a stranger and he hurt my mother. He doesn't mean anything to me.'

'Then tell him that. The funding for your refuge is guaranteed.'

Kat found his response bewildering. Was he trying to play devil's advocate? 'You know I can't. He's ill, he might...'

The hand on her shoulder was light but strangely comforting. Finding Zach Gavros comforting in any sense of the word must mean she was in a worse state than she'd thought.

'If I say something and he dies…how am I supposed to live with that?' she choked out.

'Alekis is tough and he has an army of medics on hand. Anything that happens is *not* your responsibility,' he added, suddenly angry as hell with Alekis for putting his granddaughter in this position. 'By this evening you can be swimming in the sea.'

She gave a sudden smile that lightened her expression as she responded to the tip of his head and walked towards the exit. 'That would be something. I can't swim.'

'I'll teach you.' She was looking as startled by the offer as he felt.

'Don't be nice to me or I'll cry.'

'Relax, I'm never nice. Ask anyone. Living on an island, swimming is a necessary survival skill.' As was keeping women like this one an emotional mile away, women who couldn't believe that sex could be just that, women who wanted something deeper and more meaningful, women who needed an emotional depth he simply didn't have.

It was an exaggeration to say the hotel was next door to the airport, but it was conveniently close.

'It's very nice,' she said, keeping up the same flow of polite conversation she had during the car transfer. It helped maintain the illusion of normality but was, she realised, starting to sound desperate.

Actually, the hotel, part of a luxury chain she had vaguely heard of, was *extremely* nice in a plush, up-market way.

'Thank you.'

She threw a questioning look up at Zach's austerely handsome profile. 'The chain is a relatively recent purchase. It was a bit tired, but it's amazing what a refurb can do.'

'You own it?' Well, that explained the manager who was rushing out to greet them before personally escorting them to the private entrance to the penthouse floor, where the elevator door was flanked by men wearing suits and dark glasses who spoke into the headsets they were wearing.

Kat hesitated before she stepped inside the lift, taking a moment to pull her shoulders back and lift her chin.

Stepping in after her, Zach felt a twinge of admiration. It was impossible not to. She looked as though she were walking into a lion's den, but, my God, she was doing it with style!

The swishing upward ride took seconds and then the doors were silently opening.

'He is as nervous as you.'

Kat lifted her eyes. 'I seriously doubt that. I feel like I used to when I hid.' She had always had a hiding place ready when the loud voices had started, a place to crawl into and try to be invisible.

No hiding place now, Kat! Just do it!

He sensed she had not even realised what she had said, words that might not have made sense to many but, as someone who had tried very hard to be invisible, he knew that she was talking of an experience similar to, but he *really* hoped not the same as, his own.

He found himself hoping grimly that the mother who had abandoned her had retained enough motherly feeling to protect her child from violence, the sort that had scarred his own youth.

The golden eyes lifted to his. 'I'm afraid I won't be able to stop myself, that I'll say something really bad—I'm so angry,' she whispered, pressing a hand to her breastbone as if to physically hold in the storm of emotions raging there.

'Don't be afraid. You've a right to be angry.' Maybe she would have the apologies and explanations he'd been robbed of.

'I thought you were team Alekis.' *He has a beautiful mouth...* The thought drifted through the tangled knot of thoughts in her head as she stared at the sensually carved lines... Had he *really* kissed her? The memory, like everything else, had an unreal quality.

'You won't say anything to hurt him. You're too... *kind.*' He allowed himself the comment because he spoke as an objective observer. He was not here to get involved in the relationship between grandfather and granddaughter. He carried the inescapable taint of his own family with him through life without getting involved in someone else's family conflict.

The way he said *kind*, he made it sound like a defect—not that Kat felt kind as her attention narrowed in on the figure seated in a large chair that made her think of a throne, placed centre stage in the room.

She'd seen photos online, but this man was older, much older, yet even with a craggy face, drawn, with fatigue deepening the shadowy bags beneath his eyes, you could sense the power coming off the man. Then, a second later, she saw the eyes beneath the thick white eyebrows were filled with tears.

The wave of emotion that hit her was so unexpected and so powerful that all the other emotions seething inside her were swallowed up. This was her grandfather—her family.

'Katina?'

She pressed a hand to her trembling lips as the figure in the chair held out his arms. 'I am so s-sorry, Katina.'

Zach watched her fight to hold on to her antagonism and fail.

Even the relatively short time he had spent in her company meant that it didn't cross Zach's mind that her capitulation had anything at all to do with personal gain. This was about her generous spirit, and her longing for a family, or at least her idea of what a family was.

She was homesick for an idea.

The world called Zach reckless, a risk taker with a golden touch, but it was a lie. He never risked anything he was not willing to lose. Money was not important to him in itself. Lose a fortune, make a fortune—these were not things that would ever keep him awake. They were challenges, a test of mental agility.

True recklessness was what she possessed. It was the open-hearted way she ran towards the possibility of family and love, risking having her illusions shattered.

Zach admired it, and it appalled him.

Was he team Alekis? No, but neither was he the objective observer he wanted to be. Somehow this woman had awoken a protective instinct in him. He didn't want to feel this way as he watched her cover the space between her and the old man, before dropping with graceful spontaneity to her knees beside the chair.

He turned abruptly and left, reminding himself that he was not part of this drama as he stepped into the elevator, pushing away feelings he didn't want to name, let alone feel.

Part of Kat didn't want to let go of her anger: it felt like a betrayal to her mother, but it had gone, burned away in that explosion of feeling. She'd practised her cold words but how could she be mean when he looked so frail and sounded so tearfully penitent? Though she got a glimpse of the iron man who people feared when he imperiously waved away someone who appeared to check his blood pressure.

A moment later the first man came back with reinforcements. Several nurses in uniform and the dapper figure in the three-piece suit did not react to the scowl directed at him.

'I really must insist. These readings...'

For the first time, Kat realised that there were leads trailing under her grandfather's suit, which were presumably giving readings in the connecting room.

'All right—all right!'

Kat wondered if his capitulation had anything to do with the beads of sweat along his upper lip when he caught her hand.

'As I was saying, it is a small gathering. Nothing too formal, drinks and mingling...'

Saying? she thought, playing catch up. She couldn't recall him saying anything about a *gathering*, but then the short, emotionally charged conversation was a bit of a blur.

'A small press presence…'

Her heart started to pound and she felt sick.

'Don't worry, they are friendly, all invited. One of the advantages of owning an island is that it is easier to keep out undesirable guests.' The claw-like hand tightened on her own, crushing her fingers. 'You're an Azaria, you'll be fine.'

The medics closed in, wielding scary-looking syringes, and she backed away, unable to tell him that she *wasn't* an Azaria and she didn't fit into this life.

As she walked into the lift, the feeling of sick unease in the pit of her stomach grew. What had she just agreed to? Had she agreed to anything? She didn't want to go to a *gathering*, whatever that meant, formal or otherwise.

As the lift doors opened, Zach peeled himself away from the wall he had been leaning against and stood there, hands in his pockets, looking at her.

'You look like you need a drink.' And maybe a hug? He banished the aberrant thought. He was not a *huggy* person, and with Kat hugs would not stay comforting for long. His long fingers flexed as he saw the image in his head of them sliding under that top and over her warm skin.

'I'd prefer a few explanations. Gathering? Press?'

'Ah.'

'So you know what this is about?' She wasn't sure if she was relieved or resentful.

'Basically we are talking cocktail party. Alekis invites a few tame journalists a few times a year, lets them mingle with what is actually quite an eclectic bunch—'

Her voice, shrill with panic, cut across him. 'I can't mingle.'

He didn't look impressed. 'Rubbish. Here's the car now.'

She shook her head. 'No. I'm not going anywhere until you tell me what is going on.'

'We need to control the flow of information. Denying rumours will only—'

Her eyes flew wide in alarm. 'What rumours?'

His eyes lifted. 'A story will appear tomorrow confirming that your grandfather had a heart attack. This is a story that would normally dominate headlines for weeks, excite a predictably hysterical reaction and hit market confidence.'

'You couldn't stop this story?' Kat felt a bit guilty that she was relieved this was about market confidence and not about her.

There was a ruthless quality to the thin-lipped smile he gave in response that made her shiver. 'I planted the story.'

The addition of *obviously* was silent, but quite definitely there. Confused by that as much as his admission, she shook her head. 'But you just said—' she began, feeling her way.

'I said *normally*. On this occasion Alekis's illness will be buried by the much more exciting information that he has been united with his long-lost granddaughter.'

'So, you're using me.'

She sounded shocked by the discovery. His dark brows flattened into a line of exasperation above his obsidian stare.

'This was not my idea.' He wasn't trying to deflect

her anger, but he decided it might be a good thing that she recognised that even at death's door her grandfather was not a warm and cuddly person.

It was bizarre he had to spell it out, but despite her upbringing, inexplicably it seemed to come as a shock to her that anyone had motives that were not pure and elevated.

He wasn't going to be the only one to notice her lack of guile and sophistication, but he might be the only one who wasn't trying to use it to his own advantage. You did not have to be psychic to predict that if she didn't toughen up, and quick, she was going to be a soft touch for every hard-luck sob story going. He hoped for her sake she was a quick learner, or else she was in for some painful lessons in human nature.

She glanced towards the building behind them. 'He?'

'Alekis delegated, but yes, the plan is his. It's nothing sinister. We're controlling the flow of information. Or would you prefer some tabloid breaks the story, sensationalising it? Perhaps digging up an old lover to publish a kiss-and-tell?' He saw no benefit from telling her that this might happen anyway. There were going to be disgruntled ex-lovers coming out of the woodwork once the news of the heiress hit. 'This way your exposure is controlled. Hiding you away would have photographers in helicopters flying over Tackyntha with telephoto lenses.'

Her startled eyes looked up at him as she slid into the car. 'People will want to take my photograph?' she said as he joined her.

'Are you trying to be facile?'

She shook her head.

He sighed and pushed his head into the leather head-rest. 'Belt up, Katina.'

She did and sat there looking shell-shocked.

Zach waited until the car moved away and into the traffic before he spoke. 'You are going to be one of the wealthiest women in Europe, Katina. People will all want to know what you had for breakfast, what your favourite colour nail varnish is. They will discuss what you're wearing and speculate on your sexuality, whether you have an eating disorder or a drug problem.'

He watched as the horror of the reality hit home, feeling like a bastard, but better a bastard on her side than one who could exploit the vulnerability on display in her wide eyes and trembling lips.

She half rose in her seat before subsiding, no parachute, no escape—*no escape*. 'Oh, God!' she groaned, closing her eyes. 'I can't do this.'

'Yes, you can.'

His firm, unsympathetic rebuttal made her eyes fly wide as she directed a glare of simmering dislike at him. She had seen lumps of granite with more empathy than he possessed.

'The way you handle yourself these first few weeks is important, will set a pattern. Alekis's wealth means people don't have automatic access to you. I can put up some barriers to protect you.'

She pushed away the images of walls around a gold-lined cage that flashed through her head, telling herself not to be such a drama queen. There was plenty to be nervous about without inventing things.

'You hide away and people will assume you have

something to hide. We need to create the illusion you are open,' he explained, digging deep into his reserves of patience as he explained what was obvious. 'While telling them essentially nothing.'

Her dark feathered brows lifted. *'We?'*

'All right, you. One of the first things you need to remember is trust no one, *no one*,' he emphasised grimly. 'Not *everyone* you meet will be out for a piece of you,' he conceded.

'Just ninety per cent of them. What a relief!' She quivered. He was really selling this lifestyle. 'I'm not stupid, you know. I might even be able to work out which knife and fork to use. I am a fast learner.'

'That remains to be seen. I won't pretend it isn't going to be a steep learning curve.'

'Oh, I really wish you would pretend that it is.'

He responded to her attempt at humour with a hard look. 'But you will learn to judge. Learn your own style. Until you do, that's what I'm here for.'

She fixed him with a narrow-eyed glare. 'So you mean you'll put the words in my mouth and tell me what to wear.' She folded her arms across her chest and directed a belligerent stare up at his face. 'I'm not a puppet.'

'No. From where I'm sitting you are…' He completed the sentence in a flood of angry-sounding Greek before finally dragging a hand through his dark hair as he sat there, lips compressed, dark eyes burning.

'I don't understand Greek.'

'I said,' he gritted out, 'I am trying to protect you, but if you would prefer I throw you to the wolves…?'

As their eyes connected, glittering black on gold, a

strange little shiver traced a slow, sinuous path up her tension-stiffened spine.

'What is this? Set a thief to catch a thief, or in this case a wolf to catch a wolf?' It was true, there was definitely something of the lean, feral predator about him, which she could see might appeal to some women.

'For your information, I have not spent my life in a protective bubble and I've been coping without a guardian angel—which, for the record, is *definitely* major miscasting—all my life. I resent being treated like a child.'

Were you ever a child? he wondered as his glance moved in an unscheduled slow sweep over her slim, tense figure, oozing hostility, before coming to rest on the outline of her lips. The dull throb in his temples got louder as he saw faceless wolves drawn to the delicious invitation of their plump pinkness.

The barrier of his clenched teeth did nothing to shield him from a fresh onslaught of painful desire. Alekis had put him in a 'rock and hard place' position. He couldn't lay a finger on her without betraying the trust the older man had, for some reason, placed in him and he couldn't walk away, either.

'So, we are going to the island.'

'It doesn't take long by helicopter.'

Kat felt reluctant to admit she'd never flown in one. 'And do your family live there too? Is that how you know Alekis?'

A look she couldn't quite put a name to flickered in his eyes. It was gone so quickly that she might have imagined it.

'No, my family do not live there.'

'But you have family…?' she asked, remembering how he had spoken about his mother's death. 'They were there for you after your mother died?'

'You think because our mothers are dead that gives us something in common? It does not.'

She flushed. If he'd tried to embarrass her, he'd succeeded. Did he think she didn't know they came from two different worlds? That she needed him to point out they had nothing in common, that he had been raised in a world of wealth and privilege that she knew she would never fit into.

Being orphaned was always an awful thing for any child, but in Zach's world there were cushions…nannies, good schools. None could replace maternal love, but it helped if you had the support structure of a family, especially one that meant you didn't stand out because your clothes were not the latest fashion, or you had no holiday to talk about at the start of a new school term.

'You really do worry about family, don't you? Well, relax—yes, I *did* have family.' His lips curled in a cynical smile of remembrance. 'An uncle who is now happily dead and a grandmother who is a great deal pleasanter now that she doesn't remember my name, or, for that matter, her own.'

Shock reverberated through his body, none of it showing on his still shuttered face as he realised he had just revealed more to her than he had to another living person. Not even Alekis knew the details about his life before they had met, and here he was spilling his guts to this woman, with her ridiculous sentimentality, virtually inviting her to walk around in his head!

Was this a new symptom of sexual deprivation?

She looked at his bleakly beautiful face and felt her heart squeeze with sympathy. His comment had been sparing in detail, but you didn't need to have worked with children caught in the firing line of family conflict to recognise that Zach's childhood had not been what she'd imagined.

'I'm so sorry,' she said, wondering uneasily how many of her other assumptions about him were wrong.

'There is no need to be sorry,' he sliced back coldly. 'It is the past.'

Did he really believe it was that easy? she wondered, remembering all the times when she was growing up that she had wished that her past were a painless blank. That she didn't have the snatches of memories that made her sad, while filling her with a nameless longing.

Glancing at his shuttered face, she recognised that she had pushed him as far as she could on the subject. She changed tack. 'So, what is your connection to Alekis?'

'I wonder about that sometimes myself.'

Before she could voice her frustration at this deliberately unhelpful response, he added, 'Your grandfather helped me when no one else would.'

'So, a financial loan…?' she probed.

His eyes were hidden by his half-lowered lids but the smile that quivered on his sensually sculpted mouth intrigued her. 'Not as such, but I remain in your grandfather's debt. I doubt very much if I would be where I am today without his intervention.'

'Where would you be?'

'I sometimes ask myself that, but not often. I prefer

to deal with the here and now, and in the here and now I consider myself in Alekis's debt.'

'Do you like him?'

His dark brows drew together in a straight line above his aquiline nose. 'He has many qualities I admire and many faults I accept.' His dark eyes had a mesmeric quality as he captured her gaze and there was an intensity in his words as he spoke. 'The door to the world you are about to enter is rarely opened to outsiders. I was an outsider, so maybe Alekis thought I was well placed to help your transition.'

'So you're not an outsider now?'

'I have never been a joiner.'

Did he *ever* give a straight answer? she wondered. 'But you want me to join.'

He shook his head. 'That will be your choice. I want you to be aware of the pitfalls. To learn how to—'

'Blend in?'

He gave a sudden laugh, deep and uninhibited. It melted his expression into a smile that made him look years younger and made the bottom of her stomach dissolve. She realised that if this man ever made the effort to charm there wasn't a woman alive who could resist.

Including me!

Now there was a fact to keep her awake at nights.

'What is so funny?'

'The idea of you blending in anywhere.' The laughter died from his face, leaving something much darker, much more intense, more dangerous, she realised, than mere charm. 'You're an exceptionally beautiful woman.'

His deep voice was like rumpled velvet, warm, sensuous and will-sapping. She had no idea how long she sat there staring at him before the blare of a car horn jolted her back to reality.

The reality being that Zach possessed a voice that really ought to carry a danger warning! Ah, well, the next time, should there be a next time, she would be prepared and not look like such an idiot.

She broke the seductive hold of his dark, mesmerising stare, though the effort filmed her skin with sweat as she snapped out contemptuously, 'Don't be stupid!'

Obviously she knew she wasn't *bad* to look at, but *exceptionally beautiful* was not a term used for a woman who had a mouth that was way too big for her face, a gap between her front teeth and the sort of body that looked great in clothes but without them... She hated her bony collarbones and she didn't see how anyone could consider the visible angles on her hips feminine.

Her reaction to him stating the obvious seemed strange. You could be excused for assuming, given her reaction, that no one had ever told her how beautiful she was before. Even if she had had lovers who left a lot to be desired, he thought scornfully, the woman had a mirror.

'Even if you could blend in you shouldn't. You should carry on being yourself, as much as is possible.'

She looked bemused by the advice. 'Who else would I be? I think you worry too much. I'm used to being the odd one out. The kid in care with the wrong clothes.'

If the comment had been made in an attempt to garner sympathy, Zach would not have felt any. He did not *want* to now, and yet as he looked at her he experienced less sympathy but a sudden deep anger for the childhood she had been robbed of. And yet she seemed to have her own set of values that nobody had been able to take from her.

Could he say the same? *Maybe she had come to terms with her past more than he had his?*

He pushed the thought away; the past was something he did have to come to terms with. It was gone and buried. Not only could he not imagine himself discussing it so openly as she did, but he could not imagine wanting to.

CHAPTER SIX

'YOU CAN OPEN your eyes now. We're in the air.'

She did so, taking a breath and realising that at some point during the take off she had grabbed his hand and dug her nails in hard.

With a self-conscious 'Sorry… ' she released it, her brows twitching into a front of dismay as she saw the half-moon crescents standing out white in his olive skin. Pretending to tuck a stray strand of hair behind her ears, she rubbed the skin of her cheek, which was tingling from the warm brush of his breath. It was scary that her body was so sensitive to him.

'I've never been in a helicopter before.'

She just hoped the transfer would be as short as he had promised. Kat leaned forward in her seat to loosen the hair that had got caught down the neck of her sweater. As she leaned back, her glance connected with Zach's.

The lurch in her stomach had nothing to do with their mode of transport as the moment that vibrated with unseen electricity stretched. He was sitting close enough for her to see the network of fine lines that fanned out from the corners of his eyes and the dusting of dark stubble shading his jaw, the shadow adding extra emphasis to the hollows of his cheeks.

She breathed a little deeper, unconsciously leaning forward as her nostrils flared, picking up on the clean male scent that rose from his warm skin. Sensations she had no name for shifted inside her and she paused, like someone standing on the edge of quicksand, fighting the urge to jump in with both feet.

Just before she reached tipping point, she jerked back again abruptly. The sudden adrenaline rush continued to make her head spin. She flexed her fingers before closing both hands tight, trying not to think of that unacknowledged moment when she had been within a heartbeat of reaching out and touching his cheek. It had been an instinctive thing. Kat would have been happier not knowing she possessed such instincts.

And *much* happier not having the image in her head of them lying naked together. Shame mingled with real fear as she dragged her eyes away from the firm sensual line of his mouth. Maybe there was a faulty gene responsible for being attracted to bad men…and she had inherited it? It had always been her secret fear.

Zach's eyes were hooded as he watched her, reminding himself that the task assigned him by Alekis was keeping men out of her bed, not occupying it himself. It did not assuage the ache in his groin as he watched her pupils tellingly dilate until only a thin ring of amber remained.

The muscles in Zach's brown throat rippled as he swallowed, his heavy lids lowered over his eyes as he turned his head to direct his hooded stare out of the window. He had not experienced this sort of elemental response to a woman in a long time and knowing she felt the same attraction, when they were sitting this close and she was looking at him with those hungry eyes, was not making his life any easier.

He closed his eyes to shut out the temptation, but the ache in his body did not diminish as he breathed his way through the hot elemental surge of raw desire that he had to endure because he sure as hell had no control over it.

Kat sat there, heart pounding, throat dry, wondering if he was going to acknowledge the crackle of sexual tension that shimmered in the air between them or even do something about it. Trying to decide if she wanted him to or not.

She was actually on the point of saying something, exactly what she didn't know, when he closed his eyes, and within seconds gave the impression of man deeply asleep.

She had worked herself up into a state of breathless anticipation and he was asleep!

Her cheeks stung pink with mortified heat when she realised how close she had come to utterly humiliating herself. It had felt so real, so tangible. Had it *really* been in her imagination? she wondered, studying the strong lines on his face. Sleep had ironed out some of the austerity and hardness from his face and made him seem younger somehow.

It really was odd to find yourself attracted to someone you did not even like; in fact, actively disliked, she mused, suddenly sleepy herself as the tensions of the last few hours began to catch up with her. Perhaps the *odd* thing was that she had never felt this way before.

Or maybe *she* was just the oddity, a virgin because she'd never allowed anyone to get close enough to change the situation. There had been moments of uncomfortable self-awareness when she'd recognised that this was in part at least due to her deep-seated fear of abandonment, but it was an insight she pushed away.

The same way she'd been pushing away the glaringly obvious fact that she was attracted to Zach Gavros. Of course, denial had been a lot easier when she had been able to think of him as an arrogant two-dimensional figure, but getting a glimpse of his vulnerabilities was making that a lot harder.

Would these newly aroused feelings go back into hibernation once Zach vanished from her life?

Did she want them to?

Kat hadn't worked out the answer by the time her eyelids flickered closed and did not lift.

She knew it was a dream—she'd had it before many times, but not for a long time now. The heart-thudding, stomach-clenching sense of icy dread. Except it wasn't *her*—it was someone else she was watching, crouched small in her hiding place, waiting for the monster's hand to reach in and drag her out. Kat wanted to shout a warning to the little girl, but her voice wouldn't work. Her entire body felt paralysed. She was watching, waiting, helpless to stop what was about to happen.

I'm asleep…asleep…it's not real. She kept repeating the words in her head, fighting her way through the grey layers of sleep to the surface. The process was all consuming, exhausting, then she heard a sound and focused on it, dragging herself clear of the shadows.

As she opened her eyes an indistinct face seemed to be floating there. She watched the outline grow more defined and more solid. Zach was leaning forward in his seat, talking to her.

'We have arrived.'

She blinked, had a moment utter blank, before the memories all came rushing back. She pulled herself upright in her seat with a jerk. 'Oh, God! I must have fallen asleep.' She dragged her hands over her slippery, silky hair, anchoring stray tips behind her ears as she smoothed it.

'You were dreaming.'

'Was I?' she said, thinking, *You were watching me...* and feeling quite extraordinarily exposed.

'You don't remember?'

He was looking at her with what felt like uncomfortable intensity. 'Who remembers dreams?' she said, turning her head to look out of the window, determined that whatever she saw, if her grandfather ate off gold plates and showered in champagne, she was not going to display unworldly awe. She'd show Zach she could pretend as well as anyone.

Her decision incinerated at her first glimpse of her new island home. Temporary home, reminded the voice of caution in her head.

It helped that their arrival coincided with the start of a breathtaking sunset, which, as they came in to land, had just tinged the water with feathers of red.

The landing strip seemed close to the candy-coloured village with terracotta roofs they had flown over, appearing to be cut into the rock of a peninsula that projected into the sea. She doubted her grandfather's villa could be set anywhere more spectacular.

She glanced towards the backdrop of green mountains, looking for signs of a road that might lead to the villa.

'Is it far?' she asked, releasing her white-knuckled grip on the armrest and willing her stomach to stop churning as the helicopter set down and she released the breath held in her chest in a long sibilant sigh of relief.

He angled a questioning look at her face. 'Far?'

'To the house, villa, whatever—is it far from the village?'

An amused smile deepened the lines fanning out from his deep-set eyes. 'There is no village.'

'Town, then,' she said, irritated by his pedantic response.

'Not one of those, either.'

'But…' Her brows twitched into a frown. 'I saw…' Comprehension dawned and her eyes flew wide. 'You're telling me that was a *house*?'

The incredulous uplift of her voice on the word made his lips twitch.

'But where are the people?'

'There is a live-in staff, obviously.'

Still in shock, she watched as he turned to someone who had entered the helicopter; presumably the younger man had been waiting for their arrival. He tipped his head towards Kat and spoke at length in Greek with Zach, who responded in the same language, saying something that had the other man smiling and heading for the exit.

Zach turned his eyes, stilling on her averted face. She

was struggling to loosen the clip on her safety restraint. A hank of hair had fallen across her face and he experienced the strangest impulse to push it back. Would the skin of her cheek be as smooth and soft as it appeared?

His hands clenched into fists as though they held the silky tendrils, before he brought the line of speculation to an abrupt halt. The fact that the questions had been there to begin with was a massive wake-up call. Just a warning; he was in control and in no danger of losing it now.

If the thought lacked conviction, he refused to acknowledge it. Admitting it would have meant acknowledging a chink in his armour.

Freeing herself after a tussle, Kat lifted her head and found he was looking at her with an intensity that made her stomach flip. For a moment the charge in the air, imaginary or real, was back, and it took her breath away before, heart thudding, she managed to lower her lashes in a self-protective shield. Had she imagined that moment? Had it been a creation of her over-heated imagination? *Wishful thinking?*

The sly whisper vanished like smoke but not before her spine had stiffened in utter rejection, that she would want to unleash anything in him let alone... A tiny little shudder showered through her body as she moistened her dry lips. It was ludicrous, more than ludicrous, she told herself firmly, laughable!

Only she wasn't laughing.

'Your grandfather bought the island in the sixties, I believe. At the time there was a church, a couple of houses, but the only occupants were the goats. A goatherd came over from the mainland once every couple of weeks to tend them. So no evictions. The goats are still here too, but don't try hugging them. They are feral creatures, not tame, so approach with caution.'

Kat stared at his face. In profile, there was a strength to the angles and planes that touched her now that she'd told herself it was a purely aesthetic level of appreciation.

Yes, he was beautiful to look at, but he was also *not tame.*

Luckily, she had never been drawn to the untamed, or unpredictable.

There you go with the denial again, Kat, taunted the voice in her head. *Afraid you've got more of your mother in you than you admit to?*

'All right.' She set her shoulders. 'So what now?'

'Now I escort you to the villa and introduce you to your new home.'

Standing up, her head ducked, she followed him towards the open doors.

CHAPTER SEVEN

THE TWO CARS, the first carrying the minimal baggage and the second themselves, drew up onto the illuminated forecourt. Night had fallen with a speed she found confusing, a clear starlit night scented with the smell of the sea and wild thyme.

Zach, who had gone around to open her door, left her to the assistance of the driver and moved forward to meet the woman who appeared in the massive set of double doors that were flung open to welcome them.

Dressed in a tailored black dress that suited her curvy figure, the woman was average height. It was hard to tell from this distance if the silver streaks in her dark hair were natural or a fashion statement. The chignon it was arranged in appeared as smooth and immaculate as the rest of her.

Kat felt travel-worn and untidy by comparison. She tucked the stray strands of hair behind her ears and told herself if she started worrying about what impression she made on everyone here she'd be a nervous wreck within the week.

Zach's voice drifted across the space to Kat; it sounded warm.

'Selene.'

As she watched from where she stood beside the car it seemed to Kat there was a genuine affection in his greeting as he put his hands on the shoulders of the woman, who Kat judged to be in her forties, and kissed her cheeks.

The rapid interchange was in Greek, and, as the woman glanced over in her direction several times, it didn't seem paranoid to assume they were discussing her.

Get used to it, Kat, she told herself as they began to walk back towards her.

'Katina, this is Selene Carras, your grandfather's housekeeper. This, Selene, is—'

'You have a look of Mia, my dear.'

Kat's cautiously polite expression melted in wondering disbelief. Eyes sparking eagerness, she sounded incredulous. 'You *knew* my mother?'

'Indeed I did.' The smartly dressed woman's kind brown eyes crinkled deeply at the corners as she smiled, her teeth as white as the double row of pearls around her neck. 'My own mother was the housekeeper on the island before me. When we were girls your mother and I would play together during her school holidays before we got older and…she was missed greatly by many.'

Emotion filled Kat's throat. There had never been anyone in her life she could speak to about her mother, never anyone she could ask all the questions she wanted, *needed* to ask.

'She used to tell me stories when I was little about an island where the sun always shone and the sand on the beaches was white. I thought they were stories. I never thought…' When her throat clogged with unshed tears of emotion, she turned her head, blinking hard, embarrassed less by the overspill of emotion than by the fact Zach was witnessing it.

Though, ironically, it was Zach who unwittingly came to her rescue.

'Did I hear dinner mentioned?'

'Of course, Mr Zach, but first things first. I will show Miss—'

'Kat, please,' Kat begged, not caring if this was etiquette or not.

The woman tipped her head. 'I will show Kat to her rooms, give her time to freshen up and then I'll have dinner served in half an hour?' She glanced from Kat to Zach, taking their silence as agreement, and continued cheerfully. 'Mr Zach will bring you down to dinner.' She glanced at him before explaining. 'The house is not exactly compact and it takes a little time to get your bearings.'

Not compact!

If the hallway they entered was any indication, the place was massive!

Underfoot the marble glowed while, high above, the massive antique chandeliers glistened. The central sweeping staircase ran up to the gallery above and then upwards to another floor.

It was Zach's voice, deep and inflected with dry irony, that interrupted her shocked silence.

'Alekis is not really a fan of less is more, and he really thinks that size matters. There isn't a room in the place that you couldn't have a game of cricket in. Well, not really my game, but...'

'It didn't stop you trying.' The older woman touched Kat's arm. 'The rooms *are* a little large.'

Kat only dimly registered the interchange.

'Ah.' Zach breathed and paused when he saw what had stopped her in her tracks.

'She is beautiful,' Kat said, staring.

'Your grandmother, I believe.'

Kat, her eyes wide, glanced at him and then back at the portrait in the heavy gold frame. It was positioned on the far wall lit by several spotlights. She took a step closer to study the woman, one she had never met or even knew existed.

This woman was her grandmother.

The roots she had been longing for all her life, Kat realised, were here. But did she belong? This was all so alien.

'My grandmother?'

The woman in the painting was wearing a classic shift dress that would have looked fashionable today, the knee-high boots elongated her legs and her dark hair was dressed in a slightly bouffant updo. With her dark eyes outlined by kohl, her rosebud lips pale and her lashes spiky and long, it was an iconic sixties look.

'She looks like Mum…' The face that she thought she remembered floated into her head. 'I *think*?'

Zach could not see her face, just hear the almost quiver in her voice, but it was the set of her narrow shoulders and the emotions he could feel literally radiating from her that made something twist hard in his chest. Something he refused to recognise as tenderness. An equally unfamiliar impulse to offer comfort made him move forward.

He had been so focused on the solitary figure staring up at the painting that he didn't realise he wasn't the only one affected by the poignant image she made, until the housekeeper wrapped her plump arm around the younger woman's slender shoulders. The touch was brief but enough to draw a smile of warm gratitude from Kat as the older woman moved away.

Spontaneous expressions of support and comfort were not really in Zach's comfort zone. Far better, he decided, watching the moment, to leave it to those with more experience with touchy-feely stuff. Despite his ineligibility he found the feeling that he'd been cheated out of the feel of her warm skin lingering, digging deep enough to make him ache. Everything between them seemed to come back to one thing: this desire that never quite went away and flared in an unpredictable way. Problematic but not anything he couldn't deal with—he had never allowed his appetites to rule him.

The housekeeper studied the portrait. 'She did, more so as she grew up.'

Kat sent her another look of teary gratitude. 'I don't have any photos, just what I remember, and I'm not sure how much of that is real,' she admitted.

Listening, Zach found himself wanting to tell her she was lucky; he wished his own memories of his childhood were open to misinterpretation, but his were all unpleasantly real.

'This way.'

'I'll show her the way,' he heard himself say.

'Really?' Selene shook her head and recovered her poise. 'Of course.'

'This is a lot for you to take in.'

Kat nodded. 'Pretty overwhelming. Until now I hadn't thought of my mother being here, not really.' She stopped as her throat closed over, not conscious that Zach had slowed to keep pace with her. 'Do you remember your mother?'

Midway up the sweeping staircase, he stopped. Puzzled by his rigid posture, so did Kat.

'Yes,' he said finally, and began to walk again.

'I wish I remembered more.'

He stopped again, this time at the top of the staircase, and looked down at her, his expression sombre.

'Be careful what you wish for.'

He *remembered*; he remembered a once beautiful woman worn down by single parenthood and the two or three jobs she'd needed to pay the rent on their apartment and keep him in clothes. She had always been tired, and Zach remembered promising her that one day she would not have to work. He would have a job that meant she could rest; rest had seemed like the ultimate luxury.

He never got the chance; he was ten when she died. For years he'd assumed it had been the exhaustion that had taken her life, a life that had been a constant, unrelenting grind. Only later he'd learnt by accident when he'd found her death certificate that she had succumbed to pneumonia. In her weakened condition she hadn't been able to fight the infection that had ravaged her body or afford the medicine that might have saved her.

Unable to explain even to herself this *need* in her to know more about him, more about the man who wore power so comfortably, she tentatively pushed. 'After your mother died you went to live with your grand-mother, and—?'

'Dimitri, my uncle.'

The bleakness in his voice was reflected in his face as he continued to speak. She had the impression that he had almost forgotten she was there as he continued.

'If she could love anyone, she loved him, in her way, though of course that love came a poor second to the bottom of a vodka bottle.'

'She didn't love you?' The question slipped out. She knew it was one she had no right to ask but anger pushed it through her caution.

'Me?' He laughed, the sound hard. 'She resented me almost as much as she had resented her own daugh-ter. She forgot I was there for the most part and left me to Dimitri. Dimitri was a weak man who blamed the world for anything that went wrong in his life, and, like many weak men who could not take responsibility for their own actions, he was a bully. He used me as a punching bag.'

Kat felt the tears press against the back of her eyelids. He remembered every blow, every curse. She knew it without him telling her.

'I hate bullies!'

Her fierce declaration brought his eyes back to her face as she stood there, her hands clenched into fists, the empathy shining clear in her glorious eyes. He froze. What the *hell* had he just done?

What had begun as a lesson in caution had become some sort of soul-baring session. Feelings that he had put into cold storage had been resurrected. His jaw clenched. He had every intention of putting them safely back behind the mental ten-foot-high steel-reinforced walls that had taken him years of painstaking effort to construct.

'I remembered…' The housekeeper's voice drifted up the deep stairwell and they both turned as she mounted the first few steps.

Kat tore her eyes off Zach's curiously expressionless face.

The older woman, standing at the bottom step, was breathing hard as though she'd just run back.

'You mentioned photos—I have some. They are mostly from a few summers. I will look them out for you,' she promised. 'There used to be lots about the place.'

'Thank you,' Kat called down, genuinely touched by the gesture.

'This way,' Zach said, indicating the corridor to the left. He sounded distant and cold. She was assuming he was regretting opening up to her. It was pretty obvious he was not a man who was into sharing his feelings.

'So what happened to the photos of my mother?'

'Before my time,' he said abruptly, before adding, 'I'm not sure, but your grandfather will know.'

Unless he'd destroyed them, Kat thought, imagining the angry man trying to wipe his daughter from his life. The thought left her feeling deflated as she walked beside a silent Zach down what seemed like several miles of corridors until Zach stopped at a door.

'You're here.' As he spoke a maid emerged from the room. She seemed flustered when she saw them.

Zach said something in Greek that made her smile

and tip her head towards the room and say something in her native tongue before moving away.

'What did she say?' Kat asked.

'You're not going to learn if I keep translating for you.'

Kat, who had turned to follow the girl's progress down the wide corridor, turned back to Zach. He was a lot closer than she had anticipated. She took a hasty step backwards, nothing to do with retreat and a lot to do with self-preservation. His *closeness* had a disturbing effect on her nervous system.

'So how am I going to learn? Or is that the idea—to make me feel like an outsider?' She regretted the self-pitying addition the moment it left her lips, but in reality she felt as though she always would be an outsider here. It seemed impossible that she would ever fit in.

'You could take lessons.'

She noticed he didn't offer.

'Though they say immersion's the best way to learn a language.'

'Who's they?' she jeered, unimpressed.

'Experts.'

She snapped her fingers to express her opinion of experts. 'I call it stupid, a bit like saying throwing someone in the deep end is the best way to learn to swim.'

'But you can't swim,' he reminded her, picturing her in a very small bikini, emerging from waves. It was a very distracting image. 'Well, this is your suite.' He tipped his head and walked away. 'Half an hour, then.'

She wanted to ask where he was sleeping but stopped herself. It sounded too needy. She thought of saying she wasn't hungry but she realised she was actually starving. Nerves had meant she hadn't eaten a thing all day.

Kat walked in the room and leaned against the door. The room she had entered was furnished in the style of a French chateau, the walls peachy gold in colour, the stunning fireplace with its top-heavy carving dominating the room.

She found the opulent luxuriousness of it all fascinating. The antiques, the drapes, the handmade wallpaper. This was the embodiment of money being no object. It was clear there had been an effort made to inject some personal touches. Kat was appreciative of the flowers and candles. The antique furniture, probably worth a fortune, was all a bit too ornate to ever feel comfortable; her tastes were simpler.

The bathroom was a place where she didn't mind the extravagance. It was spectacular. Someone had already lit the candles around the massive copper tub. She was sorely tempted but was conscious of the time factor and Zach's parting words. Instead, she contented herself with washing her face—her make-up was long gone anyway. She applied a smudge of grey shadow to her eyelids, two flicks of mascara, and rubbed some clear gold on her lips. Her hair, after a severe brush, she left shiny and loose, before changing her top for a clean, though slightly creased, black silk blouse from her case, which somehow had arrived in the room before her.

With three minutes to spare she was outside the bedroom in the corridor, not pausing to analyse her determination not to have him step inside her room. It wasn't as if he was going to carry her through to the French-boudoir bedroom with its canopied bed that was probably a lot of women's dream. The same women probably dreamt of having a man like Zach throw them on it and make mad, passionate, head-banging love to them…or should that be *with* them?

She had never felt that her ignorance of head-banging sex was a disadvantage in life previously, but now she found herself wondering what she was missing.

'You don't want to know, Kat. It's not you.'

The echo of her announcement had barely died away before a voice very close by responded.

'What don't you want to know?'

Kat felt as if guilt was written all over her face, but she managed a very credible recovery. 'If they dress for dinner here.' It was, she decided, inspirational but, now that she thought about it, actually quite relevant.

'Well, there is no *they*, just us, and as you see…'

She accepted the invitation of his downward sweeping gesture and felt her tummy muscles quiver in helpless appreciation as she took in the pale shirt, open at the neck, and the black jeans that clung to his narrow hips and suggested the powerful musculature of his thighs.

The wash of colour lent a peachy glow to her skin as she put effort into controlling her breathing and dragged her eyes back to his face. His dark hair was damp, as though he'd just stepped out of the shower.

'That's good, then.' She turned and began to walk briskly away. He let her go a few feet before calling after her.

'Wrong direction.'

She compressed her lips. 'You might have said!'

He might have, but the truth was he had been enjoying her rear view too much. 'Sorry.'

'I'm not really a formal sort of person.'

'Alekis rarely entertains, but I'm sure he will want to show you off when he is discharged.'

She turned her head, falling into step beside him. 'He looked...frail. How ill is he, really?'

'He has a history of what I believe he euphemistically has in the past called "cardiac events". This time, however, he had more than one cardiac arrest. He is not a young man.'

'You mean he died?' His neutral delivery made it impossible for her to figure out if he would care one way or the other. She got it that some people didn't wear their heart on their sleeve, but this was ridiculous!

Did he think it was weakness to show emotion?

'So they tell me.'

'Should I...?' She shook her head. 'No, it doesn't matter—'

He hefted a sigh. 'Your first lesson is to stop thinking about what the right thing is, and think instead about what you want.'

She skipped a little to catch him up and angled a puzzled look at his profile. 'Do you mean you *never* do anything you don't really want to?'

'Why would I?' It was a question he had been trying to answer since Alekis had foisted the task of bringing his granddaughter home. A spreadsheet would have shown that any debt he felt towards Alekis was fully paid up by the knife he'd taken for him, but some things could not be defined by spreadsheets and analysis.

His instinct, honed by his visceral hatred of bullies, had saved Alekis's life, but Alekis had enabled him to rewrite his own life. He would always owe Alekis. It was not something that he could analyse, it was just something he accepted.

His eyes drifted to the cloud of dark hair, loosened now, that fell almost all the way down to her narrow waist. His acceptance meant he would never feel that silky hair slide through his fingers.

'Oh, I don't know, because it's the right thing?'

He dug his hands deep in his pockets. 'Who decides what the right thing is? But the answer is, no, I don't. You are looking at me as though you have just discovered a different species. I promise you, Katina, I am not the one that is different.'

'You make it sound like it's a bad thing to be different.'

'When different involves you believing in the Easter Bunny, Santa Claus and the basic goodness of your fellow man after the age of nine, then, yes, it is a bad thing, a very bad thing. I believe we are eating in here.' He paused outside an open doorway and gestured for her to precede him.

'You are the most cynical man I have ever met.' She paused on the threshold. 'Oh, this is pretty,' she exclaimed as she registered the table set before the open French doors. Light, gauzy window coverings were fluttering in the light sea breeze that caused the lit candles to flicker and dance. 'I thought all the rooms were massive here.'

'I thought, after the day you have had, you might like something slightly less...formal?' He had phoned ahead to ask for the staff presence to be kept to a minimum to give her some breathing space.

Her eyes flew to his face, then, aware that her pleasure at the small consideration was excessive, she turned and walked across to the open doors to breathe in the fragrance blowing in from the water.

'I can hear the sea!'

'Hard to escape it. We are on an island.'

She swivelled around to face him. 'Well, I have never lived on a private island so I can't be quite so bored about it as you.'

What amazed him was she appeared utterly oblivious to the fact that, standing there with the moonlit, star-studded sky as backdrop, the spider's-web-fine curtains blowing around her face like a bride's veil, she looked utterly beautiful.

In this era of air-brushed perfection, she stood out, not just for her natural beauty, but her total lack of artifice. The inner sexuality that she was totally oblivious of added another transfixing layer to her appeal.

The idea of enjoying that sensuality, of wrapping himself in it, and her hair, raised his core temperature several degrees, which made him a little more effusive than he might normally have been when Selene arrived before he could say something really stupid, like, *Let's skip the food and go to bed*.

'Wow, multitasking tonight, Selene? Isn't this a bit below your pay grade?'

Mouth prim, but smiling with her eyes, the housekeeper gestured to the two maids in uniform who appeared, pushing a trolley on wheels.

'I have followed your instructions. It will be informal, but I wanted to see personally that Kat is comfortable.' She nodded to the girls and said something in Greek that prompted them both to busy themselves with the items on the trolley.

Kat approached the chair that Zach held, nodding a silent thank you as she took her seat. 'I'm very comfortable, thank you,' she said, thinking it was *almost* true now she couldn't feel the warmth of his breath on her cheek, just the tingle it had left behind. There were disadvantages to the sense of intimacy this room gave.

The housekeeper lifted the lids from the dishes on the trolley, inspecting each one before she nodded and turned back to the diners. 'Eloise…just put it down.' The young maid nodded and put a dessert she carried onto the serving table.

'Right, I'll leave you to open the wine, shall I?' She looked at Zach and at the champagne cooling in a cut-glass bucket.

'So does he…my grandfather eat here when he's alone?'

Selene gave a choke that might have been laughter before she whisked from the room.

'Did I say something wrong?'

His sensual lips quirked into a half-smile. 'Actually, Alekis eats in the main dining room, which is the size of a football pitch, and he would find it strange if he had to pour his own wine…or, for that matter, water.'

'So this is?'

'This is a private dining room used exclusively when your grandfather is entertaining one of his…*friends*.'

For a moment she looked blank, then comprehension dawned. 'He has…' Her eyes widened some more. 'But he's *old*!'

Zach's lips twitched. 'Not *too* old, apparently.' He

leaned back in his seat and looked at her. 'So is any of this what you were expecting?'

'I'm not sure what I was expecting. Mum used to tell me that one day I'd have beautiful dresses, and I have.' She had found a wardrobe the size of her flat in London crammed with designer labels. A small smile played across her soft lips as her wistful gaze drifted to the fluttering candles on the table. 'A birthday cake with lots of candles. Apart from the birthday bit, it's all here.'

'Do you like seafood?'

She jumped a little, jolting away the memories that curved her lips into a soft smile. 'I like everything,' she said honestly. 'But I'm allergic to nuts.'

Zach could tell by her expression that another memory had been triggered—he didn't want to ask, didn't want to find himself rediscovering how uncomfortable empathy was. It was masochistic, but somehow, he couldn't stop himself.

'What are you thinking about?'

Her eyes fell from his as he walked with his own plate back to his seat. 'This looks delicious.' She looked up from her plate and their glances connected. 'When Mum… When the police went to the flat.'

Kat could remember but hadn't understood at the time the glances the policewomen had exchanged when she'd given her name and address. Though pretty gentrified now, at that time it was not a *nice* area.

'She had left a note. I have it. I had access to my files after I decided to look for her,' she explained. The decision had not been made lightly. She'd known there were risks, most importantly the risk of being rejected all over again. 'I thought she might have another family and I might be a reminder of a past she wanted to forget.'

'You went ahead anyway.' They had both retraced their pasts, but with very different aims. He had wanted closure and, if he was honest, to rub his success in their faces, show them what he had achieved despite them. And she, as far as he could tell, had simply wanted to reconnect, to satisfy her craving for family.

She had forgiven, he never would. This would always set them apart.

She gave a little shrug. 'It took longer than I thought. She seemed to have dropped off the grid after she… left. It never even occurred to me that she might be… not alive.'

He watched as she lowered her eyes so he couldn't see the tears and waited as she speared a prawn onto her fork and slowly chewed it, cursing himself for asking for an answer that he knew was going to make him feel emotions that had no purpose, and yet he was being controlled by something stronger than logic—a primal need to protect.

He might have been able to fight his reaction to her beauty, but when that beauty came attached to a vulnerability not masked by her air of independent fighting spirit, it awoke something in him that he had never felt before. He didn't want to feel it.

'The note she left said…' Kat stared at her plate as she began to recite, '"He made me choose, and Katina is a good girl, and I'm no good for her anyway. PS: She's allergic to nuts."' Her flat delivery did not disguise the fact that reciting the words hurt her.

The fingers around his heart tightened as she lifted her head and said defiantly, 'She wanted me to be safe.'

If she ever had a child, Kat thought, he or she would *know* they were safe. She would never leave them, not for a man, not for *anything*.

Zach bit back the retort on his tongue. Maybe she *needed* to think that her mother had cared about her. What did he know? Maybe the woman had. Why was he worrying one way or the other? he asked himself, resenting how she had intruded into the emotional isolation. Yet when he looked at her, he couldn't be angry. He felt empathy; like a limb deprived of blood flow, the reawakening of this dormant emotion was painful.

'And were you?'

Deliberately misunderstanding him, she grinned and patted a pocket. 'I always carry my EpiPen just in case.' She speared another prawn. 'This is delicious.'

'I'll let the kitchens know about the nut allergy.'

'Don't worry, if in doubt I don't eat it. The allergy is not as serious as some. I know someone who went into anaphylactic shock because she kissed her boyfriend and he'd just eaten a curry with nuts in.'

'So your boyfriends have to swear off nuts?'

The way he was looking at her mouth made the heat climb into her cheeks, and other places. She shifted uneasily in her seat. 'I'm not that bad.' She pushed aside her plate and took a sip of the champagne. It seemed a good time to change the subject. 'So it sounds like Selene has known you for a long time.'

He arched a satiric brow. 'You mean she doesn't treat me with sufficient deference.'

The fact that he could mock himself was a pleasant surprise.

'I was quite young when I first visited the island.'

It frequently seemed to him that Selene still saw him as the young truculent teen with a massive chip on his shoulder and on more than one occasion the family silver in his pockets. His convalescence had been eventful for the new housekeeper, as Selene had been back then.

Kat, trying to imagine what young Zach had looked like, wondered if Selene had some photos of him too. She laid her napkin down on her side plate and decided against another sip of the fizz. The first had gone to her head after the long day. Her appetite after the first few bites had vanished too. She lifted a hand to hide a yawn.

'You're tired.' Of course she was—how could she not be after the day she'd had? He felt the painful twisting sensation in his chest as he watched her stifle another yawn, realising she'd been running on adrenaline all evening.

She shook her head. 'No, not really.'

'You are,' he said, laying down his napkin. 'You need your rest. Tomorrow is another long day. We'll go over the guest list in the morning.' The morning made him think of the night that preceded it. Waking up together, her head on his chest, their limbs tangled. *Tangled*—the word jolted him free of the images flickering through his head.

He did not do *tangled*—emotionally or in any other way. He liked clean-cut defined lines, minus entanglements, which were far more likely to occur if a man spent the entire night in a woman's bed. *Any* woman, let alone the granddaughter of his mentor!

Her brows twitched. 'Guest list?'

'I've compiled a who's who list of the guests for to-morrow along with a bio.'

Her eyes widened. 'Is there an exam…?'

Her comment wrenched a bark of deep laughter from his throat. Then, as their eyes connected, dark on amber, the amusement faded first from his, and then hers.

The air suddenly crackled with a sensually charged tension that seemed to suck the oxygen from the atmosphere, drawing them deeper into a sensual vortex that swirled around them.

Light-headed, Kat didn't connect the sound she could hear with her own laboured breathing, her heart thudding like a dull metronome in her chest as she experienced a surge of deep, strength-sapping longing.

Zach watched the pupils in her eyes expand until only a rim of gold remained. He could hear the roar of hunger in his blood and wanted… *Theos*, how *badly* he wanted to give himself up to it, sink into her softness and… The muscles in his brown throat rippled as he swallowed and dug deep into the reserves of his frayed self-control.

Kat blinked, confused as Zach suddenly surged to his feet, not quite meeting her eyes as he bent forward, the flickering candlelight throwing the planes and angles of his face into stark relief as he blew out the candles.

The gesture seemed weirdly symbolic to Kat because, along with the candlelight, the intimacy had vanished. Been snuffed out, to be replaced by a cool, businesslike atmosphere as he walked towards the door, having donned the persona of the ruthless tycoon with computer chips, not emotions, in his eyes.

'I'll get someone to walk you back to your room.'

She blinked, getting to her feet in confusion as his mercurial mood change made her head spin. 'Aren't you—?'

His quick smile was impersonal and distant. It seemed to her he couldn't get out of the door fast enough. 'I have some work to get through.'

In the corridor, Zach propped his broad shoulders against the wall and released a long, slow, sibilant sigh. It was not pride enhancing to realise that the only effective way he had been able to see to remove himself from temptation was to remove himself physically.

He levered himself off the wall, aware that if he had escorted her back to her room he might have ended up saying good morning and not goodnight. Even the thought of it now heated his blood in a way that drew a low snarling sound from his throat as he strode off, putting as much distance as possible between himself and the witch who had put a spell on him.

CHAPTER EIGHT

THE PLACE BOASTED a state-of-the-art gym that Zach doubted Alekis even knew existed, but he chose the beach ahead of the treadmill. Two hours of flat-out pushing-himself-to-the-limit running later, he felt he had regained a sense of proportion, enabling him to think past crippling lust and recognise that being thrown into the company of someone whose early life mirrored his own to some minor degree had dredged up some deeply buried memories, and added an intensity to his feelings when she was around.

A logical explanation, without falling back on the tired old clichés of soul mates, made him feel more comfortable and confident he was able to deal with the next few days without betraying Alekis's trust.

He just needed to keep her at an emotional arm's length and fulfil his commitment to Alekis.

Having breakfasted alone, Kat asked directions to the study, where apparently Zach was waiting for her.

The question in her mind was, *which* Zach?

It seemed to Kat that there were more than one. There was the Zach who seemed warm and interested, even sympathetic, when she told him about her past, or the one who was the distant and cool executive hiding behind defensive walls to keep emotions out.

She understood the decision to protect her heart in an emotional armour, but her heart had always ached for people who didn't realise they had imprisoned themselves at the same time. *Not your business, Kat,* she told herself firmly.

The thought had been a recurring theme through the long night that had been punctuated by fitful dreams, a session of trying on shoes from the cavernous wardrobe and minutes spent on the balcony, listening to the soothing sound of the waves.

Thank God for caffeine!

'Good morning, did you sleep well? Excellent.'

She blinked. So this was how it was going to be?

'Coffee?' He stood there with pot in hand, more good-looking than any man had a right to be in a black T-shirt and jeans. If his manner had been as informal as his clothes, she'd have been toast. It wasn't, so she wasn't. All positive—this was not the right time to develop a crush and this was not the Zach whose opinion she would ask about the outfit she had chosen for this evening.

'Yes, please, black.' Matching his manner, she took a sip of the scalding strong brew, though the effort was wasted on him as he'd already turned to the desk. 'Right, there will be thirty-five guests tonight. I have subdivided them—society, business and social.' He stabbed a long finger towards the screen of the tablet that was on the desk and tagged on casually, 'Only one royal.'

'Only one?'

He flashed her a look. 'He won't be a problem,' he

promised, dismissing blue blood with a snap of his long fingers. 'However, these might. You can see…'

She couldn't. She was still standing on the other side of the room. Seeing his look of impatience, she overcame her reluctance to move closer, and after a moment's hesitation she reacted to his gesture to step in and look, planting her hands palms flat on the surface as she leaned in.

'As you can see, I have red-flagged those who might be a problem,' he explained. 'Number one is probably Spiro Alekides.' He leaned across her, causing her breath to hitch as he scrolled down the screen before moving back to a distance she found comfortable once more as he explained, 'He can be slippery and has an unsavoury reputation when it comes to women.'

Kat turned her head. He had said that with no discernible trace of irony in his voice, and, yes, there was none at all on his face that she could see—staggering!

'Unfortunately, Alekis has a joint venture with him,' he tagged on, explaining the man's presence.

'You don't sound as though you approve?'

'Alekis does not need my approval.'

'Who is she?' Kat asked, looking curiously at the glamorous blonde woman whose photo was next to the red-flagged man.

'That's Ariana.'

Something in his voice made her turn again in response to a little spurt of something alarmingly close to jealousy tightening in her chest. 'You know her?'

'That sort of intuition will do you no harm,' he complimented her smoothly. 'We have both dated Ariana, as it happens at the same time. Spiro sent her to do a little industrial espionage and I used the situation to my advantage to plant a little false information. He has never actually forgiven me, so keep clear,' he warned.

Kat caught her breath. This was not *close* to jealousy, and more a flood than a spurt. This was the real thing with bells on! The shaft that pierced her was so intense that she would not have been surprised to see a knife hilt protruding from her chest.

Kat was as deeply shocked by her visceral reaction as she was scared by it. Lowering her gaze to hide the emotions she felt were written across her face in neon letters, she amazed herself by responding in a relatively calm voice.

'So she used you, and you used her. Does that cancel out all the using?' she wondered in a voice that sounded too bright. 'I'll look at this myself later. Don't worry, I always did my homework.'

Aware that Zach was watching her with a puzzled frown, she struggled to control her expression and presumably failed; she could hear the suspicion in his voice as he asked, 'What's wrong?'

'Not a thing.' She tucked the tablet under her arm. 'I promised myself I'd explore this morning.'

'Want a guide?'

'I think I'll be fine on my own.' She had to get out of the room before he guessed, which would be the ultimate humiliation!

He stared at the door, fighting the impulse that gripped him to follow her before he slumped down into one of the chairs. It was time to stop pretending and face facts. When it came to this woman his normal iron control did not apply.

* * *

More by luck than good judgement, she found her way back to her suite. Nobody had cleared the shoes that had littered the bedroom floor since she had pulled them out of the cavernous closet in the early hours of the morning. She kicked one of the soft-as-butter lemon-coloured pumps that were lovely, almost tripped over the striking red loafers, and picked up one of the cute kitten heels in one hand, and one of the spiky, far too high ankle boots, sexy as hell—even with pyjamas—in the other.

With a low moan, she threw them both across the room, then, feeling guilty that she was leaving someone else to pick them up, gathered up the shoes and, pairing them all up, stacked them neatly in their boxes, telling herself that she needed to get a grip. She needed to focus and *not* think about Zach Garros.

She spent the next hour lying, head propped in her hands, on the bed, poring over the guest list and the cream of Athens society. But for some reason it wasn't sinking in, so she welcomed the interruption when a maid tapped on the door.

'Mrs Carras asks me to tell you that there is morning tea in the small salon if you wish it, miss?'

Why not? thought Kat, closing the tablet.

'Lead the way,' she said to the girl, who looked startled by the informality.

An hour later, as she sipped her second cup of tea, Kat walked to the high, deep windows. The sea shone in the near distance like silvered turquoise in the morning sun. As the place was built on a peninsula projecting into the water, she assumed that most rooms would have similarly breathtaking marine vistas.

Selene bustled in. Kat found herself envying the woman's vaguely harassed air and realised she was bored. She was used to being busy. She would make a very poor lady of leisure.

'Good morning. Did you sleep well?'

'Perfectly,' Kat lied. 'I thought I might explore a little this morning, if there's nothing you want me—?' she began hopefully.

'Gracious, no. I'll send Della. She can be your guide and she's too teary this morning to be any help—she's in love,' Selene added with an eye-roll.

'No, don't worry. I'd prefer to wander alone, if that's okay?'

'Of course. Enjoy yourself.'

A little exploration had proved her assumption was right: the scale of the building was daunting and then some. She hesitated to call it a home. It seemed more to her like a massive status symbol. *Surely* no one needed this much space?

She got turned around several times during her exploration until she realised that the place was built on a grid system. After that her attempts to get her bearings got a little easier. Everything fanned out from one central living area. She supposed that you got your head around massive in time—less so the presence of staff, discreet but liable to pop up and take you by surprise. She hoped some of them were temporary additions for the evening event.

It was her first test and one she hadn't decided if she actually wanted to pass. Who was she trying to please and impress? The grandfather she didn't know, or the man who didn't care one way or the other?

Maybe, Kat, you should try pleasing yourself?

It was a plan.

The first of the two wings she explored seemed to be dedicated to private suites, like her own, and some slightly smaller guest suites. After half an hour of opening doors and admiring views she wandered back out to the terrace that ran the full length of this side of the building. Beautifully manicured lawns ran down to the sea. She took off her cardigan. It felt like spring as she took a seat on one of the long stone benches surrounded by tubs of flowers. Selene appeared, along with a young girl in a maid's uniform who she introduced as Della.

The appearance was so perfectly timed that Kat imagined her every move being picked up by CCTV cameras. She smiled at the girl, recognising the name, but didn't get a smile back, just a quick curtsey and a look that mingled tragic with sulky. She was not a recommendation for love with the black mascara rings around her eyes.

Selene noticed this, too. 'Go on, run along and wash your face,' she said, and the girl rushed off.

'It's such beautiful weather here, I can't get over it.' She had as little control over that as she did her visceral response to Zach, but the weather was much easier to live with.

'Yes, and such a relief after the heat. The summer was hot even for here. You are finding your way around?'

Kat's smile was a poor disguise for the fact she was overwhelmed by everything. She fought her way through a wave of longing for the comfortable predictability of her old life and nodded. 'There is a lot to explore.'

'Are you sure you don't want someone to show you around? Not Della,' she added hastily. 'That girl is just… She is really trying my patience today.'

'Actually, it's quite nice discovering things on my own, and if I have a guide to rely on it will take me for ever to find my way around.'

The older woman nodded and smiled. 'Oh, I should mention that the room is being prepared for this evening, so there might be a little disruption. Can I get you anything—tea, coffee, cakes?'

'Tea would be nice,' she lied, thinking, *This is how bored people put on weight.* 'So, I'm assuming the guests will be staying overnight?' It wasn't as if there weren't room.

'Normally they would, but, no, Mr Zach has arranged transport. They will be leaving by eight-thirty sharp.' Kat picked up on the 'whether they like it or not' silent addition. 'Hence the early start this evening. If you'll excuse me, the musicians have arrived and they are being a little…artistic.' She rolled her eyes and whisked away.

When the tea arrived it came with some delicious little honey pastries embedded with nuts and jewelled candy fruit, which Kat, who told herself she was still making up for her half-eaten dinner, demolished.

Exploring the second wing didn't really work off many calories, Kat discovered. It was dedicated to the domestic area. Her appearance in a food-preparation room created a bit of a shock panic moment for the staff working there.

She apologised and backed out, then promptly lost her orientation once more and ended up outside

again where she discovered that there was more than
one swimming pool, and this one was in an enclosed
courtyard. A shaded area lay to one side of the mar-
ble-floored space complete with what appeared to be
an outdoor kitchen; on a raised plinth on the opposite
side, a massive spa pool bubbled away happily.

She lay down on one of the loungers with a bump,
marvelling at how different this world was compared
to the one she was used to.

Not my world, but I'm still me.

The recognition eased the tightness in her chest. Her
chin lifted. If she was going to do this, she'd do it her
way. For starters, she'd do what she always did. Focus
not on the negative but the positive. Yes, heiress was a
bad fit for her, but she'd worn ill-fitting shoes before
now and survived, she reminded herself, and they'd always looked good.

She'd already saved the refuge… If she was going
to inherit money and power, there were a lot of worthy causes out there who just needed someone to notice them.

When a menu appeared for her lunch, Kat requested
a sandwich. She intended to explore the gardens and
beach.

'Just a sandwich?' Della looked confused. 'What will
I tell Mrs Carras?'

'That I want a sandwich.'

Her irritation fell away as, without warning, the
young girl's face suddenly crumpled and she burst into
loud sobs.

'Fine, I'll have lunch,' Kat said, alarmed. The girl
continued to sob.

'*He's* sending him away and I'll never see him again, and I love him!'

'Take a seat.' She got up and the girl took her own, scrubbing her face with her apron. 'Della, is it…? Who is *he*? The first *he*.'

'Mr Gavros. Alexi thinks he's marvellous, but he's not—he's cruel and heartless and he's sending Alexi away because he thinks I'm too young! And he doesn't want anyone to be happy!'

Kat had never been so glad to see anyone as she was to see Selene. The older woman took one look at the scene and bustled the weeping girl out. A few moments later she returned.

'I am so sorry about that.'

'It's fine. She says that Zach is sending her boyfriend away.'

'Oh, I know. She's telling anyone who will listen the same thing.'

While Kat was the first to believe that Zach was no saint, that he was cynical and manipulative, the girl's story just didn't have a ring of truth to it. Why on earth would Zach go out of his way to blight young love? Mock it, yes, but not… No, she was sure there was another explanation.

'So, is he?'

The other woman gave a chuckle. 'Well, I suppose he is. Alexi is one of the placements, one of the big successes, and, as you might know, Zach has an arrangement with the university: if the youngsters he recommends pass the interview and entrance exam they are admitted without formal exams to do a foundation year. Alexi is starting next semester. The boy, as bright as they come, is over the moon.'

Kat tried to pick her way through the information. 'So, this Alexi was originally—?'

'Much like Zach, living on the streets, though obviously his situation was not as dire as Zach's.' The older woman, unaware she had just dropped a bombshell, shook her head while Kat's imagination went into riot mode. 'Not all the youngsters end up in academia, obviously, but they are all offered a way out, a safe way out.'

Kat shook her head. Zach had lived on the streets? She knew his family situation had been bad...*outsider*, he'd said. Now she fully understood what he had meant.

'So, he escaped his family by living on the streets.' The ache in the little corner of her heart was not just for the boy he had once been, but the lone wolf he had become.

Presumably it had been her grandfather who had taken him out of that old life, which perhaps explained the loyalty he seemed to feel towards the older man.

She gave a sudden laugh as she realised that, ironically, it turned out that Zach was as much of a member of the *do-gooding* fraternity he claimed to despise as she was!

Happily, Selene misinterpreted her amusement.

'I know, young love. The thing is,' she said, lowering her voice to a confidential whisper, 'I think young Alexi is quite relieved. Della is a rather *intense* girl and very young for her age.' She hefted out a sigh. 'Better to give her the day off than risk any more meltdowns, I think. I'll leave you to your exploring.'

Her exploring took Kat to the beach, where she

peeled off the clothes over the black swimsuit she'd put on earlier. She could not swim but she could paddle. She waded out, thigh deep, staring, eyes scrunched against the sun, out to sea. She let her thoughts drift—the tide took them inevitably in the direction of Zach. Would she challenge him with his background, ask him why he was so afraid anyone might suspect he was a good guy?

It was almost as if he had tried to make her think the worst of him earlier. Maybe there was a worse but there was also a *better*. A better he seemed not to want anyone to see...*or is that just me?*

She shook her head as she collapsed onto the warm sand. The man was a confusing mass of contradictions! As she shook back her hair she let the sun dry the moisture from her skin, rubbing the sand away as it dried on her bare arms and legs.

It was only when she removed her watch from the pocket where she had put it for safekeeping that she noticed the time. With a yelp, she jumped to her feet, dragged her clothes on over her now dry swimsuit and began to jog up the deserted beach.

She had reached the green manicured lawns that ran down to the sand when she collided not with one of the palms, but a solidity that had warmth.

If his hands had not remained on her shoulders she would have fallen over. Her hands clutched his hair-roughened, sinewy forearms as she inhaled a deep breath of his warm male scent, causing her stomach to violently clench in hopeless desire.

Slowly, her eyes lifted, over the clinging T-shirt stretched across his broad chest to his face. Like the rest of his skin, it was filmed with salty moisture.

She didn't say a word; she couldn't. She ached for him. Quite literally. She hadn't thought it was possible.

It took every ounce of his willpower to resist the longing in her eyes as she looked up at him. Alekis's granddaughter who needed...*deserved* more than someone like him could give.

'You don't look in the party mood.' Hair wild, skin glazed with a sun-kissed look, her lips lightly crusted with salt that he longed to kiss off, she looked the ultimate in desirability.

Kat swallowed the occlusion in her throat; her chest felt constricted and tight. He was close, *too* close. She couldn't breathe, or think, just feel. Too much feeling.

'I'm in panic mode. I'm cutting it a bit fine, probably.' She lifted a hand to her tangled hair and took a step back. His hands fell away as she looked at him through her lashes.

'I should run,' she said, thinking, *Don't let me.*

'Yes.'

She was still running as she entered her suite, brought to a panting, shocked immobility by what waited for her there.

'Good evening,' she said pleasantly to the small army of assorted people assembled inside her private salon. *What the hell?*

She looked to Selene, brows raised, for explanation, even though the hairdryers, tongs and assorted brushes sticking out of a couple of bags was a clue.

'I thought you might like to start getting ready now?' Selene's anxious glance at the ormolu clock over the fireplace that held a massive flower arrangement suggested that she thought this process should have begun some time earlier, and, considering Kat's salty hair had taken on a life of its own, she couldn't really blame her.

'Oh, have you been waiting?'

'Not at all,' came the polite lie.

'Actually, you can all have the evening off,' she said, addressing the small makeover army. 'I'm more than happy to get myself ready.'

The expression of shock and consternation on the older woman's face almost made Kat smile. Clearly the idea that Kat could dress herself, do her own hair and apply her make-up shocked the present company deeply. They *wanted* to argue, Kat could *feel* it.

'Honestly, I've been dressing myself for years.'

Nobody smiled. Kat felt her impatience edge up; she enjoyed a spa day as much as anyone, but she couldn't see it becoming part of her daily routine, or even *big* day routine.

She'd read about freak shows and she supposed this was the modern version—she being the freak!

Damping down her mounting panic, she tried again. 'Honestly, I'll be fine, but if I have a problem I'll yell.'

She utilised a smile aimed at robbing her refusal of any offence and firmly closed her bedroom door on their collective shocked faces. It took her a moment to find the music selection she was looking for and turn up the volume. It wasn't as if there were any neighbours to worry about.

One of these days she was going to take up yoga, but in the meantime her tried-and-tested relaxation method of choice was what it always had been—a five-minute session of wild, unrestrained, let-your-hair-down dancing to a rock anthem while quite frequently singing along.

When the track came to an end, she switched the music off and fell back headlong onto the canopied bed. Staring at the ceiling, she waited for her heart rate to slow to a gentle trot.

To say she was relaxed would have been an exaggeration, but she was willing to accept exhaustion as a substitute—she was just too tired to run away. The thought brought an image of her running away from Zach on the beach. She had stopped once and he'd still been standing there staring after her. The image in her head made her stomach flip.

'Oh, God, this is crazy!' she groaned as she padded to the bathroom. Sadly, she hadn't left herself enough time for a long and lazy bath. The deep double-ended copper tub that took centre stage in the bathroom... now that was one luxury item she might get used to quite quickly.

Sniffing some of the lovely oils lined up, she stripped and walked into the shower, which was big enough to house a football team, though the image that slid into her head did not involve a team, just one man...who was constantly on her mind!

But not your bed, Kat, mocked the voice in her head.

It was about time she remembered she was not the sort of woman who undressed men, even in her imagination, let alone... She scrunched her face and threw a mental bucket of cold water over the febrile images.

Wrapped in a towel, duly anointed with some delicious moisturising lotion, her hair clear of salt, the last traces of sand washed from the crevices it had crawled into, she looked at the dress she had finally selected in the early hours from the racks in the massive walk-in closet.

It was midnight blue, so dark it looked black in certain lights—basically it was a slim ankle-length slip, not that there was anything *basic* about the cut of the heavy silk, high at the neck and low enough at the back to expose her delicately sculptured shoulder blades.

After blast-drying her long thick hair, she tried a couple of styles, almost wishing she had not rejected the services of a hairstylist, and then as she pulled her thick glossy skeins into a knot on the nape of her neck things clicked. She smoothed it properly and gathered it again, winding the sections into a smooth loose knot at the nape of her neck before sticking in several hairpins to secure it, then finally pulling out a few face-framing strands for a softening effect.

Her normal make-up was a smudge of shadow, a touch of gloss on her lips. So the fifteen minutes she did spend felt like a long time, but the end result, if not perfect, satisfied her. The dusting of blush on her cheeks lifted her pallor and the highlighter along her cheekbones worked. She carefully highlighted the almond shape of her eyes with liner before adding a sweep of mascara over her already dark and lustrous eyelashes.

She struggled to adjust the narrow straps of the dress so that they left the delicate architecture of her collarbones exposed, before slipping into the heels. She was viewing the overall effect with a critical eye when there was a knock on the door, a polite reminder from Selene.

She took a deep breath and straightened her shoulders. She couldn't pretend this wasn't really going to happen any longer, but she could pretend her stomach wasn't churning in apprehension.

Smile in place, projecting a confidence she was far from feeling, she pulled the door open. Her smile wilted and died like a rose exposed to an icy chill. A myriad sensations and emotions that were impossible to detangle hit her simultaneously as she saw the tall figure, no longer in running shorts and vest, but in the dress suit, dark hair still visibly damp as though he had just stepped from a shower. An image that did not help her composure, or her heart, which literally stalled. For several moments she felt as if it would never start again.

'You scared the life out of me!' Breathless, and sounding it, she lifted a hand to her throat, where she could feel a pulse that was trying to fight its way through her skin.

Zach cleared his own throat. It had been less a jolt and more an earth tremor to see her standing there and for several heartbeats he'd stood, literally transfixed.

'I really didn't think you scared that easily.'

She was the most fearless woman he had ever met and—as he looked at her standing there now, there was no use pretending otherwise—the most beautiful.

Against the dark fabric her skin gleamed pale gold. Her body, under the figure-enhancing cut of the midnight fabric, was slender and sensuous. The way she wore her hair displayed the length of her slender neck and her delicate collarbones. She looked exclusive and sexy—a hard look to pull off.

He leaned a hand on the doorjamb above her head. 'If you are dressing to impress you have succeeded. You look very lovely.'

Her breath caught at the compliment.

'I wanted to blend in,' she said in a small husky voice, worrying that he might assume she had made the effort to impress him. Worried even more because she couldn't swear she hadn't!

It was hard to smile with the ache in his groin, but he did anyway. 'Ah, well, you failed.' Straightening up, he gestured to her to walk beside him and after a short pause she did, her perfume making his nostrils flare.

'How was your run?'

He flashed her a frowning look. *'Hot.'*

'When is Alekis's surgery scheduled for?'

'First thing Thursday if the rest of the tests are clear.'

'Should I go there to see him before?'

'If you want to.'

'Is the surgery dangerous?'

'Another bypass and a valve replacement, I believe.'

It was weird but hearing all this life-and-death stuff suddenly made the lies she'd been telling herself all day seem petty and ridiculous.

For someone who had spent her life avoiding excitement and danger, it was not easy to acknowledge the idea that had been growing in her head. Because if danger had a name and a face and a really incredible body, she was thinking of throwing herself at him, *giving* herself to him. The thought was scary and liberating at the same time.

Zach just tapped into a reckless part of her. It had required no effort on his part; just breathing did it. Her response would require more effort. Forget instincts, she needed to use her brain.

It would have been helpful if he had remained the

unacceptable but very handsome face of capitalism; instead, she knew more, knew there was nothing two-dimensional about him. She understood when people did not want to discuss their backgrounds for fear of others assuming they were using it in some way, but why hide the things he was giving back to society?

She took a shallow breath and closed down the conflicting theories whirring around in her head. She had to get through the next couple of hours first.

'Well?'

He arched a brow. 'Well, what?' And carried on walking, requiring her to skip on her heels to catch him up.

'Well, isn't there a list? Don't eat with your mouth full, don't get drunk and dance on the tables, don't talk politics, insult the guests or slag off the powerful and influential even if they are total sleazes?'

'I think you have covered the essentials and the file had everything you need in it.' He paused. 'But actually no one here should give you a hard time. This *will* get easier.'

'Well, at least I won't get drunk so there will be no online pictures of me dancing on the table. I only got drunk once and I didn't like it.' The memory made her wince, but underneath she was feeling moderately pleased she was proving they could have a normal conversation without any sex stuff getting in the way. *It had all been in her head anyway.*

He looked amused. 'It rarely stops anyone repeating the process.'

'I had my drink spiked.'

The amusement slid from his eyes. She had the impression he didn't even know that he put his hands heavily on her shoulders, but she knew they felt very heavy; she couldn't move.

Actually, she wasn't really trying.

'What happened?'

'I was at a nightclub for someone's birthday. It was all right, my friends got me out of there.' She chose not to think what might have happened if they hadn't, if the two men trying to half-carry her out to the waiting car had succeeded. 'For a while I struggled with trust, but then I realised I was letting fear rule my life.' She stepped a little ahead of him, paused and twirled around to face him, hitting him full blast with her golden stare, leaving him no escape route.

'You have to trust someone sometime, don't you think, Zach?'

He could feel the pulse pounding in his temple. 'Is there some sort of message in there for me?'

She shrugged. 'Just throwing it out there. Some people are bad. They hurt you, but there are a lot of people that are good, too. You miss such a lot by pushing them away.'

'And if someone spikes your drink?'

'I refuse to live in fear...' Her beautiful smile flashed out. 'I had friends to look out for me and here... I have you, *I think*?'

He ignored the voice in his head that yelled *coward*, his eyes sliding from hers. 'Tonight you do, but there are a lot of tomorrows. There is such a thing as too trusting, Katina.'

'How so?'

The exhaustion came over him in a tide; fighting

the uncontrollable urge to take her in his arms became in the space of a heartbeat just too much. He stopped fighting and surrendered to the roar and the hunger, the ache of wanting.

Holding her wide eyes with his, he placed one large hand in the small of her back, noting the flare in her golden eyes as he curved his free hand around the back of her head and dragged her into him.

She did register that the combustible, exciting quality that she was always conscious of in him was not in the background but right there, in her face, reminding her he was too male, too *everything*. But nothing running through her head had prepared her for what his intention was. She was in denial right up to the moment that his lips covered hers.

The warm, sensuous movement of his mouth drew a deep, almost feral moan that emanated from deep inside her as her lips parted. Her fingers closed around the fabric of his shirt as she raised herself up on her toes, her body stretching in a slim, urgent arc as she invited the invasion to deepen, expanding the cell-deep hungry ache until she simply hung on for the ride, helpless to resist the tide of attraction, the sparking electricity between them. She felt the deep quiver run through his body.

Then it was over. She wasn't quite sure how, but she was on her feet and not plastered up against him and he was standing there looking down at her as though… Actually, she wasn't sure he was seeing her at all. There was a hot blankness in his eyes that slowly receded.

'So what,' she began in a voice that really sounded nothing like her own, 'was that about?'

'Does the unknown that waits for you in there suddenly look so very scary?'

It didn't, but as explanations went that seemed more than thin. 'Why did you kiss me?'

Breathing hard, but looking insultingly composed considering the chaos inside her body and head, he brushed an invisible speck off his shirt before replying.

'A moment… I… I wanted to know how you tasted.'

The blunt words, drawn from him almost against his will, sent a slam of hot lust through her body.

CHAPTER NINE

'OH!' HER RESPONSE gave *inadequate* a new meaning, but she didn't know what else to say. What would be an improvement?

Don't do it again wouldn't be appropriate, or, more likely, *don't stop...*

'We'll be late.' Suddenly she was the one that couldn't hold *his* eyes.

'It's allowed—you're the guest of honour.' He dragged a hand over his dark hair, thinking about how warm and perfect she had felt in his arms. The promise of passion he had always sensed in her had burnt up into life the moment he'd touched her.

It was easy to see that Kat could become the drug of choice to any man, so long as he didn't mind sharing her with a multitude of good causes.

Theos, he really didn't envy that man!

Even as he congratulated himself he recognised that, but for the obligation he felt to Alekis, *he* would be that man, at least for a night, which was in itself another problem.

The insight he had gained into Kat's character led him to doubt that she had a casual attitude to sex. He doubted she would look on it as a healthy physical out-let. For her it would come wrapped up in sentiment. Of course, there were many men out there willing to ac-cept those terms for the joy of bedding her.

Nothing of his thoughts showed in his face as they continued to walk side by side the last few yards, not touching, but he could still sense her leaping pulse.

'You'll be fine, you know.'

She gave an odd little laugh and lifted her head at the abrupt comment. 'Will I?' At that moment she didn't feel as if she knew anything. She ran her tongue across the outline of her lips and gave another laugh. Hell, she hadn't even known her own name when he'd kissed her.

'Be interested...' he said, the effort of dragging his eyes off her mouth making him sweat. 'Be yourself.'

Kat swallowed down another bubble of hysterical laughter. How was she meant to be *herself*, or even sane, after he had just kissed her like that? Being herself and kissing him back was part of the problem. *Herself* would be grabbing him and making him do it again.

'Now that is something I never thought I'd hear you say!' Wow, not even a quiver. She was extremely proud of herself.

He arched a sardonic brow. 'Why?'

'Because I get the impression me being me irritates the hell out of you tonight.' Maybe he had kissed her to shut her up, she thought, nursing her resentment.

He stopped short of the open door, from which the sounds of music and the hum of conversation and laugh-ter emanated, and looked down at her.

'It isn't you I find—'

'*Irritating?*' she supplied, slightly confused and at

the same time excited by the intensity in his manner, though next to the post-kiss confusion that still blocked her normal thought processes it barely even registered.

'Not the right word but it will do. It's the situation, Katina, that I find extremely...*irritating.*' *Theos*, wanting her was killing him.

'I don't know what you mean,' she said, thinking of the warm, clean but musky male smell of his body when he had kissed her. *Would he do it again?*

'Are you sure about that?'

She looked away, suddenly more nervous of the glow in his eyes than what lay in the room. Not nervous, excited. She ran her tongue across the dry outline of her lips. *It was just a kiss...stop trying to read things into it.*

She hefted out a deep sigh. 'Right, let's get this thing over with.'

He nodded.

She was incredibly glad for the light touch of his hand on her elbow as they walked into the room, because walking into a room beside Zach made it a dead certainty most of the room would not be looking at you. When Zach walked into a room, any room, he would always be the focus of attention.

There was a short static pause in the audible social hum as more and more people turned to look at them, from where they were already gathered in small groups, chatting, laughing, drinking the wine being offered by the staff.

The sea of faces was actually more a small pond, she told herself as she willed her feet that felt glued to the floor to move.

'Showtime, Kat.' He heard her whisper before flashing him a look from her topaz eyes and lifting her chin and walking away from him.

Zach watched her, while he wrestled with the flood of unfamiliar emotions surging inside him. He knew how scared she was but no one would ever have known it, despite her pallor, and even if they had it would have been her warmth they remembered, a warmth that could not be feigned.

He surprised himself with that thought.

He watched as she approached a man who stood excluded from a small laughing group nearby. Zach's admiration and pride went through the roof as he watched her smile and move forward, touching the arm of the housekeeper before she lifted her head to the solitary man that Selene was offering the drink to.

Zach stood, his shoulder braced on one wall, his attitude possibly not as nonchalant as he intended because nobody approached him, not even one of the guys with the fizz, which was a pity because he could really have done with a drink.

He finally managed to grab one and downed it while fighting a strong urge to march over there and tell Kat that it didn't matter what anyone thought and this wasn't a test.

What the hell was wrong with Alekis, making her jump through all these hoops? And what was wrong with him for helping? If anyone needed to change it was them, not her.

He was shocked by this thought that came from he knew not where—unlike the urge to kiss her; that source was no mystery.

He willed himself to relax. He knew she could cope

and so could he. He took a swallow and grimaced, finding he was holding an empty glass. If he could relive the moment…but he couldn't so why waste the energy? The kiss, while not being ideal, had at least taken the edge off his rampant hunger.

Yeah, you keep telling yourself that, Zach.

Tuning out the ironic voice of his subconscious, he watched as the austere diplomat melted under Kat's charm offensive and took a drink for himself before handing her the fruit juice option she must have requested. He saw her press a hand to her temple and carry on smiling… It was not the first time he had seen the gesture since she had begun to circulate.

The diplomat leaned in and said something that drew a laugh from Kat, a laugh so warm and spontaneous and *genuine* that it made other people smile, including him.

In the periphery Zach was aware of two people separate off from a nearby group and move to join Kat and the diplomat. One was a journalist that he didn't actively dislike, the other… He frowned as he recognised the other was Spiro Alekides, the business rival who had *not* been gracious in defeat and had made his humiliation worse by giving several unwise interviews that had harmed his reputation more than his financial losses.

Zach began to slowly weave his way through the jostle of bodies, not questioning or analysing the protective instincts that directed his feet.

Even without Zach's warning Kat would have summed up Spiro Alekides, who she had instantly recognised from his photo, in a heartbeat. She had encountered the type before. He smiled a lot, but not with his eyes, and tried very hard to say what he *thought* you wanted to hear.

'Oh, yes, I so agree all that talent out there is going to waste. It's not about charity, it's about investing in our future and the youth are our future.'

The man sounded as though he were reading the label on a packet of cereal, but Kat nodded, repressing a wince as the headache moved behind her eyes. Experience told her if she didn't take measures it would become a full-blown migraine and all that entailed— which was *just* what she didn't need.

'Not everyone understands that,' she said, thinking, *Like you,* before adding, 'Sorry, Mr—'

'Call me Spiro, my dear.'

'Spiro.'

The older man turned quite slowly, arranging his features into a smile. 'Why, Zach, what a nice surprise, meeting you here like this.' He beamed at Kat and the journalist and extended a well-manicured, plump hand to Zach, who raised both of his. One was holding a glass, the other a plate.

Zach smiled, making Kat think of a large sleek predator. She suspected that every woman present would have jumped straight into his mouth if the occasion arose—she had. The thought made her blush.

'So where is your lovely lady tonight?'

The reference to the woman that they had both slept with increased the tempo of the throb behind Kat's eyes. If she was going to get a migraine every time anyone mentioned a woman Zach had bedded she could spend her life with a headache!

'She couldn't make it.'

'Such a shame,' Zach murmured. 'Well, gentlemen, I hope you'll forgive me for stealing away our lovely hostess.' He planted a hand lightly in the small of Kat's back. 'But there is someone who is dying to meet her.'

Not happy that she liked the supportive feel of his hand as much as she did, she frowned and asked, 'Who?' without enthusiasm as they wove their way across the room.

'Do you have a headache?' Zach asked without looking at her.

Kat's jaw dropped and her eyes flew to his face, which sent a fresh spasm of agony along her nerve endings. *'How...?'*

His hand went to her elbow as she caught her heel in the hem of her dress and lurched. 'I thought as much,' he said grimly.

'What are we...?'

She stopped as he paused as they reached Selene and explained in an undertone, 'Kat has a headache. I'm taking her outside for some fresh air.'

'But you can't— This is— I have to stay. Some aspirin, Selene, and I'll be fine.'

'That too, please, Selene. You nearly passed out,' he condemned.

'For heaven's sake, I tripped, is all! It's the damned heels and don't blame me—you bought them for me! Not bought as such,' she tacked on hastily in case anyone had heard and got the wrong impression.

Zach stood over her as she swallowed the painkillers and, ignoring his frowning disapproval, washed them down with a mouthful of wine.

'I thought you didn't drink.'

'A mouthful and, anyway, what did you *think* I was going to do—spit them out?' She took a deep breath and massaged her temples. 'OK, back to it.'

'You need some fresh air.'

She looked up at him, exasperated by his insistence. 'I need to get back in there.'

'They can wait.'

'Make up your mind. I thought this party was ultra-important…first impressions, burying bad news with my stunning personality, and all that stuff?'

'The pain is making you cranky. You need some fresh air to clear your head.'

She sighed. It was easier to give up, and the idea of escaping for a few moments had distinct appeal. The lively music the live band struck up made up her mind.

He didn't say anything until they got outside. 'So, you met Spiro.'

She inhaled as they stepped out into the scented night and she let her head fall back. 'Uh-huh, a real charmer, isn't he? If you go for snakes, that is.'

'Not a man to be underestimated, though.'

She lifted her head and walked alongside him onto the sloping lawns that ran down to the beach. The breeze tugged at her hair, dislodging several strands from her updo. She stuck them back in haphazardly.

'He is a poor loser. He takes pleasure from revenge…'

She flashed a look at his profile in the moonlight. 'What did he do?'

'He tried to sabotage something that is…important to me.'

It had taken a while to work out there was actually a pattern to the seemingly arbitrary flurry of false, damaging stories circulating online. The near career-ending false stories about abuse, about a dedicated and vital staff member at the charity for street kids that few knew had anything to do with Zach, and simultaneously the exposé about bullying in the mentoring scheme set up for teens emerging from care.

A firm specialising in forensic investigation had taken about five minutes to reveal that the older man's grubby hands were all over the mess.

The threat of litigation had made the problem vanish. For good measure Zach had explained that he didn't need to resort to lies to bring Spiro down, and that he had in his possession several verifiable documents that would ensure the older man did jail time. As bluffs went it was a no-brainer. A man like Spiro always had dirty secrets.

'Your mentoring scheme for street kids, you mean.'

He stopped dead and looked at her in astonishment. 'How the hell do you know that?'

'What?' she said, dancing ahead and turning around to face him as she continued to skip backwards on her crazy high heels. 'That you are a bleeding heart do-gooder…?' she taunted, allowing herself a triumphant little laugh, frustrated that the shadows across his face meant she could only see his mouth, not his eyes. 'I talk to people. They open up to me. It's a gift.'

He swore.

'I don't know why you act like it's a dirty secret. I think it's marvellous!'

'You know nothing about me—the things I've—'

Her smile faded. 'I know you lived on the streets, and you survived.' That he'd had to protect himself and he had never learnt how to stop; it wasn't a matter of didn't, he *couldn't* seem to open up to anyone.

'Selene?' he growled as he strode out at a pace that made her skip to keep up with him.

'Don't blame her, she assumed I knew already. You ran away from your uncle, the one who died?'

He nodded.

'And you never went back?'

His face was in shadow and when he finally responded his voice was wiped clean of all emotion as he reacted to the question. 'I went back looking for what... I suppose some sort of closure. He was gone. Dead, I found out later, and my grandmother...dementia, final stages.'

Kat gave a little gasp, feeling his pain as sharply as if it were her own as she fell into step beside him once more. 'What happened?'

'Nothing. I put her in a home and haven't been back since the first time.'

'So, she is having the best care?' It said so much about him that he would do that for someone who had abused him so badly.

'Oh, I can provide her with the best care, but I can't... *feel*...anything.'

She reached out in the dark and curled her small fingers around his. She could feel the raw tension emanating from him in waves. 'Sorry.'

'I suppose you think I should forgive her?' he flung out.

'No, I think that you should celebrate the day you escaped every year. I'll help you if you like?'

He looked down just as the moon came out from behind a cloud. It illuminated her beautiful face with breathtaking clarity, toasting her skin with moon gold.

CHAPTER TEN

HE STARED DOWN at her, drinking in each individual feature before gorging himself on the perfect whole. Then slowly, he lifted a hand and framed her face. Kat shivered at the contact and pushed her cheek against his hand, turning her face so that her lips brushed his palm.

His hand dropped.

'How will you help me?'

Her heart gave a painful jolt; her body was humming, her nerve endings raw as though all the insulation, the protection, had been stripped from them. 'I'd do anything you need,' she whispered.

A sound like a groan was torn from deep inside his chest. 'Don't say that, Katina.'

She lifted her chin. 'Why not?'

'Because I need everything.'

The heat between them scorched the air as he bent his head and kissed her. Kat kissed him back with equal abandon, locking her hands around his neck, arching her back to crush her breast into his chest, the little gasps of shocked pleasure as she felt the hardness of his desire against her belly lost in the warmth of his mouth.

They broke apart as the sound of a helicopter over-
head cut through the sigh of the water.

Zach swore and took her hand. He studied it for a
moment, an expression almost like pain contorting his
features before his fingers tightened and he led her onto
the moonlit sand.

Kat tripped.

'You're going to break your neck on those damned
things. They are lethal.'

'But sexy.'

His eyes glowed hot and hungry. 'Hell, yes!'

The moonlight lent everything a silvered glow and
the night-time silence made the hush of the waves
breaking into a white foam hiss seem louder. There
was no wind at all, just a warm stillness as, hopping on
one foot and then the other, she whipped off the heels to
walk beside him, her heart pounding in anticipation as
they reached the point where the waves were breaking.

He turned, allowing himself to look at her. The fall
had shaken free her hair from its elegant knot and it
now spilled down her back and blew across her face in
silky tangled strands that she pushed impatiently away
with her free hand.

'I want to touch you.' He closed his eyes, trying to
get some sort of grip on the raw primal instincts that
had him in a stranglehold. The muscles in his brown
throat worked as he stared at her, but it was the heat in
his passion-glazed eyes that made her insides dissolve
and made her feet move of their own accord to close
the distance between them.

Kat, her heart thudding, forgot what she was about
to say, forgot how to speak, how to think; the raw need

stamped into his strong, beautiful features thrilled through her and into a secret place nothing had ever penetrated before.

'This is a bad idea, Kat,' he slurred, struggling to think past the roar, the tidal wave of emotion rising inside him as he dragged a not quite steady hand through his hair.

'It's too late to go back,' she said, thinking, *In more ways than one,* as a surge of sheer hopeless longing made her tremble. He really was the epitome of male beauty as he stood there in the moonlight, his shirt open to the waist, his dark hair standing in sexy tufts, the shadow on his jaw and chin highlighting the angles and planes of his face.

'You're perfect,' she whispered, utterly dazzled by his perfection.

'Agape mou!' Zach looked into her eyes, saw the heat and hunger and felt his control burn away. It was impossible to tell who moved first but suddenly they were colliding, the impetus of the contact driving the air out of her lungs; not that it mattered—Kat couldn't breathe anyway.

They sank to the sand together, lay side by side, thigh to thigh, for a moment breathing hard, staring into each other's eyes.

Zach moved first, reaching out to lay a big hand against her cheek, then, holding her gaze, he moved in with nerve-shreddingly slow deliberation to claim her trembling lips.

Kat's eyes squeezed closed as she focused on the taste of him, the feel of him, greedily absorbing the musky smell of his hard, male body mingled with the salty tang in the air.

The touch of his hand on one breast drew a soft feral whimper from her aching throat. She felt the air cool on her hot skin as he pushed the fabric away, revealing the turgid pink peak. The air around them crackled with the passion that burned away oxygen, leaving them in a bubble when, as if responding to some silent signal, they both began frantically tearing at each other's clothing, their mouths connected as they kissed with a wild lack of restraint, a desperate drowning feeling that Kat had never dreamt existed, let alone would ever feel.

Her entire body felt sensitised. She was aware of every touch, every abrasive point of friction between them and most of all the hot ache of arousal between her thighs.

Zach raised himself onto his knees, pulling Kat with him, his lips not releasing hers for a second as his hands moved to the zip at the back of her dress. The need to see her was part of the madness consuming them both.

The dress slithered down to waist level.

Kat squeezed her eyes closed and felt, rather than heard, the vibration of his deep gasp, a gasp that was drowned out by her louder groan as she felt the touch of his mouth against the tip of one quivering soft breast and then the other. Her fingers speared into his dark hair, holding his head there against her to prolong this nerve-wrenching erotic sensation, giving herself over to the bliss.

By the time his head lifted, she was shaking everywhere and burning up. They faced one another, still

kneeling as behind them the waves continued their relentless advance, retreat, hiss.

The pounding in Kat's blood did not retreat. It kept
pushing forward, harder and harder, driving her deeper
into the sensual maelstrom.

Zach leaned in to trail kisses down her neck, one
hand cupping her breast, before pressing a fierce kiss
to her parted lips.

'You feel like silk—so very soft,' he husked against
her mouth.

'I want to feel…touch you…'

Their breath mingled, their tongues tangled as they
continued to kiss with hungry, bruising intensity. Kat
felt him quiver as she pushed aside the fabric of his shirt
that hung open to allow her palms to slide down the
smooth, slightly hair-roughened skin of his chest. She
loved the feel of him, the hardness, the amazing definition of every individual ridge of muscle, every perfect contour. His skin felt fever hot under her exploring
hands as he started to kiss down her body.

His tongue had found her nipple again when he felt
the moment she encountered the scar, not from the knife
but the surgical scar where they had opened his ribcage
to save his life and massage his heart.

He lifted his head, the hot colour edging his cheekbones lending them a hard definition in the moonlight.
Holding her eyes, he fought his way out of his shirt, allowing her to see the white line that ran midline along
his breastbone and the more raised scar just under his
ribs.

'What hap—?'

Her words were lost inside the possessive heat of his

mouth as he pressed her back down onto the sand, the weight of his body pressing her deeper. The first skin-to-skin contact sent all questions, all thoughts from her head. She moved her hands over his broad shoulders, excited by his strength. The heat flaring between them as they continued to kiss and touch.

'Have you any idea how much I want you? Have wanted you from the first...the very first moment I saw you?' The expression of fierce concentration on his face, the molten hunger in his eyes as he stroked a finger down her cheek as much as his erotic admission drew a throaty whimper from Kat's throat.

'I wanted you, too. Inside me. So much.'

The admission burned the remnants of his shredded control away; he gave a grin and levered himself off her.

He watched the protest die on her lips as she realised what he was doing; he was aware of her eyes following him as he unfastened his trousers and slid them down his thighs, kicking them away.

His boxers followed.

'Oh...!' She swallowed and felt the blood pool in the juncture between her legs. He really was magnificent, the level of his arousal was shocking, yet she wasn't embarrassed; his primitive male beauty fed the urgency in her blood.

She lay there, aching for his touch, and perhaps her desperation communicated itself because his hands moved down over the feminine curve of her hips as he freed her from the folds of dress fabric that had bunched across her. Her panties—scraps of lace—followed suit and he knelt back down beside her.

Kat reached out and touched him. He gasped and she

felt him quiver as she stroked down the hot, hard length of him, then, emboldened, curved her fingers around him, touching the velvet tip with the pad of her thumb.

Nostrils flared, teeth clenched, he watched her, unable to tear his eyes from the expression of carnal concentration on her beautiful face. He bore it as long as he could before he grabbed her hand and, ignoring her protest, pushed her back, lowering his body onto her.

Hands held at the wrists above her head, all she could do at that first nerve-searingly perfect moment of skin-to-skin was moan. Then moan a lot more and squirm against him as she felt his hand slide between their bodies and in between her legs, exposing the heat in her sensitised core to his clever touch.

She tried to breathe, moving against the heel of his hand at the intimate exploration until it got so intense that she couldn't bear it. The pleasure moving close to the pleasure-pain line.

'Please,' she whispered, her teeth closing around the lobe of his ear. 'I can't...' she begged. 'It's too... You're too...'

'Relax, it's all right,' he slurred against her neck as he gave into the primal roar in his blood and parted her legs. 'Wrap your legs around me, hold me.'

She did, happy to take instruction. She was in uncharted territory, and he really seemed to know what he was doing. Zach was an intuitive, passionate and generous lover. She knew from conversations she had frequently felt excluded from that this was a rather rare combination.

She stopped thinking anything when he slid into her, his powerful thrust slowed by the tightness of her warm female body as it adjusted to him, relaxing and contracting as he began to touch deeper inside her, waking nerve endings that sent rush after rush of mindless bliss through her body.

'You feel…oh, Zach…you feel—' Her words were lost in the warm moisture of his mouth.

She felt as if she were on fire as she pushed towards an unseen goal and when she reached it the shock of release jerked her entire body as the pleasure spread from her scalp to her curling toes.

Her muscles had started to relax when she felt the hot rush of his climax; a moment later he rolled off her and they lay side by side, panting.

It felt like coming back to earth after floating far above it; it wasn't a thing that happened in a moment.

When she did Kat was smiling.

He watched as with fluid grace she rolled on her side, then he took her hand to kiss her open palm before he drew her warm, pliant body to him.

Relaxed… As it seeped through his body it took him a while to recognise the feeling. He did not associate sexual release with being relaxed; lowering your guard to that degree, opening yourself that much, required trust.

Then it hit him like a wall, the knowledge that scared him more than anything else could—in the few days he had known her she had burrowed her way through all the barriers he'd thrown up into his soul, his heart. If he loved her this much now, how much deeper, stronger would it grow if he let it?

How much harder it would be when it ended, when

he let her down; there was a terrible inevitability to it. No one had ever been there for him and he had never been there for anyone else; a genetic flaw or something he'd never learnt, it remained a fact.

It was in his genes. Who would pass on a heritage like that? It would stop with him.

He closed his eyes and lay there, feeling her hands on his body, exploring. She was a giver and he was a taker, but he didn't have the will or the strength to stop her. He wanted the moment to last.

She watched Zach. He appeared to be sleeping, his breath even and steady, his chest rising and falling. The rest of him… Her glance slid lower and she blushed, remembering the pleasure his body had given her. The rest of him was perfect. The only flaw, if it could be counted as such, was the long surgical scar she had seen.

Zach tensed and kept his eyes closed as he felt her fingers move down the scar on his chest; he'd known it was coming. In a moment she'd find the more messy, less surgically precise scars on his ribs, which the knife, luckily for him, had just glanced off, not penetrated. It was the one underneath that had thrust upwards, severing some major vessels, that had caused all the damage.

The only people who knew the truth of the scars were Alekis and Selene, plus the surgical team who had saved his life, the *real* heroes. He was indulgent of a little morbid curiosity from his bed partners. He even had a few ridiculous lies he wheeled out on occasion to amuse himself, safe in the knowledge they really didn't care about his pain or his trauma or the fact his uncle had knocked seven bells out of him—these were all pluses.

This was different. Kat's curiosity would not be morbid. Her empathy had quite a different quality and would include sympathy and pity, two things he had a strong allergic reaction to.

He opened his eyes and turned his head and, despite everything, experienced a shock-level surge of possessiveness as his eyes slid over her lovely face and beautiful body.

She smiled.

You made a mistake that was human and, if not, forgivable as such, but at least you could have a free pass; you repeated it and there were no free passes because you were a fool.

He was not a fool.

He'd made a mistake and he was not about to repeat it. This was going nowhere, because he didn't do tomorrow and she very definitely did. The kindest thing in the long run—and she might appreciate it one day, when she had her family and her brood of children— was a clean cut. Not that there would be anything clean about it if Alekis found out.

She had edged a little closer, planning to put her head on his chest, pushing her long leg against his hair-roughened thigh, enjoying the contrast in their bodies. They were two very different halves that had made a total perfect whole. At the last moment something in his face, or rather the *lack* of it, made her pause.

'Is something wrong?' Fear of losing this happiness made her tense.

'I didn't protect you.' The only time in his life.

It took a moment for his words and the self-contempt in his voice to make sense.

'I'm sorry.'

'I was there, too,' she reminded him quietly. 'It was my responsibility, too.'

He closed his eyes and shook his head. 'You would say that.' Because she was good...too good for him, but the truth was she had given and he had taken.

She reached out again and touched the scar, pale against the deep gold of his skin. 'What happened?' she asked, her tender heart aching as she thought of the pain those marks represented.

He took her hand off his chest, dropped it as if it were something contagious and sat up. 'One of those "wrong place wrong time" things.'

She blinked and felt the trace of unease already stirring in her belly take serious hold. 'Is that all I get...?' She smiled to lighten her words and added half jokingly, 'You really could do with some lessons in sharing.'

He looked at her again; the coldness in his eyes made her stomach quiver in apprehension. She reached for her dress as the self-consciousness she had shrugged off returned. Pulling herself onto her knees, she slipped it over her head but didn't attempt the zip.

He didn't offer so she knelt back down again.

'We are not sharing, Katina. Yes, we had sex, but it was not the beginning of some special sharing, caring relationship. But if you want to know, the scars are why I am who I am. I was in the wrong place but so was Alekis.'

'You saved him.'

'I am not a hero, Kat. Do not look at me that way.

I hate bullies and I didn't think before I acted…much like tonight.'

It wasn't just what he said, it was the fact he seemed to *want* to hurt her.

'You sound as though you regret it.'

She left him the space to say no, that it had been one of the best things that had ever happened to him, but the space stayed empty and instead his eyes drifted away from hers as if the contact was something that made him uncomfortable. 'It was a mistake—you must see that.'

Kat said nothing. She was actually afraid if she tried to speak she'd start crying.

'For starters, Alekis trusted me. I have betrayed that trust and betrayed someone I respect.' *But, man, is he good to hide behind.* Ignoring the sly insert of his subconscious, he appealed for her understanding. 'You must see that.'

'Why should I care about what Alekis thinks?' she flared back. 'Anyway, what about me? Don't I deserve a little bit of respect?' she choked out.

'Please do not become emotional…'

'*Seriously!* We just made love.'

'Had sex.'

The rebuttal made her pale.

'And do not imagine this is the start of some sort of love affair.'

She sat there shivering while he got to his feet and dragged his clothes on. There was a pause before he extended his hand to her; she ignored it and got to her feet.

'I know you want a happy-ever-after thing, a husband and children, which is fine, but I'm not the man for that and if I'd known you were so inexperienced I would have—' Innate honesty made him pause. If he'd known he would not have stopped—nothing would have stopped him.

'Don't put me in one of your little boxes, and don't presume to know what I want from life! You know something, Zach, I really don't think *I'm* the one with the problem. I didn't expect you to declare undying love. I just wanted a little bit of…well, respect would have been nice. But no, you had to spoil what happened by turning it into something nasty and sordid, because you're too scared to risk feeling anything that you can't control. You know what I think?'

His jaw clenched as he struggled to control his anger. 'Is there any way I can stop you telling me?'

'You won't have any sort of a future until you come to terms with your past and stop letting it rule you.'

'Who's presuming now?' he growled out.

She picked up her skirts in one hand, decided not to look for her shoes—they had killed anyway—and started back across the sand toward the lights of the house.

Zach, who experienced a stab of visceral longing as he watched her progress, dignified despite the fact her entire back, including the upper slopes of her pert bottom, was exposed, managed to wipe his face of expression as she suddenly swung back, her anger cancelling out mental censorship as she had the last word.

'You're not the only one with trust issues, Zach. Why the hell do you think I was inexperienced? Though, for the record, I was a virgin! And as it turns out a stupid one because I thought I had found someone I could let my guard down with. You know what, though, I'd prefer to be me and make a mistake than you, who spends his life pretending you don't feel anything…' Her eyes searched his face. 'But I don't believe that—you did and for me!'

The level of his self-loathing went up several notches as he watched her flounce away.

CHAPTER ELEVEN

'HOW DID IT GO?'

Selene saw Kat's face and her own melted into one of concern. 'Oh, dear, is it bad news?'

Kat shook her head as she laid her handbag down on the table and turned back to the housekeeper. 'No, no, nothing like that really.' She was not ready to share just yet what the *something* was that had put the worried look on her face. 'The doctors are really pleased with his progress. If all goes well with his next round of tests, they are willing to discharge him next week.'

Kat was visiting the clinic in Athens once a week, but talking to her grandfather during the week online. This time she had taken herself off to see another specialist after seeing her grandfather.

'Things are definitely getting more relaxed.'

'He must be pleased he's coming home.'

'No, he's mad as hell that he can't escort me to this charity auction.'

'Never mind, there's next year.'

'That's what I said only he…yes, thanks, tea would be lovely,' she said with gratitude to a maid who brought in a tea tray.

'Only?'

'He has roped in a stand-in. He says as he has donated a sports car, an Azaria should be there. I said I'm not an Azaria but, well…' She shrugged. She had discovered her grandfather was a hard man to argue with and when faced with a defeat he fell back on chest pain, and who was going to risk disbelieving him?

Not Kat.

'Join me,' Kat begged when the woman poured her tea.

Smiling, Selene poured another and took a seat. 'So who is the stand-in? Anyone we know?'

Selene had already guessed, the way she had figured out at least some of what had gone on between Zach and Kat.

'Zach,' Kat said quietly. Unlike for Selene, the news had come as a massive shock when Alekis had announced his stand-in for the charity auction.

Kat had excused herself and gone to the ladies' room to cry her eyes out, but then she had an excuse for being over-emotional. Her hormones were all over the place—she was pregnant.

She'd had her suspicions for a few days and the consultant had officially confirmed it today.

To keep things private—the island was a very small place—she'd asked Sue to post her the test kit. Her friend had been sympathetic but she had promised her that *nobody* knew that early, but Kat had, and she'd been right.

Two weeks to the day since Zach had left, never, it seemed, to return, she knew she was carrying his child. The shock was still there, even the occasional moment of blind panic, but a level of acceptance had started to kick in and, to her surprise, *excitement*.

While her emotions were all over the place, she was totally sure of one thing. This baby would have a mother who loved her or him. Her baby would never feel alone and be scared. She was absolutely determined to give this child the childhood she had not had.

Sadly, she could not guarantee the baby a father. And the great-grandfather? Well, the jury was still out, but she suspected, hoped, that Alekis would be over the moon about having a great-grandchild.

And if he wasn't, well, she would deal with it. The baby came first as far as she was concerned and if other people had a problem with that—tough!

It was the father's identity her grandfather might have a problem with. It was a problem the father himself might have, too. She had lain awake half of last night trying to decide when and how to tell Zach and had come to the conclusion that she needed to get used to the idea herself before she shared.

It made sense.

Or she might just be a big coward!

'It's a really stunning event with the cream of society and—'

'But Zach...' Kat wailed, still blaming her hormones.

Kat had taken to her room and cried for a day when Zach had left, claiming a migraine, and when she had emerged she had known that Zach wasn't the only person in denial.

Hard enough to accept she had wanted him physically, but accepting that she had fallen in love with Zach had been one of the hardest things in her life. She prided herself on being truthful but this was one truth she had been avoiding because she had known it would hurt— she just hadn't known how much!

'You could make an excuse…'

Kat's chin went up. 'Why should I?' She wasn't the one who had done anything wrong.

Zach, drawing eyes and more than a few camera clicks in his dress suit, stepped back into the shadows, and the limo that drew up disgorged the members of a new girl-band group.

The paparazzi went crazy and Zach's patience grew thin. His offer to travel over to Tackyntha to escort Kat had been politely refused by someone who was not Kat or even Selene.

He was being given the runaround. The only surprise was that nothing of what had happened between he and Kat seemed to have filtered through to Alekis as yet.

The past two weeks had been a sort of hell Zach had never experienced before. Normally in times of stress he was able to bury himself in work until it passed, but not on this occasion. He couldn't concentrate, a unique experience for him, so work was impossible.

His volatile mood had swung from anger and frustration—he hadn't asked for any of this—and then on to black despair. It was crazy but he was missing her, not just the physical stuff, although that had been incredible, but stupid things like the sound of her voice…her laugh, the way she wrinkled up her nose.

The woman was haunting him.

Logic told him that a man couldn't fall in love so

quickly, but the same logic told him that love, the romantic variety, didn't exist outside romance novels.

He'd believed that before Katina had walked into his life.

And now? Now he didn't know what the hell he felt, and her words kept coming back to him. *'You won't have any sort of a future until you come to terms with your past.'*

He was the one with the problem.

It still made him angry, but Zach had started to wonder if she could be right.

He had rejected the idea that he was a coward hiding behind his past and unable to face the future, but the more he thought about it… Tonight would give him a chance to connect again. Maybe there was some sort of middle ground?

He dashed a hand across his head. *Middle ground?* What the hell was he thinking?

He was thinking of kissing her—just sinking into her warmth—as he had been from the second she had walked away from him. He had struggled not to run after her. He had begun to wonder what would have happened if he had—maybe their passionate affair would already have burnt itself out?

Or she might have killed him.

A half-smile on his lips, he stepped forward again. This time the limos had arrived in a block of three.

The door to the first opened and a platinum blonde got out, wearing a glittery silver dress that was so figure-hugging it appeared painted on. She rocked a little on her heels as she paused to pose for cameras even though no one seemed that excited about her and her escort's arrival.

'Well, I hear that Alekis's little heiress will be here tonight. I wonder if she's as much of a slut as the mother was.'

'Was she?' the man asked.

'God, yes, and a druggie… I hear that the girl is just like her. Alekis found her in some sort of refuge and I hear that before that she was actually living on the streets.'

The woman with the uniquely unattractive voice had begun talking as she emerged from the car. Standing at the top of a long flight of stone steps, Zach nonetheless heard every word of this conversation.

He stepped in front of the doormen.

The woman looked him up and down, her painted lips widening into a smile. 'Oh, hello, how nice to see you again, Zach. Darling, it's Zach.'

Zach, who had not to his knowledge ever seen either of them before, waited until she had finished listing to her long-suffering partner all the times they had met him previously.

'I heard you speaking—actually I think several people heard you speaking—about Miss Katina Parvati,' Zach observed, pitching his own voice to carry. It was a message he did not mind sharing. 'I did not like what I heard. Obviously anyone with an ounce of sense will recognise spiteful lies and malice when they hear it. But I feel it only fair to warn you that should I hear those lies repeated anywhere online or in person I will have no compunction but to put the case in the hands of my *very* litigious legal team. And after they have finished with you I am sure that Alekis Azaria might enjoy watching his own team picking at your bones. His granddaughter is a person so superior to the likes of you that I find it offensive that you breathe the same air!'

'Zach!'

At the sound of the voice he turned. Kat was standing at the bottom of the steps, wearing a dress a shade paler than the one he remembered stripping off her body. This one was much more formal: a strapless bodice that revealed the upper slopes of her breasts and the dazzle of a diamond necklace.

He rushed down to her, taking the steps two at a time, shedding his doubts with each step he took. What he felt for her was not going to burn itself out. She was part of him and if he ever won her back he would never let her go!

'Do you make a habit of making public scenes?' Oh, God, he looked so gorgeous she could not take her eyes off him. The ache of longing she had struggled to deny was a physical ache that went soul deep.

He looked blank for a moment, a little dazed, and then glanced up the stairs. The couple had vanished.

'Not usually.' His shoulders lifted in a shrug.

There was so much he needed to say but now she was here and he was acting like some tongue-tied kid, or maybe just the Neanderthal who had taken her virginity on a beach she probably thought he was.

Kat lowered her eyes and struggled to collect her fractured composure. Seeing him standing there had shaken loose a million conflicting emotions. The idea that she could distance herself from him emotionally or any other way had vanished.

He was the father of her child and she loved him.

'I heard what you said,' she said, not even bothering to try and project the illusion of calm control—who was going to believe it? 'I think maybe a lot of people did.'

That was the problem: there were way too many people and he wanted her all alone. 'Let's get this over with,' he said, taking her elbow and mentally figuring out just how soon they could reasonably leave without causing massive offence. While he had zero problem with offence, he suspected that Kat might not be on the same page as him with this.

'You've not lost any of your charm,' she said, hating the fact he had the ability to hurt her.

He looked down at her, frowning. 'No, I didn't mean... I need to talk to you alone and I avoid these things like the plague normally.'

Warning herself not to read anything into his words or the possessive blaze in his eyes when he looked at her, she allowed herself to be escorted into the room.

Selene had warned her that everyone crowded into the small space for drinks and finger food before the auction, which was to be held in the marquee outside. And it was crowded, very! The jewels she had been so reluctant to wear were not the most extravagant baubles on display. Kat had never seen so much bling in such a small space in her life, though maybe the impression was exaggerated because the walls felt as if they were closing in on her.

'Fruit juice, please,' she said as she was offered champagne. 'I feel like everyone is staring at me.'

'They are. You're the most beautiful woman in the room.'

It might have given her more pleasure to hear him say this had her head not started to spin in a really sickening fashion. She lifted her head as the lights above began to blur.

'Zach?'

He caught her before she hit the floor and when she opened her eyes, he was kneeling beside her looking pale while he emptied the contents of her small bag onto the floor.

'Where's the EpiPen...? Does anyone have an EpiPen? This is anaphylactic shock. Will someone call an ambulance?'

'No, Zach, it isn't.'

A look of intense relief washed over his face. '*Agape mou*...no, don't move, you fainted. I think you might have eaten something with peanuts in.'

'No, I haven't.' She hadn't eaten a thing; she'd been too nervous about tonight. 'You remembered!'

'I remember every word you have ever said to me.'

She ran her tongue over her dry lips and tried to lift her head. 'No, stay there, wait for the ambulance.' A large hand on her chest made it impossible for her to defy this edict.

'Will you stop it?' she said, batting his hand with both hers. 'I'm not ill, you idiot, I'm pregnant!'

Her exported admission coincided with a lull in the conversation that had started up when people had guessed she wasn't dead. The room had excellent acoustics so at least eighty per cent of the people present heard the happy news.

Beside her, Zack had frozen. The blood had quite

literally drained from his face; he looked much more in need of an ambulance than she did.

'Pregnant.'

She nodded.

A long sibilant hiss left his lips as he leaned back onto his heels.

'Only just…obviously.'

His hand lifted from her chest, but her relief was short-lived. He needed both hands to scoop her up and carry her out of the place, magnificently oblivious to the hundred pairs of eyes watching them.

Outside, a car appeared as if by magic. Zach slid her into the back seat as if she were a piece of porcelain before joining her.

'I don't know… I don't know what to say.' His dark eyes slid to her belly. 'You're sure?'

She nodded. 'Sorry.'

His dark brows lifted. 'Do not say sorry. A child is, is…' A child was scary. 'A blessing. At least that was what one of the nuns who taught me in kindergarten said. I think she decided I was an exception when I asked her how many she had.'

'You don't have to pretend, Zach,' she said, sounding understanding but feeling miserable as hell. If he could allow himself to love her even half as much as she loved him, they could have a wonderful life. A family, because, even if he did not know it, she knew he was a marvellous man who had overcome more than most people could imagine. 'I know that this is the very last thing you would have wanted and I'm not going to ask you for anything.'

'You shouldn't have to ask.' He stared at her for a

moment before giving a cracked laugh. 'And you don't have to. Obviously, we're getting married.'

It was Kat's turn to laugh. 'Is that meant to be funny?'

'You tried telling Alekis that yet?'

'This is nothing to do with Alekis.'

Rather to her surprise, Zach nodded. 'No, it isn't.' He leaned forward and lifted a hank of hair from her face, tucking it behind her ear with such tenderness that it brought tears to her eyes. 'I came here tonight wanting to talk to you, to say some things. How about I do that first and then we talk about…?' His eyes dropped, a smile curving his lips, as her hand lifted to cover the flatness of her belly protectively.

'So you don't want to discuss the elephant in the room.'

'I want very much to discuss it, but there are things I need to say first to put what has happened into perspective. Would that be okay with you?'

She nodded warily and glanced at the partition between them and the driver.

'He can't hear us.'

'All right.'

'Firstly, you were right. I do have a problem. The past is…has been stopping me moving on. I've been alone for a long time and I decided that was a strength, but I realise now that it is in fact a weakness.'

'It's lonely,' she said quietly, her heart aching for the lonely boy he'd been. 'I know. It's not weak, Zach, it's just…sometimes you need to give a bit of yourself to get something back.' Kat knew she'd been lucky she'd had foster parents who had taught her that. Zach had had no one; he'd been alone.

'It's *easier* to be alone,' he said with a self-recrimina-tory grimace. 'I was willing to walk away from the best thing that ever happened to me because I was scared. A coward. I've been wrong about a lot of things in my life but this here with you… I was insane to let you walk away.'

'You didn't let me walk, Zach, you threw me away.'

A look of shame crossed his face as he heard the bit-terness in her voice. 'You're right. I'm an idiot. I think that part of me cannot believe that I am allowed to be happy in that way—to have something so precious and lose it… I think that was my fear. I was afraid that I couldn't look after you like I couldn't look after my mother.'

Heart aching for the pain drawn on his face, she caught his hand and pressed it between both of her own. 'You were a child, Zach. It wasn't your job to do the looking after.'

'Being alone was my way of feeling in charge…but I'm not going to think of being alone now, and I'm going to think of that time when I was as the time I was wait-ing for you, until that moment I saw you, in that grave-yard, looking like a sexy angel.'

'There was someone there!' she breathed, recalling the day when she had sensed a presence as she'd laid flowers at her mother's grave.

He gave a half-smile. 'I couldn't get your face out of my head.' He took his phone from his pocket and showed her the snapshot. 'Have you any idea how many times a day I have looked at that?'

The tears that had filled Kat's eyes as he spoke

spilled out, sparkling on her lashes. 'You're not saying this just because of the baby? I really couldn't bear that.'

'The baby… Now that is something I never thought I would have, but now I am claiming it.' He pressed a possessive hand to her stomach and his mouth to her lips.

The kiss was deep and tender and life-affirming.

'I love you, Kat!' Just saying it felt liberating, so he said it again, aching sincerity throbbing in his voice. 'I love you and I hope you will one day learn to love me. Marry me, Kat. Let us be a family.'

'That's not possible, Zach, because I'm already totally insanely in love with you!' she cried, throwing her arms around his neck.

EPILOGUE

'I WANT TO see the person in charge!'

Kat's eyes lifted from the baby in her arms to see her handsome husband standing at the side of the bed.

'He is just so perfect…yes, I think Alek suits him?' Her husband looked as exhausted as she had felt, but it was a good tired that came with a deep feeling of contentment.

'I think so. You should really get some sleep, you know.'

She nodded. 'We have a family, Zach.' There was wonder in her face as she looked down at the baby who had arrived at six that morning.

Zach covered her hand with his own. 'We are a family,' he corrected, looking deep into her eyes.

The bellowing voice interrupted the tender moment, making itself heard once more. This time the baby's eyes opened; they were dark, flecked with amber.

'Hush, Alek, we will not let Great-Grandpa wake you up. You'll get used to him.'

'If he's anything like his mother he'll have the old man wrapped around his little finger in no time at all.'

'What can I say?' Kat said with a smile. 'I'm irresistible. You know, you really *should* go and tell him to come in. You know he's creating havoc out there.'

Zach gave a resigned sigh and levered himself off the bed, pausing to touch the dark head of his son and press a warm kiss to his wife's lips. 'You did good, kid.'

'A joint effort,' she protested.

'Hardly. My contribution required much less effort,' he said with the wicked grin she loved so much.

'Oh, I helped a little bit with that too, as I recall.'

His grin deepened. 'Well, I have to say I'm really relieved he doesn't look like Alekis. That was my secret fear all along.'

'Oh, was that what your secret fear was?' she teased lovingly. 'I thought it was I might slip, I might get too hot, I might get too cold, I might—'

'All right, all right, a man is allowed to be protective, isn't he? And now we have this… He is very beautiful, isn't he?'

'Of course he is, he looks just like his papa.'

'Doctor!' the voice outside thundered scornfully. 'I wish to speak to the person in charge, not a child.'

'Oh, really, Zach, go and give him the news before he starts telling everyone how there would be no baby if he hadn't thrown us together, and that it was all part of his grand plan…' She broke off and gave a laugh of delight as the baby's tiny perfect fingers curled around one of her own. 'He is so strong, aren't you, my precious?' She looked up. 'You don't think there was a grand plan, do you?'

'You know something, *agape mou*? I really don't care. I am here with you and our baby. I don't care if the devil himself arranged it. I am just happy.'

Kat nodded. 'Me too.' She lifted a hand to stifle a yawn. 'Tired and happy.'

The addition made him smile. 'Right, I will go and tell your grandfather that you are not allowed visitors until tomorrow.'

'But the midwife said—'

Zach kissed her to silence. 'Tomorrow.'

'You are a very good husband.'

'I am a work in progress, but my heart,' he promised, pressing his hand first to his own chest and then against Kat's beating heart, 'is definitely in it.'

'Seen the name outside the surgical wing, young man? That is *my* name. I think you'll find I have some influence in this place!' Alekis shouted from the hallway.

'But he doesn't in this room,' Kat promised the sleeping baby in her arms.

Zach nodded his agreement. 'Oh, everyone at the refuge sent their love when I texted the news. Sue made a flying visit to the new refuge and she said to tell you there were no problems.'

'Oh, that is good news!' In the months after they had joined forces there had been five more refuges opened and Zach's mentoring scheme had started up in two UK cities.

'She also says everything is under control, so relax and enjoy the baby.'

'I—' Kat broke off as a loud bellow outside made the sleeping baby stir. 'Go and save the poor staff, Zach.'

Laughing, he obeyed, because after all Kat had saved him from a lonely life. She had given him the greatest gift there was—unconditional love.

* * * * *

ONE NIGHT WITH THE FORBIDDEN PRINCESS

AMANDA CINELLI

For Zara and Mia

CHAPTER ONE

'You will receive a marriage proposal this week.'

Olivia's ears still rang with her father's words, even as she moved through the motions of greeting the rest of the guests at the formal luncheon. It was not every day that your father informed you that you were set to marry a stranger, after all.

But, then again, her father was a king.

And the King clearly thought that the best time to impart news of this magnitude was no less than thirty seconds before he introduced her to her intended fiancé—a complete stranger. It was a wonder that she had managed to greet their guest of honour at all before she'd hurriedly made an excuse to leave.

Princesses were generally not permitted to sneak away during royal functions. Especially when that royal function concerned a very esteemed guest of honour from a faraway kingdom. Still, Olivia found herself making her way slowly across the room in search of fresh air.

'Another glass of champagne, Your Highness?'

Olivia stopped her progress and gracefully accepted the crystal flute from the waiter's hand, noticing the way his fingers trembled slightly as he tried to balance his tray. He was quite young—fresh out of school, she would bet.

'Is this your first Royal Races?' she asked, glad of the distraction while her eyes scanned the room, plotting her escape.

'It's my first day, actually. In general,' he replied.

'You are doing a wonderful job.'

She smiled, hoping her words might help to calm his nerves somewhat. It couldn't be an easy start, balancing priceless crystal while surrounded by some of Europe's wealthiest and most famous people.

'Thank you, Princess Olivia—I mean, Your Highness. Er…thank you.' He stumbled over his words, then smiled nervously, showing a mouth full of shiny metal braces.

Olivia smiled back with genuine warmth as the boy made a wobbly attempt at a bow and moved away. She sighed, taking a small sip from her glass. She would happily have spent the rest of the afternoon chatting with the teenager simply to avoid thinking of the bombshell that had just completely taken her by surprise. As if these royal functions weren't difficult enough.

The usual array of eager guests had predictably occupied her afternoon so far, with wave after wave of polite, banal conversation. Her parents, King Fabian and Queen Aurelia of Monteverre, stood at the opposite side of the long balcony surrounded by people and bodyguards. Her own personal security team stood at strategic points around her, trying and failing to blend into the crowd in their plain black suits and crisp white shirts.

The Royal Monteverre Races were infamous around the globe for their week-long parade of upper-class style and glamour. The historic racetrack was spread out below them, and thousands of guests had gathered in their finery for a day of sport and socialising.

No one's style was more closely watched than her own. Her morning had consisted of three hours being transformed by her own personal styling team. Her naturally wavy long red hair had been ironed and pressed to perfection, and her fair skin polished and highlighted in all the right places.

The public hailed her as a stunning natural beauty, but she knew the effort that went into upholding that image was far from natural at all. She was a public brand—a symbol for an entire country with her every single step followed closely by the whole world.

Even her older sister, Crown Princess Eleanor, was not given the same amount of attention. Perhaps it was because she was already married. The press took much more pleasure in the single siblings than they did in the 'taken' ones. And yet her younger sister had the excuse of her studies in London to avoid the limelight.

For the past five years Olivia had been very much at the centre of public attention—since taking her official role in palace life at twenty-one. She did not shy from the pressure—she had been trained for it after all. She knew to expect intense scrutiny. And yet there was nothing that could make her feel more alone than being surrounded by thousands of people who treated her like an ornament to be admired from afar.

A sudden crash jolted her out of her thoughts and she looked up with a groan of empathy to see that the young waiter seemed to have lost his balance and gone crashing into a nearby couple.

'You absolute imbecile!'

The roar came from an elderly duke, a close friend of her father, who seemed to have been the sole recipient of the tray's liquid contents. Shards of priceless crystal lay scattered across the floor in a pool of expensive champagne while the teenage server stood frozen with a mixture of embarrassment and fear.

'Have this clumsy idiot taken back to the schoolroom. Out of my sight!' the Duke spat, his eyes bulging as his equally outraged wife hurriedly tried to dry his sodden shirt with a napkin.

As Olivia watched with horror, a single bodyguard materialised from the crowd and took the boy roughly by the shoulders.

'Stop!' She moved forward suddenly, her body seeming to propel her towards the dramatic scene of its own volition.

'A princess should never concern herself with such matters.'

Her late grandmother's voice seemed to warn her from her subconscious. But she pushed the thought away, arriving by the boy's side and looking up at the burly guard with all the authority she could muster. A hush had fallen over the crowd around them.

'I think there is a better way of managing this, don't you?' She addressed the guard, then turned her attention to the elderly Duke and his wife. 'Duque L'Arosa, this young man is a friend of mine. I know he would appreciate your kindness on his first day of work.'

The Duke's eyes widened horribly, his face turning even more red as his much younger wife gripped his arm and snorted her disapproval. Olivia stood her ground, flashing her best royal smile as the guard immediately released the boy. The young waiter avoided her eyes as he hurriedly gathered his tray and rushed off in the direction of the kitchen.

Olivia became suddenly painfully aware of the quiet that surrounded her. Members of the Monteverrian nobility and various public and government figures all averted their eyes, no one daring to speak or whisper about a member of the royal family while she stood in their midst.

A strange sensation began to spread over her bare shoulders, and she instinctively turned her head and found herself pinned by the gaze of a man who stood a few feet away. He was remarkably tall—taller than most of the men in the room. Perhaps that was what had drawn her attention to him.

She tried to look away, feeling uncomfortable under his obvious scrutiny, but there was something about the way he looked at her. She was quite used to being stared at—she was a public figure after all. But his dark eyes seemed to demand her complete attention. It was quite inappropriate, she told herself. She should be annoyed. But even with the length of the room between them, having his eyes on her seemed to make her heart beat faster.

A strange quiver of anticipation jolted to life in her chest, making her want to close the gap between them just to hear how his voice sounded. She raised one brow in challenge and felt her heart thump as a sinful smile spread across his full mouth, making him appear all the more rakish and infinitely dangerous.

No man had ever looked at her that way before— as though she was a tasty snack he might like to sample. She shook her head at the ridiculous turn of her thoughts and forced herself to look away.

When she finally looked back he had vanished.

She steeled her jaw, nodding politely to the Duque and Duquesa before making a slow and graceful exit through the main doors. Her own personal team of guards made themselves known as she walked faster, all five of them closing in from their previous placements. She had never felt more frustrated at her newly heightened security than she did at that moment. There was no immediate threat—no need for the ridiculous new measures her father had put in place the week before.

'I'm feeling ill,' she announced to the men once they had exited into the empty corridor outside the racetrack's function room. 'Surely there is no need for all of you to accompany me into the bathroom?'

The men reacted predictably, coughing awkwardly before moving aside and allowing her to walk unchaperoned into the ladies' restroom. She searched the for an exit point, her eyes landing on a second door on the opposite side of the bathroom.

She smiled with triumph. Sometimes a little rebellion was necessary.

Roman Lazarov had never been particularly comfortable at high society functions. It had been sheer curiosity that had led him to accept the Sheikh of Zayarr's invitation to attend the Royal Races while he was already in Monteverre. Small European kingdoms were one of the few niche markets he had not yet entered with his security firm, as monarchies largely tended to keep to their own traditional models of operation. Old money aristocrats also tended to show a particular disdain towards new money Russians.

His fists tightened as he thought of the scene he had witnessed after only being in the room mere moments. Nothing made him feel closer to his own humble beginnings than watching a rich man treat his server badly. There was something particularly nasty about those who had been born to immense wealth. As though they believed the world should bend to their will and that those with less than them were somehow *worth* less as well. A sweeping generalisation, to be sure, but a painfully accurate one in his own experience.

The redhead had surprised him. She was clearly upper class—he could tell by the way she was dressed. Diamonds and rich yellow silk. He had noticed her the moment he'd entered the room. She had stood proud and untouchable near the centre, all alone, with her delicate fingers holding on to a champagne flute for dear life. And yet she had stepped forward for the servant and caused an obvious scene.

He should thank her, really. She had provided the perfect distraction for him to move on to his main purpose of business.

He would have liked nothing more than to stick around at the pretentious party and see if Lady Red lived up to his expectations. But really this brief detour to the races had been a mistake on his part. Time was of the essence when you had a royal palace to break into, after all…

The early summer afternoon was pleasant as Roman rounded the last bend on the dirt path, finally bringing the high walls of the palace into view. The overgrown abandoned hunting track wasn't the easiest route, but when you were about to break into the home of Monteverre's royal family you didn't usually use the front gate.

The forest was quiet but for the sounds of wildlife and the occasional creak of tree branches protesting as he methodically pulled them out of his way. Reaching the medieval stone wall, Roman looked up. It had to be at least five metres high and three metres thick—rather impressive and designed to be impossible to scale, especially when you weren't dressed for the occasion. He checked his smartwatch, zooming in on the small map that would guide him to the access point.

In another life Roman Lazarov had found pleasure in breaking the law. Bypassing even the most high-tech security system had been child's play for a hungry, hardened orphan with a taste for troublemaking. But in all his time in the seedy underworld of St Petersburg an actual palace had never made it onto his hit list.

That life was over now—replaced by a monumental self-made wealth that his young, hungry self could only have dreamed about. And yet here he was, his pulse quickening at the prospect of what lay ahead. The fact that this little exercise was completely above-board made it no less challenging. The palace had a guard of one hundred men and all he had was a digital blueprint of the castle tunnels and his own two hands.

The thought sent adrenaline running through his veins. God, but he had missed this feeling. When the Sheikh of Zayyar had first asked him for a favour, he had presumed it to be assembling a new security team for a foreign trip or something of that nature. Khal was in high demand these days, and his guard had been assembled almost entirely from Roman's security firm,

The Lazarov Group. But Khal's request had intrigued him—likely as it had been meant to. The challenge had been set, and Roman was determined to enjoy it.

As for whether or not he would succeed—that question had made him laugh heartily in his oldest friend's face.

Roman Lazarov never failed at anything.

The daylight made it seem almost as though he were taking a leisurely stroll rather than performing an act of espionage. He finally reached the small metal hatch in the ground that would provide the cleanest and most ridiculously obvious point of entry. An evacuation hatch, more than likely from long-ago times of war. He had hardly believed his eyes when his team had uncovered it on an old blueprint.

Although it looked rather polished and clean for a decades-old abandoned grate, he thought to himself, sliding one finger along the sun-heated metal.

A sudden sound in the quiet made Roman go completely still, instinctively holding his breath. He felt the familiar heightened awareness that came from years of experience in the security business as he listened, scanning his surroundings. Footsteps, light and fast, were coming closer. The person was of small build— possibly a child. Still, Roman couldn't be seen or this whole exercise would be blown.

Without another thought he took five long steps, shielding himself under cover of the trees.

A shape emerged from thick bushes ten feet away. The figure was petite, slim and unmistakably female. She was fast. So damned fast he saw little more than a set of bare shapely legs and a shapeless dark hooded coat before she seemed to pirouette and disappear through the hatch in the ground without any effort at all.

Roman frowned, for a moment simply replaying the image in his head. Evidently he was not the only one who had been informed of the hidden entryway. He shook off his surprise, cursing himself for hesitating as he made quick work of reaching the hatch and lowering himself.

The iron ladder was slippery with damp and led down to a smooth, square-shaped concrete tunnel beneath. Small patches of sunlight poked through ventilation ducts at regular intervals, giving some light in the otherwise pitch-blackness.

Roman stilled, listening for the sound of the woman's footsteps. She had moved quickly, but he could hear her faint steps somewhere ahead of him in the tunnel. As he began his pursuit a half-smile touched his lips. He had come here today tasked with proving the ineptitude of this palace's security, and now he would have a genuine intruder to show as proof.

This cat burglar was about to get *very* rudely interrupted.

Olivia held her shoes tightly in one hand as she slid her hand along the wall of the tunnel for support. The ground was damp and slippery under her bare feet—a fact that should have disgusted a young woman of such gentle breeding. But then she had never really understood the whole 'delicate princess' rationale. It was at times like this, after escaping palace life for even one simple hour, that she truly felt alive.

Her sudden disappearance had likely been noticed by now, and yet she did not feel any remorse. Her attendance at the international horse racing event had been aimed at the King's esteemed guest of honour, Sheikh Khalil Al Rhas of Zayyar. The man that her father had informed her she was intended to marry.

Olivia paused for a moment, tightness overcoming her throat for the second time in a few short hours. The way he had phrased it, as her 'royal duty', still rung in her ears. She was only twenty-six, for goodness' sake. She wasn't ready for this particular duty.

She had always known it was customary for her father to hold the right to arrange or refuse the marriages of his offspring, but she had hoped the day would never come when she was called upon in such an archaic fashion. But now that day was here, and the Sheikh was set to propose to her formally any day now—before he completed his trip.

Olivia pressed her forehead briefly against the stone wall. She felt cold through and through, as if she would never be warm again.

'Drama queen.' Cressida's mocking voice sounded in her head.

Her younger sister had always been such a calm, level-headed presence in her life. It had been five years since Cress had moved away to study in England. And not a day passed that she didn't think of her. With barely a year between them, they had always been more like twins. Cress would know exactly what to say to alleviate the unbearable tension that had taken residence in her stomach today. She was sure of it.

The tunnel was a straight path along the south boundary of the palace. It seemed like an endless mile before the staircase finally appeared. Olivia climbed it in the near darkness, relying solely on memory to make her way up to the partially hidden door in the stone wall. She pressed a slim crease, sliding open a panel and stepping through easily.

The brightness of her dressing room was a welcome shock of cream and gold after the prolonged darkness. She took a moment, breathing in the clean air, before turning to slide the secret door closed.

Olivia stilled at the sound of footsteps in the tunnel below. But that was impossible. In almost fifteen years of roaming she had never seen another soul down there. She had never even told her sisters.

She stepped back down to the small landing at the top of the steps. She braced her hands on the stone balustrade to peer down into the darkness, biting the inside of her lip. Had one of the guards followed her?

The footsteps suddenly disappeared and an eerie silence filled the stone caverns. Still she held her breath. *Eight, nine, ten...* Olivia exhaled slowly, cursing her overactive imagination. The silence of the tunnel tended to play with your mind after a while—she was clearly going insane.

She turned around to move back to the doorway to her apartment—only to be blocked by a wall of muscle. Warm muscle that smelled of sandalwood and pine.

Strong hands—definitely male—appeared like chains across her chest and turned her towards the wall. Her arms were pulled behind her and she instinctively pushed her body backwards, aiming the hardness of her skull towards her assailant's nose. Even princesses were taught self-defence.

'You have some skills, I see.'

His voice was startling in the quiet darkness. A

heavy accent made his threat even more worrying. This was most definitely *not* a palace guard.

Olivia hissed, turning away and trying in vain to pull against the bands of iron strength. She squinted in the darkness, trying to see his face, a uniform, an insignia—anything that might tell her who he was and why he was here. If she could remember anything from the Palace Guards' kidnapping talk it was one thing: *Don't say a thing.*

He pressed on what seemed to be a watch and turned a faint light downwards, lowering its beam to her over-sized black trench coat and bare feet. She had swapped her designer blazer with someone else's coat in the cloakroom before bolting. The vintage lemon cocktail dress she wore underneath was hardly ideal for going unnoticed in public.

She turned her head and caught a brief glimpse of a hard jaw and gigantic shoulders before he plunged them into darkness once more.

'You're not exactly dressed for a quick escape,' he mused.

She almost laughed at that—almost. But being held captive by a mysterious hulk of a man had kind of dampened her infamous ability to see the bright side of every situation. As far as she could see there was nothing positive that could come of being abducted, which was the only logical solution for whoever this man was. He would recognise her any moment now and the game would be up.

Perhaps they would ransom her, she thought wildly. How much was her life worth? Hopefully not too much…the kingdom was already facing complete financial ruin as it was.

She gulped hard as she felt his hand slip just under her left armpit—a strange place to grope, indeed.

'Don't! Don't you dare touch me.' She gasped, arching her body away frantically. He tightened his hold on her slightly, barely even noticing her attempts to free herself.

'You are in no danger from me,' he gritted. 'I must ensure the same can be said of you. Stand still.'

Such was the authority in his voice that she stilled herself. She held her breath as his touch moved almost mechanically to her hip. His movements were calm and purposeful as he did the same to her other side, feeling inside the pockets of her coat and underneath to slide along the indentation of her waist.

Her mind suddenly realised that he was searching for a weapon. She sucked in a breath as strong fingers brushed her ribcage, just underneath her breasts. Of all the situations in which to become excited by a man's touch, this really wasn't it. And yet her traitorous body had begun to respond to the intensity of the situation even as her heart thumped with fear.

His breathing did not alter at all, and nor did he show any signs of noticing her response. As his hand finally moved to her thigh Olivia could take no more. She kicked out. Partly in shock at his boldness, but mostly because of the discomfort of her own reaction.

She took a deep breath. 'Do you honestly believe that I'm hiding a weapon in my underwear?'

The stranger cleared his throat. 'I have known people to hide weapons in the most ludicrous places. Women especially tend towards a certain…creativity.'

'Do *not* put your hands on me again.'

He was silent for a moment, and the only sound in

the dark tunnel was that of their steady breaths mingling in the air between them.

When he spoke again his accent was more pronounced, his voice deep and intimidating. 'Tell me who you are and why you are attempting to break into the palace.'

She paused at that. So he hadn't recognised her yet. Surely if he was a kidnapper he would have come here knowing the faces of the royal family. Although it was dark, she supposed. Her choices were limited. She had no panic buttons down here—no guards within shouting distance.

She needed to get away.

She turned her head towards the door, breathing a little faster with anticipation as his shrewd gaze followed the movement and he saw the sliver of light coming through the gap.

'You managed to find a way inside, I see,' he said with surprise. 'Come on, then. Let's see what you were after, shall we?'

He held her forearm tightly, dragging her behind him up the steps and into the lavish dressing room. Her eyes adjusted quickly once again, to take in the rows and rows of her wardrobes. The room was empty, as it would be for a while, seeing as her staff presumed her to be at the races for the rest of the day.

Olivia gulped hard. She had just led an uncleared intruder right into the heart of the palace.

She took a moment to look at him for the first time in the light.

'It's you…' she breathed, realising it was the man from the racetrack.

To his credit, he also looked momentarily stunned as he took in her face in the light.

He was taller this close—almost an entire foot taller than her five feet three inches. All the self-defence classes in the world wouldn't give her a hope against such a brute. Dark hair, dark eyes and a jawline that would put Michelangelo's *David* to shame. He had a fierce beauty about him—as if he had just stepped off a battlefield somewhere—and he thrummed with vitality.

Her grandmother had always said she watched too many movies. Here she was, in very real danger, and she was romanticising her captor.

'You have taken a break from saving servants, I see.' His eyes lowered to take in the coat that covered her cocktail dress. 'You seem to be a woman of many talents.'

Olivia stayed completely silent as he spoke, knowing the more she said the more chance there was that he would put two and two together and guess her identity. She glanced to her left, searching the room for possible weapons for when the time came to run. If she could find something to kick at him, perhaps…

She looked down at her bare feet, cursing her own stupidity.

'We are in the south wing,' he mused, looking around the room. 'One of the royal apartments. How did you find out about the hidden tunnel?'

She shrugged, looking down at her feet and taking one tentative step away from him while his attention wandered.

'I saw how you slid down there. You knew exactly what you were doing. Just like you know what you are doing right now.' He grabbed her arm, stopping her progress.

She couldn't help herself then—she cursed. A filthy word in Catalan that would make her father blush if he heard her.

The stranger smiled darkly. 'We're going to get absolutely nowhere if you don't speak to me. Why are you here?' he asked again, releasing her arm and pushing her to sit down in the chair in front of her dressing table.

Exactly where she needed to be.

'I could ask you the same question,' she replied, slowly reclining backwards under the pretext of stretching her tender muscles.

'That's simple. I'm here for people like you,' he said simply, crossing his arms and staring down at her.

'People like me?' she asked breathlessly, her hand feeling blindly along the dressing table behind her for where she knew an alert button had been placed. She tried to calm her breath and prayed he would not see what she was doing. She felt a smooth round bump and pressed it quickly, holding her breath in case she needed to run.

No sirens sounded…there were no flashing lights. She moved to press it again, only to have his fingers encircle her elbow and place her hands in her lap.

'Keep your hands where I can see them.'

It was clear this wasn't going to be over any time soon.

He tilted his head to one side, looking at her in such an intense way it made her toes curl into the carpet under her feet. His eyes lowered, darkening as they swept down her legs.

The way he looked at her, the blatant male appreciation on his striking features, made something seem to uncoil in the pit of her stomach. She felt warm under his gaze and turned her face away in case she blushed.

'Whomever you think I am, I can tell you now that you are very wrong.'

His answering smile was raking, and made goosebumps break out across her arms.

The stranger bent down so that their faces were level. 'I think that, whoever you are, beautiful, you are a lot stronger and a lot more dangerous than you seem.'

CHAPTER TWO

'YOU SOUND LIKE quite the expert,' she purred, her cat-like eyes seeming to glow in her pale features.

Roman frowned. 'I can tell by your eyes that you're worried about being caught in the act, and yet you mock me.'

'You're quite arrogant and you deserve some mocking, I think,' she replied sweetly.

He fought the urge to laugh at this situation. Here he was, with a thief held captive inside the palace walls, and he was enjoying their verbal sparring too much to make a decision over what to do with her.

He couldn't simply waltz up to the King's offices and present him with this gift. Problem one being that the King was out of the palace today, along with the rest of the royal family. Problem two being that the Palace Guard had no idea he would be here today. As far as they were concerned he would be just as much a criminal as the sharp-tongued redhead who sat staring at him as though she'd like to claw his eyes out.

He would have to call Khal and tell him that their plan had encountered a minor diversion. It was no matter, really. He had identified a serious security blind spot and provided the Palace Guard with an attempted burglar to boot. All in all, quite a success.

So why did the thought of handing her over make him feel so uneasy?

He had got where he was by trusting his gut, and right now his gut was telling him that something wasn't quite right here. That this woman was not all that she seemed. Something made him pause, his brain weighing the situation up piece by piece.

'You are quite possibly the most ladylike thief I have ever encountered,' he mused. 'Do you always go barefoot on a job, or was today an exception?'

'You assume that I make a habit of this?' She glared up at him.

'Correct me, then.' He held her gaze evenly until she looked away.

'You have quite an intense stare. It's making me uneasy.'

She crossed one slim leg over the other. Roman felt his throat go dry, and looked away from the expanse of creamy smooth skin below her dress.

'I'm in the business of being observant,' he said, clearing his throat. 'You might benefit from it yourself, then maybe next time you won't get caught so easily.'

'I assume you are the almighty authority on how to break into palaces?' She raised her brows, sitting straighter in her seat.

'Seeing as you arrived here first, I disagree,' he countered.

'Oh, *now* I see. You're angry that you were beaten to the punch by a woman.' She placed both feet flat on the floor, smoothing her dress over her knees. 'This whole body-searching, intimidating act has all been one big ego-stroke for you.'

'I searched you because I am not so pig-headed as to believe that you pose no threat to me simply because of your sex.' Roman shook his head in disbelief, hating himself for rising to her bait. 'Why would you assume that the fact you are a woman has anything to do with it?'

She looked away from him then. 'Because it always does.'

'I think that's far more telling of your low opinion of men than anything else.' He raised his brows. 'Trust me, I am an expert in assessing risks. Women are not somehow physically destined to surrender to men. I have seen it first-hand. I have trained women, watched them down men twice their size without breaking a sweat.'

'You *train* women? To become…thieves?' she said with disbelief. 'Who on earth *are* you?'

Roman laughed, not bothering to correct her assumption. 'Let's just say I am the last person you wish to meet while you're on a job. Not just here, in this castle. Anywhere. I know how the criminal mind works. I have made it my business to be an expert in it.'

'So if I'm a criminal, you'll know what I am thinking right now?' Her eyes darted towards the door once more.

'I'm trying to.' Roman poised himself in case she ran. 'Just tell me what it is you're after and I can make this easier for you. Tell me your name.'

'No,' she said plainly.

Her body language was telling him that she was becoming increasingly more agitated with the situation. A flight risk if ever he'd seen one.

Even as the thought crossed his mind she jumped from the chair, her speed surprising him for a split second before he moved himself. She made it a few steps before his arms were around her waist, holding her body tightly against his as she struggled in vain.

'Please—just let me go,' she breathed.

The fear in her voice startled him, but his training had taught him not to release anyone until he had another means of restraining them.

'You are making it very difficult for me to help you here. Do you know that?' he said, holding her arms tightly to her sides and trying in vain to ignore the delicious scent of vanilla that drifted up from her hair.

'Why…? Why would you offer to help after what you think of me?'

He thought for a moment. 'Because I believe in second chances.' He spoke without thought, his answer surprising even himself. 'You always have a choice— no matter how impossible it seems.'

A strange look came over her face as their eyes locked. Her breath was coming hard and heavy against his chest but she'd stopped fighting him. Her eyes drifted away from him, settling on the distance with a mixture of resolve and deep sadness.

'I'm not who you think I am.'

Without warning a heavy weight came down behind him, followed by what he presumed to be a palace guard shouting in furious Catalan.

Roman pushed the man backwards, holding his hands up in what he hoped resembled a peaceful motion.

'I have authorisation,' he began, motioning towards the lapel of his suit jacket. 'The King knows I am here.'

Roman felt his hands being pulled behind him into handcuffs and fought the urge to laugh as he looked up into a second guard's furious face.

'You will regret this.'

He grunted at the pressure of a knee between his shoulder blades, knowing that they most likely did not speak a word of English. As his face was crushed against the carpet he looked sideways, just in time to see a pair of dainty bare feet appear by his side. Up close, he could see that a tiny hand-drawn daisy adorned each red-painted toenail.

The woman spoke in rapid-fire Catalan, her voice muted and fearful yet with a strange backbone of authority. The nearest guard nodded, uttering two words that made his body freeze.

'*Si, Princesa.*'

Roman crushed his face further into the carpet with disbelief and sheer dread.

He had just body-searched a damn princess.

His Majesty King Fabian of Monteverre stood up as Olivia entered the private sitting room flanked by two stony-faced members of the Royal Guard.

'Of all the days to pull one of your disappearing acts, Libby,' her father said angrily, motioning for the guards to leave them with a flick of one hand.

Her mother, elegant and perpetually silent, did not acknowledge her entry. Queen Aurelia sat poised in a high-backed chair, her eyes trained solemnly on nothing in particular.

'Where have you *been*? You were informed of the intruder hours ago,' Olivia said, breathing hard.

'And naturally you expected us to abandon the

event? Honestly, Libby...' The King frowned in disbelief, reaching down to take a sip of whisky from a thick crystal tumbler.

Her father was the only one who still called her Libby. It reminded her of being five years old and being scolded for trying to sneak chocolate from the kitchens. But she was not a child any more, and she was damned tired of being treated like one.

'I was attacked,' she said slowly. 'A man held me hostage in my own dressing room. And yet I've been left to pace my apartments completely alone for the past five hours.'

'The matter has been resolved. It was a simple misunderstanding.' King Fabian avoided his daughter's eyes. 'Best to forget the whole business.'

Olivia felt all the outrage and pent-up frustration freeze in her veins as she registered her father's words. Had he actually just told her to *forget* this afternoon? She opened her mouth, then closed it, completely at a loss as to what to say in response.

'Your absence was noticed by Sheikh Khalil,' he said, scolding, his brows drawing down as they always did when he was unimpressed.

'Well, as I have just said, I was rather busy being held against my will by a dangerous intruder.' She took a deep breath, looking briefly across to her mother's uninterested blank features before returning her furious gaze to her father. 'Have I gone mad? Or are you both completely unaffected by today's events?'

'I understand it might have been...alarming...' King Fabian began solemnly.

'"Alarming" hardly covers it.' Olivia fumed. 'Why are you both so *calm*?'

The last word came out in a disbelieving whisper. She fought a distinct urge to walk over and bang her fist on her father's chest, to knock over her mother's glass, to make them both react in some way other than with this muted nothingness.

Today's events had shaken her to her core, and yet she felt as though she were intruding on their peace with her inconvenient outrage. Surely her own father should be shocked and outraged that his daughter's safety had been at risk inside their own home. Unless… Unless he wasn't shocked at all.

'What do you mean by a misunderstanding?' she asked, not bothering to hide the challenge in her voice.

'Libby…' Her father sighed, raising a hand for her to quieten.

'Please, don't "Libby" me.' She placed one hand on her hip. 'Tell me exactly what is going on. Did you know about this man?'

The King twisted his mouth in discomfort. 'Well… not directly, no.'

'Indirectly, then. You *knew* that someone would be here today? In our home.'

King Fabian strode to the window, placing one hand on the sill and looking out in silence. 'The man you met today was Roman Lazarov, founder of The Lazarov Group, an international security firm.' Her father sighed heavily. 'He is a very close friend of Sheikh Khalil and I have been assured that he is *the* authority on high-class security operations. But after the complete muddle he made today, I'm not so sure of his expert status…'

He laughed weakly, his voice trailing off as he took in her expression of horror.

'Don't look at me that way. It was a gift from Sheikh Khalil—very thoughtful of him to want to ensure your safety, I thought.'

Olivia felt a headache begin at her temples. This was all becoming too much. She closed her eyes a moment, unable to bear her father's apparent disregard for his daughter's privacy or independence.

'No, Father. In fact I find it horribly thoughtless. And intrusive, among other things.' She felt her breath coming faster, her temper rising like a caged bird set to take flight. 'This is the last straw in a long line of things I have overlooked since you began vaguely mentioning a possible marriage. I am not a piece of livestock to be insured and fenced in, for goodness' sake.'

He sighed. 'You are overreacting.'

'No, I'm really not. Did anyone consult me before all my charity events were cancelled? Was I informed when I was assigned five new bodyguards for all trips outside the palace?' She shook her head, her knuckles straining with the tightness of her fists by her sides. 'And now this. Did you even think to ask me before you sent a bloody *mercenary* into my room? I'll never feel safe there again!'

'Lazarov was simply going to *attempt* to gain entry to your rooms. To find any weaknesses in our security. Besides, you were supposed to be at the races with your fiancé.'

The tightness in her throat intensified. 'I have not yet agreed to this marriage. Until today I had no idea that you were truly serious about it! And if this is how the Sheikh shows his concern…'

She tightened her lips, willing herself to say the

words. To tell her father that the whole deal was off. She didn't want this. *Any* of it.

King Fabian's voice lowered in warning. 'Olivia, these negotiations are months old—we have discussed why this is a necessary step.'

She blinked. *Months old?* 'For the kingdom, yes. I understand what we stand to gain from a political union.' She cleared her throat, her voice sounding all of a sudden smaller. 'But what about for *me*?'

Her father's brows rose imperiously. 'You will be serving your kingdom.'

'I don't see why I must get married to a complete stranger in order to serve Monteverre. I am doing good work with Mimi's Foundation—I am making a difference.'

'Your grandmother and her damned charities...' Fabian scowled darkly, draining the last of his whisky. 'You think teaching a handful of scrawny kids to read will change anything about our situation?'

'My grandmother taught me that charity is not always about money. It's important to nourish the youth as well as to do our best to help those in need. She was beloved by this kingdom.'

'Ah, yes, the eternally perfect Queen Miranda! My mother spent so much time on her charities she didn't even notice her country's economy crumbling beneath her feet.' His mouth twisted cruelly. 'Don't you *see*, you silly girl? We are facing financial ruin without this union.'

Olivia opened her mouth to protest, only to have her father's scowl stop her as he continued on his own personal rant.

'The Kingdom of Zayyar is overflowing with

wealth, thanks to this man. He is an economic genius. But the civic history of his country still stands
in the way of true acceptance from the west. To put it
bluntly, they need our political influence and we need
their money.'

'Money...' Olivia bit her lip, wanting to ask just how
much she was worth, considering he was essentially
trading her body for cash.

'Sheikh Khalil has the capabilities to take Monteverre back to its glory days—surely you want that for
your people? What good is being able to read if they
have no money to feed themselves?'

She had never heard her father speak so frankly,
and his eyes were red-rimmed with half-madness. Olivia knew that Monteverre was in trouble. A series of
bad leadership decisions and banking crashes had left
them neck-deep in debt and with many of the younger
generation emigrating to greener pastures. They were
bleeding, and it appeared that this Sheikh had come
offering a magic bandage. At a particular cost...

'Trusting an entire country's economic future to one
man's hands? That seems a bit...reckless. Surely there
is another way without the marriage—?'

'No,' he cut across her, his voice a dull bark in the
silent room. 'There is no going back on this. I won't
hear another word.'

Her father's eyes were dark in a way she had never
seen them before, as though he hadn't truly slept in
months.

'Everything you have had since birth is thanks to
your position. It's not like you have an actual *career* to
think of—you spend most of your time looking pretty
and waving. None of that would even change. Your

life would continue just as it has been—only as the Sheikha of Zayyar.' He took a breath, smiling down at her as if he had just bestowed upon her some enormous gift. 'This is your *duty*, Olivia. To Monteverre. It's not about you.'

She felt his words sink into her skin like an icy breeze, setting off goose pimples down her bare arms. Did being born a Sandoval really mean surrendering every aspect of your life to the good of the kingdom?

As the second daughter she had naïvely believed that her life would be different from her older sister's. She was not first in line to rule Monteverre—she didn't bear that crushing weight of responsibility and she had always been infinitely glad of it.

'The Sheikha of Zayyar...'

Her mother's melodic voice intruded on her thoughts, sounding absurdly serene.

'Sounds like something from a film...'

'I don't even know where Zayyar is,' Olivia said numbly, almost unable to speak past the tickle of panic spreading across her throat.

'Somewhere on the Persian Gulf,' Queen Aurelia offered, twirling the liquid in her glass. 'They have a hotel shaped like a boat sail.'

'That's Dubai.' King Fabian rolled his eyes. 'Zayyar is halfway between the desert and the Arabian Sea. Gorgeous scenery—you will love it.'

'Thank you for the sales pitch, Father.' Olivia sighed, looking across to her mother, who had once again turned to gaze into the empty fireplace.

It was customary for her mother to permanently nurse a glass of the finest cognac after midday. In Olivia's memory no one had ever questioned it or raised any concern. There had always been an unspoken understanding among the Sandoval children that their mother and father each did whatever they pleased and things would always be that way. They did not welcome personal discussions.

She looked up to the ceiling, feeling the familiar sense of exhaustion that always accompanied any meeting with her parents. For that was all they ever were. Meetings.

'Sheikh Khalil simply wanted to ensure your safety, Libby. Surely you find that romantic? I know you are prone to the sentiment.'

Her father looked down at his wife, but she had drifted off, her eyes dull and unfocused as she stared into nothingness. The look on his face changed to outright disgust and he turned away, busying himself with retrieving his jacket from a chair.

Olivia's heart broke a little for her parents' fractured marriage. She had fleeting memories of a happier time, when her parents had seemed madly in love and the Kingdom of Monteverre had been a shining beacon of prosperity and culture. Now there was nothing but cold resentment and constant worry.

'Father...' Olivia took a breath, trying to calm her rapid thoughts. 'This is all happening very fast. Perhaps if I just had some more time—'

'Why do you think the Sheikh arranged this trip? He plans to propose formally this afternoon so that the announcement can be made public before he leaves.'

Olivia's breath caught, expanding her throat painfully. 'He...he can't do that...'

'Oh, yes, he can—and you will be grateful for his patience.'

His voice boomed across the room, the sudden anger in it startling her, making her back away a step.

He took a breath, deliberately softening his tone. 'Can't you see that you are a vital part in this? There is power in your position.'

'Power...' Olivia repeated weakly. Her shoulders drooped. Even her bones felt heavy. *Women are not always destined to surrender to men...* Those words—*his* words—had struck something deep within her.

Roman Lazarov.

She bit her lip hard. For a moment she had regretted her decision to have him captured. He had seemed to glow from within—a fiery protector and proclaimer of women's strength. Now she knew he was just like the rest of them. Here to ensure that her cage was kept good and tight. That she had no hope of freedom.

King Fabian tightened his lips, forcing a smile before shrugging into his navy dress jacket and fixing the diamond cufflinks at his wrists. He paused by her side, looking down at her.

'You will have a private lunch with Sheikh Khalil tomorrow.' He placed one hand on her shoulder, giving it a light squeeze. 'I know you will give him the answer he wants. I'm so proud of the beautiful woman you have become.'

Olivia closed her eyes, not wanting him to see the tears that glistened there. Her heart seemed to slow in her chest as she nodded her head in defeat, glad when he was gone, with the smell of cigar smoke wafting on the air in his wake. How could he be proud of the woman she was when she had no idea who she was herself?

'I can't do this,' she breathed, silently hoping her

mother would look up. That she would hold her and listen to her worries, then kiss her forehead and tell her everything would be okay.

But sadly she knew that would never happen. She had no memories of ever being in her mother's arms, and even if she had the woman who now sat like a living ghost in the sitting room was not truly her mother.

She stood still for a long time, letting the tears fall down her cheeks and stain the neckline of her dress. Eventually she wiped her face and turned away from the unbearable silence, walking through the long main corridors of the private suites.

As usual, the guards pretended not to notice her.

She took her time, idling through the gardens on her way back to her rooms. With a few deep breaths she calmed the tremor in her throat. It had been a long time since she had let a single tear fall—probably not since the day of her grandmother's funeral. Crying was a fruitless activity when her future had already been neatly packed up and arranged.

She sat heavily on a marble bench in the centre of the courtyard. This was her favourite part of the palace, where a low stone square fountain provided the perfect vantage point to sit and listen to the staff as they went about their daily duties. Here, partially concealed by bougainvillea and foliage, she had been privy to the most heart-stopping live-action dramas outside of television.

The fights, the wicked gossip, the passionate clandestine embraces. A reluctant smile touched her lips. She had seen it all.

Just in the past month it had been revealed that one of the upstairs maids had engaged in an affair with the head gardener's handsome son. Olivia had overheard the whole sordid situation developing—right up to the point when said housemaid had found out that her beau was also heavily involved with one of the palace florists. The ensuing slap had resounded across the courtyard and earned the young Romeo a speedy transfer outside the palace.

The housemaid had moved on quickly enough, accepting a date with a palace guard. The look of delirious happiness as she'd described their first kiss to her friends had haunted Olivia for days.

She stood restlessly, leaning against the side of the fountain. Was that look the very thing she was sacrificing by agreeing to a loveless marriage?

She frowned, drawing her hand through the water and watching the ripples spread across her own solemn reflection. Love was about falling for the wrong guy, having your heart broken and then ending up with your handsome Prince Charming—not that she had ever experienced it. But she had watched enough old movies to know it was always true love's kiss at the end that gave her that butterflies feeling in her stomach. That moment when the couple swore their undying devotion and fell into each other's arms…

She wanted to feel like that. At least once in her life.

There had been a handful of kisses in her past; she was twenty-six, after all. But never more than a brief touching of lips. The kind of men who had been permitted near her just happened to be the kind of men who got aroused at the thought of their own reputations inflating with a real-life princess on their arm. Not one of the men she'd dated had ever tried to get to know her *really*.

A prickle made its way along her skin as she thought of a certain pair of grey eyes, raking their way down her body. It was madness, the way her body had seemed to thrum deep inside just from a man's gaze. It was ridiculous.

She looked down at her forearms, seeing the goose-flesh there. Why did he have to affect her so violently when no other man had managed to inspire so much as a flicker of her attraction?

She bit the inside of her cheek with frustration and turned to begin walking back to her apartments—only to find a large male frame blocking her path.

'Good evening, Printsessa.'

CHAPTER THREE

'I SEE THEY have released you... Mr Lazarov.' The Princess straightened her shoulders defensively, moving a long silken curtain of vibrant red hair away from her face as she directed her gaze upon him.

Roman ignored the strange tightening in his stomach at the way she said his name, focusing on her pale features to better read her mood.

She seemed less colourful than he remembered—as if something had stolen the fire he had witnessed earlier in the day, both at the racetrack and afterwards.

'Once they realised their mistake they were quite accommodating. I hope you were not worried for my welfare.'

'If it were my choice I would have had you detained for the night.'

She held her chin high as she delivered the blow, but Roman saw the telltale convulsive movement in her throat as she took a breath. He leaned casually against a nearby column, raising a single brow in challenge.

Far from bowing under his scrutiny, she held his gaze evenly. 'I assume you are here to make your apology?'

Roman fought the urge to laugh. 'I'm no stranger to handcuffs, Princess.' He smiled darkly. 'It would take more than five hours in a cushy palace detainment room to force me to my knees.'

Her gaze lowered a fraction and Roman gave in to his mirth, a darkly amused smile spreading across his lips.

'I don't want you to be on your...' She shook her head, exhaling hard. She crossed her arms below her chest—a gesture likely meant in defence, but all it served to do was draw his attention to the resulting swell at the neckline of her delicate yellow dress.

'Well, you are free to go,' she said, sarcasm dripping from her tone as she gestured towards the door to the main palace.

For the first time in his life Roman was at a complete loss as to what to say. How he had not recognised that she was a royal instantly, he did not know. The woman before him seemed to exude class and sophistication in every inch of her posture. She eyed him with suspicion, her brows lowering in a mixture of challenge and defence.

He should have left the moment he had been freed, and yet he had sought her out. He had told himself he needed to apologise, but right now, remembering the honest arousal in her eyes as he'd been pressed close to her... He wasn't feeling quite so apologetic.

He stood taller, hardening his voice. 'In case you are planning another escape, the tunnel has been blocked. It is no longer passable.'

'You certainly work fast,' she said quietly, leaning back against the lip of the fountain. 'I assume the Sheikh asked you to make sure my cage was good and tight?'

'Your...cage?'

She was oblivious to his confusion. 'Of course it matters to no one that I am an adult with free will. By all means let him have the run of the palace. There will be bars installed on my bedroom windows next.'

Roman raked a hand across the shadow beginning to grow along his jaw. He allowed her to a rant a moment, before clearing his throat pointedly. 'You seem upset.'

'"Upset" does not even begin to cover it. Everything about today has been unbearable.'

Something about the faraway look in her eyes bothered him. It was as though she were on the edge of a complete meltdown, and he worried that it was his mistake that had brought her there. Perhaps there was a need for his apology after all—much as it pained him to admit it.

'Princess, I need you to understand that I am not in the habit of holding a woman against her will,' he said solemnly. 'Earlier…when I searched you…'

She looked back at him, her lashes half lowered with something dark and unspoken. 'Will you be telling your fearsome Sheikh about that, I wonder?'

'The Sheikh is not the villain you seem to think he is,' Roman said quietly, inwardly grimacing at the thought of telling his best friend how he had manhandled his future wife. 'I have never known someone as loyal and dedicated.'

'Perhaps the two of you should get married, then,' she said snidely.

'I did not expect an actual princess to be quite so… cutting.' He pressed a hand to his chest in mock injury. 'Is it any wonder I mistook you for a common thief?'

That earned him the hint of a smile from her lips.

The movement lit up her eyes ever so slightly and he felt a little triumphant that he had caused it.

Roman smirked, turning to lean against the fountain, taking care to leave a good foot and a half of space between them. It had been a long time since he had been this conscious of a woman's presence.

'You seem like quite the man of mystery, Mr Lazarov,' she said, turning to look at him briefly. 'Best friends with a sheikh…founder of an international security firm.'

'You've been researching me?'

'I only found out your name twenty minutes ago,' she said honestly. 'Does the Sheikh always fly you in for such favours?'

'No, he does not.' Roman felt the corner of his mouth tilt at her mocking. It had been a long time since a woman had been so obviously unimpressed by him. 'I have my own means of transportation for such occasions.'

'Let me guess—something small and powerful with tinted windows?'

'It is black.' His lips twisted with amusement at her jibe. 'But my yacht is hardly small. No tinted windows—I much prefer the light.'

Her gaze wandered, the smile fading from her lips as she looked away from him. 'A playboy's yacht… of course.'

'These things have not magically fallen into my lap, I assure you. I have worked hard for the lifestyle I enjoy.'

'Oh, I didn't mean…' She turned her face back towards him quickly. 'I envy you, that's all.'

He raised a brow, wondering not for the first time

what on earth was going on inside her head. 'There is an entire fleet of vessels moored in the harbour with the royal crest on their hulls. You're telling me you couldn't just choose one at will?'

'I spent years learning how to sail at school. But I have yet to go on a single trip by myself,' she said, looking up and meeting his eyes for a long moment. 'It's strange…' she began, before shaking her head and turning her face away. 'I've spoken more frankly with you today—a complete stranger—than I have with anyone in a long time.'

Roman did not know how to respond to that statement. He swallowed hard, looking ahead to where a group of housemaids walked and chatted their way across the second-floor balconies. When he finally looked back the Princess had moved from beside him.

He stood up, looking around him for a sign of where she had gone, only to see a glimpse of pale yellow silk disappearing through the archway that led to the royal apartments.

He took a step forward, then caught himself.

She was where she belonged—surrounded by guards and staff.

It was time for him to get back to his own life.

The afternoon sun was hot on his neck when Roman finally walked out onto the deck of his yacht the next day. In his line of work he was no stranger to going to sleep as the sun rose, but his restless night had little to do with work. Being handcuffed in a room by himself had given him far too much time with his own thoughts. A dangerous pastime for a man with a past like his.

Nursing a strong black coffee, he slid on dark sunglasses and sank down into a hammock chair. They would set sail for the *isla* soon enough, and he would be glad to see the back of this kingdom and all its upper-class pomp.

He surveyed the busy harbour of Puerto Reina, Monteverre's main port. Tourists and locals peppered the busy marble promenade that fronted the harbour— the Queen's Balcony, he had been told it was called. A glittering golden crown insignia was emblazoned over every sign in the town, as though the people might somehow otherwise forget that it was the crown that held the power.

Never had he met a man more blinded by his own power than His Majesty, King Fabian. Khal had insisted on them meeting two nights previously, so that the three men could discuss the situation of the Princess's security—Khal was notoriously meticulous when it came to bodyguards and security measures.

It had been clear from the outset that Roman would be treated like the commoner he was, so he had made the choice to leave, rather than sit and be spoken down to. His tolerance levels only stretched so far. It seemed His Majesty still harboured some ill will, as made apparent by the gap of five hours between the time he had been informed of the incident at the palace and the time at which he'd authorised Roman's release.

Roman's fists clenched by his sides. He was no stranger to dealing with self-important asses—he'd made a career of protecting arrogant fools with more money than sense. But it was hard to stay professionally disengaged when one of the asses in question was your best friend. Khal had never treated him as 'lesser'—he knew better. But he had not so much as made a phone call to apologise for his oversight.

His friend knew, more than anyone, what time locked in a room could do to him.

Roman tilted his head up to the sun and closed his eyes. He was not in a locked room right now. He was on his own very expensive yacht, which would be out in open water just as soon as it was refuelled. He exhaled slowly, visualising the clear blue waters of Isla Arista, his own private haven.

Moments passed before his visualisation was interrupted by a loud car horn. He opened one eye and sighed as he saw a sleek black limousine edging its way through the crowds on the main street, flanked by four Monteverrian policemen on Vespas.

The Sheikh of Zayyar did not simply take a taxi, he supposed dryly as he reached forward to drain the last of his coffee and then tilted his head back to the sunshine. When he finally looked up again Khal was standing a foot away, his face a mask of cool fury.

'It was nice of you to finally come to my rescue, *bratik*.' Roman raised a brow from his perch on the deckchair, but made no move to stand and greet his oldest friend.

Khal's mouth twisted. 'I was under the impression that the untouchable Roman Lazarov never *needed* help.'

'And *I* was under the impression that our friendship came before brown-nosing the King of Monteverre.' Roman spoke quietly, venom in every word.

Right now, looking at Khal in his perfectly pressed white royal robes, a good old-fashioned punching match didn't sound like the worst way to start his day.

Back on the streets of St Petersburg it was the way most fights were resolved. Fighting had sometimes been the only way not to starve.

Roman scowled, realising the hunger in his gut was doing nothing to help his already agitated mood and the dark memories of his past threatening his control.

'I was not aware that you had been held in custody until this morning.'

Khal interrupted his thoughts, frowning with genuine concern.

Roman tipped his head back, propping one foot lazily up on the low table in front of him. People generally afforded the almighty Sheikh of Zayyar a certain level of ceremony and pomp. But not him. He usually went out of his way to take Khal down a peg whenever they were alone.

'Oh, just five hours in a windowless room with my hands cuffed behind my back—no big deal.'

'I find it hard to sympathise, considering you'd held my future wife hostage like a common criminal,' Khal said simply.

'An interesting choice of words, *Your Highness*,' Roman snarled, derision in every syllable.

A silence fell between them—not the comfortable kind that came from years of close friendship. This was a silence filled with tension and frustration.

A friendship like theirs had no clear rules, different as they were.

Khal came from a long line of royalty—had been educated and privileged and born with power in his blood. Whereas Roman had fought for everything he owned, clawing his way out of the gutter he had been abandoned in as a child. Over the years he had refined his harsh manners and learned how to act like a gentleman, but underneath he would always bear the marks of his past. The darkness had branded him—quite literally—and that was something his friend had no experience of.

Khal cleared his throat loudly. 'You know, in ten years I don't think you've changed one bit.'

Roman ignored the barely veiled insult, shrugging as he put one leg casually across the table. 'I have a lot more money.'

'And an even bigger ego.' Khal frowned.

'Need I remind you that I came here as a favour? I did not *have* to dirty my hands for you, Khal. No matter what debts I may owe you.'

'Is that the only reason you came? And here I was thinking you cared for my happiness.' Khal's mouth tightened. 'Four years is a long time to hold on to your guilt, Lazarov.'

Roman shook his head, standing to pace to the railing that edged the upper deck. He had enough painful memories affecting his concentration today—he didn't need more reminders of the long line of blackness he left in his wake.

'I came here because you needed help, *bratik*. Nothing more.'

For the first time Khal looked weary as he rubbed a hand across his clean-shaven face. He sat down in the deckchair Roman had vacated and stared up at the clear sky above them.

'This whole situation is rapidly getting away from me. My trip was supposed to be simple and straightforward, tying everything up. And now I stand to lose everything I have staked.'

Roman frowned at his friend's unusual display of weakness. 'It will be fine. I will apologise to the Princess and smooth things over for you.'

Khal looked at him, realisation dawning on his dark features. 'You don't know? The Princess has disappeared, Roman. Half the Palace Guard is out searching for her.'

Roman froze with surprise. 'Disappeared? I just spoke with her last night.'

'You *spoke* with her?' Khal's voice raised an octave. 'What on earth would possess you to speak with her after what you'd put her through?'

'She had me put through far worse, trust me.'

'So this is even more your fault than I had originally thought?'

'Khal, I had the tunnel blocked, extra guards assigned. How on earth could she have just walked out of there?'

Khal shook his head. 'Clearly she wanted to get away badly enough to risk her own safety. What did you say to her?'

'We barely spoke two words. Mainly she insulted me and then she walked away.'

Both men were silent for a long moment, facing off in the midday heat.

'The girl is reckless,' Roman said darkly. 'Are you sure that you want to marry someone so...unpredictable?'

'My kingdom needs it. So it will be done.' Khal smoothed down the front of his robes. 'I have been heavy-handed with my approach so far. I worry that perhaps I have scared her off completely.'

'How so?'

'I ordered a stricter security regime. I needed to make sure she was protected adequately before her name was linked with mine. In case…'

Roman saw the haunted look in his friend's eyes and immediately stopped. How had he not realised before now?

He moved towards him, placing a hand heavily on his shoulder. 'Khal… I understand why you felt the need to ensure her security…believe me. But there *is* such a thing as smothering with safety.'

'We both know the risks for any woman who is by my side,' Khal said, standing to his feet.

The moment of weakness had passed and he was once again the formidable and controlled Sheikh of Zayyar. But Roman could still sense the heaviness in the air, the unspoken worries that he knew plagued his friend and had likely tortured him for the past four years.

Nothing would bring back his friend's wife. Her sudden death had shifted something in the easy friendship that had once bonded them together, and nothing would erase the pain of knowing that he hadn't been there in Khal's time of need.

Roman cleared his throat. 'I will go and find the Princess,' he said gruffly.

'No. Definitely not.' Khal turned back to him, crossing his arms. 'Your presence would only aggravate the situation further.'

'If it was my actions that caused her to rethink the engagement, then let me be the one to apologise and bring her back.' Roman pushed his hands into the pockets of his trousers, feeling the weight of his own error settle somewhere in his gut. 'This is *my* fault.'

'Yes. It is.' Khal raised one brow. 'And I hate not knowing if I can trust you to fix it.'

Roman's jaw clenched. Khal was like a brother to him—his *bratik*. The closest thing to a family member he had ever chosen for himself.

'You have trusted me with your life in the past. Are you telling me you don't think I'm capable of retrieving one errant little princess?'

'This is important to me, Roman.'

'I will bring her back. You have my word,' Roman said, meaning every syllable.

He would find the little siren and bring her back to her royal duty if it was the last thing he did.

This had been a terrible plan.

Olivia slumped down in her seat, tucking an errant strand of bright red hair back into her dark, wide floppy-brimmed hat. Because of the dark sunglasses she wore, and the rather plain white shift dress, thankfully so far nobody had looked at her twice.

Olivia sighed. Had she really been so naïve as to think that she could just check in to the next commercial flight without question? The realisation of what she had almost done suddenly paralysed her with fear. She had almost broken the law, for goodness' sake.

She was hyper aware of her surroundings, noticing every little movement of the people in the departures hall. Every time one of the airport security guards looked at her she unconsciously held her breath, waiting for the moment when they would realise who she was and unceremoniously haul her back to the palace. And to her father.

She didn't even know exactly what she was trying

to achieve here. Honestly, had she really been so immature as to think that her father would take her more seriously just because she had attempted to run away from her engagement? In reality this little stunt had done nothing but ensure that she would have even less freedom than before.

She closed her eyes, leaning her head back against the seat and wishing that she had never come up with this stupid plan. She felt the air shift to her right, a gentle breeze bringing with it an eerily familiar scent of sandalwood and pine.

'A risky choice, hiding in plain sight,' a deeply accented male voice drawled from beside her, bringing memories of strong, muscular arms and eyes like gunmetal.

Roman Lazarov lowered himself casually into the seat beside her and lazily propped one ankle on the opposite knee.

'You really didn't think this through.'

From this angle, all she could see were powerful thighs encased in designer trousers and a pair of expensive leather shoes. She exhaled slowly, realising from the sound of his voice that he must have his face turned towards her. Watching to gauge her reaction.

He was probably congratulating himself on finding her so easily, the brute.

He cleared his throat loudly, waiting for her response.

Olivia pursed her lips and kept her eyes focused straight ahead. She wondered if, perhaps if she waited long enough, he would simply disappear into thin air.

'You have ten seconds to give up your silent act before I announce your presence to this entire airport.' He spoke low, his voice a barely contained growl.

She stiffened. 'You're bluffing.'

'Look at me.'

She turned her head at his demand, hardly realising she had obeyed until it was done. His eyes were focused on her, steel-grey and glowing, just as she remembered them. His lips, so full and perfectly moulded, seemed to quirk a little at the sides as his eyes narrowed. It took a moment for her to realise he was silently laughing at her.

'I *was* bluffing.' He smiled in triumph, showing a row of perfectly aligned white teeth.

His smile was aggressively beautiful, just like the rest of him, she thought, with more than a little frustration. She noticed the rather delicious hint of dark stubble that lined his jaw. It somehow made him appear rugged and unrefined, even in his finely tailored clothing. She felt her throat go dry and silently cursed herself.

'If you're wondering how I found you, I simply followed the enormous trail of breadcrumbs you left in your wake, Printsessa.'

'Don't call me that here,' Olivia murmured. The hum of noise in the airport was loud enough, but she didn't want to draw any more attention than was needed.

He raised one brow, but nodded.

Olivia took a sharp breath, a slight tremor audible in her throat. 'If I asked you to go, and pretend you'd never found me...'

'That will never happen.' He half smiled as he spoke the words, a small indentation appearing just left of his lips.

The man had dimples, she thought wildly. That was hardly fair, was it?

Before she could react, he had reached down and grabbed the small document she had been holding tightly in her hands. As she watched, he opened it, tilting his head to one side as he read.

After a long moment he looked up, meeting her eyes with disbelief. 'You planned to use this?'

'Initially, yes. But then I thought better of it.'

'A wise choice, considering identity fraud is a very serious crime. Even for princesses.'

Olivia remained silent, staring down at the red mark on her fingers from where she had clutched the maid's passport so hard it had almost cut off her circulation.

It had been a careless plan from the start, one borne of desperation and anger. If she had got caught... The thought tightened her throat. Fraud simply wasn't something that was in her nature, luckily. Meaning that she had come no closer than eight feet from the check-in desk before she had turned on her heel and run. Leaving her sitting on this damned chair for the past two hours, frantically wondering where to go next.

Olivia shook off the ridiculous self-pity and forced herself to get a handle on her emotions. She was emotionally and physically exhausted. Any sleep she had got last night had been plagued by dreams of being trapped in tunnels with no way out, and a man's voice calling to her from the darkness. When she had finally got up this morning it had been with the grim intent of getting as far away from Monteverre as possible, and yet here she was, less than an hour's distance from the palace and already captured.

The entire plan had been stupid and impulsive from the start. Honestly, where had she really thought she would go once she'd walked out of the palace gates? She didn't even have the right to hold her own passport, for goodness' sake. Everything in her life was planned and controlled by others. She didn't even have enough freedom to run away properly.

Roman was still looking at her intently. She could feel the heat of his gaze on the side of her face, almost as though he burned her simply by being near. He made her feel as though she were on show and he was the only person in the audience. The intensity of his presence was something she simultaneously wanted to bask in and run far away from.

'I'm not running from my title.' She spoke solemnly, knowing he could never understand.

'Then what are you running from?' His voice was low and serious, and his gaze still pinned on hers with silvery intensity.

Olivia took a deep breath, knowing this conversation had to end. He was not on her side, no matter how sympathetic he pretended to be.

'It's not safe for you to be wandering alone.' His voice took on a steely edge. 'I feel responsible for your decision to leave the palace. Perhaps you felt that yesterday reflected badly on your future husband—'

Again the 'future husband' talk. Olivia stood up, feeling her blood pressure rise with sheer frustration.

Roman's hand took hold of hers, pulling her back down to a sitting position. His voice was low, somewhere near her right ear, as he spoke in chilling warning, 'Don't make any more impulsive moves, Printsessa. I might seem gentle, but I can assure you if you run from me again I might not be quite so civilised in hauling you back where you belong.'

Her heart hammered hard in her chest, and the skin along her neck and shoulders tingled and prickled with the effects of his barely veiled threat.

'My car is parked at the door. We can do this the easy way or the hard way.'

Olivia briefly considered her options—or lack thereof. Was she really prepared to risk what might happen if she resisted? The memory of his powerful arms encircling her in her dressing room sprang to her mind. For a moment she sat completely still, wondering if the frisson of electricity that coursed through her veins was one of trepidation or one of something infinitely more dangerous.

She stood, spine straight, and began walking towards the entrance. He followed, as she'd expected, his muscular frame falling into step by her side. His hand cupped her elbow, steering her out into the daylight towards a gleaming white luxury model car with privacy-tinted windows. Not the kind of car she would have expected from a new money playboy with a taste for danger.

Her silent captor slid into the driver's seat across from her, his warm, masculine scent filling the small space. He didn't look at her as he manoeuvred the car out of the airport and through the maze of roads that led to the motorway.

She covertly glanced at him from behind the safety of her sunglasses. Strong, masculine hands handled the wheel with expert ease. She noticed the top two buttons of his black shirt lay open and his sleeves had been rolled up along forearms that practically bulged with muscle. Strange black markings encircled his skin just above his shirt cuff—tribal, perhaps, but she couldn't see more than the edge.

Of *course* he had a tattoo, she thought, biting her lip as she wondered just how many he might have. And where they might be...

'You are staring. Something you'd like to say?'

His low, accented voice jolted her and she averted her eyes, looking straight ahead, curling her fingers together in her lap. 'I was simply wondering if you will be delivering me to my father or to the Sheikh.'

'So dramatic.' He sighed. 'You make it sound like you are a shipment of goods.'

'I might as well be,' she muttered under her breath. 'It's hard not to feel like a piece of livestock. Being traded from one barbarian to another.'

His hands seemed to tighten on the wheel. 'I'd prefer if you didn't use your pity party to insult my friend in that fashion. "Barbarian" is not a term he would take lightly.'

'Mr Lazarov, at this point I can't say that I particularly care.'

'I suggest that you start caring,' Roman gritted, moving the car off the motorway and towards the mountain range that separated them from the Grand Palace.

Twenty minutes in this pampered princess's company and he was tempted to stop the car and make her walk the rest of the way.

She was a puzzle, this fiery redhead. A spoilt, impulsive, dangerous puzzle, all wrapped up in one very tempting package. He would not feel guilty for being attracted to Khal's fiancée. A man would have to be blind not to see the raw sensual appeal in Olivia San-doval. But, unlike her, he had his impulses under con-trol. It was not hard to brush off attraction when he could tell that all that lay beneath her flawless skin and designer curves was a spoilt, bored little royal on the hunt for a thrill.

'Your father has asked that you be returned to the palace as soon as possible,' Roman said, noticing how her body seemed to tense at the mention of the King. 'But I feel that you and your fiancé need to speak first.'

'He is *not* my fiancé,' Olivia gritted.

'Oh, so that's what is going on here. You decided to break the engagement by running away. How very mature.'

Roman felt his jaw tighten with anger for his friend, for the future of two nations that was hanging in the balance all because of one woman.

'No, *I* haven't decided anything. That's the point!'

Roman heard the slight tremor in her voice and turned briefly to see she had her head in her hands. 'Look, if this is bridal jitters, I'm sure there's plenty of time before the wedding—'

Her head snapped up and she pinned him with the most ferocious icy blue-green gaze. 'Do you honestly think I would risk my reputation, my safety, over a little case of *bridal jitters*?'

'I only met you yesterday.' He shrugged.

It was true—he didn't know very much about her except that she had a deep-rooted mistrust of men and a mean left hook.

'This isn't something to speak about with a stranger.'

'At least you're listening…somewhat.' She sighed. 'Even if you think the worst of me.'

He said nothing, concentrating on the road as they edged around the mountain face. He could have taken the new, modern tunnel that bisected the mountain entirely. But this was a new country for him and he enjoyed the scenic routes.

Olivia lay her head back on the seat, her voice low and utterly miserable. 'How can a woman suddenly have a fiancé when she hasn't heard or even decided to accept a marriage proposal?'

'You mean... Khal didn't formally propose? This is what's upset you?'

'No. He did *not* formally propose,' she said, mocking laughter in her voice. 'I only met the Sheikh yesterday for the first time—at the races. Five minutes after my father informed me that I would be marrying him.'

CHAPTER FOUR

ROMAN FELT HIS brain stumble over her words. 'That is impossible.'

'Welcome to my life.' A deep sigh left her chest. 'Apparently Monteverre has reverted to the Middle Ages.'

'The Sheikh assured me that all the arrangements have been made. That he is simply here to make the formal announcement of your intended marriage.'

'The only arrangement that has been made is a business one. Evidently the bride was not important enough to be let in on the plans.'

She laughed once—a low, hollow sound that made Roman's gut clench.

'I'm twenty-six years old and suddenly I'm expected to tie myself to a stranger for the rest of my life.'

A tense silence fell between them and Roman took a moment to process this new information. Khal had not been honest with him. And if there was one thing that Roman Lazarov despised it was being taken for a fool. Khal had said the Princess was his future bride, leaving him with the assumption that the woman had consented to the marriage. Now, knowing that she hadn't…

Call him old-fashioned, but he believed a woman

had a right to her own freedom, her own mind. Growing up on the streets, he had seen first-hand just what happened when men decided simply to assume a woman's consent.

The Princess had called Khal a barbarian, but Roman knew that was the furthest thing from the truth. He wanted to believe that this was all a misunderstanding—that Khal had been misled by the King into believing his intended bride was a willing participant in all this. However...he knew the single-minded ruthlessness that possessed the Sheikh whenever his nation's future lay in the balance.

He had said himself that this marriage was vital to Zayyar's future. Perhaps it was vital enough to overlook a reluctant bride?

They rounded a particularly sharp bend and the road began to descend towards the lush green valley that spread out below. This country had its own particular charm—there was no denying it, he thought as he took in the glittering sea in the distance.

A small lay-by had been built into the outer curve of the road—a safe place for people to stop and take photographs while stretching their legs. Making a snap decision, Roman slowed down, manoeuvring the car into a vacant spot in the deserted lay-by and bringing them to a stop.

'What are you doing?' Olivia's brows furrowed.

'I need a moment,' he said, taking the keys with him as he stood away from the car, just in case his passenger had any ideas. The lay-by was deserted, and the road far too steep for her to get anywhere on foot.

He braced his hands on the glittering granite wall and took a moment to inhale the fresh mountain air deeply. There was something about the sight of completely unspoiled nature that deeply affected him. He had spent far too much of his youth surrounded by concrete buildings and garbage-scented air.

The sea beckoned to him in the distance. His yacht was ready to leave the moment he returned—ready to sail out into the open sea, where he would be free of this troubled royal family and their tangled web.

All he had to do was drop her off at the palace and he was home free.

Why he was hesitating all of a sudden, he did not know, but something was stopping him from completing his directive without questioning it further. He heard the car's passenger door close gently and turned to see the Princess come to a stop at the wall beside him.

'This is my favourite view in all of Monteverre,' she said. There was not a hint of sadness in her voice. It was just fact, stated without emotion.

He realised that since the moment he had held her captive in the tunnel he had not seen her resort to tears once. No one, including him, would have judged her for breaking down in the face of an unknown captor. She had a backbone of steel, and yet she had not been able to follow through with her plan to use the fraudulent passport. She clearly drew the line at breaking the law, and could not blur her own moral guidelines even in apparent desperation.

'What exactly were you hoping to achieve by running?' he asked, directing his question to the side of her face as she continued to stare out at the distance.

'I don't know.' She nipped lightly at her bottom lip. 'I just needed the chance to come to a decision myself.

Some time to weigh up my options. I have no idea what life is like away from my guards and my responsibilities, and yet here I am, expected to blindly trade one set of palace walls for another.'

He couldn't disagree with her logic.

'When I agreed to perform the security operation yesterday, I presumed that your marriage had already been arranged.' He ran a hand across his jaw, the memory of his handling of her raw and uncomfortable. 'Had I known the situation was not what it seemed I would not have agreed to it.'

She shrugged, defeat evident in the downward slope of her slim shoulders.

'I will take you to Khal. You can address your concerns to him directly. That is generally how adults resolve such situations.'

Olivia stared at him with disbelief. 'I am not a child. Despite being treated like one time and time again.' She braced her two hands on the wall, her perfectly manicured nails in stark contrast against the stone. 'I have no interest in pleading my case to a man I do not know. Besides, do you think I would have done this if I wasn't already completely sure that my voice will hold no weight in this situation?'

Roman pinched the bridge of his nose, a low growl forming in his chest. 'Damn it, I do not have time for this. I could have been halfway across the Mediterranean by now.'

She turned to him, one hand on her hip. 'I'm sorry that our political situation is such an inconvenience to your playboy lifestyle, Mr Lazarov.'

She took a step away, her shoulders squared with frustration, before she turned back to face him.

'You know what? I'm tired of this too. You may as well just take me to the Sheikh right now, so that I can reject his proposal in person. If his choice in friends is anything to go by, I'm sure I won't be missing out on too much.'

'You presume I *care* how you pampered royals resolve your issues?'

'You wouldn't be here if you didn't.'

'The only reason I am here is because you chose to be a coward rather than face the situation head-on.'

Hurt flashed in her eyes and he suddenly felt like the world's biggest heel.

'I don't know what to do,' she said honestly, her eyes meeting his with sudden vulnerability. 'I know that marrying the Sheikh is the right choice for my people. Despite what you might think, I *do* care about this kingdom—very much. If I didn't, I would have already said no.'

The silence that fell between them was thick and tension-filled, although the air was cooling down now, as the sun dropped lower in the sky and evening fell across the mountain.

She had accused him of tightening her cage yesterday, and today it couldn't be more true. The idea of pretending he hadn't found her in the first place was tempting...but no matter how much it would simplify his life he knew that a woman like her wasn't safe alone in the world. He knew more than anyone that there were far too many opportunistic criminals out there, just waiting for a chance at a high-class victim. Keeping rich people safe was his business, after all.

'I have never been out in public away from the Palace Guard for this length of time. It's nice…not being surrounded by an entourage.'

'You want a taste of freedom,' he said plainly, and the sudden realisation was like clouds parting to reveal blue sky after a storm.

'Isn't that what all runaways want?' She smiled sadly. 'But we both know how that has worked out for me so far.'

'I can't just let you walk away from me, Princess. You know that.'

He pondered the situation, despising his own need to problem-solve. Khal needed this marriage to go ahead. That was his directive here. There was no point returning the Princess only for her to reject the marriage completely. But maybe he could offer a solution that would benefit everyone involved.

Everyone except him, that was.

He frowned, hardly believing he was even entertaining the idea, but words escaped his mouth and he knew he had to trust his instinct. 'What if I could offer you a temporary freedom of sorts?' he asked slowly, watching as her face tipped up and her eyes regarded him with suspicion.

'I would ask what exactly you mean by "temporary".'

'I can offer you some time alone in which you can come to a decision about your marriage.'

'Or lack thereof?'

'Exactly.'

'How would you do that?' she asked. 'And, more importantly, *why* would you?'

'Don't worry about how—just trust that I am a man of my word. If I say you will be undisturbed then I mean it. But you would have your side of the bargain to hold up.'

'I'm listening.'

'All I ask is that you take time to consider all aspects of the union. I believe that you would be making a mistake in walking away from this engagement. Khal is a great man,' he said truthfully.

He was careful not to mention the small fact that she was a flight risk who would likely end up in real trouble if the situation wasn't contained. This was containment at its most extreme. He had somehow gone from holding a princess hostage to volunteering to take one on as his guest.

He waited while she visibly weighed up her options before him, worrying at her lower lip with her teeth. Her mouth was a dusky pink colour, he noticed. No lipstick or gloss, just pure silky rose flesh. She flashed him a glance and he quickly averted his gaze, looking back out at the view.

In that moment he instantly regretted his offer to salvage his friend's union. He had the sudden uncomfortable thought that perhaps he had just voluntarily offered to step out onto a tightrope with everything hanging in the balance.

But even as he began to regret his offer she nodded her head once, murmuring her acceptance.

And just like that the deal was done.

He had never gone back on a deal in the past, and he wouldn't be starting now. Self-doubt held no place in his life. He trusted his own self-control, his own loyalty to those he cared for. And so he walked her back to the car and dutifully avoided looking down at the swell of her curves as she sashayed in front of him.

'I still don't understand why you are doing this for me.' She looked up at him through long russet lashes, and he saw a smattering of freckles appearing high on her cheeks in the evening sun.

'Consider it a wedding gift,' he gritted, shutting the door with finality and steeling himself for the drive ahead.

Olivia stepped out on the deserted deck of the yacht and watched as they drew nearer and nearer to land. The evening was fast fading to pink as dusk approached. She wondered if maybe she should be worried that she had no idea where Roman was taking her, but really the destination itself didn't matter. So long as it was far enough away from the palace for her to be able to breathe again.

With every mile that had passed since they'd set sail from Puerto Reina harbour she had felt the unbearable tension begin to ease and a sense of sharp relief take its place. But her newfound sense of freedom still held an unpleasant tinge of guilt around the edges. As if a dark cloud was hovering somewhere in her peripheral vision, just waiting to spill over and wreak havoc on her fleeting sense of calm.

She was doing the right thing, wasn't she? Taking time away from the royal bubble in a controlled manner was the mature course of action. Despite what others might think, she knew she had a very important decision to make. This wasn't so simple as making the best choice for herself—putting the rest of her life first and repercussions be damned. She had been raised always to hold Monteverre in greater esteem than herself. To value the people more than she did her own family.

But what happened when her own family didn't seem to value her happiness at all?

Her eyes drifted across the deck to where her slim black handbag sat atop a sun lounger. Inside that bag she held all the information she had found about the foundation that her grandmother had left in her name. Information on all of the amazing work that it had carried out since her passing ten years ago.

She wasn't quite ready to share what she had uncovered with anyone just yet.

At the moment, the bottom line was clear. Her father had said that she had no alternative but to marry the Sheikh and she had agreed with him, Going against a union arranged by the King now would have very real, very severe ramifications. Either way, her life was about to change drastically.

It was no big deal, really, she thought with a slightly panicked intake of breath. Sign her life away to a loveless marriage in order to save her kingdom or have her title stripped away for ever. No big deal at all.

She closed her eyes, breathing in the cool sea air and willing her mind to slow down. She had spent two days going around and around in circles already, and the effect made her temples feel fit to burst. Was it any wonder she had made such a rash decision to run away from it all?

She exhaled slowly, opening her eyes to find that the yacht was now sailing alongside the coast of the seemingly deserted island they had been approaching. The place looked completely wild—like something from a movie. But as they rounded an outcrop of rocks she was suddenly looking at a crescent-shaped coastline formed out of ragged black rocks and golden sand. A tall white lighthouse stood on the far coast in the distance, atop a lush green cliff. And a small marina was situated at the furthest end of the bay, in the shade of the cliffs.

She gradually felt the yacht lose speed until it began the process of mooring at the end of the long white floating dock.

Roman was still nowhere to be seen, she thought as she scanned what she could see of the upper decks. The yacht was huge, and he had disappeared almost immediately after depositing her in one of the lower deck living rooms.

She was still not quite sure why he had decided to give her this time in the first place. She doubted he felt pity for her, considering his disdain for 'pampered royals', as he had so delicately labelled her. But he had seemed genuinely surprised to hear that the marriage situation was not all that it seemed.

She was not naïve enough to believe that he was on her side, but she hoped that he understood her motivations a little more at least.

Still, she would do well to remember where his loyalties lay. He was determined to see her accept Sheikh Khal's proposal—there was no doubt in her mind about that. She imagined that Roman Lazarov was not the type of man to give up on something without putting up a good fight first.

Surprisingly, the thought of debating her future with him didn't fill her with the same dread that she had felt in her father's presence the day before. She couldn't quite explain it… He spoke to her like a person, not as someone lesser. Or, worse, as a princess. He wasn't afraid to look into her eyes as he spoke, unlike most others who met her.

He had listened to her today. She would never let him know how much that had meant to her. He was not a friend—she knew that. But maybe he didn't have to be her enemy.

As though conjured by her thoughts, Roman suddenly emerged from a door to her right, speaking to someone on the phone in a deep, throaty language she presumed to be his native Russian. He had made no move to interact with her in the hours since they had set sail from Monteverre.

He looked tired, she noticed, and yet his dark shirt and trousers barely held a single crease. She, on the other hand, was rumpled and in dire need of a shower and a full night of sleep. She smoothed the front of her dress self-consciously and turned herself to face him, shoulders held high.

He ended the call with one click and took a moment to tilt his face up to the view of the vibrant overgrown landscape around them. For a moment the harsh lines around his mouth relaxed and his eyes seemed to glow silver in the evening light. She realised with surprise that the look on his face was something very close to contentment. She'd not yet seen him with anything but hostility in his features, and she had to admit the man had very inviting lips when he wasn't smirking or insulting her.

'We still have a short drive from here,' he said, taking a quick look at his watch and motioning for the single cabin porter to take care of their luggage. 'I hope you don't get motion sickness.'

Before she could question that statement, he gestured for her to follow him down the steps onto the whitewashed boards of the marina. She practically had to run to catch up with him.

'Where are we?' she asked, her short legs struggling to keep up with his long strides.

'My very own island paradise,' he said simply, not bothering to slow down until they'd reached a dirt road at the end of the dock. Roman stopped beside a small, open-sided white Jeep and turned to face her, one hand braced lazily on the mud-spattered door frame as he held it open for her.

'Jump in, Princess.' His lips quirked.

That was a challenge if ever she'd heard one. He likely expected her to throw a fit of pique, demanding transportation that better befitted her station.

She smiled sweetly, holding up her white skirt to protect it from the worst of the dirt, and hoisted herself up into the cab without complaint. Within minutes the engine was roaring loudly and a cloud of dust flew around them as they began a steady climb up the cliffs.

'When you said you could guarantee privacy, I didn't realise you meant to maroon me on a desert island.' She forced an easy tone, trying to hide the breathlessness from her voice.

He didn't immediately respond, so she filled the silence by commenting on the views of the coast below as they drove higher and higher, weaving in and out of the treeline. As they bounced over a particularly rough stretch of terrain her shoulder was jammed hard against the window and she let out a little squeak of alarm.

She turned to see that he was smirking once more. She fought the sudden, irrational urge to punch him in the bicep.

'Judging by the transportation, am I to expect a rustic mud hut for my stay?' She gripped her seatbelt with all her might, her resolve slipping fast.

'I'm not here to act as your tour guide.' He shrugged, uninterested, his jaw tightening as he shifted gears and the terrain seemed to level out. 'I'll be sure to have your tent inspected for cockroaches, at least.'

She had never actually slept in a tent. It would be a drastic change from her usual surroundings, but she rather thought she might enjoy the novelty.

Just as she turned to say this to him she caught sight of something sparkling in the distance. The land began to slope downwards towards the lower terrain again, revealing a spectacular side view of a very large, very sleek, modern villa.

As they descended a short driveway Olivia felt her breath catch at the view that spread out before them. She could see the entire island from this vantage point. The evening sky was tinged pink and orange as the sun sank lower and lower towards the jade-green sea.

'Wow…' she breathed, her awestruck brain not quite able to form anything more eloquent after the stunning visual onslaught.

A small white-haired man appeared at the door as they stepped out of the car. He looked immediately to Roman with raised brows.

'You did not mention a guest, sir,' he said, his smile forced and pointed.

'Jorge, how many times do I have to tell you not to call me sir just because we are in company?' Roman grunted.

'It's more professional.' Jorge shrugged, trying and failing to keep his voice low.

'You are *far* from professional.' Roman smirked,

clapping the other man on the shoulder with friendly familiarity. 'Ridiculously capable and efficient? Of course. But not professional in the least. That's why I hired you.'

The two men looked back to see Olivia watching the odd exchange with interest.

'Olivia, this is my right-hand man, Jorge. He travels with me to my homes as housekeeper and chef.'

Roman seemed suddenly preoccupied as he took out his phone and clicked a few buttons.

'Show her around and set her up in the white guest room.'

Olivia frowned as he began to walk away without another word. 'You mean you won't be giving me the grand tour yourself?' she called, half joking but actually quite shocked at his blatant disregard.

A harsh laugh escaped his lips as he continued to power across the hallway, away from her. 'I am not in the hospitality business. I thought you would have noticed that by now.'

And with that he disappeared through a doorway at the end of the hall, leaving her alone with his very apologetic housekeeper.

Roman ended the call with a double-click and laid his phone down hard on the marble patio table. In almost ten years of friendship he had never heard his friend curse.

Khal had been stunned at the revelation that the Princess was being strong-armed into their union by her father. But, ever practical, he had asked if there was a chance she might go ahead with it. Roman had answered truthfully—saying that he believed the Princess was just seeking a break from the heightened security measures.

'Give her time,' he had said. 'I will ensure she returns to accept your proposal.'

Khal trusted him to guard his future bride. There wasn't another person on this earth that Roman would be doing this for. He was not a personal bodyguard. He specialised in hard security. Elite risk assessments, intruder prevention, high-tech electronic systems and such. He did not have the refined people skills that were needed to work one-on-one in this kind of setting.

And yet here he was, babysitting a runaway princess on the island that he made a point to keep free of unwelcome guests.

If he had ever been a drinker now would be an excellent time for copious amounts of alcohol in which to drown his dark mood. He leaned heavily against the glass rail that lined the balcony of his master suite, looking out at the horizon where the sun had begun to dip into the Mediterranean Sea.

A sudden splash from below caught his attention and he looked down to see a creamy silhouette cutting easily across the bottom of the pool.

She had started her holiday straight away, it seemed, he thought darkly as his fist tightened on the rail.

Her head and bare shoulders broke the surface of the water as she reached the infinity ledge. Her red hair was dark and heavy on her shoulders; she hadn't bothered to tie it up. She leaned against the side of the pool, pale shoulders glistening with moisture above a bright red one-piece bathing suit. He could see the outline of long, slim legs under the water.

Roman felt the darkness inside him roar to life.

He wanted her.

He growled to himself, turning away from the tantalising view with a jaw that suddenly felt like iron. He stalked across his suite into the large white and chrome bathroom. The large floor-to-ceiling mirror showed his frustration in high definition. His pupils were dark, his nostrils flared with anger as he began unbuttoning his shirt.

It had been a while since he had been with anyone—that was all this was. His body was reacting to its recent deprivation in the most primal way possible. He had never been good at denying himself something he wanted with this kind of intensity.

A more emotionally charged person might say it had something to do with a childhood full of being denied, he thought darkly. *He* knew better. It was simply a part of him—a part of how he was put together. It was what drove him to the heights of success, always wanting more.

All he knew was that his wealth had brought along with it the delicious ability to gratify his every whim instantly. Whether it was a new car or a beautiful woman, he always got what he wanted with minimal effort.

But not her.

She was not his to think about, to look at, to covet.

He was long past his days as a thief, he thought dryly as he divested himself of the rest of his clothing and stepped under the white-hot spray of the shower, feeling the heat seep into his taut shoulder muscles and down his back.

Another man might have opted for a cold spray, but he had spent too much of his life in the cold. He had the best hot shower that money could buy and damn it, he would use it. Even if it only spurred on the heat inside him.

He was unsure whether he was angry with his friend for trusting him so blindly or angry that he did not fully trust himself. He was a sophisticated man, well capable of resisting flimsy attractions. And yet he felt a need to keep some distance between himself and the fiery-haired Olivia, with her sharp wit and unpredictable nature.

He had built his fortune on trusting his own instincts, and everything about Olivia Sandoval signalled danger.

CHAPTER FIVE

As was usual when he stayed on Isla Arista, Roman had instructed Jorge to prepare an evening meal to be served on the terrace. The scent of aromatic rosemary chicken filled his nostrils as he stepped outside and his stomach growled in anticipation.

Olivia already sat at the table, waiting for him. He was surprised to see she had not changed after her swim; instead she was wrapped in an oversized white terry-cloth robe from the pool cabana. One bare foot peeked out from where it was tucked under her. His stomach tightened at the sight of a single red-painted toenail.

'I see you are taking your holiday quite literally,' he said, taking the seat opposite her at the long marble table.

She looked down at his crisp white shirt and uncertainty flickered across her features, followed closely by embarrassment. 'Your housekeeper said it was just a quick meal. I wasn't aware that we would eat together,' she said, standing to her feet.

'Sit down,' he said and sighed.

But she vehemently shook her head, promising to be just a few minutes as she hurried away through the terrace doors at lightning speed. He fought the urge to laugh. How ironic that out of both of them it was the member of royalty who felt unfit for polite company.

True to her word, she returned less than ten minutes later. He was relieved to see that she hadn't opted for another dress, and amused that once again she wore white. The simple white linen trousers hugged her curves just as sinfully as the dress had, but thankfully she had chosen a rather sober white button-down blouse that covered her up almost to her chin.

Still, her slim shoulders were completely bare, showing off her perfect alabaster skin. He consciously lowered his gaze, to focus on filling their water glasses.

He made no move to speak. He was tired and hungry and in no mood to make her feel at ease. In fact it was better that she wasn't completely comfortable. That would make two of them.

Ever the efficient host, Jorge soon had the table filled with delicious freshly cooked dishes. Roman loaded his plate with tender chicken, garlic-roasted baby potatoes and seasonal grilled vegetables. No matter where they were in the world—New York, Moscow or this tiny remote island—his housekeeper always managed to find the freshest ingredients. He really should give him another raise...

Roman ate as he always did—until he was completely satisfied. Which usually meant two servings, at least, and then washing his meal down with a single glass of wine from his favourite regional *cantina*.

'Where on earth do you put all that food?'

Roman looked up to see Olivia watching him with open fascination, her fork still toying with the same handful of potatoes she had spooned onto her plate ten minutes previously.

'In my stomach,' he said, keeping his tone neutral. 'You had better follow suit or risk offending the chef.'

'We are not *all* graced with fast metabolisms.' She smiled tightly, putting down her fork and dabbing the corners of her mouth delicately.

'I exercise hard so that I can eat well. Good food is there to be enjoyed.' He fought annoyance as she sat back, clearly done with her food.

'The meal was wonderful—thank you.'

'If you say so, Printsessa,' he said, with just a hint of irony, considering she had barely eaten more than a child's portion. At least she didn't seem to be downing the wine to compensate for her self-imposed starvation.

'Why do you call me that?' she asked. 'I presume it's Russian? Printsessa?'

'My apologies. Do you harbour a preference for the term your subjects use? Your Highness, perhaps?'

She frowned. 'Do you enjoy mocking people for no reason?'

'I enjoy nothing of this situation, Olivia.' He exaggerated the syllables of her name with deliberate slowness and watched with satisfaction as she visibly swallowed.

'I don't understand,' she said, sitting forward, a frown forming between perfectly shaped russet brows. '*You* are the one who offered to bring me here, remember? Nobody forced you to do that. We are practically strangers, and yet you have been nothing but rude and downright hostile since the moment we met.'

'I offered to bring you here so that you would stop running away like a teenager,' he gritted. 'This is not a holiday. And I am not here to entertain a pampered royal seeking one last thrill ride before marriage.'

Her blue-green eyes narrowed with some of the fire he remembered from her dressing room the day before. 'You have made a lot of assumptions about my character in the past twenty-four hours.'

'Like it or not, right now you are in *my* charge. If I am making assumptions, it's because I can.'

'You think you know who I am? Please—enlighten me.' She sat back, crossing one slim leg over the other.

Roman watched the movement, his pulse quickening slightly as his eyes followed the curve of her thigh down to the slim silver-heeled sandals on her feet. 'I do not pretend to know who you are—nothing quite so philosophical.'

He leaned back in his chair, stretching one arm behind his neck. She followed the movement, eyelashes lowered.

'I know your type well enough,' Roman said darkly, and his mind surprised him by conjuring up an image of a familiar face. A pair of blue eyes that had haunted him for almost two decades.

His night of imprisonment must have affected him worse than he thought. The cold sweat from being handcuffed still seemed to coat his skin like dirt, even after the hot shower and plentiful meal.

Thoughts of his past were not a common occurrence these days. Thoughts of Sofiya even less common.

He cleared his throat, irritated at himself and his momentary lapse in keeping his own demons at bay. 'You are young, beautiful and privileged, frustrated with the strict rules designed to protect you. So you go out in search of adventure. A little danger to shake up the monotony.'

'So I'm just another spoilt brat looking for a bit of fun? Is that it?'

Roman shrugged noncommittally, draining the last of his wine. 'You are telling me this *isn't* about rebellion?' he asked, knowing he had hit a nerve when her eyes darted away from his to look out at the inky darkness of the sea in the distance.

'You know, insulting me and my motivation is hardly going to send me running back to accept your friend's proposal.'

'The only reason you feel insulted is because you are likely used to always hearing what you want to hear.'

Olivia sighed, leaning her head back for a moment and pinching the bridge of her nose. 'I am simply taking a brief reprieve before making one of the most important decisions of my life. No big deal, really.'

'I hate to tell you, but that's just a fancy way of saying you're running away.' He couldn't help but smirk.

'So you have me all figured out, then?' She crossed her arms over her chest, meeting his eyes head-on. 'It must be nice, being so untouchable and faultless.'

Roman shrugged. 'It is not my fault that you dislike being told the truth.'

'What I *dislike*, Mr Lazarov, is that you find it so easy to shove all my class into one pile, simply because we were born with money.' She exhaled heavily. 'In my opinion, that says far more about you than it does me.'

'Is that so?'

'Yes, *it is*. I may have been born into wealth, but that does not automatically take away the fact that I am human.' She stood up, pacing to the stone ledge of the terrace before turning back to him. 'You know nothing of my life—just as I know nothing of yours.'

Roman watched as she looked out at the distant black waves for a moment, with that same faraway look in her eyes that he had seen the night before. He almost felt guilty for goading her.

He cleared his throat loudly. 'We are getting off-track here. This is about repairing your trust in Sheikh Khal.' He sat a little straighter and laid one leg over his knee. 'Not that it will pose much difficulty. Khal is a good man.'

'I appreciate the vote of confidence,' she said, her voice rasping slightly. 'But I believe the point of this time away is for me to come to a decision alone.'

'No one knows him better than I do. Allow me to put your mind at ease.'

'You are not my friend. And I would do well to re-member that. I am taking advantage of some time to clear my head—nothing more. I won't speak of this marriage business with you again.'

Roman raised a brow in question, getting to his feet and walking to stand beside her. '"Business…" An in-teresting word choice.'

She shrugged one slim shoulder, still looking away from him. 'It's the reality.'

'It is a very complex arrangement, from what I know—it's not just about *you*.'

It was as though he were reading straight from a script her father had written. The sudden reminder of her di-lemma settled painfully like a dead weight in between Olivia's shoulders. She was so tense she could scream. She had barely slept in the past twenty-four hours, and that coupled with being in this man's presence made every nerve in her body feel completely on edge.

She felt her throat tighten. 'I may be more sheltered than your average twenty-six-year-old woman, but I know what kind of situation I am in.' She cleared her throat, steeling herself. She would *not* show weakness. 'It's *never* been about me—that's the point.'

'Are you telling me you feel you truly have no choice in the matter?' he asked, a sudden seriousness entering his eyes. 'Because a woman being forced into marriage is something I know Khal would never condone. Nor would I.'

Olivia looked up, taking in his broad stance and the furrow between his brows. Logically, she knew that his concern was for his friend, and not for the inconvenient charge he had been landed with. But for a moment she imagined what it might be like to have that kind of protectiveness completely to herself. She imagined that when a man like Roman cared for a woman he would do it fiercely—no prisoners taken. It seemed that he brought intensity into all aspects of his life.

She shook off the fanciful thoughts, suddenly hyper aware of his broad presence looming mere feet away from her. The warm headiness of his cologne teased her nostrils on the night air. His was the kind of scent that made a girl want to stand closer, to breathe it in. It was dangerous, that smell. It made her want to do dangerous things.

'Your silence doesn't exactly give me any insight.' He leaned back on the stone ledge so that he faced her, his grey eyes strangely dark and unreadable in the warm light of the outdoor lamps.

Olivia sighed, shrugging one shoulder with practised indifference. How could she tell him that the only alternative she had to this marriage was to walk away and lose everything she had grown up to value?

'I am not going to be handcuffed and frogmarched up the aisle, if that's what you mean.'

He raised a brow. 'But there would be consequences if you refused?'

She nodded once, unable to stand still in the face of his intense gaze and unwilling to discuss those consequences with a man who'd made it clear he was firmly on the opposite side. She might have escaped her father's imperious presence, but it seemed she had simply swapped one judgemental know-it-all male for another.

She suddenly felt more alone than ever. Her restless feet took her to the end of the terrace, where the stone tiles gave way to soft, spongy grass.

'I can't remember the last time I walked barefoot in the grass,' she said, more to herself than him, and she took a few tentative steps and sighed with appreciation.

One look back showed her that he was still watching her with that same unreadable expression. It was as though he were trying to categorise her, to pin down exactly what he needed to do to fix the very problem of her.

He had said the Sheikh trusted him to problem-solve. That was all she was to him—a problem. It seemed that was all she was to everyone these days, unless she shut her mouth and did what she was told.

'Olivia, come back from there.' Roman's voice boomed from behind her. 'This time of night it's—'

'You know, I think I can make that decision for myself,' she said, cutting him off mid-speech. It was rude, but she was too irritated to care. 'If I want to walk in the grass, I will. I don't need someone to manage every second of my day.'

She took a few more steps across the grass, putting some space between herself and the surprised, strangely amused smirk that had suddenly spread across his face.

'Suit yourself,' he said quietly, looking down at the expensive watch on his wrist. 'But you're going to regret changing out of that bathing suit.'

She frowned at the cryptic statement, turning to face him. Just as she opened her mouth to question that statement the heavens seemed to open above her. Thick droplets of ice-cold rain fell hard and heavy onto her face, making her gasp as the cold spray got heavier and heavier, spreading through her clothing and down her neck and spine.

She was instantly wet through, and her mind took at least ten seconds before telling her to sprint back towards the house. After a few feet the rain suddenly stopped, and she was left looking into Roman's laughing face.

'I would have warned you about the sprinklers,' he said, crossing his arms. 'But I didn't want to manage your day too much.'

She gasped as the cool night air hit her sodden skin. She looked down at her wet clothes and, to her surprise, felt hysterical laughter bubble up her throat.

Roman frowned, also with surprise, 'What? No angry tirade about my appalling lack of consideration?'

'I'm done with being angry today.' She shook her head. 'If I don't laugh right now I might cry. And I make a point of never doing that.'

She leaned to one side, laughing once more as she

began to squeeze the water from her hair. A sudden wicked urge grabbed her, and before she could stop herself she pooled the excess liquid in the palm of her hand and threw it in his direction, watching as it landed with a satisfying splash directly in his face.

'I'm sorry,' she said quickly, trying to curb her laughter as she took in his thunderous expression.

He took a step towards her and she felt her breath catch.

'You can't throw the first punch and then retreat with an apology.' His voice was dark and silky on the night air. 'You sell yourself short. That was an excellent aim.'

'I'm not sorry, then.' She smirked, realising with a sudden jolt that she was flirting with him. And that he was flirting back.

The way he was looking at her coupled with the silent darkness of the night surrounding them made her almost imagine that this was a different moment in time entirely. That they weren't just strangers forced into each other's company by circumstance.

She imagined normal people laughed like this and poked fun at one another without fear of making a faux pas. It felt good, being normal.

'You've got quite a wild temper hidden underneath all those royal manners.' He took another step closer.

'I manage to keep it in check most of the time.'

'But not around me.' It was a statement, not a question.

'Don't flatter yourself.' She smiled nervously.

He stood little more than a foot away now, his warm scent clouding around her. She was wet and bedraggled, but she didn't want to leave just yet. She didn't want to end this—whatever it was that was passing between them. After a day filled with confrontation and being on the defensive, it was nice to lose the serious tone—even if for a brief moment.

She crossed her arms under her breasts, feeling the cold air prickle her skin into gooseflesh.

'*Khristos*, why didn't you say you were freezing?'

He reached out to touch her arm, the movement shocking them both as their eyes met in the half-darkness. It was a touch too far. They both knew it. And yet his hand stayed, gripping the soft skin just above her elbow. She shivered again, and this time it was nothing to do with the chill.

She noticed his expression darken suddenly. The air between them filled with a strange sizzling energy and his fingers flexed against her skin just a fraction.

She realised his gaze had moved below her chin. Self-consciously she looked down—and felt the air rush from her lungs in one long drawn-out breath.

Her white blouse.

She might as well be standing in front of him completely naked for all the coverage the wet piece of fabric was offering her. Of *course* tonight had to be the night when, in her haste to dress, she had decided a bra wasn't necessary. And of *course* the cool breeze had resulted in both taut peaks standing proudly to attention.

'Oh, God…'

She took in another breath, silently willing herself to laugh it off, but her mind stumbled clumsily over itself as she took in the obvious heat in his gaze. His eyes were dark and heavy-lidded as they lifted to meet hers. There was no mistaking it now. The silent strum of sensual heat that thrummed in the air between them.

It was a strange feeling—wanting to hide from the intensity of his gaze and bask in it all at the same time. He made her feel warm in places she hadn't known she could feel heat. It was as though her body was silently begging her to move towards him.

What would she do if he suddenly closed the gap between them and laid his lips hungrily on hers? Would he taste as sinfully good as he smelled?

She could suddenly think of nothing else.

What felt like hours passed, when really it was a matter of minutes. All the while his hand remained where it was, scorching her skin. Branding her.

When he finally turned his face away she fought the urge to step closer. To take the moment back. But then she followed his gaze and spied the housekeeper, quietly tidying their dinner dishes away nearby, with all the practised quietness of a professional.

She took one deliberate step away and crossed her arms over her chest, covering herself. His hand fell to his side and the haze of open lust disappeared from his features almost as quickly as it had come.

She wondered how he managed to look both furious and guilt-ridden at the same time. What would have happened if she had given in to that impulse and simply leaned forward to close the gap between them?

As though he'd heard her thoughts, a furrow appeared on his brow. He cleared his throat loudly, turning back to his housekeeper without another glance in her direction. 'Grab a towel for Miss Sandoval before she freezes.'

His cold, uncaring tone only added to the sudden chill that spread through her.

Without saying goodnight, or even looking in her direction, Roman disappeared through the terrace doors, leaving her standing alone, confused and embarrassed in her sodden clothes.

The walls of his master suite were bathed in a cold powder-blue light when Roman awoke. As usual he had not dreamed, but sleep had taken much longer than usual to claim him. And even then it had been fitful and broken at best. It was as though his entire body had thrummed with an intense nervous energy that refused to allow him any real rest.

Never one to remain in bed once his eyes had opened, Roman stood and threw on his jogging shorts.

In less than five minutes he was stretching on the steps that led to the beach. Within another ten he had completed two laps of the mile-long sandy inlet and worked up a healthy sweat. He ran barefoot on the damp sand until his chest heaved and his muscles burned with effort. And then he ran some more.

Usually a good run was enough to rid him of any thoughts strong enough to affect his sleep. A self-inflicted punishment of sorts, for those times when he knew his mind had begun to grow weak and was in need of strengthening. A weak mind had no place in his life—not when so many relied on his razor-sharp instincts to protect their homes and indeed their lives.

He prided himself on always being able to separate his personal and professional life—especially when it came to affairs with women. Lust never clouded his judgement.

The women he pursued were usually professional workaholics, just like him. Women who were sophisticated in and out of the bedroom and who weren't looking for sweet nothings to be whispered in their ear once they had scratched their mutual itch.

He had a feeling a sheltered young princess wouldn't be quite so worldly when it came to no-strings sex.

He picked up speed as he chastised himself for even entertaining the thought of a no-strings affair with Olivia. Guilt settled heavily in his chest as he thought of the night before, of the thoughts that had run through his brain as he had openly ogled his best friend's intended bride. *Stupid, weak fool.* The words flew by along with his breath as he exhausted his body with a final punishing sprint.

He had always believed that he deserved punishment for the multitude of sins he had committed in his youth. That no matter how complacent he grew in his wealth, in his power and success, there was always a darkness in him just waiting to ruin everything. It was beginning to seem that Olivia had been sent into his life to tempt that darkness to the fore. To tease him with her elegant curves and squeaky-clean nature.

He had a certain code for how he lived his life—certain people he did not betray and certain things he did not do. A rule book, of sorts, that kept him on the straight and narrow when the impulsive bastard inside him threatened to rise to the surface.

Khristos...

He exhaled hard. He had never been more tempted to break his own rules than in these past two days. Olivia reminded him of one of those perfect, luscious cakes that had always been on display behind the glass of his local bakery as a child. He had stood outside in the cold, salivating over the idea of breaking through that glass and claiming the treat for himself. But at that stage in his life his innocent boyhood self had innately known that would have been the wrong thing to do.

The Roman Lazarov of the present day did not have that luxury. Telling himself to walk away last night had been like standing in front of that bakery window all over again—hungry and frustrated, but unable to do a damn thing but fantasise about how the icing would taste in his mouth.

A delicious torture.

With his breath hard and even, he turned to the horizon and watched as the first flickers of pink and orange began to colour the dawn sky.

One of his favourite things about Isla Arista was the unspoilt view of both the sunrise and sunset from various points on the island. In those few dark months after the tragedy in Zayyar he had often spent an entire day walking here. He could completely circumnavigate the island in a few short hours because he knew the right tracks to take. It was an island of many personalities—smooth and habitable in some places, but fiercely wild and impassable in others.

He turned to begin walking back up to the villa, stopping as he spied a familiar feminine silhouette emerge from the open glass doors onto the terrace.

Olivia had been unashamedly watching Roman's progress up and down the beach with interest. It had been imposssble not to stare at his broad, muscular form as he powered up and down the sand with seeming effortlessness.

She had debated hiding in her room all day, and avoiding breakfast with him altogether, but she'd decided that was something the *old* Olivia would do.

She was done with avoiding conflict and simply daydreaming of what she might say if she had the bravery in certain situations. She would sit across the table from him this morning and she would show him how completely unaffected she was by what had happened last night. Or almost happened, rather.

Aside from wanting to prove a point to herself, she had to admit that she desperately wanted to speak with him again. He was so unlike any man she had ever known. It was addictive, talking to him.

She had possibly taken slightly more time than usual in washing and preparing her hair, so that it fell in soft waves around her face. And so what if she had tried on three of the five dresses in her suitcase before committing to one?

The pale pink linen day dress was perhaps a little much for breakfast, but the way it nipped in at the waist and flowed out softly to her knees made her feel feminine and confident. And besides, she was simply taking pleasure in choosing her own outfit without a styling team surrounding her.

After twenty minutes of waiting, her stomach rumbling, with a beautiful display of fresh fruit and pastries spread out before her on the breakfast table, Jorge informed her that Mr Lazarov would be working all day and had decided it was easier to eat in his office.

She told herself that she wasn't bothered in the least as she poured herself coffee from the French press and nibbled on a piece of melon. She didn't care that he had chosen to avoid her. It was better, really. There was no one here to goad her, to push her to think about things she wanted to avoid. No all too perceptive slate-grey eyes watching her, making her skin prickle.

Eventually she gave in to the tantalising breakfast display and grabbed a large sugar-frosted croissant, smearing it liberally with butter and strawberry marmalade. The sticky sweet treat was like heaven itself as she washed it down with the fragrant gourmet coffee. Pastry was firmly on her list of *never* foods.

Regret was inevitable, and it washed over her as she self-consciously smoothed her dress against her stomach. Another result of the life she led was the constant pressure to stay slim, to stay as beautiful as possible in order to live up to her persona.

She had always harboured a soul-deep envy of her sisters and their seeming lack of pressure to play a part for the public. As the oldest, Eleanor was to be Queen one day—a position she took very seriously. She was naturally rake-thin, and always immaculately dressed, but the only media pressure *she* had to deal with was speculation on when she would start producing little heirs of her own.

Cressida was rarely, if ever, seen in the media. As a respected researcher in her field, she had somehow been allowed to study and live an almost civilian lifestyle in London, with only the barest minimum security detail.

Olivia sighed. The only skills *she* had were those best suited to what she was already doing, along with the uncanny ability to daydream herself out of any situation.

She had always adored the more dramatic movies— the ones where the heroine went through hell in order to get her happy ending. Maybe this was her punishment for refusing to adapt fully to real life?

Now, the information that lay inside that folder up in

her room had the potential to change her life. To give her a little of the freedom she had longed for, for the past ten years. But, as with every choice, there would be some fall-out. And that fall-out would affect the people of her kingdom for many years to come.

Roman had said that she was spoilt and selfish. If that were true then she would have simply walked away from her place in the royal family as soon as she'd legally become an adult. Or when she had been made aware of her private inheritance three years ago.

It was her 'Get Out of Jail Free' card—a golden ticket to civilian life. But she was a royal of the realm at heart, and her father knew that. Hence why he so easily used her own loyal nature against her and made sure that she knew the consequences of her actions if she were to defy him.

She knew her father spoke the truth when he said that this marriage had the potential to solve all of Monteverre's problems.

Could she really be the person to stand in the way of that?

CHAPTER SIX

OLIVIA SAT UP quickly in the bed, feeling a sharp pain shoot through her neck. In her exhausted state she must have fallen asleep with her head propped on one arm. A quick look in the mirror showed that not only was her hair an unsightly nest, but she also bore a hot red patch on her left cheek from her uncomfortable position.

She stood up and walked to windows. A silvery moon had risen high above the bay below, casting pretty shadows all along the gardens that surrounded the villa. It was certainly past dinner time, she imagined, but still her eyes widened as the clock showed it was almost midnight.

Disorientated and groggy, she quickly ran a brush through her hair before making her way downstairs.

The villa seemed to be completely empty, and devoid of all human presence. The air was cool out on the terrace, and she half wished she had thought to take a sweater. From her vantage point she had a spectacular view of the glass-fronted villa in all its warm, glowing glory. At night, somehow the place seemed even more beautiful than it was during the day. Soft lighting warmed the space from within and made it look like a wall of glowing amber stone.

The garden was lit up with small spherical lights that appeared to float in mid-air. Tall, thick shrubbery blocked her view of the moon and its hypnotising glow on the waves. She was filled with energy, and suddenly wanted nothing more than a brisk walk along the moonlit beach.

As she made her way towards the edge of the lights she paused, briefly wondering if it was wise to venture away from the villa. The island was completely private, so she felt she was in no real danger so long as she kept to the well-lit parts. But that didn't mean that her brooding guard would take kindly to her exploring without permission…

That thought was immediately banished once she remembered how her host had effectively barricaded himself in his office for the day. She hadn't so much as caught a glimpse of him since seeing him running on the beach.

Her arms instinctively wrapped around her midriff, shielding herself from both the cool breeze and her thoughts as she made her way down the steps to the beach. Who the hell did he think he was anyway? Did he think that she would shadow him around? Begging for his attention?

She had much more pressing things on her mind than brooding Russians with ridiculously inflated egos.

The steps at the back of the house were steeper than she had anticipated. The drive up in the Jeep had not truly given her an appreciation of how high up the house was perched above the marina. She momentarily considered turning back, but stubbornness and curiosity made her keep moving. There was a safety rail on each side, and small lamps to light the way—it was not truly dangerous.

The soles of her sandals slid suddenly against the stone surface, making her gasp as she teetered forward precariously. The world seemed to shift for a split second before she clambered back, grabbing the rail for dear life.

She slid off her sandals, abandoning them on the steps. Her bare feet gave much better grip for the rest of the way down, and soon she reached the very bottom. The sand was cold and damp under her toes but the midnight air was balmy. She took a moment to stop and simply bask in the utter stillness of it all.

It reminded her of the warm nights her family had spent out on the terrace at their summer estate. The beautiful countryside manor in the southern peninsula of Monteverre was the setting of most of her fondest childhood memories. Back in the days when her grandmother had reigned over the kingdom as Queen and her father had simply been the young, handsome heir to the throne.

There had been no palace for the three young Princesses—no twenty-four-hour bodyguards. Her grandmother had ensured they were given as normal a childhood as possible, considering the circumstances.

And even as father had grown ever more reckless, and her mother had retreated into her brandy glass, Mimi had been there. Until all of a sudden she hadn't.

Olivia shivered, taking a few long strides across the sand until she reached the long whitewashed jetty of the small marina that she had arrived at. It looked different in the semi-dark, with only a few lamps illuminating the shadows. Roman's sleek yacht was a dark shadow in the distance. The moonlight glowed against its polished glass body, smooth, severe and striking—rather like the man himself, she thought.

The marina also housed a handful of other vessels. A couple of top-of-the-range speedboats—likely for sporting use—a small rescue dinghy, and the one that had caught her eye the moment she had disembarked the day before: a magnificent vintage sailboat.

In the dark, it was hard to see any of the fine detailing. She reached out, running her hand along the smooth silver lettering emblazoned just above the waterline.

'"*Sofiya*",' she said out loud. 'Just who are you named after, I wonder?'

'That is none of your business.'

The deep voice boomed from behind her, startling her enough to make her lose her footing and fall hard against the side of the boat. She fell for what seemed like minutes rather than milliseconds, before strong arms grabbed her around the waist and lifted her swiftly upright.

'Planning a midnight escape?' Roman asked, his accent both intimidating and strangely welcoming after the prolonged silence of her day.

'You…you startled me,' she breathed hard, her voice little more than a breathy whisper.

His hands were still on her waist, the heat of him seeping through the material of her dress. She reached down, covering his hands with her own for a moment before pushing them away and taking a tentative half-step back.

The loss of heat was instant. Her skin prickled with tiny bumps, as though calling his touch back.

'If you insist on sneaking around outside in the dark, I might rethink the terms of your stay here.'

'The *terms*? I assumed I had been abandoned to my own devices.'

'Fine, then. Let's get this straight. You will only leave the house in daylight hours, and you will clear it with me first.'

'You expect me to just sit around all day and go insane from my own thoughts?' She half laughed. 'This is an island—where could I even go?'

'I have learnt not to underestimate you.'

He crossed his arms and for the first time she noticed he wore only a dark-coloured sleeveless workout shirt and cut-off shorts. Her eyes took in the bulging muscles that lined his shoulders, his lean, hard biceps and strong forearms. Her gaze wandered once again to the strange black band that stretched around his left arm, just under the elbow. The design seemed intricate, but she quickly looked back up to his face, aware she had been gawking.

'Are we clear?' he asked, scowling down at her from his impressive height.

Olivia fought the urge to roll her eyes at him in all his perpetually sardonic glory. She had a feeling this was what it would be like to have a surly, unimpressed guardian angel following her every move.

In this light he certainly looked the part. The glow of the moon emphasised his harsh features, making him even more darkly attractive. But good looks and incredibly broad shoulders would never account for a severe lack of sense of humour. Did the man *ever* smile?

'Are you like this all the time or just around me?'

she asked, turning on her heel and walking away from him, back towards the sand.

'Oh, you're telling me how I am now?' He fell easily into step beside her, mild amusement on his voice. 'Please enlighten me.'

'You are controlling. And rude.' She said, counting off on her fingers. 'Judgmental, intimidating, far too serious—'

'You are accusing *me* of being rude?' He clutched a hand to his chest as though mortally wounded.

Olivia stopped just short of where the wooden planks gave way to hard sand and turned to face him in the dim light of the spherical lamps that lined the small marina. 'You've just instructed me that I cannot leave the house without your permission.'

He smirked, reaching out to stop her when she made to move away with irritation.

She crossed her arms and met his eyes, determined to have this conversation like an adult.

'Olivia, closely controlled security is only required if there is a risk of the client putting themselves in danger. Unfortunately for me, in your case, that means, yes, it's needed.' He sighed. 'And I am not prepared to shadow you around this island simply to provide you with a more enjoyable experience.'

'Are you telling me I'm under house arrest just because you're determined not to spend any time alone with me?' she said with disbelief.

'I don't think it would be the best idea,' he said plainly. 'For obvious reasons.'

She watched him silently for a moment, wondering if he was actually openly referring to the chemistry between them. 'Are you really so unable to control a flimsy attraction?' she asked bravely, shocked at the words coming from her own mouth.

His eyes widened. 'I'm a grown man, Olivia. Older than you by almost a decade.'

'I fail to see what age has to do with it.'

He stepped forward, a dangerous glint in his slate-grey eyes. 'I'm not a mindless teenager who can be waylaid by a set of curves.'

'Well, then, what's the problem?' She shrugged one shoulder, fully committed to her act now, even as her insides quaked. 'I'm not about to jump your bones, and you've made it clear that you are far too mature to do anything quite so...*primal*.'

He smiled the kind of smile that screamed danger as he allowed his gaze to take her in slowly from her head down to her bare toes. 'Primal? Is that what you'd call it?'

She gulped.

He noticed.

Roman took a single step forward, closing the gap between them so that they stood almost toe to toe. 'I'd like to wager that you've never jumped anyone's bones in your life, Printsessa.'

'I'm not about to divulge that kind of information to you.' She tried her best to keep up her confident act but he'd rattled her. He knew it too.

Cursing her lack of practice in these things, she turned as nonchalantly as possible and began walking back towards the villa, hoping she'd simply seem bored or tired.

'I did not mean to offend you.' His voice drifted from behind her as she began climbing the steep steps.

'I'm sure you are perfectly capable of jumping my bones.'

'Don't flatter yourself,' she breathed, aware that she was barely a quarter of the way up and already feeling winded from the incline.

She hadn't eaten nearly enough today to fuel this kind of exertion, and tiny spots had begun to appear at the edges of her vision. She paused, holding on to the rail for a moment as she caught her breath.

'Problem?' he asked, coming to a stop beside her.

He was barely even breathing heavily, the great brute.

She shook her head, not wanting to admit that she had been moping around the villa for most of the day and had refused Jorge's offers of lunch and dinner.

Standing up straight, she continued to climb, begging the gods of never-ending stairs to have mercy on her. Eventually she reached the top—and not a moment too soon. She caught one glimpse of the amber lights of the villa before her ears began to pop and her legs started to shake.

Roman instantly noticed the change in her demeanour. 'Was the climb *really* so tough?' he asked, half mocking.

She groaned, moving to the grass and half sitting half falling onto her rear end with an unceremonious grunt as the world tilted around her.

'You look as though you are about to be ill.' He crouched in front of her, the mocking tone completely vanished from his voice. 'Olivia?'

'I need some water,' she managed to rasp, looking up at the blurred outline of his face. 'Just a little light-headed.'

* * *

Roman took one look at Olivia's pale features and cursed under his breath. 'When did you last eat?' he asked, a mixture of anger and concern filling him as her eyes darted away from him with embarrassment.

'Just give me a moment to catch my breath.'

'No, you need a damned sandwich and some common sense,' he gritted. 'Can you walk?'

She nodded—far too quickly. Her eyes were still unfocused and her face pale as moonlight. Still, to her stubborn credit she rose to her feet and attempted two whole steps before her legs buckled and she tipped into his waiting arms.

'This is mortifying!' she groaned, her face mashed against his chest.

Roman ignored the all too welcome sensation of having her slim figure pressed against him. With a deep breath he lifted her against his shoulder and closed the distance between them and the villa.

Once inside, he deposited her roughly onto the bench in the kitchen and set about preparing a cold meat sandwich on crusty white bread and a tall glass of ice-cold orange juice.

She sipped at the juice with gusto, and a hint of colour reappeared in her cheeks after a moment as she nibbled on the crust of the bread.

'You eat like a rabbit,' he commented, when after five minutes she hadn't taken more than a series of tiny bites.

'I eat enough.' She shrugged.

Roman remained silent. She was watching him closely over the rim of her orange juice glass, but did not speak until the sandwich was completely gone.

'White carbs are my weakness.' She sighed. 'You've just sent me down a path of total and utter ruination in the eyes of my stylist.'

'I'm sorry its not gluten-free, but true hunger can't afford to be picky.'

'What would *you* know of true hunger?' She raised a brow. 'You eat enough to feed a small army.'

'I grew accustomed to eating as much as I could fit in once I got out of prison.' He spoke without thought, and then watched as stark realisation dawned over her delicate features. 'Old habits, I suppose.' He shrugged, instantly regretting his words.

'I never thought…' She let her voice trail off. 'I'm sorry.'

'You're sorry that I was in prison?' He leaned down, grabbing her plate and turning to deposit it in the sink. 'Don't be. I deserved every year I got. Trust me.'

'No, I'm sorry you had to experience hunger like that. I didn't think when I spoke. I was just being… snarky.'

'Don't worry about it.'

In all the years that had passed since his time in jail, he couldn't remember anyone ever commiserating with him over the hardships he must have endured. She didn't even know why he had been landed there in the first place. She knew nothing of the man he had been. No, he corrected himself, the *boy* he had been.

'You're not a bad guy,' she said quietly.

Roman looked up, unable to conceal his surprise at her words.

'I mean, obviously I've only known you a couple of days…' She shrugged her shoulders, heat lightly warming her cheeks. 'But a bad guy wouldn't have brought me here to begin with. He wouldn't be making sand-wiches at one in the morning to stop me from fainting like a helpless damsel.'

'Don't paint me as some hero, Olivia.' He shook his head. 'You have no idea how far that is from the truth.'

She made to continue talking, but he'd suddenly had enough. He put a hand up, silencing her. 'I've had a long day, and I'd appreciate it if you considered what I said about obeying my rules tomorrow.'

'I'll consider it.'

She shrugged, then walked past him into the hall-way and began ascending the stairs, effectively rob-bing him of the chance to walk away first.

'That didn't sound like a yes.' He sighed, trying and failing to avoid the delectable sight of her shapely bare calves below the hemline of her dress.

'That's because it wasn't one.'

She disappeared from his view.

Olivia shielded her eyes as her hair whipped around her. The wind was like razor blades at this altitude, but the hour-long hike had definitely been worth it. She braced herself, taking one step out onto the balcony of the lighthouse. Heights had never really been an issue for her, but then again she had never been alone on a ledge in coastal winds before.

But all fear was forgotten once she stepped out and felt the sun spread across her face, warming her through.

There was nothing but ocean ahead of her for miles. She turned and caught her breath. She could see the entire island in all its glowing emerald glory. A heavy sigh escaped her lips and she leaned her elbows against the metal railing.

The villa was little more than a pea-sized white blur from here, partially hidden in the trees far over to the north. Likely Roman was still holed up in his office there, determined to spend as little time in her company as possible.

She had almost been tempted to go and ask him to show her the lighthouse. She had walked boldly up to his office door and stood poised, ready to knock. But then she had remembered his face as he'd called her Princess. The patronising tone as he had all but called her a child in need of supervision. She had not actually agreed to his terms, so technically she wasn't breaking any promises.

The hike had been just what she'd needed to shake off the extra energy that had plagued her all morning. She had made a point of eating a good wholesome breakfast before setting off, not wanting to make the same mistake as she had the night before. Now her thighs burned from exertion and her cheeks were warm and she finally felt as if she was *doing* something. And the best part of all was that she was entirely alone.

A harsh male roar caught her by surprise and her hand almost slipped on the railing. She looked down, wide-eyed, and caught sight of Roman powering across the plane at the base of the lighthouse, angry determination in his posture as he stopped and looked up at her.

He shouted something entirely inaudible, his voice fighting against the noise of the wind and the waves below. Olivia couldn't help it—she laughed. The smile that erupted on her lips made him scowl even more as he powered ahead once more and disappeared through the door beneath her.

There were at least three storeys between them, made up of one long winding staircase, and yet it seemed like barely a minute passed before she heard him step out onto the platform behind her.

'What the hell do you think you're doing up here?' he growled.

Olivia turned to look at him over her shoulder. 'I'm enjoying the view.'

'Oh, of course. Of *course* you'd have to perch yourself fifty feet in the air. You couldn't just stand on the deck below like a normal person.'

'The door was unlocked and I've never seen the inside of a lighthouse before.' She shrugged, holding onto the railing to pull herself up. 'It's not half as quaint as I'd imagined.'

She turned to face Roman, seeing his look of cold rage turn quickly to disbelief.

'This isn't a game, Olivia,' he said darkly. 'What if you'd fallen?'

'I'm quite capable of using stairs without supervision.' She stood tall, wishing he wouldn't keep looking at her that way. 'Please, just…stop treating me like a child.'

'Well, then, stop acting like one!' He raised his voice.

She sidestepped him, neatly sliding through the doorway and starting down the steps at a rapid pace.

He followed quickly behind her.

'You are the most reckless, difficult client I have ever had.' Roman stalked behind her, his voice still holding that dark edge.

'Because I wanted to explore a little?' She paused, turning to look back at him. 'This entire island is more secure than the royal vaults. You knew exactly where I was—as evidenced by the fact that you are *here*.'

'I was at least ten minutes behind you.'

'You are seriously overreacting, and I would like to know why.'

He met her eyes easily, his height making him tower above her even more than usual. 'I'm reacting as anyone would if they found the woman they are supposed to be protecting dangling her legs from a fifty-foot balcony.'

'It would hardly be your fault if I fell, would it?' She shrugged, turning back to continue down the steps. 'I'm sure your beloved Khal would find a replacement princess eventually.'

Strong hands encased her shoulders, effectively barring her from moving. Roman moved around her so they stood face to face.

She was almost completely level with him on the step below. The expression on his face completely took her breath away.

'Do you honestly have a death wish?' He grasped her shoulders tightly, his eyes blazing with real, deep concern.

'I... No, of course not.' She turned her face away from him, only for him to turn it right back.

His fingers were hot and hard against her cheek, and this close she was surrounded by the warm, delicious aroma of him that she had come to recognise so well.

'Your eyes tell me a different story.'

'Isn't that against the rules? Looking into my eyes?'

Was that her voice? That husky murmur? She could

feel her heart hammering hard and slow in her chest. It was as though the simple act of being near him sent her vitals into chaos.

'I've always hated rules.'

His mouth tightened, and tension spread through his hands and up his arms so that they felt like bands of iron on her shoulders rather than flesh and bone.

She bit her bottom lip as shivers spread down her arms. Roman's eyes lowered to take in the movement, his pupils darkening as he pressed his lips together hard. She thought he might kiss her. He certainly looked as though he wanted to.

But she saw the moment that something changed in his eyes—something that made his mouth harden and his eyes shift away from her once more.

For one crazy moment she wondered what it might be like to lean across and kiss all that tension from his mouth. To just take a wild leap and not care about the consequences.

And then all of a sudden she was doing it.

She closed the gap between them and laid her mouth against his, feeling his shocked intake of breath as their lips connected and her breasts pressed flush against the hard, strong plane of his chest.

He was going to hell.

There were no two ways about it.

Roman felt something inside him roar to life the moment Olivia's lips gently touched his, her feather-light caresses against his mouth almost completely undoing him. His hands found their way to her hair, releasing the clasp that held it wound at the nape of her neck.

He was letting this happen.

More than that, he wanted it so badly it made him ache.

She gave just as good as she got, her hands travelling over his shoulders and down his waist. Sharp fingernails grasped his hips just above his jeans. The sensation sent pulses of heat southwards and he felt himself grow hard against his zip.

The fleeting thought of stopping the madness came and went quickly as Olivia moved against him, her abdomen in direct contact with his erection. Far from being shocked or appalled, she kissed him even harder.

Their breath mingled into one frantic cloud of white-hot need. He kissed a trail down her neck, his hands sweeping deftly to the front closures of her blouse. With each satisfying click he was treated to a delicious sliver of creamy soft skin and the smallest glimpse of white lace.

Her breasts were small and firm, perfectly rounded and straining against the lace fabric of her bra. With one hand he reached behind her, undoing the clasp.

She exhaled long and slow, biting her lip as he pulled the garment away and lowered his mouth to her breast. Her skin tasted like a smooth ripe peach, the softness unbelievable against his tongue.

As he drew one peak into his mouth she hissed out a breath. 'Roman…' she breathed in awe.

Her fingers wound through his hair, anchoring him to her as he explored one taut peak and then gave ample attention to the other.

Their position on the steps made things difficult. It would be so easy to carry her down to the landing below and take her hard and fast on the floor. He could tell she was ready for him by the way she moaned at the slightest touch. She was his for the taking…

Except, she wasn't, was she?

The thought stilled him, stopping his body mid-motion.

She wasn't his.

Roman stepped away from her as though he'd been burned. His breath escaped his nostrils in harsh bursts as his body screamed in protest. He cursed out loud, his voice echoing in the cavernous space as he realised what he had been doing. What his body was still deeply invested in doing.

Olivia fell back at an uncomfortable angle, her breasts still bared to him. She looked up, confused and flushed.

'That shouldn't have happened,' he breathed, bracing his back against the cold wall and forcing himself to look away from the tantalising curves on display.

In his peripheral vision he saw Olivia stiffen, her hands quickly moving to cover herself. A prolonged silence ensued as he turned his back and listened while she frantically tried to button up her blouse and calm her breathing. When he finally turned around it was to find her gone—back up the stairs to the top of the lighthouse.

He followed, stepping out soundlessly onto the narrow balcony alongside her.

'Olivia…' he began, exhaling on a long sigh.

'Whatever you are about to say, just *don't*,' she said, her voice tight with recrimination and something else—regret, perhaps?

'It won't happen again, between us,' he said, almost as though he were trying to convince himself along with her. 'It was a mistake, bringing you here at all. This just proves what I already knew.'

'And that is?'

'That you are incapable of controlling your impulses.'

'And *you* are the most arrogant man I have ever met.' She turned to face him. 'Are you actually trying to blame *me* for this?' she asked. 'I may have kissed you first, but at least I'm emotionally mature enough to admit it was because I wanted it.'

'Excuse me?'

'I wanted it.' She spoke slowly and deliberately, her eyes blazing emerald in the brightness of the mid-afternoon sun. 'I wanted to know how it would feel, being kissed by you. To get under that wall of stone you surround yourself with. And I may be unpractised in these things, but I know that you wanted it too.'

His mind caught on one single word she had uttered. *Unpractised.* He coughed on the sharp intake of breath that filled his lungs.

Olivia's eyes widened, her face rapidly warming with embarrassment. 'I simply meant that I'm not accustomed to making the first move,' she said quickly, her eyes wide with mortification.

'Chert voz'mi,' Roman cursed under his breath, suddenly despising his own ability to see through to the truth. 'You have never had a lover, have you?'

He watched as her shoulders tensed and she tightened her grip on the rail in front of her. She hid her face from him but he could read the signs in her body. Surprise rapidly turned to self-defence. She didn't speak, but she didn't have to. He already knew he was right.

She was a virgin.

As if there weren't enough reasons already for this attraction to be the worst kind of wrong…

He turned, bracing one hand on the balcony rail and gripping it with all his might. 'Have you any idea what kind of game you are playing?' he gritted.

'I was not playing a game.' She turned her face to him, her shoulders stiff and unyielding.

'How would you even *know* what you were doing?' he said harshly. Anger raged in him—towards her, towards himself. He felt as if he was drowning in it. 'What did you think? That you could use me as a damned test run? Lose your virginity with the rough and tumble ex-con before I sent you back to your royal fiancé's bed?'

Her eyes narrowed, her fist flying out to thump him squarely in the middle of his chest. 'How dare you?'

He grabbed her hand in his fist, stopping her movement and inadvertently pulling her closer to him.

'You are angry at me because it is the truth. You think you are attracted to me? You don't even *know* me. You're attracted to my lack of refinement, Olivia. You see me as some big, uncivilised fool who you can charm with your delicate skin and innocent eye-flutters.' He shook his head, his mouth hardening into a cruel line.

'I don't think of you that way.'

'Well, maybe you should start. I might come from the gutter, but that doesn't mean I make a habit of living like a street thug. I do not sleep with virgins or with other men's fiancées. I have morals, Olivia.'

'What? And I don't? I am not engaged. I have done nothing wrong here.'

'You are as good as spoken for,' he ground out.

She looked up at him. Eyes that moments ago had been blue-black with desire were now wide and blazing with anger. 'I will *never* be spoken for. Never again.' A tremor passed through her throat. 'I am not another man's property, to be protected and transported.'

'You are going back to the palace as soon as possible.'

'Roman, is it so hard to believe that I am just as overwhelmed as you?'

'Don't flatter yourself, Princess,' he said cruelly. 'It would take a lot more than an innocent's clumsy kisses to overwhelm *me*.'

Her face fell and he knew he had gone too far.

But she was already turning to walk out through the door. 'If you don't mind, I'd like to walk back alone.'

He made to walk after her but stopped, thinking it might be best if they both had some time to calm down.

'Fine. You can take the time to prepare your explanation. I will deliver you to your fiancé tonight.'

CHAPTER SEVEN

OLIVIA REGRETTED STEALING Roman's boat almost as soon as she had set off, but stubbornness kept her from turning back. As the wind pulled her hair around her face and the salty air filled her lungs she felt the awful tension inside her loosen a fraction.

She hated him.

Every single word that Roman had thrown at her had swum around in her head as she had hiked across the craggy woodland towards the villa. His indignant accusations. His refusal to see the truth in their situation. He seemed determined to power through any argument she had.

It was the thought of his final words that had cemented her decision to change course and hightail it for the marina. *'I will deliver you to your fiancé tonight.'*

She gripped the wheel even tighter, steering the boat as the mainland drew nearer on the horizon. The distance between Isla Arista and the small mainland town of Puerto Arista was a mere fifteen minutes, but as the small dock came into view she contemplated turning around.

What *was* it about her breaking the law when she was around this man? Once again she had proved him right by giving in to an emotional impulse without a thought for the consequences.

Still, pride kept her from doing the intelligent thing and returning with her tail between her legs. She busied herself with mooring and disembarking safely, taking pleasure in the manual work.

She had always enjoyed her national sport—there was something quite peaceful about letting her mind wander as she followed through all the steps.

This small speedboat was much more streamlined and modern than the complex sporting sailboats she was used to, so before she knew it she was climbing the limestone steps up from the dock and emerging into a busy little Spanish village. Thankfully she had worn large sunglasses and a floppy-brimmed hat on her hike, to protect her from the sun, both of which now helpfully concealed her face from possible recognition.

The streets were cobbled and sloped upwards towards the impressive white cliffs that dominated the landscape. A long row of whitewashed houses and shops lined the seafront, with terracotta roofs and vibrantly coloured windows. The village was small, and seemed almost pristine in its appearance.

It was quiet. There was none of the hustle and bustle of the coastal spots in Monteverre. It was like stepping into a well-kept secret. People smiled as they walked past, shopkeepers tipped their sunhats in her direction. No one approached her or called her name. No one cared.

It was a revelation.

After she had walked to the top of the hill and back down her stomach began to growl. The thought of returning to the island—to Roman—filled her with trepidation. Without a second thought she walked into a nearby café and eyed the delicious selection of handmade pastries and freshly cut fruit. The smell of warm butter and melted chocolate permeated the air and made her stomach flip.

Yes, this was exactly what she needed.

'Can I help you, miss?' A middle-aged man smiled jovially from behind the counter, his white apron smeared with powdered sugar.

Olivia smiled in response, really enjoying not being recognised. 'Yes—what's good here?'

'It's all good, of course.' He laughed. 'We have a special on today: three *magdalenas* for the price of two.'

Olivia looked down at the elegant golden-brown pastries and instantly felt her stomach drop.

She had no money.

With a murmured excuse she practically ran from the shop, embarrassment fuelling her as she walked swiftly down the hill back towards the marina. She stopped on the promenade, taking a seat on a bench that overlooked the small inlet.

As her breathing slowed, a heavy sadness replaced her embarrassment. She had no idea how to prepare for living in the real world. For all her thoughts of leaving her bubble and making a difference, the reality was that she had absolutely no idea how to function outside the privilege of royal life.

Her father had been right.

She had told herself that she would find a way to become the woman she wanted to be outside of her parents' expectations and royal obligations. She had believed she could fulfil the vision her grandmother had had for the foundation alone. But she didn't have a business mind—she didn't have that kind of common sense or leadership skill. She certainly didn't have the kind of innate intelligence and passion that could support her, as her siblings did.

Maybe she was delusional. Maybe her father was right and she should stick to where her strengths lay. Just another Sandoval princess, destined to stand and smile by her husband's side.

But one thing was for sure: she was *not* what Roman had accused her of being. She had not seen him as some sort of base creature to use for her own amusement. The thought that he saw her as someone capable of such cruelty…it bothered her.

She ambled towards the marina with the intention of returning and paused, watching as a familiar sailboat moored itself next to her smaller vessel. The name *Sofiya* was emblazoned across its hull.

Roman jumped down athletically onto the boards of the jetty before striding purposefully in her direction.

She turned away quickly, not quite ready for the confrontation she knew was bound to happen. He was likely furious, and he had every right to be. But she had hoped for more time to compose herself before the inevitable. Even now, the memory of his hands on her bare skin made her short of breath.

She shook off the heated thoughts, walking along the promenade at a brisk pace.

A man was walking towards her—the man from the pastry shop, she realised suddenly. He was walking quite fast and had a slightly odd expression on his face. Olivia paused, feeling suddenly very exposed on the empty promenade. As he neared her he reached into his jacket, his large hand fumbling for something in his breast pocket.

A loud growl erupted from somewhere over her left shoulder. Roman was running past her in a matter of seconds, moving to stand in front of the older man with ferocious agility and strength. His large body manoeuvred the man to the ground and he shouted to Olivia to move away. She could hear the man calling out underneath him—a strange muffled cry of one word, over and over.

Finally Roman moved from his position and the other man managed to gasp. 'Camera! Camera!'

Olivia spied the small black object that lay shattered near Roman's left knee. She rushed forward. 'Roman, it's just a camera!' She gasped, tugging at his sleeve for his to remove his body from the man. 'Roman, please stand up. He's not dangerous,' she urged, pulling at his shoulder.

Roman looked into the blue-green depths of Olivia's eyes and something inside him shifted. All at once he became aware of the man's fleshy paunch beside his knee. The roar of the waves hitting the promenade to his left. He could hear Olivia's panicked tone and his own fiercely ragged breathing.

Khristos, it had happened again.

He stood to his feet, looking away from where his unsuspecting, seemingly innocent victim had stood up and shuffled away. The roaring in his ears was deafening, the hammering in his chest making him feel as though he might pass out.

Without thinking of the lack of logic in his actions, he grabbed Olivia roughly by the wrist, ignoring her protests. Eventually she gave in and allowed him to lead her down to where his sailboat lay in wait. Within moments they were on board, and he closed the door of the spacious interior saloon with a harsh exhalation of breath.

'Sit down,' he commanded, watching confusion enter into her eyes.

'Roman, what on earth—?'

'Just sit down,' he repeated harshly, his breath still raw and uneven in his chest as he fought to control the ridiculous racing of his treacherous mind.

Sofiya.

His mind whirled against the onslaught of terrible memories threatening to overcome him as his sister's face broke through to his consciousness. As if in slow motion he could see the life leave her baby-blue eyes as the bullet tore through her body, silencing her scream.

He shook his head, swallowing past the dryness of fear in his throat.

Olivia moved in front of him, concern in her wide eyes as she placed her hands on his chest.

'You're shaking,' she said softly, in the kind of placating tone one used when trying to soothe a wild animal. 'Has this happened before?'

Her warm hands on his chest both irritated and calmed him. 'Don't push me, Olivia,' he warned. 'I don't want to hurt you, too.'

'You won't hurt me, Roman.'

She shook her head just a fraction, her innocent eyes so wide and confused it made him want to growl with frustration and bask in her concern all at once.

'Let me help you,' she whispered, moving her hand uncertainly to rest on his face.

The touch of her soft, feminine hands on his skin undid him completely.

He leaned forward, capturing her words roughly with his mouth, showing her just why she needed to run from him.

Her lips were soft against his, trying in vain to offer him comfort even as he plundered and deepened the kiss. He wound one hand around the back of her neck and twisted the fine silk of her hair in his hands. His rough touch anchored her to him while his other hand bunched into a tight fist by his side.

This was wrong, he told himself. He was using her in the aftermath of his own weakness, losing himself in her, and it was so wrong he hated himself. She was innocent to situations like this, he reminded himself, talking himself down from his own madness. She deserved better than this—than him.

He moved to away an inch and she looked up at him, lust clouding her vision.

'I can't keep my hands off of you,' he gritted, running his fingers down one side of her face and wincing as he noticed the small patch of blood staining the front of her dress.

Logic told him that the blood was likely from his own cut knuckles, but the sight of her pale skin next to the red smear was enough to sober him just for a moment. He tried to fish though the haze of his memory but drew up nothing but blankness.

'Roman, I need to know what happened back there.' She spoke slowly, as though afraid she might set him off again.

'I don't want to talk right now.' He shook his head,

pulling himself away from the heat of her, inch by inch, even as his body screamed in protest.

It was colder without her in his arms, but safer.

'Talk to me,' she said simply.

'I'm not good at talking, Olivia.' He turned to sit heavily on the leather sofa of the saloon. 'Guns trigger something inside me. Even the *thought* of guns, apparently.' He laughed cruelly.

'There was no gun, Roman,' she said. 'No danger.'

He stood, his anger boiling over to the surface. 'You think I don't *know* that?' he asked. 'But in that moment, when my mind goes there…'

'You are powerless to stop it?' she offered helpfully.

Powerless. God, how he hated that term. Was there anything in the world more terrifying than being out of control of your own mind and body, even if only for a few moments?

Olivia moved to sit beside him, her thigh brushing his on the small settee.

'You can talk about it with me, if it helps,' she offered.

'We are not all built for flowery conversations and sharing our dreams.'

Her eyes dropped and he realised he was doing it again—being needlessly cruel.

'None of this would have happened if you hadn't run off with my damn boat,' he continued, seemingly unable to stop himself.

'You deserved it,' she said harshly.

'For trying to protect your reputation?' he said incredulously.

'I don't think my reputation has a thing to do with it, Roman. You attacked a stranger, dragged me back here like the hounds of hell were chasing you and then you kissed me like your life depended on it.'

She met his eyes without hesitation.

'I kissed you to shut you up,' he argued, turning towards the bridge that housed the control panel so they could get the hell out of here and he could find some space.

'Now who's running away?' she challenged.

'You'd prefer to wait around until local law enforcement arrives to question us both?' he said darkly. 'I didn't even stop to see if I had hurt him.'

'He was fine—just shaken. You don't remember *any* of it?' She frowned. 'I got the chance to apologise quickly before you pulled me away.'

'If you think an apology is enough to stop him from pressing charges...'

'I told him that you were just a jealous lover.' She winced, half smiling with embarrassment.

Roman took a moment to look at her, and the situation suddenly replayed in his mind like a bad movie. He pursed his lips and then, before he knew it, dark laughter erupted from his chest.

Olivia smiled, also seeing the humour in their situation, and soon she was laughing too. She had a great laugh, he thought to himself as they both returned to silence after a moment.

'Thank you,' he said, looking deeply into her eyes for a moment.

He wasn't accustomed to thanking anyone for anything quite so personal; he made a point of not needing anyone enough to necessitate heartfelt apologies. But this woman had lied for him—protected him in a way. After he had treated her horribly.

It was a strange feeling—one he didn't want to examine too closely. For now, the ability to laugh it off was a novelty in itself.

Olivia nodded once—a graceful acceptance.

He took a step away from her, looking out at the harbour around them. It was late; the sky was already in full darkness around them. He suddenly did not want to return to the island—to the silence of the villa and the self-imposed exile he had placed himself in.

'Are you hungry?' he asked hopefully.

Simply named Faro, the small restaurant was partly built into the rocks that stood proudly at the tip of the peninsula. Olivia felt butterflies in her stomach as Roman's hand encircled hers, helping her down the steep steps to the low wooden door of the entrance.

'It doesn't look like much from the outside, but I assure you it's the best paella in all of Spain.'

'I'll take your word for it.'

She smiled, following him into a small hallway. Roman led the way down a corridor and out onto a large terrace that overlooked the coast as far as the eye could see. Warm glowing lanterns adorned the walls and brightened the space, making it seem like the terrace at the back of someone's home rather than a restaurant.

The overall effect was so welcoming she felt instantly at ease, all her tension from the afternoon leaving her shoulders as the waiter led them to a table on the very edge of the space. A man rushed over to take Roman's hand and clap him on the back. The pair began conversing in perfect English, and Roman ordered bottle of red wine.

When it came, Olivia took a sip of her wine, thanking the waiter and looking out across the bay. They were so close to the water she could see the waves crashing into the rocks below them. The after-effects of the day made her forehead tighten painfully.

Roman seemed determined to avoid the subject of their kiss entirely.

Both kisses.

She shivered at the memory of his rough handling after he had all but dragged her back to his boat. He had been completely raw and out of control, and yet she had felt nothing but excitement. Maybe he was right—maybe she *was* just looking for a taste of danger. Maybe she was naïve for not fearing him.

He had made one thing clear: he did not trust her. She desperately wanted to ask him about the incident on the promenade—find out why a man who ran a company of armed bodyguards would have such a deep issue with guns. But maybe she was a fool for worrying about him when he'd continuously told her she was no more than a job to him.

She had told him that she was a virgin and he had made it clear that the fact only cemented his view of her as being completely untouchable. She had never resented her own pesky innocence more than at that moment. When had he stopped being just a glowering bodyguard and become the object of all her fantasies?

She swallowed hard past the dryness in her throat as Roman sat down across from her and apologised for the interruption. After checking with her first, he ordered them both a light starter followed by the chef's special paella.

Once the waiter had taken their order they were

left completely alone. The moment of uncomfortable silence was not lost on Olivia. She cleared her throat, making a show of looking up at the vaulted ceiling that partially covered the open terrace.

'You seem to know the staff quite well,' she offered.

'It's been five years, I believe, since I started coming here for lunch every day when I was overseeing building work on my island.'

'They seem to like you.'

'The chef—he is also the owner. And the waiters are his sons.' He smiled, looking over at the young men bustling around the small restaurant. 'The first day I found this place, my architect brought me for lunch. The owner, Pedro, had an argument with his oldest boy and the kid ran off, leaving him with a pile of dishes and a line of hungry guests. I rolled up my sleeves and offered to help.'

'Not many people would do that.'

'Not many princesses would do what you did at that racetrack.' Roman shrugged, sitting back as their bread and gazpacho were laid out on their table.

Olivia couldn't mask her surprise at his mention of the incident with the young waiter and the champagne. 'That afternoon seems like a lifetime ago.'

He nodded. 'Perhaps we are both destined for the sainthood?'

She smiled. 'If you are hoping to convince me that you are not entirely heartless, it's working.'

'I might not have the benevolent influence of a royal, but I'm not afraid to get my hands dirty.' He shrugged again. 'Charity isn't always about money.'

'That's…' She shook her head, frowning at the memory of her argument with her father. Of those very words that she had spoken so vehemently. And here was Roman, echoing them as though it were simply a fact.

'Is something wrong?' he asked, frowning.

She shook her head, ignoring the painful throb in her chest at hearing his words.

She took another sip of wine, clearing the fullness from her throat. 'I adore my work in the community...' Olivia sighed, unable to hide the wistfulness that crept into her voice. 'I swear it's the only time I feel like I'm doing something worthwhile with my life.'

'That sounds like a vocation,' he said, sipping from his own glass. 'And yet you don't sound fulfilled.'

She shook her head. 'This might surprise you, but princesses don't have much sway when it comes to promoting new education laws or increasing expenditure on public schooling.' She sighed again. 'Since the crackdown on my security I've missed several important events. Perhaps the children won't even have noticed. Perhaps I'm only helping *myself* by going out there, boosting my own self-importance. Maybe I'm just an egomaniac.'

'I highly doubt that,' he said, all seriousness. 'This bothers you? Your lack of power?'

'Of course it does. How would *you* feel if you had people holding you back from living your own life at every step?'

A strange look passed over his face, disappearing just as quickly.

'I can only do so much.' She shrugged. 'Potential future innovators of my kingdom are sitting in homeless shelters and all I am allowed to do lately is hold charity balls. It means absolutely *nothing*.'

'Your work means more to those children than you could ever know.'

'How can you know that?'

Roman was quiet for a long time, his hands held tight in front of him. Then, 'I've lived that life. A long time ago, now. But you never forget.' He forced a smile, draining his glass. 'I know that a stranger's kindness means more to a homeless child than you would ever believe.'

Olivia took in the tightness on his features, the guarded emotions in his dark steel-grey eyes. 'Roman, I had no idea…'

'My past is not something that I like to relive. I just want you to know that your work has value. I owe much of my success to men and women I never even knew. They received no thanks, no rewards. I never understood such selfless giving—it was not something I had grown up to feel. Never doubt such honest goodness, Olivia.'

'I am sorry that you had such a difficult upbringing.'

'I'm not. It made me who I am today. But I am not arrogant enough to forget that the world would be an awful place if it was only filled with cynical men like me.'

Olivia understood him then—a little more than before, at least. 'You're not so bad.'

He laughed. 'You don't know the half of it.'

'Tell me, then,' she said quickly. 'Tell me whatever it is you think is so awful about yourself and let me be the judge.'

'Mine is not the kind of story you tell over paella and wine.' The laughter died from his voice, making it clear that the topic was not open for further discussion.

Their main course was laid in front of them, providing a welcome distraction. The food was delicious, and yet as Olivia watched Roman eat she couldn't help but imagine him as a young boy. Thin and hungry... helpless. It was a jarring thought—one that filled her throat with emotion.

She hated to think of anyone suffering through such hardship—especially considering the luxury she had been born into. It had never sat well with her, the enormous divide between the wealthy and the poverty-stricken. She had always felt a weight on her shoulders and an obligation to do her part.

'That was delicious,' she said, forcing a smile as the waiter came to clear their plates and replenish their wine glasses.

'I hope this meal has done something to make up for my behaviour so far,' he said, lowering his glass and looking at her. Sincerity darkened his eyes as he held her gaze. 'For some reason the idea that you see me as cold and cruel bothers me.'

'I don't think you are cold at all,' she said, in all seriousness. 'I think that's just what you prefer people to believe.'

The night had grown cold by the time they embarked at the Puerto Arista harbour and set sail for the short trip back to the island.

Olivia apologised once again for the fact that they had had to abandon his luxury speedboat, but Roman assured her it was fine. They fell into silence as he concentrated on moving the boat along the harbour safely towards open water, each of them deep in thought.

A spark in the sky behind them startled her, and she turned back just in time to see an explosion of red and blue lights erupt into the perfect black sky.

'It must be midnight,' Roman said from behind her.

She could feel him lower their speed and allow the boat to drift slightly.

'This firework display is not one to be missed, trust me.'

'There's no need to stop just for my benefit,' she said quickly.

'Consider it part two of my apology.'

He guided her to the sun deck and pulled two cushions from the built-in sofa, laying them on the cold tiled floor. It was slippery with mist, and just a little chilly, but as a cascade of golden lights began to spread across the inky black sky she knew she wouldn't have changed the night for anything.

After the final booming red spinning wheels had faded into the air, she turned to see he was watching her intently. She took in the heat in his gaze and knew he was battling with the aftermath of that kiss just as she was. She had never wanted to be kissed again more in her life.

'We should be getting back,' he rasped, his eyes not leaving hers.

'I'm really tired of doing what I *should* do all the time.' She licked her lips, silently urging him to give in one more time to the madness between them.

'Olivia...' He shook his head a fraction, lowering his eyes from hers.

She reached out to lay her hand just under the collar of his shirt, knowing she was being brazen but needing to do *something*. To show him in definite terms what her mind was struggling to convey with words.

He took her hand in his, lowered it back to her lap. 'You're not the only one who has to live by the rules,' he said quietly. 'Sometimes they are there to stop us from getting in too deep where we don't belong.'

'I am a grown woman, Roman. If I decide to take a leap into something unknown, you'd better be sure that I've got my reasons.'

'You might *think* you know what you want—'

Olivia stood quickly, looking down at him. 'I told you that I won't be spoken for again,' she warned him, feeling her temper bubble to the surface as she alternated between wanting to hit him and wanting to beg him to take her into his arms.

'Speak, then,' he said plainly, sitting back to look up at her. 'What is it that you want?'

'It's more what I *don't* want,' she said. 'Being here— away from the bubble of royal life—being with you...' She took a breath, urging the words out, needing to say them even if he simply walked away.

Roman shook his head, not giving her a chance to continue as he jumped to his feet and moved back downstairs to start up the engine once more.

The rest of their journey back to the island was silent and tense, unspoken words heavy in the air between them. She wanted to ask him if he still planned to take her back to the palace tomorrow. If he still believed that she should go ahead with the marriage.

The Jeep ride was bumpy, and all too quickly they were standing in the dim empty hallway of the villa. Jorge must have closed up for the night and headed off to his quarters on the opposite side of the island.

'Goodnight, Olivia.'

Roman's voice was dark and final as he made to walk away from her.

'Wait,' she said quietly. 'I've realised something.'

He turned around, crossing his arms over his chest as he waited for her to speak.

Olivia cleared her throat, suddenly feeling very much on show. 'I've realised that I don't want to walk away from my kingdom, and if marrying a stranger is the way to keep it safe then perhaps that's what needs to be done.'

She took a deep breath, wondering if that was relief or disappointment that flickered momentarily across his features. She couldn't tell in the dim hallway.

'You are quite the sacrificial lamb,' he said quietly, with not a hint of emotion in his tone. 'So you plan to return to the palace and accept the marriage?'

'I've decided to return, yes. And face the situation like an adult, at least.' She met his eyes, challenging him in the darkness. 'But I can't fully commit to the marriage knowing there is one thing I have yet to experience in life.'

'I thought you ran away because there were *many* things you hadn't experienced?' he said, sarcasm dripping from his tone.

'There is only one that truly matters to me. I cannot agree to an arranged marriage without allowing myself to experience one of the things I truly have control over.'

His gaze was pure heat as he moistened his lips with one smooth flick of his tongue. She felt heat spread down through her veins and pool in her stomach. If a simple look could make her feel this way, she needed to know what else he could make her feel. It was suddenly the only thing she wanted.

'I want my first time with a man to be on *my* terms, with someone who wants me just as badly as I want him.'

CHAPTER EIGHT

IN HIS MIND Roman simply gathered her into his arms and carried her up to his suite as fast as his legs could take him. Surely this was far more torture than one man was expected to endure? But in reality he remained silent for a long moment, his throat dry as his mind fought to sort between loyalty and lust.

She was offering herself to him on a silver platter.

'You think you can separate sex from love?' he said softly.

'If the sex is good enough.' She shrugged one delicate shoulder, biting her lower lip gently as though embarrassed by her own words.

She couldn't even say the word without blushing and she wanted to fall into bed with him. He took one step towards her, then another, until they were almost toe to toe.

'Men like me don't make love, Olivia,' he said darkly. 'They don't make empty promises just to play into some fantasy.'

She gulped, looking up at him through hooded lashes. 'What if I don't want the fantasy?'

'I have a thousand fantasies I could tell you about,' he whispered. 'Each one more risqué and physically demanding than the last. I would have you naked in my bed quicker than you could beg me to take you. Is that what you want me to say?'

'I...' Her voice trailed off, her eyes wide with uncertainty.

Roman let one finger trace the curve of her shoulder. 'You're not ready for me, Princess,' he said cruelly. 'You need a man who is going to whisper sweet nothings in your ear and make sugar-coated promises. I'm not that man.'

Roman braced his hand on the door of his suite and laid his forehead against the wood—hard.

Loyalty be damned. He wanted nothing more than to break down every door between them and take her like the unrefined street thug that he was.

But she was a virgin. She was not his to take.

Even as his mind thought the words his fist tightened in protest.

He took another deep, rattling breath, feeling the stale air of the room fill his lungs to bursting point.

She was not his.

With more force than necessary he turned and swung open the door to the terrace, silently thanking his housekeeper for placing his guest in the opposite wing of the villa. What would Olivia think of him now? Standing out in the night air, trying desperately to calm his raging libido like a scorned youth?

He looked across to where the light shone out from her rooms.

No. He shook his head, turning to vault down the stone steps in the direction of the pool. He had made his decision, just as she had made hers. And by God he would live with it.

The night was surprisingly mild, with barely a breath of breeze blowing in from the bay. The moon was full and high in the sky, casting a silvery glow on the water of the pool.

He took no time in stripping down and diving in, shock coursing through him as the cold water encased his skin, penetrating through to his very core. The pool was deep and he pushed himself to his limit, waiting as long as possible before breaking the surface.

As the balmy air refilled his lungs he saw the un-mistakable silhouette of Olivia, standing near the water's edge.

Roman stood, so that the water reached his waist, very aware that he was completely nude in the water. His heart beat slow and hard in his chest. They were silent for a long moment, his eyes never leaving hers.

'You decided to take a late-night swim,' she said, her voice strangely husky in the dim light.

'And you followed me.'

She moved to the entry steps of the pool, dipping one toe in before stepping down ankle-deep in the water.

He noticed for the first time that her legs and feet were bare, that she wore a thin robe that stopped just above her knee. He wondered if she had anything underneath. He felt an ache in his gut, so deep, and he knew right then that he would move heaven and earth to have her out of that robe and in his arms.

He moved forward in the water, closer to her with every breath.

'I decided I couldn't leave here tomorrow without

knowing more about those fantasies,' she said, her voice carrying across the space between them loud and clear.

Her hands moved to the tie of her robe and Roman paused, feeling the breath freeze in his lungs as he simultaneously willed her to stop and to keep going.

'How much more?' he asked, his voice husky as it echoed off the pool walls.

'Everything,' she said, her eyes never leaving his.

Roman took another step and watched as Olivia's eyes dropped to where the water level now completely exposed him to her. Her eyes darkened as she looked, and looked, before finally dragging her gaze back up to meet his. What he saw there ignited a fire in his blood. Raw desire darkened her eyes and coloured her cheeks as she undid the tie of her robe.

The white silk slid from her skin and darkened as it touched the water, leaving nothing between them but space. He was within arm's length of her now, unconsciously moving towards her. But he stilled at the sight of her, completely nude and offered to him like the living statue of a goddess. Her skin glowed under the moonlight. Every perfect curve of her body was on display in high definition and it was a revelation.

She stood still for a moment, before modesty got the better of her and she self-consciously moved one hand to shield her most intimate parts from his hungry gaze.

Roman closed the distance between them in a single movement, encircling her waist with his hands and pulling her with him into the water. With her body partially hidden, she relaxed in his arms and pressed herself tightly against him.

'I changed my mind too,' Roman said throatily, his mouth tracing a path along the exposed curve of her neck.

Her hands refused to stay clasped at his neck, instead preferring to explore the muscles of his back and down his waist.

She bit her lip seductively, removing her nails from where they had pinched quite roughly. 'I have wanted to do that for quite a while now.'

'Oh, so we are making up for lost time?' He gathered her higher, to his chest, wrapping one of her legs around his waist before doing the same with the other and pressing her back against the wall of the pool. 'In that case…'

Olivia groaned at the sensation of having Roman's lean, hard body cradled between her thighs, and his mouth captured hers in a kiss filled with barely restrained want. She could feel the heat of his chest pressing against hers and silently prayed for him to kiss her there again. As if he'd heard her plea, he broke the kiss and began trailing a path down her neck. By the time his mouth reached her breast, her breath was coming in short bursts. His mouth, hot and sinful, captured the entire rosy peak and tortured her with slow, languorous circles.

She began writhing against him as his free hand cupped her bottom and squeezed hard. The pleasure that rocketed through her was like being shot with lightning, and suddenly it was not her mind but her body that knew exactly what she wanted and just where she wanted him.

Her hips rolled against him and she moved herself lower, startled as she felt the hardness of his erection press erotically against her skin.

'Slow down,' he whispered, nipping the skin of her ear with gentle pressure.

'I don't think I can,' she breathed, moving against him, silently urging him to move against her. To place himself against her.

She tried to be embarrassed at her wanton response, but found she was quite past caring. Roman held her hips tightly in his hands, effectively stopping her movements. She looked up to find his dark eyes trained on her face and his jaw tight with restraint.

'That is possibly the most beautiful torture I could experience,' he breathed, leaning forward to gently nip her bottom lip with his teeth. 'But I want this to be good for you.'

'It feels pretty good so far.' She licked the curve of his lower lip, her gut clenching as he pressed the full length of himself against her in one quick slide.

'Olivia… I'm so hard right now that taking you fast and furious against this wall is *not* a good idea.'

He moved again, letting the tip of his erection slide against her sensitive throbbing flesh.

'Oh…' She moaned low in her throat as he moved, making slow, aching circles over just the right spot. 'Roman…don't stop.'

She closed her eyes, tilting her head back as his mouth found her breast once more. The double effect of his touch made her heart jump into overdrive and she could feel her pulse thrumming hard, as though it tried to escape her skin.

He urged her on in a mixture of English and Russian, his low, husky words sending her soaring higher and higher until she swore she could take no more. She dug her fingernails deep into his shoulders, wanting him to stop but wanting him to keep going for ever. It was like being trapped in her own personal hurricane—being swept up into a power so much stronger than herself.

When she finally found her release Roman was right there to catch her and hold her as she fell back down to earth. Heat spread out across her body, sending electricity right down to the tips of her toes. She opened her eyes and realised she was being lifted out of the water as her skin came into contact with the cold lip of the pool.

The contact was brief, as Roman lifted himself out and gathered her up into his arms as though she weighed nothing at all. It was strange, allowing him to carry her naked across the terrace. They were completely alone on the island, so privacy was guaranteed, and as she looked up at him she realised the feeling she had was not one of nervousness but one of anticipation.

He carried her easily up the stairs to his master suite. She had barely taken in the cool grey sheets on the gigantic bed when she felt her anticipation quickly intensify to mild panic. He was advancing on her now, his perfect muscular torso glowing in the light of a single lamp as he lowered himself over her and cupped her face with one hand.

As his lips lowered to touch hers she turned her cheek, grimacing when she realised what she had done.

'Is everything okay?' he whispered from above her, one hand trailing down her shoulder in a slow, sensual path. 'Are you…rethinking this?'

'No,' she said quickly, noting his features soften with relief. 'No, I'm definitely not rethinking *any* of this.'

'Relax,' he murmured, kissing a path down between

the valley of her breasts. 'This is one of those fantasies I was telling you about.'

'It is?'

She lay back, staring up at the ceiling and willing herself to calm down. His mouth was doing a very good job of distracting her. That was until she realised just where those lips were headed. She tensed, reaching down for him just as his lips began to trace a path below her navel.

'This is *my* fantasy, remember?' he said, gripping her wrists and holding them by her sides. 'And I haven't even got to the good part yet.'

'Roman...you can't honestly—'

'Do you trust me?' he asked, his eyes dark with passion as his lips pressed gentle kisses along the inside of her thigh.

Olivia watched him kiss her, watched him draw closer to the centre of her, and felt herself nod once. She did trust him. Completely.

The nerves fell away with each gentle kiss on her skin and her eyes never left him, watching as he drew his tongue slowly against the centre of her sex. Her back arched and her eyes fluttered closed for a moment. When she looked back down his eyes were on her, dark and possessive, as he moved his hands to spread her wide and kiss her even deeper.

Her head sank back against the pillows as her body was enveloped in wave after wave of hot, wet pleasure. She reached down and knitted her fingers through his hair, anchoring him to the spot that felt most intense. He growled his appreciation, sliding one finger inside her in a slow rhythm.

'Oh... Roman...' She gasped at the feeling of delicious fullness, hardly believing it when he added a second digit to join the first without breaking rhythm.

Just as she began to feel that pressure mounting once more he removed his mouth, sliding up her body in one fluid movement. He reached across to the nightstand, grabbing a small foil packet and sheathing himself with lightning speed.

'I can't wait another second. This time I want to be inside you when you come,' he rasped, his voice half demand, half question as he met her eyes in the dim glowing light.

She spread her legs wide, silently answering his question with her body.

She could feel the tension in his shoulders as he positioned himself at her entrance, slick and ready from his expert attentions. His breathing hitched as he entered her with exaggerated slowness. Olivia raised her legs to encircle his waist, showing him that she was ready. That she wanted to feel him inside her for the first time.

The feeling of fullness was so intense she almost begged him to stop. After a moment she wanted to ask if there was much more of him to go.

There was.

She breathed deep as the sensation became uncomfortable, and was vaguely aware of Roman's voice intruding on her thoughts.

'I'm hurting you,' he said, deeply concerned, and began to withdraw from her.

Olivia held him with her thighs, keeping them connected as her body adjusted to his sizeable girth. 'Now it's your turn to be patient,' she breathed.

She tested her hips once, then twice, in a slow rolling movement. What had begun as a dull sting of pressure soon gave way to a more pleasurable pulse of heat.

Roman's breath hissed from between his teeth as she moved against him, but he remained exaggeratedly still above her.

'Does that feel good for you?' Olivia asked, taking in his tense jaw and serious expression as she tightened her innermost muscles, feeling the delicious hardness of him buried inside her.

Roman lowered his face into the crook of her neck, groaning low in his throat as though he was in pain. 'Oh, yes. Oh, God, yes.'

Olivia smiled, moving against him and feeling his breathing quicken in response. Suddenly he moved over her, his body arching slowly to press more firmly against her. She looked up into his eyes and somehow knew just what he needed.

He moved her thighs high on his waist, spreading her wide so that he could thrust right to the hilt. She gasped in pleasure, her hands on his chest as he braced himself on his forearms above her. His rhythm was deep and purposeful as he moved over her. He was powerful and entirely lost in his own pleasure.

Release reached them both at the same time, crashing down in wave after wave of pleasure. Olivia closed her eyes as the last of the ripples flowed through her, feeling the mattress move as Roman lay himself down heavily beside her.

CHAPTER NINE

ROMAN LAY STILL for a long time, his brain working overtime to fight through the heavy fog that always came after orgasm. This was different—heavier, somehow. He had never experienced a climax so intense.

Thoughts of why he should not feel so relaxed threatened the edges of his consciousness but he fought them off. He would analyse the repercussions of what they had just done in the morning, for now he thoroughly intended to repeat the experience just as soon as she was able.

He turned on his side, looking down at her where she lay curled on her side. Her eyes were closed, and for a moment he wondered if she was asleep, but then her lashes fluttered open and he was pinned by that blue-green gaze. Her hair had come undone at some stage, and its long lengths were spread across his sombre grey pillows in all their vibrant red glory. If possible, it looked even redder in that moment.

He reached out, taking a strand in his hands and running his fingers along the length of it. He was suddenly overcome by the realisation that it had been her first time and he had almost taken her in the swimming pool. Thankfully his brain hadn't been too far gone to realise that she deserved an actual bed for such a delicate moment, and that they needed to use protection. He *never* forgot to take precautions.

'I hope that was…satisfactory?' He smiled, a glow of male pride in his chest as he took in the slow smile that spread across her face.

'I never even dreamed that it could be so…' she began, shaking her head. 'Earth-shattering.'

'It isn't always that way.'

He ran a finger down the valley of her breasts, watching the play of light on her flawless skin. He had only just finished making love to her and he yet he couldn't stop touching her.

'I'm glad my first time was with you,' she said softly.

Roman stilled, taking in the look of deep emotion in her eyes. Knowing his own personal warning bells should be ringing at full blast. She was not experienced enough to separate the physical side of what they had just shared from her emotional reaction. And yet even as he told himself to remind her of his rules he found that he himself was having a hard time abiding by them.

He fought the urge to lean in, to kiss her mouth and lay a trail of kisses down her neck. He frowned. Such actions were dangerously close to tenderness. He was not a tender lover—to a virgin or not.

But he cared what she thought of him, that she'd enjoyed her first time—that was entirely normal, wasn't it?

Maybe that was the problem. He had nothing to compare it to, having steered clear of virgins up to now. He had never enjoyed the idea of being a woman's first, of having that much pressure on the act. But now, knowing he was the only one to have touched her, been inside her, heard her scream out in her orgasm…

He wanted more.

It was a dangerous madness, feeling like this. He had always prided himself on remaining detached and aloof from the women he chose to spend time with. They knew he wasn't in it for commitment. They got what they needed and left his bed satisfied as a result.

Olivia sighed deeply and moved so that she lay against his side. Her hand stroked up the inside of his wrist to his elbow and he looked down to see her curiously tracing the thick black band of ink that encircled his forearm.

He didn't think of the tattoo often—it was usually covered up and out of sight. But every now and then he found himself looking at it, thinking of the man who'd branded him, of the *life* that had branded him. And yet he had never had it removed.

'It's a gang tattoo,' he offered, not knowing why he suddenly felt the urge to explain. 'Not my own personal choice of design.'

Her lips formed a delicate little O as her fingers stilled over him. 'From your time in prison?' she asked quietly.

'Long before prison.'

A silence fell between them. Roman wondered if perhaps she was regretting her choice of lover after his revelation, but after a moment she sat up on her elbow, pinning him with her gaze.

'This gang—did they use guns a lot? Is that where your fear stems from?'

Roman frowned, laying his head back against the

pillows as he remembered the events of the day before in painful detail. 'No. That's not where it comes from.'

She seemed suddenly self-conscious. 'I'm sorry if this isn't exactly pillow-talk material. I know you are probably the kind of guy who doesn't like to talk afterwards.'

'I don't,' he said honestly. 'But I can compromise.' He turned smoothly onto his side, so that they were face to face. 'You can ask me *one* question about my past and I will answer it—truthfully.'

Her eyelashes lowered momentarily. 'Who is Sofiya?'

Roman was silent for a moment. Then, 'Sofiya was my little sister,' he said. 'She died a long time ago.'

'Oh, I'm sorry.' Olivia's brow deepened into a frown. 'She must have been very young.'

'Sixteen.' He shrugged. 'It's in the past. Almost twenty years ago.'

'Grief doesn't care about time.' The corners of her lips tilted down sadly. 'My grandmother was buried ten years ago and I still visit her grave often.'

'I have never visited Sofiya's resting place,' Roman said, surprised at how easily the words spilled from him. 'Her parents despised me.'

Olivia sat up slightly. '*Her* parents? Not yours?'

'We were both abandoned by our birth mother at a very young age. Sofiya was a tiny blonde cherub with big blue eyes. She was adopted very quickly. I was not.'

'Oh…' She sat up slightly, looking down at him with concern.

He hated the feeling of being so vulnerable, and yet somehow he was unable to stop the words from coming once they'd started. 'Unlike my sister, I wasn't the most appealing child. I always had too much to say. It became a part of me to cause as much trouble as I could manage.'

He frowned, remembering the uncontrollable rage that had filled him as a child. He had broken toys, furniture—even bones on a few occasions.

'I was fuelled by anger and hatred. I was kept at the orphanage until I grew too big to contain. After I ran away for the third time they stopped trying to bring me back.'

'That is when you became homeless?'

Roman nodded. But the truth was he had never known a home. The only difference was that once he'd left the orphanage he'd had the added struggle of finding a safe place to sleep at night.

'I can't imagine how that was for a young boy.'

'I was thirteen—practically a man.' A low, harsh laugh escaped his lips as he thought of his gangly young self, so cocky and self-assured. 'When the local thugs saw the size of me they asked me to run errands. I didn't mind that they were criminals. They took me in…gave me a warm bed. One of the guys even bought me shoes.'

His chest tightened at the memory. He had worn those shoes until his feet had burst out of them. Then he had gone out and stolen himself a brand-new pair.

'I was thin and fast. They used me to climb through windows and vents and such on jobs. I felt very important.'

Olivia was quiet as he spoke on, telling her of his ascent into the criminal gangs of St Petersburg. To her credit, she did not react in any way other than to ask a question or to clarify a point. She just listened.

She listened when he told her of Alexi—the father of 'the brotherhood', as he'd called it. She nodded as he told her how, when he had grown broader and stronger, he had advanced to being a part of the main crew. They'd held up banks, intercepted cash in transit and generally just taken whatever they wanted. More than once he felt the old shame seep in, threatening to silence him, but she urged him on.

'This Alexi guy…he sounds dangerous,' she said softly, tracing a small circle on his chest as she watched him.

Roman thought for a moment of the man who had simultaneously given him everything and then torn his life to pieces.

'I wanted nothing more than for Alexi to be proud of me. He was the only dominant male figure I had ever known. It made me feel needed, validated—I don't know.' He shook his head, uncomfortable with the conversation all of a sudden. He didn't like to think of Alexi, of the hold he had once had on him.

'I think that was only natural. You were easily groomed—an easy target. You were vulnerable and he exploited that.'

'I never truly relaxed into the so-called brotherhood, and Alexi could see that. I had seen how quickly some of their drunken brawls escalated and I made a point to always stay sober. More than once he questioned my loyalty using violence.'

'Is *that* where your issue with guns stems from?' she asked quietly.

Roman frowned, realising he had gone off on a tangent. How had he kept on speaking for this length of time? Usually talking of the brotherhood and its fearless leader was enough to send him into silence for days, but something about Olivia had kept him talking...opening up.

Unwelcome memories assaulted his brain. Memories of the last night he had seen Alexi. Of the blood and the outrage and that pair of terrified, lifeless, baby-blue eyes.

Suddenly he couldn't talk any more. He stood up, walking to the terrace doors to look out at the night beyond. He shivered, feeling a cold that was not actually in the air but inside him. Ingrained in him.

Olivia bit her bottom lip hard as Roman remained completely silent by the doors and then watched as he walked into the bathroom, shutting the door behind him with finality. She had pushed too hard—her curiosity had been too overbearing. He was likely already planning the best way to tell her to leave.

He had made it perfectly clear that he was a one-night-only, no-snuggling type of guy—and here she was, initiating a psychotherapy session.

She lay back, throwing one arm across her face in mortification. She had just made love with this physically gifted specimen of a man and still she kept digging deeper, wanting more from him than he had warned her to expect. Trying to peek under his armour.

She angrily swung her legs over the side of the bed and stood, feeling her inner muscles throb with just the barest hint of exertion. She didn't feel too different, she thought with a frown. A little sore, perhaps, but not monumentally transformed as she had expected.

Still, it had been...utterly perfect.

Maybe it was best that it ended this way. She would

arrange to have a helicopter pick her up in the morning and that would be it. No awkward morning-after encounter, no hurt feelings. They both knew what this was, that it could be nothing more. She was completely fine with that.

But still some small naïve part of her made her linger for a moment outside the bathroom door until she heard the shower turned on. He couldn't have sent a clearer signal if he'd shouted the words *Go away!* at the top of his lungs.

The night was over.

She returned to her bedroom in darkness, not bothering to turn on any lights as she slipped in between the cool white covers and let stillness wash over her. Her mind raced, thoughts of what tomorrow might bring seeping through to her consciousness as the afterglow of her one experience of lovemaking dimmed.

Was one night of perfect lovemaking with a man of her choosing really enough to carry her through a lifetime of a loveless marriage?

As her exhausted brain admitted defeat and she drifted into half-sleep, she imagined what her wedding day might look like. Only in her mind the man at the top of the aisle was Roman. Devastating in a dark tuxedo as he took her hand and professed his eternal love for her.

All of a sudden her dream shifted to their wedding night, becoming infinitely more erotic. She sighed as he leaned in and pressed his lips to hers, the scent of him so familiar and overwhelming it was as if she could actually feel the heat of his skin pressing against her.

'You are so beautiful…'

His voice rasped near her ear, sending shivers down her spine and even lower.

Her eyes snapped open. 'Roman?'

He was draped across her, the scent of his shower fresh and warm on the air as his mouth laid a trail of kisses down the side of her neck.

'You left without giving me a chance to say goodbye,' he said, a dark glint in his eye as he moved lower to take one of her breasts into his mouth.

'You were the one who left.' She exhaled on a slow hiss as his teeth grazed her skin. 'I thought you were a one-night-only kind of guy.'

A wicked smile spread over his dark features as he poised himself over her, one hand snaking a path down her abdomen to slip between her thighs.

'The night isn't over yet, Princess.'

His kisses became more heated as his fingers took her higher and higher towards climax. Before she could completely shatter, he turned onto his back and urged her to straddle him.

'You will still be tender... I don't want to hurt you,' he rasped, his breath coming hard and fast, evidence of his arousal.

Olivia moved over him so that her breasts grazed the smattering of dark hair on his chest. She was clumsy at first, uncertain in her own movements as she poised her body over the sizeable length of him. He was rock-hard and already sheathed, waiting for her. She took a moment to slide the tip of him against her most sensitive spot, enjoying the sensation of molten heat that spread through her.

She repeated the motion a few times, wondering if he would grow impatient and take over himself. He didn't. Even as his rigid jaw showed the extent of his control he remained still, allowing her this moment of exploration.

'I'm not quite sure if I'll be any good at this,' she said uncertainly, lifting herself so that he was poised at her entrance.

'I'm right here, holding you.' He ran his large hands down her back, cupping her buttocks with possession as he guided her.

Her body stretched around him as she took him deep inside her in one smooth movement. The barest hint of discomfort faded quickly to an impatient need to roll her hips, to ride him and increase the delicious pressure she could feel with each movement.

'Is that...good?' she asked, her breath coming faster as arousal pooled and tightened inside her.

'You are driving me insane in the best possible way,' he groaned, his eyes never leaving hers. 'Don't come yet. Not until I'm right there with you.'

Olivia tried to slow down, to control her movements and somehow hold off the mounting climax that seemed ready to shatter her entire being at any second. He held her gaze, his hands gripping her hips as he began thrusting upwards slowly, in time with her.

Their rhythm was so smooth, so gentle, and yet somehow it was filled with a barely restrained madness as they both rose closer and closer to climax. Roman's breath fanned hard and fast against her cheek as she leaned forward, her breasts crushed against his chest. His hands moved up her back to hold her close, a deep primal groan escaping his lips as he slowed down even further and moved deeper inside her.

Olivia gasped at the overwhelming intensity of

being so absolutely cocooned in his strength, and then the intense friction tipped her over the edge and she fell headlong into an orgasm that seemed to ripple through every inch of her body.

As she fell she felt a tightening in her throat, and prayed he wouldn't see the sheen of moisture in her eyes as she watched him lose control entirely beneath her.

Roman kissed her neck, growling something deeply erotic in his native tongue as the muscles of his abdomen began to ripple with the force of his own orgasm.

Afterwards, as she listened to his breathing deepen with sleep, she wondered if she had ever felt closer to another human being in her entire life.

The thought made her feel sad and grateful all at once. She had got her wish, without a doubt. He had made her first time the most sensual, real experience of her life.

His long, hard body was partly covered, but she still let her gaze sweep over him in the darkness, lingering on his features. His face was transformed in sleep, the hard lines of his mouth completely relaxed. It made him seem younger…more carefree. It dawned on her that she had never seen him look at peace. Here, in sleep, Roman the great and powerful master of security, was completely vulnerable.

The thought of returning to the palace, to her own empty bed, was suddenly inconceivable. And even worse was the thought of sleeping alongside another man.

Marrying another man.

Her throat tightened painfully with the force of her emotion. Roman would not offer her any more than this night—she knew that. He was not the marrying kind, no matter what she suddenly hoped. He was not even the relationship kind.

But as she lay staring up at the play of shadows on the ceiling she knew one thing with more certainty than she had ever known anything in her life.

She would not marry the Sheikh.

When she awoke the bed was empty beside her in the early-morning light. Ignoring the sting of loss, she grabbed a white robe and stepped out onto the terrace, taking a moment simply to breathe and take in the gorgeous view of the bay spread out below.

Her hair was a nest of tangles, and she was in dire need of a shower, but for once she had no formal breakfast to attend, no official functions. She could stand here all morning if she chose, enjoying the last few hours of her freedom.

Roman would expect her to leave today, and that was perfectly understandable.

She thought of his revelations last night, the deep, dark secrets he'd shared, and wondered if he would regret sharing so much now that their night together was done.

He had told her only briefly of his life in St Petersburg. Of the orphan who had been abandoned to sleep in cold gutters, but she remembered every word in vivid detail. Every little piece of the puzzle he had revealed that made him what he was.

Roman had lived through hell itself. It was no wonder he seemed harsh. The world had hardened him from the moment he was born. He shouldn't have had a chance—and yet he had risen from his old life, determined and hungry for better. He had created his own empire without a single care for his social class or his chequered past.

He was the master of his own destiny.

Here, in the rosy glow of dawn, she felt utterly transformed simply by having known him. She laughed at her own thoughts. Romantic, indeed, or maybe simply foolish. Perhaps all virgins felt this way about their first lover?

How would he react to the news once he found out that her marriage was not going ahead? She imagined he would be frustrated with her—with himself. He would blame it all on their brief affair.

But, truly, Olivia wasn't sure her decision was completely down to their night together. On some level she had known she was not destined for a loveless marriage from the moment her father had thrust the idea upon her.

No amount of loyalty to Monteverre would outweigh the value she needed to feel in herself. Roman had made her see that, somehow.

She told herself that it didn't bother her that he was completely unaffected by their time together. She was not going to read anything into last night, and nor would she expect anything more from their liaison. He had made it very clear that he was not the kind of guy who slept with the same woman twice.

CHAPTER TEN

ROMAN HAD TOLD Jorge to take the day off, to ensure them some privacy, wanting as little intrusion as possible so that he could deal with the aftermath of their night together.

Olivia arrived down to breakfast dressed in pink. The dress had the kind of high waist and flowing, knee-length bell-shaped skirt that made her appear like something straight from a vintage movie.

She was breathtaking.

Her eyes were shuttered and her smile forced as she sat at the table across from him. The silence was heavy and uncomfortable, and his mind scrambled to find something to break the tension. In the end he accepted that there was simply nothing to say.

To his amazement, Olivia demolished two full plates of fresh fruit and a cream-drizzled pastry. She moaned as she devoured her last bite of pastry, looking up to find his eyes trained on her.

'I was hungry,' she said, a light blush on her cheeks.

'I've seen prison inmates eat with more decorum,' he found himself saying playfully. 'One night with me and you've completely forgotten how to behave like a princess.'

Her eyes widened at his mention of last night, as though he had broken some unwritten rule by acknowledging that it had happened.

She sat back in her seat, a smile crossing her lips as she met his eyes boldly. 'Whatever will my subjects think?'

Roman raised a brow. 'That you've been taken down the path to ruin by a disreputable mongrel.'

'Mongrel?' She looked both amused and shocked.

'You come from a world where breeding is everything, after all.'

'Have we suddenly become *Lady and the Tramp*?' She laughed.

'I have no idea what that is,' he said honestly, smiling at the look of horrified surprise on her face.

'I can't believe you've never seen such a classic. It's wonderful—the lady dog comes from a fancy home and gets lost, and the tramp dog saves her?'

'You are likening me to a tramp dog?' He raised one brow in disbelief. 'I'm flattered.'

'*You* likened yourself to a mongrel—not me!' she exclaimed. 'It's not *my* fault that my brain associates everything with movies.'

'Film and television were not a regular part of my childhood,' he said, disliking where this conversation was headed. 'But let me guess: they all live happily ever after at the end?'

'Yes, exactly.' She smiled.

'That's why I don't waste my time on movies. It's not reality.'

'Well, of *course* it's not reality.' She laughed. 'That's what makes them an escape.'

Roman stood, gathering their plates and placing

them less than gently into the sink. 'You spend far too much of your time escaping real life—you know that?' he said, knowing he had hit a nerve when he looked up and saw both of her hands balled into fists on the tabletop.

'You're being cruel now, and I have no idea why.'

'This is not cruelty, Olivia,' he said calmly. 'You have no idea what true cruelty is. What true hardship is, even. You dislike it when people put real life in front of you—that's your problem.'

She shook her head slowly. 'I have no idea why you're being like this right now. We were just talking about a movie.'

'Life is not like the movies, and the sooner you realise it the better!' He raised his voice, surprising himself with the force of his outburst.

Olivia stood, closing the distance between them. 'I may not have known the kind of hardship that you have experienced in your life, but that does not negate the fact that I have feelings too.'

'I thought it was clear that last night was not about feelings,' he said stiffly.

'And yet here you stand, shouting at me, when I was perfectly prepared to leave here on good terms.' She shook her head. 'It's probably best that I wait outside until my helicopter arrives.'

'You are leaving?' he said, the words tasting like sawdust in his mouth.

'I called the palace first thing this morning. They are sending someone to get me.' She nodded, moving to the table to pick up her coffee cup before returning to place it in the sink.

Even with her perfect posture and impeccably

coiffed hair she seemed quite at ease, clearing up after herself. Far from a domesticated goddess, but still not too far above herself to consider leaving the mess for him to clean.

He thought of their conversations the evening before, of her talk of charity work. She was not the pampered royal he'd accused her of being and it was high time he admitted it to himself.

It was easy to place her in that box—to see her as stuck up and untouchable. It made her less real. But here she was, the woman who had shattered something inside him with her lovemaking last night, all too real.

And all too ready to leave him.

He knew then why he was being cruel. He simply wasn't ready to give this up. To give *her* up. Not yet. And yet he knew it had already gone on too long as it was.

He was the worst kind of bastard, he thought darkly. Khal had trusted him with this—had entrusted him with the care of the woman he hoped to spend the rest of his life with. Whether the union was cold and political or not, it did not matter. He had rationalised his actions simply because their passion had been mutual. He had got lost in the novelty of feeling so utterly out of control.

Olivia deserved more than this. She deserved more than a brief fling with a man like him. And that was all he could offer her. Once the passion wore off he would only end up hurting her when he left. Roman Lazarov did not *do* relationships. He did not make declarations of love and commitment or plan lifetimes together.

In the past he had never been good at returning the things he had stolen. He refused to repeat his mistakes.

And yet the idea of Khal knowing what had happened made him balk. Not for himself, but for Olivia. She deserved his protection.

'I'm coming with you,' he said, surprising himself.

Olivia turned around, her eyes wide with confusion. 'There is no need to escort me home, noble as it seems.'

'This is not about being noble—it's about being honest with Khal.'

Guilt entered her expression at the mention of the Sheikh's name. His gut churned at the realisation that by rights he should be displaying the same emotions himself, seeing as he had spent the past twelve hours in bed with the woman his best friend hoped to marry.

'Do you honestly want us to tell him about last night?' she said with disbelief.

'I will speak to him alone. There is no need for you to see him.' He found himself saying the words— words he had meant to protect her—and yet he could tell by the dark look on her face that they had come out wrong. As usual.

'You presume that I need you to explain on my behalf.' Her gaze seemed to darken as he took a step closer to her. She stood tall. 'I am quite capable of speaking for myself.'

'Clearly you are not. Otherwise none of this would have happened.' Roman shook his head, anger at the whole ridiculous situation coursing through him.

'Feeling some remorse, I see.' She pursed her lips.

'*One* of us should. Do you simply plan to go back and accept his proposal with the heat from my bed barely gone from your skin?'

'Is that actually what you think of me? Do you even know me at *all*?' She was completely still, unnaturally still, like the eerily calm glass of the ocean before a hurricane.

'I'm trying to—God help me. But you're not making it very easy.'

'And just what will you tell him? Seeing as you've got this covered.'

'Whatever needs to be said. Bottom line: he needs to know that we have slept together. I cannot let your marriage go ahead with him in the dark.'

'Bottom line?' Olivia's eyes widened. 'You know that telling him will essentially be ending the engagement before it can even happen? Why the sudden change of heart? Two days ago you were doing everything in your power to make this union go ahead.'

'Do I truly need to explain to you what has changed?'

Olivia's eyes darkened. 'Yes. You do.'

And there it was. The gauntlet, large and heavy, hanging in the tension-charged air between them.

'You spent the night with me, Olivia,' he said. 'I took your virginity.'

'That does not qualify as an explanation.' She bit one side of her lip, taking a few paces away from him before turning back. 'You said it yourself—it was just sex.'

Roman met the unmistakable challenge in her blue-green eyes. He had not lied when he'd told her that sex was not always so intense.

'Sex is never "just sex" when it is one person's first time,' he said quietly, knowing he was being a complete coward.

'I think that is up to me to decide.'

'You wouldn't need to decide anything if I had done the right thing and walked away last night.'

'How utterly male of you to think that.' She rolled her eyes. 'Spending the night in your bed was *my* choice too, Roman. I wanted it just as much. I wanted *you*.' Olivia took a step towards him, the sunlight glowing on her Titian waves. 'You did not *take* my virginity. You can't take something that is given freely. I took last night just as much as you did.'

She looked so beautiful at that moment—all strength and feminine power. Hadn't he told her she needed to let this woman be free?

The unmistakable sound of helicopter blades in the distance intruded on the moment. Roman looked out of the windows and sure enough a scarlet-coloured chopper was coming in from the coast, the gold crest of Monteverre emblazoned along its side.

I wanted you.

Her words echoed in his mind as he analysed his own motivation for wanting to tell Khal of their night together. He knew that telling his friend would stop the engagement, knowing Khal as he did. He still wanted her. He was not fool enough to deny the fact. One night was just not enough when it came to Olivia. She was the best and the worst thing that he had ever stolen in his life, and the bastard in him wanted to keep her here until they were both truly done with each other.

Was he really that selfish? To manipulate her situation and push Khal out of the picture simply so that he could get her out of his system?

He ran one hand through the short crop of his hair, trying to make sense of his own thoughts.

'What if I told you that I plan to refuse the marriage?'

Her voice was quiet from behind him, strangely uncertain after the power of her speech moments before.

'You said yourself that your loyalty to your country is important.'

'Yes, but that was before I realised how it felt to take control of my own life for once.' She bit her bottom lip. 'Being with you…it's made me realise that I can have more. That I want more.'

'I can't give you what you want,' he said plainly, panicking at the look of open emotion on her face. 'If you plan on placing your entire future on the hope of something more between us then you are more naïve than I originally thought.'

She flinched at his harsh words and he felt like the worst kind of bastard. Hearing her speak of their time together so tenderly did strange things to his chest. As if with every word she uttered, bands grew tighter around his lungs. And it made him want to lash out with words to make her stop. To make her see him for what he was.

It was ridiculous, and immature, and yet he could no more stop himself from reacting that way than he could stop his brain from seeing guns where they didn't exist.

Olivia fought the tightness in her throat, refusing to let him see how deeply his words had cut. She met his gaze evenly. 'I will be returning to the palace alone. I trust that you will respect my privacy when it comes to last night. I should at least have the right to that from you.'

'I never said I didn't respect you,' he said harshly.

'Good. We have an understanding.'

She kept her voice even, walking over to the terrace doors to watch as the helicopter finished its landing and a familiar assistant exited the door, making her way towards the villa.

'This is goodbye, then,' she said, not wanting to turn to look at him but knowing she would regret it for ever if she didn't. She felt anger, hot and heavy, burning in her chest. 'Thank you for allowing me to be one of the many women in your bed.'

His eyes narrowed, a cynical snarl appearing on his lips. 'Indeed. I will always have the pleasure of knowing that when it comes to you I was the first.'

'You are using the past tense already—how honest of you.'

'I have been nothing but honest with you about the kind of man I am,' he said harshly.

'Last night… I just thought that things seemed different somehow. That *we* seemed different.' She spoke calmly, trying and failing to hide the hint of insecurity in her voice.

'Everything seems different in the heat of passion, Printsessa.'

The silence that followed might only have lasted a matter of seconds, but to Olivia it felt like an eternity. In her mind she willed him to say more. Even a hint that he felt something more would be enough. Had she truly imagined that last night was momentous for them both?

And then he turned from her. Every step that he took across the kitchen seemed to hammer into her heart. Dampening down any flicker of hope she might have had.

She listened as his footsteps echoed across the marble tiles. Did he pause for just a split second in the doorway or did she imagine it? For a moment she thought he had taken a breath, preparing to speak. But then his steps kept going, out into the hallway, echoing as he moved further and further away from her.

She let out a breath that she hadn't even realised she'd been holding. The air shuddered through a gap in her teeth, like a balloon deflating and making a spectacular nosedive towards the ground. It was the ultimate heartbreak…knowing she had been just another woman in his bed.

She wanted to be *the* woman. The *only* woman.

But hadn't he made it abundantly clear that he would never be that kind of man? Was she really such a clichéd, naïve little virgin that she had fallen head over heels in love with him and expected him to do the same?

Typical that there wasn't a drop of vodka on the damned boat when he needed it.

Roman threw the empty bottle down hard on the glass bar-top, feeling it crack and shatter in his hand as it hit the surface.

'*Chert voz'mi!*'

He held his hand over the sink as the first drops of blood began to fall. The cuts were not deep, just surface wounds.

'*Damn* whoever is in charge of stocking the damned bar.'

'That would be me, sir.'

Roman turned to see Jorge in the open doorway, the man's face filled with concern.

'I came to see if you want me to close up the house.'

'Do whatever you like. I won't staying around long enough to check.'

'I see that Olivia has left us,' Jorge said tentatively.

Roman lowered his voice. 'I do not want to speak about Olivia. I want to relax and enjoy the rest of my vacation on my damned boat—alone.'

'With vodka?' Jorge added.

'Yes. With vodka. Is there a problem with that?' Roman spat. 'I am a grown man and you are not my father.'

'No. No, I am not,' Jorge said, a hint of sadness in his voice. 'But you have made it clear in the past that you at least see me as a friend of sorts.'

Roman grunted, wrapping a strip of linen carelessly around his injured hand.

'Can I speak frankly with you?' Jorge asked.

'You always do.'

The older man half smiled, crossing his arms and taking a deep breath before speaking. 'I think that you are hurting right now.'

'Believe me, I've had worse in my lifetime. I'll heal.'

'I'm not talking about the cuts on your hands.'

'Neither am I.'

'The Roman I know would never concede defeat so easily. You are not the kind of stupid man who would let pride stand in the way of what he wants.'

'Just because I want something, it doesn't mean I should have it. I have learnt that lesson in the past, Jorge. She is meant for a better man than me. A *good* man.'

'She loves you.'

'No. She is in love with the *idea* of love and nothing more.'

'I watched her get into that helicopter and, believe me, I know a heartbroken woman when I see one.'

'Well, that's not my fault. I did not hide from her the man that I am.'

'The man that you are would never come railing into his liquor cabinet unless he was deeply hurt by something. Or someone.'

'Jorge, you really must add psychoanalysis to your list of skills.'

'Tell me I'm wrong,' the other man said. 'Tell me she doesn't mean anything to you and I will fill that bar with vodka and send you on your way.'

'She is nothing to me,' he said the words, willing himself to believe them. Willing himself to ignore the burning pit of anger in his stomach.

'So if Khal marries her you will stand by his side and wish them well? I can see it now. You can visit them each summer in Zayyar. If you are lucky, their children might even call you Uncle.'

Roman's eyes snapped up to meet the gaze of his all too knowing housekeeper.

'*There.* That's all the reaction I needed to see.'

'Just because I feel the marriage is the wrong choice for both of them, it doesn't mean there is something deeper going on. I know Khal, and I know he would not be happy with a woman like Olivia. She is too adventurous, too unpredictable. She wants to see the world, to be surprised by life. Not trade one palace prison for another.'

'And have you said any of this to the woman herself?'

Roman sat down on the bar stool, pulling the linen tighter on his hand and feeling the sting of pain that came with it. Jorge was right. He had not told Olivia how he felt about the marriage. Not honestly. He had spent half his time with her trying to convince her to marry Khal, and the other half trying to make her forget.

Was it really surprising that she had run from him

again at the first chance? From the start he had handled her badly.

Women like Olivia were out of his league. She was too open, too caring and kind-hearted for a cold, unfeeling bastard like him. She deserved love. She deserved the happy-ever-after that she craved. And if he couldn't give it to her himself then he would make damned sure that she had a decent chance of finding it elsewhere.

'Shall I have the boat readied for departure?' Jorge asked hopefully.

Roman nodded once, watching as his housekeeper practically skipped from the room. He really should give that man a raise, he thought darkly as he moved to look out at the waves crashing against the lighthouse in the distance.

The marriage would not go ahead—not if he had anything to do with it.

CHAPTER ELEVEN

THE FIRST THING that Roman noticed as he entered the Sheikh's penthouse hotel suite was the utter stillness of the place. A single palace guard welcomed him inside before returning to his post outside the doorway. There was no butler to accept his coat or announce his presence—in fact no one at all roamed the halls as he passed through from room to room.

He had almost given up when finally he reached a large dining room that looked out over the lush green mountainscape of Monteverre's famous rolling hills. Khal stood alone at the head of the long dining table, his back turned as he stared out at the view.

Roman cleared his throat, feeling as though he had interrupted a moment of quiet meditation and wishing he had called ahead of his arrival.

'Roman. Now, this *is* a surprise,' Khal said, surprise filtering into his dark features as recognition dawned.

But Roman had not missed the mask of dark stillness that had been on his friend's face. That look bothered him deeply, and yet he knew that if he asked his concern would be met with a stone wall.

They were much alike, he and Khal.

'I need to speak with you,' Roman started, finding the words much more difficult than he had anticipated.

Truthfully, he was unsure where to begin. He had come here, all guns blazing, ready to rock the boat and make sure this ridiculous marriage did not go ahead. But how exactly did he tell his best friend that he had not only broken a rather important promise, but that he had done it in the worst way possible? He had promised to bring the Princess back to Monteverre to take her place as Khal's future wife, and instead...

Well, instead he had found himself consumed by a passion and a need so intense it had bordered on obsession.

He had not stopped thinking of Olivia in the few hours they had been apart. Memories of her assaulted him at every turn. If he closed his eyes he could almost smell the warm vanilla scent of her hair as it had lain spread across his pillows. He could almost hear her throaty laughter. She consumed him like no other woman ever had.

In fact, it was a mark of the strength of his feelings for her that he chose *not* to fight for her.

He was not here to lay claim to her.

He was here to set her free.

Khal sat heavily in one of the high-backed chairs, putting his feet up on the marble tabletop and surveying Roman with one raised brow. 'By all means, speak.'

'The Princess is the wrong choice for your bride.' He met Khal's gaze purposefully, making sure that there was no mistaking the seriousness of his tone.

'You sound quite sure.'

'I am. And I would like you to take my concern

into account. There are things more important in life than politics.'

'Such as friendship, perhaps?' the Sheikh suggested, a strange hint of cynicism in his voice.

'I was thinking more along the lines of personal happiness.'

'I'm touched, Roman. Truly.'

'I'm trying to do the right thing here. To stop you from making a mistake that will last the rest of your life.'

'If you were doing the right thing you would be telling me the truth. You see, you need not worry about my personal happiness at all, Lazarov. Princess Olivia has already made her refusal of marriage to me quite clear.'

Roman felt his chest tighten painfully. 'Olivia? She came to you?'

'Not long before you, actually. Strangely, when she spoke of you she bore the same look on her face as you do right now when I mention her name.'

Hot guilt burned low in his stomach as his friend stood up and met his eyes with a cold detached evenness he had never witnessed before.

'I'm trying to control my temper here, Roman, because I don't want to jump to conclusions. But I'm struggling. Three months of planning. The future of two kingdoms hanging in the balance. And after a few days with you she's ready to give everything up.'

Roman remained silent for a moment, taking in the glint of barely controlled temper visible in his oldest friend's eyes. He knew he should walk away before things became any more heated. Olivia had already refused the marriage—he had no reason to be here.

But something held him rooted to the spot. In his

mind all he could picture was King Fabian, planning Olivia's life for months before informing her of her impending engagement. Using an innocent woman as a pawn in his own political games. The man was cold enough to practically sell his own daughter to the highest bidder—as though she were a commodity rather than his own flesh and blood. It made the proud, possessive street thug inside him roar to life and demand justice.

'Tell me something,' he said calmly. 'In your three months of planning did you ever think to speak to the woman herself to see if she *wanted* a political marriage?'

He watched Khal's mouth harden into a tight line as they stood toe to toe in the utterly silent dining room. There were no onlookers here, no palace guards or servants. They did not need to maintain any level of propriety. Right now they were just two men.

'I will ask *you* this question, because I deemed it inappropriate to ask the lady herself.' Khal's voice was a low whisper. 'Did you sleep with her, Roman?'

'Yes. I did,' Roman said the words harshly, feeling the air crackle with tension between them. 'And I am not going to apologise. Not to you, or to her damned father, or anybody.'

'Well, I'm glad to see you showing some remorse.'

'She is a *person*, Khal,' Roman spat. 'Not mine or yours. She can make her own damned choices—which you would know if you had ever bothered to treat her as such.'

'Right now this has nothing to do with her and *everything* to do with you,' Khal snarled, taking a step forward and jamming one finger hard against Roman's shoulder. 'You just couldn't control yourself—admit it. You wanted a woman and so you had her. Does the Princess *know* that she is just another notch on your bedpost? Or perhaps you are both just as selfish and impulsive as each other?'

Roman surged forward. Their noses were now mere inches apart. 'She is *nothing* like me,' he said coldly. 'She is kind and giving and she deserves more in a man than either of us could ever offer her.'

He paused, watching the anger drain from Khal's face as his brows furrowed with surprise. With a deep, shuddering breath he stepped away, turning to face the window.

A long moment of deathly silence passed before he heard Khal exhale slow and hard behind him, a slight whistle escaping his lips. 'I don't believe this… You are in love with her.'

Roman braced one hand on the window ledge, looking out and seeing nothing. 'Don't be a fool. You said it yourself—women have only ever served one purpose for me.'

Khal's low whistle of laughter sounded across the room. 'I never thought I'd see this day. Roman Lazarov—brought to the edge of his infamous personal control by love.'

Roman shook his head, turning to take in the look of amused wonderment on the Sheikh's dark features. 'I am not prone to the sentiment. I simply believe Olivia has been treated poorly and I want to see it made right.'

'You poor, naïve fool. Sadly, love is not something we can choose to feel or not to feel. Trust me—I know.'

'I am not like you, Khal. I am not made for family life.' He took a deep breath, knowing it was finally time to say out loud the words that he had wanted to say for a long time. 'Look at my history with protecting the women I care for. My sister, your wife… I break things. I always have. I am simply not the kind of man she needs me to be.'

The mention of his late wife was usually enough to put an end to any conversation, but Khal surprised him, standing and placing a hand heavily on his shoulder.

'It was not your fault that Priya was killed. I have told you this time and time again. Just as it was not your fault that Sofiya was killed. You cannot take on the blame for everything that goes wrong around you.'

'What about Zayyar?' Roman said, shaking his head. 'This marriage was part of your great plan and now it's all gone to crap.'

'Perhaps not,' Khal said cryptically. 'I am not completely out of options just yet. Once Olivia ran away, the King and I discussed a possible fallback plan.'

Roman was silent for a moment. 'The youngest Princess?'

Khal shrugged. 'If she is willing, so be it. If not, I will retreat and regroup—as always.'

Roman nodded, glad that all hope was not lost for the two nations.

Olivia stood in her dressing room and placed the elegant emerald tiara upon her head for the last time. She met her own eyes in the mirror with a mixture of sadness and excitement, knowing that after tonight everything would change.

And yet everything had already changed for her.

Would anyone notice that everything inside her

had undergone a massive transformation in the past few days?

With sudden momentous clarity she realised that for the first time in her life she truly didn't care. From tomorrow she would be giving up her right to succeed to the throne voluntarily, and making the leap into actually leading Mimi's Foundation. She was done with being a pretty face who smiled and waved. The time had come for her to use her own two hands to make the difference she craved.

Perhaps once all of this was over she might appreciate this moment more—the sudden power she felt as she left her suite and began to descend the grand staircase on the way to take her life back into her own hands. But at that moment she felt neither powerful nor relieved.

She had given her virginity and her heart to a man who had repeatedly warned her that he would treasure neither. She knew now that romantic souls could not simply choose to behave otherwise. She could not switch off the part of herself that yearned to feel loved, no matter how much she willed herself to.

A lifetime of training had taught her how to relax her facial muscles into a polite mask of indifference, even while emotions threatened her composure. Harsh decisions would likely need to be made, and comfort zones abandoned. But for the first time in her twenty-six years she was not worried about the unknown.

Olivia couldn't recall the grand palace ballroom ever looking more beautiful. As she descended the long staircase into the crowd of guests below she reminded herself to smile and hold herself tall and proud.

Perhaps one day in the far future she might look

back on this night and yearn for a moment like this. But even as the tug of uncertainty threatened she pushed it away. She had made her decision and the time had come to put herself first.

The Sheikh had not been half as forbidding as she had anticipated—in fact he had seemed more pensive than anything as she had carefully outlined her reasons for refusing his proposal. His gaze had seemed knowing as he had enquired about Roman's treatment of her, but perhaps that was just her own sense of guilt.

She had her own reasons for keeping her affair with Roman private. She wanted to treasure her time with him, not have it sullied by the judgement of others. Either way, she had taken her power back and it felt great. The marriage would not be going ahead.

But she was not naïve enough to think that the hardest part was over.

Even as the thought crossed her mind she looked up to see her father watching her from across the ballroom. They had not yet formally met, but by now she assumed he would have spoken with the Sheikh. He would know that she had refused the proposal and he would be planning his punishment for her supposed betrayal.

Let him plan, she thought with a solemn shake of her head. He had no control over her. Not any more.

A commotion near the entrance caught her eye and she looked up to the top of the staircase to see a man pushing past the guards to descend the steps with ease. Two Royal Zayyari guards in crisp white and purple uniforms flanked him, holding off the Monteverre palace guards with ease and forcing them to stand down.

Roman.

Her mind went completely blank as the man she loved advanced towards her, his powerful frame accentuated by a perfectly tailored tuxedo.

'What are you doing here?' she blurted, so taken off balance by his appearance that it made her insides shake.

'It's good to see you too, *milaya moya*.'

His voice was like a balm to her soul. She hadn't realised how much her silly lovesick heart had yearned to hear it again. Just one more time. It had barely been twenty-four hours since she had left Isla Arista, and yet it felt like a lifetime since she had stood in front of him. Since she had looked into his slate-grey eyes as he had broken her heart with all the practice of a pro.

He opened his mouth to speak, but was cut off by the booming voice of her father as he advanced upon them from the other side of the room.

'Guards! Get this criminal out of my palace this instant!' King Fabian was livid, his cheeks a bright puce as he came to a stop a few steps away from where Roman stood.

The ballroom seemed to have become very quiet all of a sudden, and Olivia was thankful that the room was only half full as the guests had only just started to arrive.

'King Fabian—I was hoping I would see you tonight.' Roman's eyes narrowed, his shoulders straightening with sudden purpose.

Olivia reached out as Roman took a step towards her father, her hand on his arm stilling his movements. 'This is my fight, not yours,' she said, steeling herself as she turned to her father.

'The Sheikh has said that you refused his proposal

after your little trip with this thug,' King Fabian spat. 'Judging by the lovesick puppy expression on his face, I can take a good guess as to why.'

Roman snarled, but remained dutifully silent.

'Father, I had planned to have this conversation at a better time,' she said, looking around to see that the palace guards had descended to herd the guests to the other side of the room, offering the royal family some privacy.

'There is nothing you can say to save yourself now, girl.' Her father shook his head sadly. 'I hope he's worth giving up your place in this family.'

'He has nothing to do with me giving up my place,' she said, as Roman frowned. 'Well, he does—but not in the way that you think.'

She took a deep breath, facing her father head-on.

'By giving up my right to succeed to the throne I am free of your control. That's worth more to me than being a princess ever could be.'

Roman reached out to touch her arm, 'Olivia, you don't have to do this.'

'I do. You see, my father has made more life-altering decisions on my behalf than this one.' She looked back at her father, noting his gaze darken. 'Such as when I inherited sole ownership of my grandmother's foundation ten years ago and he had me sign away my rights to him. At sixteen years old I didn't understand the repercussions. But now I do. And I know that by stepping out from under your thumb I'll get to take control of my own destiny for once and truly start helping people.'

'You can't do that.' King Fabian laughed cruelly. 'You can't simply walk away from this life.'

'I already have, Father,' she said sadly. 'I've been in

contact with external advisors over the past few months to discuss the legalities. Once I relinquish any claim I have to the throne the foundation goes back into my name alone. Just as Mimi wished it to be.'

She hated it that her own father could look at her with such open disgust simply because she had chosen to go against his wishes.

Her own personal happiness did not matter to him.

Roman's eyes had widened as he listened to the exchange but he did not speak for her again. Nor did he attempt to interrupt as Olivia finished her conversation with her father and simply turned and walked away.

He took a moment to stand toe to toe with His Majesty, King Fabian. The urge to say everything he wished to say was so intense it consumed him. But Olivia had handled the situation with all the style and grace of the Princess she truly was. There was nothing he could add that wouldn't ruin it.

And so he walked away, following the woman he loved and ignoring the slew of vulgar curses in Catalan shouted in his wake.

He followed her in the direction of the outer terrace, instructing the two Zayyari guards Khal had lent him to stand sentry by the doors and make sure they were undisturbed.

Olivia stood with her back to him, staring out at where the moonlight shone across the ornamental pond in the gardens.

He moved to her side, reaching out his hand, needing to touch her. She flinched away and something inside him flinched too, with the hurt of that small movement.

'You're angry with me…of course you are,' he said softly, silently urging her to turn to look at him.

She didn't speak. Instead she wrapped her arms around herself defensively and stared resolutely ahead.

'I came here because I wanted to save you,' he said. 'I never even entertained the possibility that you were completely capable of saving yourself.'

'I'm glad I surprised you,' she said, irony dripping from her words as she turned to face him.

'Olivia…' he breathed. 'I came here to make sure that the marriage would not go ahead. I told myself that I was doing it for *you*, to save you from making a mistake that would last a lifetime. But I know now that I was only lying to myself.'

He braced one hand on the balustrade beside her, making sure to keep some space between them.

'I have never told anyone the things that I told you about my past.' He looked away for a moment, out at the darkness of the water. 'Something about you makes me want to tell you everything. To confide in you and trust you, even though I have spent a life-time trusting no one. It scared me to death, to be quite honest.'

'Oh, Roman…' she said softly, reaching out her hand to touch him.

He raised his hand, holding her off. 'Wait just another moment. I've been thinking all evening about what I would say when I got here, you see.' He inhaled sharply, felt the adrenaline coursing through him. 'I've spent years—decades—blaming myself for my sister's murder at the hands of a man I trusted. She was shot right in front of me by Alexi, to teach me a lesson.'

Olivia's hands covered her mouth and tears filled her eyes. This was all going wrong, he thought. He hadn't meant to upset her—he just needed her to understand.

He stepped forward, taking her hands in his and kissing her knuckles gently. 'No, please don't cry. Anything but that.' He looked deeply into her eyes. 'I'm telling you this because I want you to understand why I'm such a cold, unlovable bastard. That monster wanted me to see love as a weakness. So he could break me down and make me easier to control. I have unknowingly let that lesson stick to me like tar for the past twenty years. I let that man's actions shape me, even from beyond the grave.'

'You are so brave to have overcome that…' She shook her head. 'To have become what you are now…'

'My success is nothing so long as I am alone,' he said simply, taking a breath and steeling himself for possible rejection.

She was utterly breathtaking, her long fiery hair backlit by the glow of the lights in the garden. The dress she wore was utter perfection in emerald silk, but truly she could have worn rags and he would have found her breathtaking. She was beautiful, it was true. But knowing her as he did now…knowing what lay below that surface beauty… It was infinitely more spectacular.

'I came here to tell you that I love you, Olivia,' he said softly, watching as his words resonated. 'I didn't know how much I needed you until I thought of seeing you on another man's arm. *Any* other man. Of watching you become his wife and have his children… I cannot bear the thought of you marrying anyone… other than me.'

* * *

Olivia's heart thumped wildly in her chest as she looked into the solemn, emotion-filled eyes of the man she loved. 'Is that a proposal?' she breathed.

'I hadn't planned on laying it all out like that so quickly,' he said uncertainly. 'I understand if I've done too much. If I've been too cold for you to ever trust me or feel the same way.'

She shook her head, a small smile forming on her lips. 'I trusted you from the moment you offered to take me away with you.'

'Foolish girl.' He smiled, uncertainty still in his eyes.

'But love…?' she said, taking a step closer and running her hand over the lapel of his suit jacket. 'That didn't come until I truly knew you. Knew the man you are underneath all the bravado and the ice. Then I fell in love with you so deeply it took my breath away.'

He finally took her into his arms. His mouth was hot and demanding on hers as his hands held her tightly against him. His embrace filled her with warmth and strength. When he finally pulled away she groaned with protest, never wanting the moment to end.

'Are you sure you want to marry me? Even though I am no longer a princess?' She let a smile seep into her words as he tipped her back in his arms.

Roman shrugged. 'I suppose it's okay to settle for a simple philanthropist as my wife.' He sighed, sweeping his hands down her sides. 'If you're okay with the fact that *I* don't run an entire kingdom?'

She pretended to consider her options for a long moment, until his hands began to move lower on her hips and he pulled her hard against him in mock warning, with playfulness and a joy that mirrored her own in his eyes.

'I love you, Roman Lazarov,' she said solemnly. 'And nothing would make me happier than becoming your wife.'

The kiss that sealed their engagement was one filled with passion and promises. Olivia sighed with soul-deep contentment as she looked up into the face of the man she loved. The man she had chosen for herself.

Her own destiny.

* * * * *

POSSESSED BY
PASSION

BRENDA JACKSON

To the man who will always and forever be the love of my life, Gerald Jackson, Sr.

To all my readers who waited patiently on another novel about those 'Bad News' Steeles, this one is especially for you.

And to my readers who gave me their love, support and understanding as I endured a difficult time in my life, I appreciate you from the bottom of my heart.

Though your beginning was small, yet your latter end would increase abundantly.

Chapter 1

"I understand you became an uncle last night, Tyson. Congratulations."

Tyson Steele glanced over at the man who'd slid onto the bar stool beside him. Miles Wright was a colleague at the hospital where they both worked as surgeons. "Thanks. How did you know?"

"It was in this morning's paper. Quite the article."

Tyson shook his head as he took a sip of his drink. Leave it to his mother, Eden Tyson Steele, to make sure the entire city knew about the birth of her first grandchildren. Twins. A boy and a girl that represented a new generation of Steeles in Phoenix. Everyone was happy for his brother Galen and his wife, Brittany, but his mother was ecstatic beyond reason. Within the past three years, not only had three of her six die-hard bach-

elor sons gotten married, but as of last night she also had
a grandson and granddaughter to boast about.

He wondered if Galen was aware of the article in
this morning's paper since he hadn't mentioned it when
Tyson had spoken to him earlier. Knowing their mother,
Tyson wouldn't be surprised if the announcement appeared in the *New York Times* next. A former international model whose face had graced the covers of
such magazines as *Vogue*, *Cosmo* and *Elle*, his mother
still had connections in a lot of places and had no shame
in using them.

Miles's beeper went off and with an anxious sigh he
said, "Need to run. I got an emergency at the hospital."

"Take care," Tyson told his colleague, who moved
quickly toward the exit door. He then glanced around.
Notorious was a popular nightclub in Phoenix, but not
too many people were here tonight due to the March
Madness championship basketball game being held in
town. Usually, on any given night, Tyson could have
his pick of single women crowding the place, but not
tonight.

His brothers had tried talking him into attending the
game with them, but he'd declined after his team had
been eliminated in the previous round. It didn't matter one bit when they'd laughed and called him a sore
loser. So what if he was.

Tyson took another sip of his drink and checked his
watch. It was still early, but he might as well call it a
night since it seemed he would be going home alone,
which wasn't how he'd envisioned spending his evening.
Taking some woman to bed had been at the top of his

agenda. Scoring was the name of the game. Women hit on him and he hit on women. No big deal. It was the lay of the land. His land anyway.

He stood to leave at the same time the nightclub's door swung open and three women walked in. Three good-looking women. He sat back down, thinking that maybe the night wouldn't be wasted after all.

Not to be caught staring, he turned around on the bar stool. The huge mirror on the wall afforded him the opportunity to check out the women without being so obvious. Good, he noted. No rings. That was the first thing he looked for since he didn't believe in encroaching on another man's territory. Tyson figured it must be his lucky night when they were shown to a table within the mirror's view. The women were so busy chatting that they didn't realize he was checking them out.

For some reason his gaze kept returning to one of the women in particular. She looked familiar and it took a second or two before it hit him just who she was.

Hunter McKay.

Damn. It had been years. Eighteen, to be exact. She had been two years behind him in high school, and of all the girls he'd dated during that time, she was the only one with whom he hadn't been able to score. She'd had the gall to ask for a commitment before giving up the goods, and unlike some guys, who would have lied just to get inside her panties, he'd told her the very same thing then that he was telling women now. He didn't do commitments. His refusal to make her his steady girl had prompted her to end things between them after the first week. It had been the first time a Steele had ever been shot down. For months his brothers had teased him, calling Hunter "the one who got away." He frowned, wondering why that memory still annoyed him.

When he'd returned to Phoenix after medical school he'd heard she attended Yale to fulfill her dream of being an architect. After college she had made her home in Boston and returned to town only occasionally to visit her parents. Their paths had never crossed until tonight.

He'd also heard she had gotten married to some guy she'd met while living in Boston. So where was her ring? She could be getting it cleaned, resized or…maybe she was no longer married. He couldn't help wondering which of those possibilities applied.

Hunter had been a striking beauty back then and she still was. It had been that beauty that had captured his interest back in the day and was doing so now. It didn't appear as if she'd aged much at all. She still had that young-girl look, and those dimples in both cheeks were still pretty damn pleasing to the eyes.

The shoulder-length curly hair had been replaced with a short natural cut that looked good on her, and he couldn't help it when his gaze lingered on her lips. He could still remember the one and only time he'd kissed her. It has been way too short, yet oh so sweet.

He felt an ache in his groin and didn't find it surprising since it was a familiar reaction whenever he saw a beautiful woman. But it was Hunter who was affecting him, not the other two women. He remembered them from high school as well, but had forgotten their names.

What he did recall was that they had been Hunter's best friends even back then.

"Ready for another drink, Doc?"

He glanced up at Tipper, who'd been the bartender at Notorious for years. "Not yet, but do me a favor."

Tipper grinned. "As long as it's legal."

"It is. Whatever drinks those three ladies are having, I want them put on my tab."

Tipper glanced over at the table where the women sat and nodded. "No problem. I'll let their waiter know."

"Thanks."

Tipper walked off and Tyson's gaze returned to the mirror. At that moment Hunter threw her head back and laughed at something one of the women said. He'd always thought she had a sensuously shaped neck, flawless and graceful. He'd looked forward to placing a hickey right there on the side of it. It was the place he would brand all the girls in high school who'd gone all the way with him. It had been known as the Mark of Tyson. But Hunter had never gotten that mark. What a pity.

His cell phone pinged with a text message and he pulled his phone out of his jacket to read his brother Mercury's message. My team is up four. Be ready to celebrate later tonight.

Tyson clicked off the phone and rolled his eyes. *When hell freezes over*, he thought. If his brothers thought he was a sore loser, then Mercury could be an obnoxious winner, and Tyson wanted no part of it tonight. After returning the phone to his jacket, he let his gaze return to the mirror and to Hunter. He couldn't help but smile when he made up his mind about something. Her name might be Hunter but tonight he was determined to make her his prey.

Hunter McKay appreciated sharing this time with her two best friends from high school—Maureen Santana, whom everyone fondly called Mo, and Kathryn Elliott, whose nickname was Kat. Both had been bridesmaids in her wedding and because they'd kept in touch over the years, they'd known about her rocky marriage and subsequent divorce from Carter Robinson. Mo, a divorcée herself, thought Hunter had given Carter far too many chances to get his act together, and Kat, who was still holding out for Mr. Right, had remained neutral until Carter had begun showing his true colors.

"Here you are, ladies," the waiter said, placing their drinks in front of them. "Compliments of the gentleman sitting at the bar."

Their gazes moved past the waiter to the man in question. As if on cue, he swiveled around in his seat and flashed them a smile. Hunter immediately felt a flutter in the pit of her stomach, a flutter that should have been forgotten long ago. But just that quickly, after all these years, it had resurfaced the moment she stared into the pair of green eyes that could only belong to a Steele.

"Well now, isn't that nice of Tyson Steele," Mo said with mock sweetness. "I wonder which one of us he wants to take home tonight."

"Take home?" Hunter asked, while her eyes remained on Tyson. For some reason she couldn't break her gaze. It was as if she was caught in the depths of those gorgeous green eyes.

"Yes, take home. He doesn't really date. He just has a history of one-night stands," Mo replied.

"Do we have to guess which one of us he's interested in?" Kat asked, chuckling, and then took a quick sip of her drink. "If you recall, Mo, that particular Steele was hot and heavy for Hunter back in the day."

"That's right. I remember." Mo turned to Hunter. "And if I recall, you dumped him. Probably the only female in this town with sense enough to do so."

With that reminder, Hunter tore her gaze from Tyson's to take a sip of her drink. In high school, Tyson, along with his five brothers, were known as the "Bad News" Steeles. Handsome as sin with green eyes they'd inherited from their mother, the six had a reputation as heartbreakers. It was widely known that their only interest in a girl was getting under her dress.

Galen Steele, the oldest of the bunch, had been a senior in high school when she'd been a freshman. Tyson was the second oldest. After Tyson came Eli, Jonas, Mercury and Gannon. Each brother was separated the closest in age by no more than eleven months, which meant their mother had practically been pregnant for six straight years.

"Tyson gave me no choice," Hunter said, finally replying to Mo's comment. "I liked him and for some reason I figured he would treat me differently since his family had been members of my grandfather's church. Boy, was I naive."

Kat chuckled. "But like Mo said, when you found

out that you'd be just another notch on his bedpost, at least you had the sense to dump him."

"I didn't dump him," Hunter said, sitting back in her chair. She didn't have to glance over at Tyson to know he was still staring at her. "When he told me what he wanted, I merely told him I saw no reason for us to continue to date, because he wasn't getting it."

"That's a dump," Mo said, grinning. "And be forewarned, nothing about the Steeles has changed. Those brothers are still bad news. Hard-core womanizers. Getting laid is still their favorite pastime."

"At least three had the sense to get married," Kat added, taking another sip of her drink.

"Oh? Which ones?" Hunter inquired.

"Galen, Eli and Jonas."

Hunter vaguely remembered Eli but she did remember Jonas since they'd graduated in the same class. And she couldn't help but recall Galen Steele. He had gotten expelled from school after the principal found him under the gymnasium bleachers making out with the man's daughter. His reputation around school was legendary. "So, Galen got married?"

"Yes, a few years ago, and his wife just gave birth to twins," Mo explained. "Last night, in fact. The announcement was in the papers this morning. It was a huge write-up in the society section."

Hunter nodded as she tried ignoring the fact Tyson still had his eyes on her. "What does Tyson do for a living?"

"He's a heart surgeon at Phoenix Baptist Hospital," Mo responded.

"Good for him. He always wanted to be a doctor."
She recalled their long talks, not knowing at the time
their conversations were just part of his plan to reel
her in. Unfortunately for him, she hadn't been biting.

"Don't look now, ladies, but Tyson has gotten up off
the bar stool and is headed this way."

Although Kat had told them not to look, Hunter
couldn't help doing so. She wished she hadn't when
Tyson's gaze captured hers. He'd been eye candy in his
teens and now eighteen years later he was doubly so.
She couldn't miss that air of arrogance that seemed to
surround him as he walked toward them. He appeared
so powerfully male that every step he took conveyed
primitive animal sexuality. There was no doubt in her
mind that over the years Tyson had sharpened his game
and was now an ace at getting whatever he wanted.

He was wearing a pair of dark slacks and a caramel-
colored pullover sweater. She was convinced that on any
other man the attire would look just so-so. But on Tyson,
the sweater emphasized his wide shoulders, and the
pants definitely did something to his masculine build.

"I understand whenever a Steele sees a woman he
wants, he goes after her. It appears Tyson's targeted
you, Hunter," Mo said as she leaned over. "Maybe he
thinks there's unfinished business between the two of
you. Eighteen years' worth."

Hunter waved off her friend's words. "Don't be silly.
He probably doesn't even remember me, it's been so
long."

It took less than a minute for Tyson to reach their
table. He glanced around and smiled at everyone. "Eve-

ning, ladies." And then his gaze returned to hers and he said, "Hello, Hunter. It's been a while."

Hunter inhaled deeply, surprised that he *had* remembered her after all. But what really captured her attention were his features. He was still sinfully handsome, with skin the color of creamy butternut and a mouth that was shaped too darn beautifully to belong to any man. And his voice was richer and a lot deeper than she'd remembered.

Before she could respond to what he'd said, Mo and Kat thanked him for the drinks as they stood. Hunter looked at them. "Where are you two going?" she asked, not missing the smirk on Mo's face.

"Kat and I thought we'd move closer to that big-screen television to catch the last part of the basketball game. I think my team is winning."

Hunter came close to calling Mo out by saying she didn't have a team. She knew for a fact that neither Mo nor Kat was into sports. Why were they deliberately leaving her alone with Tyson?

As soon as they grabbed their drinks off the table and walked away, Tyson didn't waste time claiming one of the vacated seats. Hunter glanced over and met his gaze while thinking that the only thing worse than being deserted was being deserted and left with a Steele.

She took a sip of her drink and then said, "I want to thank you for my drink, as well. That was nice of you."

"I'm a nice person."

The jury is still out on that, she thought. "I'm surprised you remember me, Tyson."

He chuckled, and the sound was so stimulating it

seemed to graze her skin. "Trust me. I remember you. And do you know what I remember most of all?"

"No, what?"

He leaned over the table as if to make sure his next words were for her ears only. "The fact that we never slept together."

Chapter 2

Tyson thought the shocked look on Hunter's face was priceless. He also thought it was a total turn-on. Up close she was even more beautiful. There had been something about her dark, almond-shaped eyes and long lashes that he'd always found alluring. But what was really getting to him was her lips, especially the bottom one. The curvy shape would entice any man to want to taste it. Nibble on it. Greedily devour it.

She interrupted his thoughts when she finally said, "And if you recall that, then I'm sure you remember why."

"Yes, I remember," he said, holding tight to her gaze. "You weren't one of those high school girls who slept around. You wanted me to make you my steady girlfriend and I had no intention of doing that."

"You just wanted me in the backseat of your car," she said.

He smiled. "The front seat would have worked just fine, trust me. I wanted you and my goal was to get you. For me it was all about sex then."

"Just like it's all about sex for you now?" she asked smoothly.

"Yes." He had no problem being up front with her or any woman, letting them know what he wanted, what he didn't want and, in her particular case, what he'd missed out on getting. She was the lone person in the "tried but failed" column. He intended to remedy that.

"I heard a while back that you'd gotten married, Hunter."

She took another sip of her drink and he remembered the one and only time he'd sampled the beautiful lips that kissed her glass. "Yes, I got married."

He looked down at her ringless hand before glancing back up at her. "Still married?"

"No."

Her response was quick and biting, which only led him to believe the divorce had been unpleasant. That might be bad news for her, but he saw it as good news for him since he was known to inject new life into divorcées. Over the years he'd taken plenty to bed, not necessarily to mend their broken hearts, but mainly to prove there was life after a shitty marriage.

"How long ago?"

Her eyebrows lifted. "Why do you want to know?"

"Just curious."

For a second, she didn't respond, and then she said, "Two years."

He nodded as he leaned back in his chair. "Sorry to hear about your divorce," he said, although he was anything but. Although his parents had a great marriage and it seemed his three brothers' marriages were off to a good start, he was of the opinion that marriage wasn't for everybody. It definitely wasn't for him and evidently hadn't been for her.

"No need to be sorry, Tyson. I regret the day I ever married the bastard."

He'd heard that line before. And as far as he was concerned there was no need for her to expound. It really didn't matter to him what she thought of her ex. What mattered was that divorcées were his specialty. He would gladly shift her from his "tried and failed" column to his "achieved" category. Every one of his senses was focused on getting her into his bed.

"So what brings you back to Phoenix, Hunter?" he asked with a smile.

Hunter was glad a waiter appeared at that moment to place a drink in front of Tyson. Evidently he was a regular, since the man had known just what to give him. It took only a minute but that had been enough time to get herself together and recover from Tyson's charismatic personality. It was quite obvious that he was a man on the prowl tonight and had set his sights on her. Mo and Kat had said as much, but at the time she hadn't believed them. The man had been a player in high school and eighteen years later he was still at it. She couldn't help wondering why he hadn't gotten past that mentality.

"Now, where were we? Oh, yes. I asked what brings you back to Phoenix."

She took another sip of her drink. There was no way she would tell him how after their divorce and the dissolution of their partnership, her architect husband had underhandedly taken all their clients. Starting over in Boston would not have been so bad if he hadn't deliberately tried to sabotage her reputation as an architect. Tyson didn't have to know that because of her husband's actions she'd decided to start over here. Instead of telling him all of that, she decided to tell him the other reason she'd come back home.

"My parents."

He lifted a brow. "Are they ill?"

She shook her head. "No, they aren't ill. My brother thinks they're having too much fun."

Hunter realized just how ridiculous that sounded and added, "A few months ago they purchased 'his and hers' Harleys, and before that they signed up to take skydiving lessons. Lately, they've been hinting at selling the house and buying a boat to sail around the world."

Tyson appeared amused. "Sounds to me like they're enjoying life. Maybe your brother needs to take a chill pill."

"Possibly, but his hands are full right now with his teenage sons and he feels Mom and Dad are driving him as crazy as they claim he's driving them. I decided it was best I came home to keep peace." Hunter had no idea how she would manage to do that. Her parents were intent on having fun and her brother was intent on getting them to act their age.

"You're an architect, right?" he asked her.

"Yes. How did you know?"

"Someone mentioned it at one of the class reunions that you never attended."

He was right, she hadn't attended any. At first it had been school keeping her away, and later trying to build her career and finally trying to save her marriage. Although Carter had made sure they attended all of his high school reunions, he had been dead set against attending any of hers, and as usual she'd given in to him.

"I understand you're a doctor."

He nodded. "Yes. A heart surgeon."

She smiled. "And I bet you're a good one."

"I owe it to my patients to do my very best."

And there was no doubt in Hunter's mind that he did. She remembered he was devoted to whatever he did, even if he was chasing girls.

"I'm glad you're back in Phoenix, Hunter."

"Why?" She really couldn't understand why he would be.

He leaned in closer. "Because we have history."

She couldn't keep the smile from tugging at her lips. "History?"

"Yes."

"What kind of history?"

"I think of you as the one who got away."

She had to keep from laughing out loud at that. "You mean the one who never made it to the backseat of your car?"

"Pretty much."

"It's been eighteen years. I would think you'd have gotten over it by now."

He shook his head and chuckled. "I had. However, seeing you again brought it back home to me, so I've come up with a plan."

She lifted a brow. "What kind of plan?"

"A plan to seduce you."

Hunter's breath caught in her lungs. His audacity was almost as great as his arrogance. What man told a woman he planned to seduce her? "Seriously? Do you think it will be that easy?"

The smile that appeared on his face almost made her heart miss a beat. Although all the Steele brothers had those killer green eyes, she recalled that Tyson and Mercury were the only ones with dimples. Why was it that whenever he flashed those dimples, her pulse rate went haywire?

"I didn't say it would be easy," he said smoothly. "What I said was that I had a plan. I see no reason that we can't rekindle what we had years ago."

"There's nothing to rekindle. Need I remind you that we didn't have anything mainly because you were only interested in one thing?"

His smile widened as he lifted his drink to his lips. Without saying a word, he was letting her know that nothing about him had changed and that he was still only interested in one thing.

"I suggest you go find someone else to seduce."

He shook his head. "I can't do that. I want you."

"You can't always have what you want. That's life."

Whatever he was about to say was lost when Mo and Kat appeared. "My team lost," Mo said, grinning. She glanced at her watch. "Tomorrow is a workday so we figured it's time to go."

Great timing, Hunter thought, and she stood.

Tyson stood as well and shoved his hands into his pockets. "I'll take you home, Hunter, if you aren't ready to leave just yet."

If he thought for one minute she would go with him, especially after admitting his plan to seduce her, he wasn't thinking straight. "Thanks, but I am ready. It was good seeing you again, Tyson."

"Same here, Hunter," he said, and she thought she saw something akin to amusement in his eyes. "I have a feeling we'll be running into each other again."

Hunter hoped not. She had enough to worry about with her parents, without being concerned about Tyson Steele trying to get her into bed. "Good night." She walked toward the door with Mo and Kat, feeling the heat of Tyson's gaze on her backside.

As soon as they were out the door she turned to her friends. "Why on earth did the two of you leave me alone with Tyson?"

Kat grinned. "Because we knew you could handle him."

"Besides, it was quite obvious you were the one on his radar and not us," Mo added. "So how did it go?"

Hunter shook her head. "You guys were right. Nothing has changed with Tyson. He's still looking for a pair of legs to get between."

"And you didn't make yours available to him again?" Kat asked, grinning. "What a shame."

"For him I'm sure it was, especially since he told me of his plan to seduce me."

Mo's eyes widened. "He actually told you that?"

"Without cracking a smile or blinking an eye."

Both Mo and Kat stopped walking to stare at her. "You don't sound worried."

Hunter stopped and glanced at her friends, lifting a brow. "Why would I be?"

"We're talking about Tyson Steele, Hunter. The man who's known to get what he wants. I heard from women that he's so smooth you won't miss your panties until they're gone. And for him to already have a plan of seduction for you sounds serious."

"Only in his book, not mine."

Kat tilted her head. "And this from a woman who's gone without sex for two years now."

"Actually four. If you recall, Carter and I slept in separate bedrooms for two years before our divorce. You can't miss what you never got on a regular basis anyway. I haven't had an orgasm in so long I've honestly forgotten how it feels."

"Then you're in luck," Mo said with a huge smile on her face. "There are quite a few women around town who claim the orgasms those Bad News Steeles give a girl can blow her mind to smithereens and have her begging for more. Rumor has it that you haven't truly been made love to unless it's been by a Steele. They're supposed to be just that good in the bedroom."

Hunter rolled her eyes. "I'm sure it's nothing more than a lot of hype."

"But what if it's not?" Kat asked seriously. "And just think. One of those Bad News Steeles has plans to seduce you. If Tyson succeeds then you'll never forget how an orgasm feels again."

"Whatever," Hunter said as they resumed walking. By the time they reached the car, Hunter decided whatever plan Tyson thought he had for her was no big deal, since she doubted their paths would cross again anyway. And even if they did, she was certain it was just like she'd told Mo and Kat. All those rumors about the Steeles were probably nothing more than a lot of hype.

"Is there a reason you're visiting me this time of night, Tyson?" Eli Steele asked gruffly, moving aside for his brother to enter his home. "And why aren't you at the basketball game with Mercury and Gannon?"

"I had better things to do."

Eli rolled his eyes. "In other words, your team didn't make it to the finals. Everyone knows what a sore loser you are."

Tyson frowned. "I'm not a sore loser." He then glanced around. "Where's Stacey?"

His once die-hard bachelor brother had defected and married, just like his brothers Galen and Jonas. The only thing redeeming about that was he'd married Stacey Carlson. She was the sister of a good friend and former colleague of Tyson's by the name of Cohen.

"Stacey's in bed, where most people with good sense are by now," Eli said, dropping down on the sofa. "I hear Brittany and the babies might be going home to-morrow."

Tyson nodded. "So I heard."

"Word also has it that Mom has volunteered to help out for a few days. I hope she doesn't get on Galen's nerves."

Tyson chuckled. "I doubt that she will. He's been in her good graces ever since he was the first to get married. Besides, helping out with the babies will keep her busy."

"And the busier she is the less chance she has to get into your business—and Mercury's and Gannon's—right?"

"Right," Tyson said, knowing Eli understood. Before he married, he'd gotten the Eden Tyson Steele's "sticking her nose where it doesn't belong" treatment, just like the rest of them. Now, with three sons married, she was relentless on the other three, prodding them along to get them to the altar. Tyson vowed it wouldn't work on him. "So who do you think the babies look like?"

Eli chuckled. "With those green eyes, forehead and lips, they favor Galen all the way. I haven't heard their decisions on names, have you?"

"Nope, but rumor has it they're allowing Mom to do the honors."

Eli shook his head. "No wonder she's blowing up the newspapers. She's up there on cloud nine."

"Fine. She can stay there for a while," Tyson said. "Just as long as she's not into my business while she's up there."

"You and Mercury and Gannon will get a slight reprieve, but don't think she'll let you guys off the hook for good." Eli didn't say anything for a minute as he stared across the room at his brother and then he said, "Okay, get it out. There's a reason you dropped by so late."

Tyson sat down in the wingback chair across from the sofa. "There is. Hunter McKay's back in town."

Eli's forehead bunched. "Who's Hunter McKay?"

Tyson rolled his eyes. "I can't believe you don't remember Hunter. But I shouldn't be surprised. Back in the day, the old Eli remembered bodies and not names."

A smile curved Eli's lips. "True. So was she one of those bodies?"

"Hell, no! She was my girl."

"You never had a girl, Tyson."

His brother was right and for the life of him Tyson wasn't sure why he'd said what he had just now. "Sorry, saying that was a huge mistake."

"I hope there's not a reason why you made it. And lower your voice or you'll wake up my wife and she needs her rest."

Tyson didn't need to ask why. It seemed that all his married brothers had wedded women they enjoyed spending time with in and out of the bedroom. "There's not a reason."

Eli stared at him for a long moment and then asked, "So what's the big deal about this Hunter McKay being back in town?"

"It just is."

"Hey, wait a minute," Eli said, sitting straight up on the sofa. "That name is coming back to me. Isn't Hunter

McKay the girl who dumped you in your senior year of high school?"

"She didn't dump me."

"That's not the way I remember it. And why are you interested in Hunter McKay? Didn't I hear something about her getting married some years back?"

"She's a divorcée now. I saw her tonight at Notorious and got that much out of her. And it was a nasty divorce."

"How do you know?"

Tyson stretched his long legs out in front of him. "She called her ex a bastard."

"Okay, her ex was a bastard. That doesn't explain why you're here at midnight."

Without hesitation Tyson said, "I want you to find out information on her."

Eli rolled his eyes. "Do I look like a friggin' detective?"

"No, but she's an architect and as president of Phoenix's business council, you would know if she's set up her own business in town or was hired by an established firm."

"And you want to know that for what reason?"

Tyson's lips curved into a smile. "Because I plan to seduce her. And before you conveniently forget your own reputation before marrying Stacey and start acting holier-than-thou, just for your information, I gave Hunter McKay fair warning of my intentions tonight."

"You actually told her that you plan to seduce her?"

"Yes. You know how I operate, Eli. I don't play games and divorcées are my specialty. I'll be doing her a favor, especially if her ex was the bastard she claims he was."

Eli frowned. "You claim you gave her fair warning, so now I'm going to give you the same, Tyson. I had a plan for Stacey, although my plan was different from yours. My plan backfired. In my case it was for the best. My advice to you is to tread lightly and with caution, or you're liable to get possessed by passion. Once that happens, it will be all over for you."

Tyson frowned. "Possessed by passion? What the hell are you talking about?"

"You're cocky enough to think that once you get Hunter McKay in your bed, you're going to blow her mind."

Tyson smiled confidently. "Of course."

"Have you given any thought to the possibility that she'll end up blowing yours?"

Tyson stared hard at his brother. "No, I haven't given it any thought because *that* won't be happening."

Chapter 3

Hunter studied the older woman sitting across her desk. Pauline Martin had come to her highly recommended by Hunter's brother, Bernie, who was a good friend of the woman's son. Ms. Martin's husband had died last year and she wanted to do something other than stay in the house and stare at the walls. The administrative assistant position seemed perfect for her. From the interview, Hunter had known she was just what McKay Architecture Firm needed. Now if she could only get some clients.

She was scheduled to meet with an advertising firm later that day to discuss ideas on how she could promote her business. There were a number of architectural companies in Phoenix and the key to succeeding was to make sure hers stood out.

Hunter stood. "I'm looking forward to us working together, Pauline, and I'll see you in the morning."

"Thanks, Hunter."

An hour or so later Hunter had snapped her briefcase closed to leave for the day. Starting over in a business wasn't easy but, as her parents had reminded her that morning when she'd stopped by their house for breakfast, she was a fighter. What Carter had done was wrong, but instead of getting bitter, she had to do better. She had to look ahead and not look back. No matter what, she couldn't let him break her.

And more than anything, she couldn't believe all men were like Carter Robinson. Had he really expected her to remain his wife while he engaged in all those affairs? And when she had confronted him about it, he'd only laughed and told her to get over it. He'd said she wouldn't leave him because she had too much to lose, and that no matter what she accused him of, his family would stick by his side.

And they had.

Even his mother, who'd said she sympathized with Hunter over her son's wretched behavior, had stuck by him in the end. For Hunter, that had hurt more than anything because she'd assumed she and Nadine Robinson had had a good and close relationship. At least they had until the day Hunter had decided to bring her eight-year marriage to Carter to an end. Then Nadine had proven Carter right. Blood had been thicker than water.

Even with Carter's high-priced divorce lawyer, at least the judge who'd handled the divorce had sided with her and ordered Carter to give her fifty percent equity out of the company. He hadn't even wanted to do that. And the judge had been more than fair in making sure he did the same with their home, as well as all the other assets Carter had acquired over the years. Some she hadn't known about until the day the private investigator she'd hired had uncovered them.

So now she was back in Phoenix. In a way she felt like a stranger in her own hometown, since she'd made Boston her home ever since enrolling in MIT for her graduate degree. She'd been working a few years when she'd met Carter at a fund-raiser her architecture firm had given. He was a member of the Boston Robinsons, a family that took pride in their old-money status and the rich history that came with it.

They'd been married three years when she'd first found about Carter's affairs. He swore they meant nothing and begged her to forgive him, and she had. He became attentive for a year or two, and they'd even tried having a family, but with no success. Hunter wasn't exactly sure when his affairs had picked back up again, but she'd begun noticing the usual—lipstick on the collar, the scent of another woman's perfume and suspicious text messages. That's when she hired a private investigator. The PI's report had been the last straw. There was no way she could remain married to Carter after that, regardless of what her in-laws thought. In the end, they had sided with Carter in his campaign to destroy her.

She drew in a deep breath, refusing to give in to her sorrows. Somewhere out there were women in far worse situations than she. Her grandmother used to repeat that adage about making lemons into lemonade and Hunter intended to do just that.

At that moment the image of Tyson Steele came into her mind. Not that it had actually ever left since they'd run into each other last night. In fact she had dreamed about him. Of all things, in her dream she had let him do what she had refused to let him do eighteen years ago, and that was to take her in the backseat of a car.

Hunter shook her head. She couldn't believe how scandalous that dream had been and it was even worse that she had totally and thoroughly enjoyed it. Luckily it had been just a dream and not the real thing. But the dream had been enough. She had awakened panting, with heated lust rushing through every part of her. It had taken a long cold shower to calm down her body.

During the four years of her sexless life, the last thing she had thought about was having an affair. So why now? And why Tyson Steele? He was arrogant, confident and too cocky to suit her. They hadn't held a conversation for more than a few minutes before he was telling her of his plans to seduce her.

She shook her head as she headed for the door. Some men's attitudes simply amazed her. But then again, he was a Steele. Hearing three of his brothers had married meant there could be hope for him, but she wouldn't be crazy enough to put any money on that assumption.

But what really should be hilarious was that Tyson Steele thought he could seduce her. She figured he'd been all talk and that his words had been meant to get her sexually riled up, and they had…to a point. After her shower this morning her common sense was firmly back in place. All it had taken was a look around her apartment to remember all she'd lost because of a man. The last thing she needed was to get involved with another man for any reason.

But what about just for sex?

She almost missed her step when the idea popped in her head. Where had such a thought come from? She was a good girl. The granddaughter of a retired minister. A woman who'd always worked hard, played fair and been a good wife to her husband. And as Nadine had often claimed, the best daughter-in-law anyone could ask for.

Yet, regardless of all those things, she'd gotten royally screwed. And because of all those things Carter had figured she would never leave him. That she would stay married to him regardless. What he'd failed to take into consideration was that everyone had a breaking point. When she had taken as much as she could, she had walked away without looking back. She only wished she'd been strong enough to do it sooner.

As she locked up her office she figured she might as well dream about Tyson Steele again tonight. Dreams were safe. Besides, she had no reason to think their paths would cross again. For one, she didn't intend to return to that nightclub where he apparently hung out.

His parents attended the same church as hers, the one where her grandfather had been pastor before he'd passed away years ago. During breakfast this morning she'd deliberately asked her mother to bring her up-to-date on church members, former and present. It seemed the Steeles were still members of their church, and her mother said that although she would see Eden and Drew Steele on most Sundays, she rarely saw their sons and couldn't recall the last time one of them attended church.

Deciding she didn't want to think about Tyson Steele, she stepped inside the elevator to leave the office.

Tyson had stepped out of the shower and was toweling off when his cell phone rang. He recognized the ring tone. It was Eli. With three surgeries today back to back, he hadn't time to think about much of anything but his patients. The surgeries had gone well and he'd delivered good news to the families. Before leaving the hospital, he had made his rounds, completed his reports and given final instructions to the nurses caring for his patients. Now he was at home, on full alert and eager for any information his brother had for him.

He grabbed the phone off the vanity. "Eli, did you find out anything?"

"This is going to cost you."

Tyson rolled his eyes. "Who do you think I am? Galen?"

It was a running joke in the family that Galen worked the least but made the most. While attending college Galen and his two roommates had decided to do something to make money and since all three were computer-savvy, they created video games. After their games became a hit on campus, they formed a business and by the time they graduated from college they were millionaires. The three were still partners today and usually released one game a year around the holiday season. Galen enjoyed flaunting the fact that he was able to work less than twenty hours a week and still make millions.

Eli chuckled. "With twins Galen won't have as much free time on his hands."

Tyson smiled at the thought. "You think?"

"We can hope."

Tyson tossed the towel aside to slide into a pair of briefs. "So what did you find out about Hunter McKay? Did she establish a company here?"

"Yes. She opened an architect office in the Double-Row building a week ago." Eli paused a minute and then said, "And you were right. Her divorce from her husband was pretty nasty."

"How do you know?"

"The one good thing about being president of the business council of a major city is getting to meet other such individuals. The one from Boston, John Wrigley, and I have become pretty good friends. I gave John a call today. According to him, Hunter divorced her husband on grounds of adultery and had the goods from a PI to prove it. Her ex hired this high-priced attorney to fight to keep Hunter from getting a fifty-fifty split of the architectural firm they owned together, but the judge sided with Hunter. In the end Hunter's ex retaliated by making sure she didn't get any of their clients."

The man was a bastard just like Hunter McKay said, Tyson thought, easing a T-shirt over his head. "I think I'll pay her a visit tomorrow."

"That doesn't surprise me."

"As a client," Tyson added.

"A client? That *does* surprise me. I didn't know you were interested in getting a house designed."

Tyson smiled. "I wasn't before now."

"Hell, Tyson, you don't even own any land."

Tyson's smile widened. "Shouldn't be that hard to buy some." Even through the phone line Tyson could imagine Eli rolling his eyes.

"And you would go to all that trouble just for a woman?"

Tyson thought about his brother's question. "But she's not just any woman. She's the one who got away. And now she's back."

The next morning Hunter walked into her office and stopped dead in her tracks. Her eyes did a double take. Was Tyson Steele actually sitting in her reception area, chatting so amiably with Pauline that neither noticed her entry?

"Good morning," she said, breaking into their conversation.

Pauline and Tyson both glanced up, and Pauline smiled brightly. Tyson stood as he gave her a slow perusal, his gaze moving over her from head to toe. His eyes returned to meet hers and she tried ignoring the acceleration of her heart, a result of the intensity of his stare.

What were the odds that the same man she had been dreaming about for the past two nights would be in her office this morning? And they were the kind of dreams that heated her just by remembering them.

An excited Pauline interrupted her thoughts. "Good morning, Hunter. I think we might have our first client."

"Do we?" Hunter asked, her gaze switching from Tyson to Pauline.

"Yes. Dr. Tyson Steele is here to see you about designing his home."

Hunter found that hard to believe, especially after what he'd told her two nights ago. He was more interested in seducing her than anything else. "Is he?"

"Yes, I am," Tyson said.

She tried ignoring the slow, languorous heat that flowed through her body at the sound of Tyson's deep, husky voice. She looked back over at him and wished she hadn't. She'd thought he was sinfully handsome when she'd seen him at the nightclub, but as he stood in the sunlight streaming through her office window he looked triply so. The man was totally gorgeous, one hundred percent male perfection. He looked like scrumptious eye candy in his jeans and dark gray hooded sweatshirt. For her, there was just something about a nice male body in a pair of jeans and it was almost too much for her this early in the morning.

"In that case, Dr. Steele, you and I definitely need to talk," she said, moving toward her office.

She heard Tyson close her office door behind him the moment she set her briefcase on her desk. She turned around and fought back the urge to moan. The way he was leaning back against the closed door, he was sexiness personified. And his razor-sharp green eyes were on her. Why, today of all days, had she worn a dress, one shorter than she would normally wear? Shorter but still appropriate for conducting business. Yet from the way Tyson was staring at her, one would think otherwise. In fact, one would think she didn't have on any clothes at all. Sexual vibes were pouring off him in droves and she could feel desire flowing through her veins.

Clearing her throat as she tried getting control of the situation, she said, "Please have a seat, Tyson, and tell me just what it is that you want."

Realizing that wasn't a good question to ask him, she rephrased it. "Tell me what design of home you're interested in."

Tyson thought she had asked the right question the first time. He certainly had no problem telling her exactly what he wanted. But first he had to get his libido back in check. It had begun smoldering big-time when he'd glanced up from his conversation with her administrative assistant to see her standing there. She was what sexual fantasies were made of, and when it came to her he had plenty.

She was a constant visitor to his nightly dreams. If that wasn't bad enough she'd also crept into his daytime thoughts. All this from a woman he hadn't seen in years. Usually he didn't waste time fantasizing about any one woman before moving quickly to another. But it seemed he was focused on Hunter McKay and no one else, and he couldn't figure out why.

Eli thought he was obsessed with her and Tyson was beginning to wonder if that was true. He had never been obsessed with a woman before and was convinced he only wanted her in his bed, nothing more. Every time he thought about them having sex his pulse went crazy. He couldn't help wondering if there was more to his desire for Hunter than her being the one who got away. Why was he turned on by almost everything about her? Like her dress, for instance.

He knew it was just a dress, but on her it looked simply fantastic. He especially liked the way it complemented her legs. The other night she'd been wearing slacks so today was the first time he'd seen them. Now it came back to him that in high school, she had been a majorette, and the one thing he had liked was that she had a gorgeous pair of legs. She still did. And in that dress and a pair of three-inch pumps, she was definitely presenting challenges to his peace of mind. She looked neat, professional and way too appealing.

"Tyson?"

Hunter's voice brought his focus back to their conversation. He stepped away from the door and slid into a chair across from her desk. Doing so put him in close proximity to her and he enjoyed inhaling her scent. She was wearing the same perfume she had the other night and he thought the fragrance was definitely her signature. He met her eyes and said, "I have no problem telling you what I want." He let that statement hang in the air between them for a moment before adding, "As far as a design for a house, of course."

"Of course," Hunter said, moving around her desk to sit down behind it. "Before I can help you there are a few things I would need to know," she said, picking up a notepad and pen.

"Like what?"

"Like the location of the property the house will be built on. I need to verify there aren't any restrictions in the area that might prevent you from building the type of home you want. And I need to make sure your lot is large enough to fit whatever design you have in mind."

He nodded. "I find your inquiries interesting. Why don't we have dinner tonight and talk about them?"

She leaned back in her chair and stared at him. "We need to discuss it now, Tyson, because I have no intentions of having dinner with you."

"Why?"

"Because after work is my time. A business dinner means extending my work time into my pleasure time."

"We can make it both."

Her mouth flattened into a hard line. "No, we can't, and I don't have time to play games. If the only reason for your visit is to—"

"Try my hand at seducing you?"

She held his stare. "You warned me the other night that would be your main objective."

A soft chuckle escaped his lips. "It still is. Trust me. I haven't changed my mind about it. But I do want to talk about a house design, as well."

Tyson was serious about that. Although he would admit he'd initially had an ulterior motive for seeking her out today, all it had taken was for him to wake up to the noise outside his window to know he had put off moving long enough. Currently, he leased a condo in a very prestigious area of Phoenix not far from the hospital. It was large and spacious and had a great view of the mountains. But unfortunately it came with some drawbacks. Like the close proximity of his neighbors. Over the years he had gotten used to car doors slamming, horns honking and the early morning ruckus of parents hustling their kids off to school. Maybe it was time to pursue his dream of living in the countryside.

She was still staring at him, as if she was trying to figure out if he really was serious about getting a house designed. He decided to put her mind at ease. "What you might see as a problem is the fact that I haven't purchased the property yet. It doesn't matter, Hunter. You design my house and when I get ready to build it I'll buy enough land for it to sit on."

She was still staring and he had no problem with her doing so because he knew she was also thinking about him. Sizing him up. Trying to figure him out. He wished he could tell her not to bother because he was too complex for her to try.

"I need to ask you something, Tyson," she finally said after a few moments had passed.

"Yes?"

"When did you decide you wanted a house designed, and why did you come to me?"

He could tell her about his conversation with Eli yesterday, but decided to omit that part. "To be honest with you, I hadn't given much thought of designing a house. I live in a condo and that suited me just fine. However, I knew you were an architect and I knew my plans for you, so I decided I wanted to see your work."

"Let me get this straight," she said, sitting up in her chair. "You planned to seduce me so you came up with the idea to have me design a home for you. A home you never thought about owning until after you saw me the other night. You would go to all that trouble to get a woman in your bed?"

He couldn't help the smile that curved his lips. "No. I wouldn't go to all that trouble to get a woman in my bed, Hunter. But I would go to all that trouble to get you there."

She frowned. "Don't waste your time."

"It won't be. I know women, Hunter. I can read them as well as any book that's ever been published. You gave me the same looks I was giving you at Notorious. The 'I want to sleep with you' looks."

"I was not!"

"Yes, you were. Maybe you didn't realize you were doing so, but you were. The sexual chemistry between us was strong that night. I felt it and I saw no need to play games. That's why I told you my intentions up front. Did you honestly expect me not to explore all those heated vibes you and I were giving off that night?"

"But to invent this—"

"I didn't invent anything. What I've done is take another look at my living situation. Of my brothers I'm the only one who doesn't own a home. Never gave much thought to doing so. My condo is not far from the hospital and pretty convenient to everything I want. But this morning I noticed things I had chosen to ignore. Like the closeness of my neighbors. The noise and such. And the more I thought about it, the more that house in the country, the one I had thought about building years ago when I first got out of med school, suddenly appealed to me again. So I thought—"

"That since I was an architect and you had plans to seduce me anyway, that you would kill two birds with one stone?"

"I guess that's one way to look at it."

Hunter shook her head. After a minute she said, "That night after I left the club I thought about you a lot."

"You did?"

She heard the delight in his voice. "Yes, I did. I tried convincing myself that I imagined it. There was no way that at after eighteen years you were as arrogant and conceited as you were back in high school. But, Tyson, I was wrong. You are. You assume all you have to do is say what you want and you'll get it. You love women, although you'll never fall *in* love with one. You enjoy sharing your bed with them but that's about all you'll ever share. You—"

"Don't blame me," he interrupted. "Blame my father."

She lifted a brow. "Your father? What does your father have to do with it?"

Tyson smiled. "I'm Drew Steele's son. My brothers and I inherited his genes. We got some from Mom, of course, but the womanizing ones came from my dad. He used to be a player of the worst kind in his day, and even got run out of Charlotte because of his scandalous ways."

"And you're actually using your father's past behavior as an excuse for yours?"

"Like I said, it's in the genes. But since my father

is happily married to my mother and has been for over thirty years, I figure there's hope for me and my brothers. At least my mother is convinced there is and she might be right. Three have gotten married within a three-year period. Not that I have any interest in getting married, now or ever."

"I don't blame you," she said, not able to stop herself. "I tried it once and once was enough." He would never know just how much she meant those words.

"Are you going through the 'I hate all men' stage?"

She tried not to notice the breadth of his shoulders when he leaned back in his chair. Or the way his jeans stretched tight over his muscular thighs. "I have no reason to hate all men, Tyson. In truth, I don't hate my ex. I pity him."

He held her gaze. "So the reason you won't share my bed has nothing to do with him."

"No. It's mainly because of your attitude."

"My attitude?"

"Yes."

"What's wrong with my attitude?"

"You act entitled."

"Do I?"

"Yes. I guess it's from women always letting you have your way. Giving you whatever you want. They make it too easy for you."

"And you intend to make things difficult, Hunter?"

A smile touched her lips. "I intend to make things impossible, Tyson."

"Nothing is impossible."

He stood and she couldn't help but admire how sexily

his body eased out of the chair. "And since you won't have dinner with me, how about lunch tomorrow?"

"Give me one good reason why I should."

"Because I'm a potential client who merely wants to discuss ideas about the kind of country home I want you to design for me."

Hunter stared at him. Was he really serious about wanting her to design his home? There was only one way to find out. "Lunch tomorrow will be fine. Make an appointment with Pauline on your way out."

"No, I'm making one with you now. Put me on your calendar for tomorrow. Noon. At Gabriel's. I'll meet you there."

He headed for the door. When he reached it, he turned around and smiled. "And you look good today, by the way. Good enough to eat."

And then he opened the door and left.

Chapter 4

Hunter was convinced she should have her head examined when she arrived at Gabriel's the next day at noon. Meeting Tyson for lunch wasn't a smart move. So why was she here? Even if Tyson wanted her to design his country home there were ulterior motives behind it. He had been up front about his plans for her. It was all about seduction. Plain and simple. But he would discover there wasn't anything plain or simple about it.

The last thing she needed was to get mixed up with Tyson, or any man for that matter. She had put her divorce behind her, moved to be closer to her family and start over in her business. Hard work lay ahead of her and she had very little time to indulge in an affair. Besides, hadn't a failed eight-year marriage proved she was lousy at relationships?

"May I help you, madam?"

"Yes," she said, glancing around. "I'm meeting Tyson Steele for lunch."

The maître d' smiled. "Yes. Dr. Steele arrived a few moments ago and requested one of our private rooms in the back. I'll lead the way."

"Thanks," she said, following behind the man. A private room? In the back? She didn't like the sound of that and had a mind to turn around and walk out. But Tyson was a client. And so far, he was the only one she had. She kept telling herself that once the advertisements she'd approved finally ran, business would pick up. She certainly hoped so.

The maître d' opened the door then stepped aside for her to enter. She looked around and saw Tyson. He stood and she could feel the air between them sizzle. She knew he felt it as well when she saw heat smoldering in the depths of his green eyes.

He must have come straight from the hospital since he was still wearing his physician jacket. Tightening her hand on her briefcase, she moved forward and tried to fight the attraction she felt toward him. "Tyson."

"Hunter. Glad you could join me." As if only realizing his attire, he took off his white coat. "Sorry, an emergency detained me."

No need to say she hoped it wasn't anything serious, because he was a heart surgeon, so anything he did was serious. "No problem. I know your time is valuable so we can go ahead and—"

"You look good again today."

"Thanks." Knowing they would be meeting for

lunch, she had worn a pantsuit. The way he had checked out her legs yesterday had been too unnerving. "As I said yesterday, usually a client has purchased property, but since—"

"We'll discuss business later. Let's order first. I'm starving. I've been in surgery all morning and missed breakfast."

"Oh. Of course." She glanced down at the menu and tried ignoring the tingles of awareness going through her. It wasn't easy sitting across the table from such a sexy man. So far he seemed all business and hadn't said anything she considered inappropriate. She wouldn't hold that compliment on how she looked against him. In fact she appreciated him making the observation. Carter had stopped telling her how good she looked even when she'd gone out of her way to please him.

"I already know what I want."

She glanced up and swallowed deeply at the look she saw in his eyes. She wasn't imagining the sizzling undercurrents flowing between them. "Do you?"

"Yes."

She held his gaze and the sexual tension surrounding them began mounting. He had been referring to what he wanted off the menu, hadn't he? With Tyson, one could never be sure. She'd discovered that often his words had a double meaning. "That was fast," she said, breaking his gaze to look back down at her menu.

"I've never been accused of being slow, Hunter."

She glanced back up at him again. "And what did you decide to get?"

"The pork chops. That's what I usually get whenever I come here."

She nodded. He had been talking about what was on the menu, after all. "The pork chops sound good."

"They are and that's what I want for now. What I really want I'll put on the back burner until…"

She glanced up to find his focus totally on her, making the undercurrents between them sizzle even more. "Until what?"

"I can bring you around to my way of thinking."

Hunter couldn't help but chuckle.

"And what do you find amusing, Hunter?"

She leaned forward in her chair. "For a minute there I thought this would be one of those rare times that you would be good."

"I am good. Always."

His words flowed through her and with supreme effort she tried not to imagine just how good he would be. "I was referring to your behavior."

"Now, *that*, not always. According to my mother I can push the envelope at times."

She bet. Hunter was glad the waiter returned and with the amount of food Tyson ordered it was apparent he hadn't lied about being hungry. She wondered where he would put it all.

As if reading her thoughts, he said, "I plan to work it off later."

"I don't doubt that you will."

He reached across the table and his fingers caressed her hand. "I don't mean with another woman, Hunter. I have a membership at the gym."

She wondered what had given away her thoughts and figured it must have been her tone. Why had the thought of him sleeping with a woman bothered her? And why did him caressing her hand send shivers of desire through her? "You don't owe me an explanation. What you do and with whom is your business, Tyson. And need I remind you," she said, pulling her hand back, "that this is a business meeting?"

"Duly reminded," he said, smiling. "Temptation got the best of me."

Although she wouldn't admit to it, temptation had almost gotten the best of her, as well. She had loved the feel of his touch and could still feel the imprint of his hand on her skin. It was becoming pretty clear that this attraction between her and Tyson could lead to big trouble if she wasn't careful. Deciding to break up the sexual tension flowing between them, she steered the conversation to an innocuous topic. "So how are your niece and nephew?"

He lifted a brow. "I take it you read that article in the paper, as well."

She shook her head. "No, Mo did and mentioned it the other night."

He took a sip of his water before answering. "Brittany and the twins are home now. I got a chance to see them before they left the hospital yesterday and they're doing fine. Galen is doing okay, too. In fact, he's on cloud nine."

"I can't picture him married."

"I couldn't, either, but it happened. And I'll admit

there's something pretty special between him and Brittany."

"She's not from here, right?"

"No. She's from Florida. She was in town on business when they met."

"Have they named the twins yet?"

"They gave my mother the honor and she came up with Ethan and Elyse."

A smile spread across Hunter's lips. "Oh, I like that."

"My brothers and I figured she couldn't help but seize the opportunity to give the twins names starting with the letter E to match hers."

Then he smiled and Hunter was amazed he could be even more handsome. But he was.

As they ate, Tyson tried not to glance over at Hunter. Conversation between them had stopped, and he couldn't help wondering what she was thinking. Although whatever thoughts going through her head were a mystery to him, those going through his own head were not. Simply put, he wanted her. How could a woman he hadn't seen in eighteen years hold his interest like she was doing? It didn't make sense. No woman had ever gotten to him this way and without any effort on her part. At least not any conscious effort. He doubted she was aware of just how alluring she was without even trying.

Even wearing a pantsuit he didn't miss her small waist and sexy curves. And on more than one occasion when he'd glanced at her while they were eating, he hadn't missed the hardened tips of her nipples be-

neath her blue silk shirt. That meant she wasn't as im-
mune to him as she pretended to be. And when he had
reached out to stroke her hand, he'd felt the sparks and
knew she had, as well.

Somehow Hunter had managed to eradicate thoughts
of other women from his mind. He hadn't even bothered dropping by Notorious last night. Instead, he had
gone to his brother Jonas's house and stayed for dinner.
Jonas's wife, Nikki, was an excellent cook and spoiled
Jonas with all her delicious meals. Luckily neither Jonas
nor Nikki seemed to mind his drop-in dinner visits.

He glanced over at Hunter again and liked the way
she worked her mouth while chewing her food. He felt
a tightening in his gut at the thought of her working
that same mouth on him. And although his pork chop
tasted good, as usual, he had a feeling she would taste
even better. He closed his eyes and in his mind he could
taste her. As sweet as honey.

"It's *that* good?"

He popped his eyes back open. "What?"

"Your pork chop. You had your eyes closed as if savoring the taste."

He wondered what her reaction would be if he con-
fessed that he'd been thinking about her and not the
pork chop. "Yes, it is good. Moist. Tender. Just the way
I like it. What about your meal?"

"The baked chicken is delicious, as well. I'm glad
you suggested this place. It's pretty new, right?"

"Gabriel's? It wasn't here eighteen years ago if that's
what you're asking. Actually, it opened a few years after
I returned home from medical school. The owner is a

good friend of my brother Gannon so I tend to drop in occasionally."

"What made you decide to come back to Phoenix after medical school?"

And what made you stay away? As much as he wanted to ask that question, he answered hers. "I couldn't imagine living anywhere else. I missed home. I missed my family. I figured this was where I belonged. Phoenix is a beautiful city."

"Yes, it is."

"Yet you stayed away," he pointed out.

Regret darkened her eyes. "After living here all my life I figured it was time to see the world and going to school on the east coast helped. In Phoenix I was Reverend Hugh McKay's granddaughter and everyone expected me to act a certain way. In Connecticut, where no one knew me, I could be myself."

"I can't imagine you getting buck wild."

She chuckled. "I didn't go that far but I had my fun. I figured I deserved it because I studied hard. I was lucky to get a job with a top architectural firm after college in Boston. I felt my life was set."

"Then you met your ex."

He saw the regret in her gaze deepen. "Yes, then I met Carter Robinson. He worked at another firm. We met at a party and dated a year and then got married."

Tyson didn't say anything, but his mind was filled with thoughts of how different things might have been had she returned to Phoenix after college. Then maybe their paths would have crossed. *And then what?* he silently asked himself. *You aren't a serious kind of guy, never was. All you could have offered her was a romp between the sheets.* He took a sip of his water knowing that was true.

Hunter tipped her head to the side and stared at Tyson. When he wasn't trying to get a girl on her back, he was surprisingly easy to talk to. But then he very well might be so engaging just to reel her in like he'd tried doing in high school.

When the waiter came to remove the dishes she placed her briefcase on the table, opened it and pulled out her notepad. "Now for business."

"All right."

He was agreeable. She was surprised and had expected him to make some attempt to delay things. "So tell me what you would like in your house."

"Besides you in my bed?"

Now the Tyson Steele she knew had returned. "Won't happen, Tyson, so get over it."

"Doubt if I can, Hunter."

Whenever he said her name she felt a tingling sensation in the lower part of her belly. "Try real hard." With her notebook and pen in hand she forced herself back into business mode. "How many bedrooms would you like in your home?"

"At least six."

When she lifted her brow, he said, "A room for each of my brothers in case their wives ever put them out."

"At the same time?"

He shrugged. "You never know. And they're smart

enough to not to move back home. Mom would drive them to drink."

She fought back a smile. "Not your mom. I remember her from church. I was always in awe of her. She was beautiful."

"She still is beautiful. However, she does have one major flaw."

"What?" Hunter asked, taking a sip of her water.

"She likes getting into her sons' business too much to suit us. If she had her way we would all be married."

"And, of course, that's a bad thing."

"For me it is. I can't speak for my brothers since she got to three of them already."

Hunter shook her head. "I'm sure it wasn't your mom that 'got to them.' I would think it was their wives. From what I hear they fell in love."

He gave her a smile. "You're right. They're pretty damn smitten. Now they're looking at me, Mercury and Gannon like they expect us to follow suit."

"But you won't."

"I won't. I like being single."

"I bet you do. Now, to get back to your design. You want six bedrooms, one of them the master. Any specifics there?"

"Umm, I want it big and spacious. Huge windows. Large walk-in closet and the regular stuff that goes in a bedroom. Nothing far-out like what Galen has. He built a house in the mountains and his bedroom has glass walls and a glass ceiling. He likes lying in bed and looking up at the stars."

"Sounds beautiful."

"It is if that's your taste. Not mine. I want regular walls and when I lay in bed and look up the only thing I want to see is a ceiling fan."

"What about the kitchen?"

"I want a large kitchen."

She raised a brow. "You cook?"

"No. But for some reason women are impressed by the size of a man's kitchen."

She fought the urge to laugh. "Are they?"

"Yes. Some think if they get in your kitchen and cook you a good meal then you'll sweep them off their feet."

"Hasn't worked yet, I gather."

"When I sweep them off their feet I head for the bedroom and not the wedding chapel as they would like."

For some crazy reason the thought of him heading for the bedroom with any woman annoyed her. "What's the range of square footage you want?"

"Minimum of thirty-five hundred and max of fifty-five."

"That's a lot of house for a single person."

He smiled. "I figure I'll eventually have plenty of nieces and nephews and would want a big enough place for them to enjoy themselves when they come visit their uncle Tyson."

Over the next half hour Tyson continued to add on to his wish list. And there were a few things she suggested that he hadn't thought about. With additional land, a home in the country would be different from one built in the city. Already ideas were forming in her head and she couldn't wait to get started on this project.

"I think that will be enough information for now,"

she said finally, putting her notepad away. "I should have some preliminary sketches for you within a week to ten days. You can call Pauline and make an—"

"I prefer calling you directly."

"Why?"

"I just do."

"I hired Pauline for a reason."

"Tell that to your other clients."

She glared over at him. What she should do is get up, thank him for lunch and leave. But he was her client and at the moment he was the only one she had. She pulled her business card out of her purse and scribbled her mobile number on the back of it. "Don't call unless it's about business."

He took the card and slid it into his pocket while smiling at her. "I'm beginning to think you don't like me."

He didn't know how close to the truth that was. Just when she thought he might have some redeeming qualities, he proved her wrong. "Time for me to get back to the office. Thanks for lunch."

"We need to do this again. Maybe dinner the next time."

Deciding not to address Tyson's suggestion, she stood. "Goodbye, Tyson." And then she walked off. Try as she might she couldn't ignore the heat of his gaze on her back...and especially on her backside.

Chapter 5

A week and a half later, with his heart heavily weighing him down, Tyson entered his condo. Losing a patient was never easy. Although Morris Beaumont and his family had known the risks, the married father of two—and grandfather of four—had chosen to have the surgery anyway. And he hadn't survived. Delivering the news to the Beaumont family hadn't been easy. They had been hoping to beat the odds and had taken the news hard.

Tyson clenched his jaw, trying to keep his emotions at bay. Sure, he was a doctor, saw people dying every day, and accepted death as part of life. But still, doctors were human. Caring and experiencing grief didn't make one weak, as some people thought. Staying detached, as one of his professors had stressed in medical school, wasn't always easy.

Needing a beer, Tyson headed toward his kitchen to grab one out of his refrigerator. This had been a rough week with a full load of scheduled surgeries and a few unscheduled ones as well. One such emergency had been a newborn with a hole in her heart. She was doing great and if her condition continued to improve, she would be leaving the hospital and going home in another week.

Because of his workload, he hadn't followed up with Hunter, nor had she followed up with him, which probably meant she hadn't completed the initial sketches she'd talked about. Over the next number of days, which he had off, he'd get in touch with her.

The first thing on his agenda was getting laid. He needed sex like he needed this beer, he thought, popping the tab and taking a long, pleasurable gulp. He licked his lips afterward. He was beginning to feel restless and edgy. At least twenty-four hours of sleep would alleviate the former problem, but the latter would only be relieved between the legs of a woman. But not any woman. Hunter.

He took another swig of his beer. That thought filled him with concern. When had he begun lusting after just one woman? Even worse, when did his dreams just center on one woman? At night, whenever his head hit the pillow, he deliberately shut out unpleasant thoughts and only allowed his mind to conjure up pleasant ones. Hunter always headed the list.

Why was he focused on getting her to the one place

she'd made it clear she didn't want to be, which was his bed? And why did he think that once he got her there the real thing would be far better than any dream?

Tyson's cell phone rang and the ringtone indicated which brother it was. He pulled the phone off his belt. "What's up, Mercury?"

"Just checking on you. Mom told us why you didn't make last Thursday night. You okay?"

Over the years his mother had deemed Thursdays as family dinner night at their parents' home. Eden Tyson Steele expected all six of her sons to be present and accounted for, grudgingly or otherwise, unless one had a good excuse. Tyson and his brothers knew their mother used the Thursday night dinners as a way to show her sons that although their father had once been a die-hard womanizer, after meeting her all that had come to an end. She wanted them to see with their own eyes that a man like Drew Steele, who'd been known for his wild ways, could fall in love one day, marry and be true to one woman for the rest of his days. Galen, Eli and Jonas had gotten the intended message. The jury was still out for him, Mercury and Gannon. As far as Tyson was concerned, the jury could stay out for him because he wasn't changing his mind about marriage.

He was having way too much fun being single and sharing his bed with any woman he wanted.

Except for one by the name of Hunter McKay. The one he wanted with a passion.

"Tyson?"

He'd almost forgotten his brother was on the phone. "Yes, sorry. Rough stretch at work. I plan to sleep it off."

"Good idea. I'm leaving town later today for Dallas. Might have a new client with the Cowboys."

"That's good." Mercury was a former NFL player turned sports agent. He enjoyed what he did and traveled a lot.

"I thought I'd check on you before I left. By the way, I visited with the twins yesterday. They're so tiny."

Tyson figured there was no need to mention to Mercury that most newborns were. "Yes, they are. But they'll grow up fast and be walking before you know it. Getting into all kinds of stuff."

"I can't see laid-back Galen trying to keep up with them."

Neither could he, but then he hadn't figured his oldest brother would ever marry, either. "What's Gannon up to?" His youngest brother had taken over the day-to-day operations of their father's trucking company when the old man had retired a few years ago. Gannon even enjoyed getting behind a rig himself every once in a while.

"Gannon is planning to drive one of his rigs for a pickup in Florida later this week."

"That's a long ride."

"Yes, but knowing Gannon, he'll have fun along the way."

Tyson frowned. That was what worried him. While growing up, since he and Galen had been the oldest two Steeles, his parents—especially his mother—had expected them to look out for Gannon, who was the baby in the family. Although Gannon was now thirty-two, Tyson was discovering that old habits were hard to break. "I'll talk to him before he hits the road."

"It might be a good idea for you to do that. I'll talk with you later, Tyson."

"Okay and have a safe trip." Tyson clicked off the phone and returned it to his belt.

After he finished off the last of his beer, he released a throaty, testosterone-filled growl. It was a testament to how long he'd gone without a woman, which was so unlike him. He needed to step up his game, be the conqueror he knew he could be. Turn up the heat and do what he had warned Hunter he planned to do and seduce the hell out of her.

A smile touched his lips as he headed for his bedroom. First he would get the sleep he needed and then he would make it his business to seek out the object of his passion. Hunter McKay thought she'd given the last word, but he had news for her.

"Yes, and thanks for calling, Mrs. Davis. I'm looking forward to meeting you as well."

Hunter hung up the phone as a huge smile touched her lips. That would be the third new client she'd gotten in a week. It didn't even bother her that all three referrals had come from Tyson. The first, Don Jamison, was a colleague of Tyson's at the hospital. Dr. Jamison and his wife were new to town and currently living in an apartment. They had recently purchased land on the outskirts of town and were anxious to build their home.

Tessa Motley's mother was a patient of Tyson's. When she had mentioned that she and her husband planned to build a house on property that Tessa had inherited from a grandmother, Tyson had recommended Hunter.

Then there were the Davises, an older couple with dreams of building a house on beachfront property they had recently purchased in Savannah.

Hunter rose to her feet and walked over to the coffeepot to pour herself a cup. Her thoughts couldn't help but dwell on the man who'd helped to give her business a kick start. It has been two weeks since she'd seen or talked to him. She had called and left a message with him two days ago that the preliminary sketches for his house were ready. However, he hadn't bothered to call her back.

In a way she should be glad he'd given up on pursuing her, but for some reason she wasn't. Mainly because if he wasn't chasing her that meant some other woman was holding his interest now. Why did that bother her? Probably because he still managed to creep into her nightly dreams, which were getting steamier and more erotic. Going without sex for four years had finally caught up with her. Even now the thought of being seduced by Tyson Steele wasn't as unappealing as it had been originally. She took a sip of her coffee, not believing she was actually thinking that way.

She turned when she heard the knock on her door. "Come in."

The door opened and the very subject of her thoughts walked in. Tyson strode in with the casual arrogance that was so much a part of him. She was forced to admit the man was the most sensuous piece of artwork she'd ever seen. So much so it was mind-boggling. He was the last person she'd expected to see today and his surprise visit had her breathless.

He gave her a sexy smile that made her knees weaken. She could actually feel the sexual chemistry sizzling between them. "Hunter."

The sound of his voice actually made her skin tingle. What were the odds that the very man she'd been thinking about suddenly appeared? How strange was that? Somehow she found her voice to ask. "Tyson? What are you doing here?"

"I got the message you left on my phone."

"That was two days ago." She hoped he hadn't heard the testiness in her voice.

"I know. I slept for almost two days."

Hunter fought back the temptation to ask the question that burned in her mind. *With whom?* Instead she put her coffee cup down and moved to stand in front of her desk. She felt the heat of his gaze with every step she took. Every other time, the fact that he closely watched her every move had annoyed her, but not now. It thrilled her.

When she reached her desk she turned and looked over at him to find his piercing green eyes staring her up and down. She fought back a heated shiver and asked, "Is anything wrong?"

"What makes you think something is wrong, Hunter?"

She wished it didn't do things to her whenever he said her name. "You're staring." She'd worn a dress today and his gaze continued to roam up and down her legs.

"I am, aren't I? My only excuse is that you're good to look at."

Carter had rarely given her compliments, so hearing them from Tyson definitely boosted her feminine confidence. He might be checking her out but she was doing the same with him. She couldn't help but appreciate how good he looked in his jeans and the way his shirt fit over his well-toned muscles. She forced her eyes away. "I'm sure that's a line you've used on a number of women."

"No. It's not."

Deciding not to believe him, she looked past his shoulder to the door. "How did you get into my office without Pauline announcing you?"

He shrugged. "I told her she didn't have to bother. I like announcing myself. Besides, she was packing up to leave, and she told me to tell you that she would see you Monday morning."

Hunter glanced at her watch. She hadn't realized it was so late. That meant they were alone and that wasn't a good thing right now with her present frame of mind. The best thing was to send him packing. Picking up the manila folder off her desk, she offered it to him. "Here's what you came for."

Tyson moved toward her with calm, deliberate strides, and when he came to a stop directly in front of her, she tried ignoring the sparks going off inside her. Instead of accepting the folder, he reached out and brushed the tips of his fingers across her cheek. "That's not what I came for, Hunter. This is."

And before she could draw her next breath, he leaned in and captured her mouth with his.

* * *

Tyson hadn't lied when he'd told Hunter that this was what he'd come for. He refused to suffer through another dream where he'd kissed her madly without getting a taste of the real thing. And now he was discovering that no dream could compare. It didn't come close.

He'd known when he took her mouth that he risked getting his tongue bitten off. Evidently she needed this kiss as much as he did if the way her tongue was mating with his was anything to go by. He could taste her hunger in this kiss, and he could feel the passion and the desire engulfing them. He was greedily lapping up her mouth.

He'd kissed her once before, years ago behind the lockers at school. It had been way too short and at the time he hadn't known how to use his tongue like he did now. He hadn't known how much kissing could thoroughly arouse a man when done the right way and with the right woman.

Tyson wrapped his arms around Hunter's waist to bring her closer. Never had any woman's mouth tasted so delicious, so hot that it was heating the blood rushing through his veins. In seconds he had her purring and himself moaning.

He heard the folder she'd been holding fall to the floor seconds before she wrapped her arms around his neck as he continued to feast on her mouth. He moaned again when he felt her hardened nipples press into his chest. And if that wasn't bad enough, her scent was all around him, seducing him in a way no other woman had ever been capable of doing.

He knew this kiss was the beginning and was determined for it not to be the end. He had succeeded in breaking through her shell, but it was imperative not to push too hard and too soon. So he did what he really didn't want to do—pull back from the kiss.

Before she could say anything—he was certain it would be something he didn't want to hear right then—he leaned close and whispered against her moist lips. "Have dinner with me, Hunter."

Hunter could only stand there, feeling weak in the knees, while she gazed into the green eyes staring back at her. One minute Tyson had been standing in front of her and the next he had his tongue in her mouth. And the minute she tasted it she was powerless to resist him.

His kiss had been possessive. It had sent her emotions in a tailspin, accelerating out of control. At the time, something had convinced her that she desperately needed the urgent mating of his tongue with hers and she'd given in to it. Now that the kiss was over, common sense had returned and she was thinking more rationally. At least she hoped so.

"Hunter?"

She drew in a deep breath. He had asked her to have dinner with him and there was no way she could do that, especially after that kiss. He had shown her what could happen if she lowered her guard with him just for one moment. "I can't have dinner with you."

He frowned down at her. "You can't or you won't?"

It was basically the same thing in her book. "Does it matter?"

"Yes."

"Not to me, Tyson."

"What are you afraid of?"

That question irked her. "I'm not afraid of anything."

He crossed his arms over his chest. "Do you know what I think?"

"Not really."

"I'm going to tell you anyway. I think you're afraid that I have the capability to make you feel like a woman again."

Hunter swallowed deeply, knowing what he said was true, but she'd never admit to him. "Sorry to disappointment you but—"

"You could never disappoint me, Hunter. Only pleasure me."

If his words were meant to take the wind from her sails, they succeeded. She wished he wouldn't say things like that. Words that could slice through her common sense and make her want things she shouldn't have. "Doesn't matter."

"It does to me. Let's have dinner and talk about it."

That was the last thing she wanted to do—discuss how she'd come unglued in his arms. "I'd rather not."

"I wish you would. What I told you earlier was true. I've been sleeping for almost forty-eight hours."

"Why?"

"A lot of surgeries at the hospital." He paused a moment and then added, "And I lost one of my patients during surgery last week."

His words sliced through her irritation. "Oh, Tyson,

I'm so sorry to hear that." Without realizing she was doing so, she reached out and touched his arm.

He drew in a deep breath. "Doctors aren't super-heroes and we can only do so much but…"

"But you did your best."

"Yes," he agreed somberly. "I did my best. Unfortunately for Mr. Beaumont, my best wasn't good enough."

A part of Hunter understood how Tyson was feeling. All she had to do was to recall that time when her grandfather had first taken ill. She had been at the hospital with him when a commotion out in the hall had drawn her attention. She'd stepped out in time to hear some family member of a person who'd just died accuse the doctor of not doing enough. The doctor had tried to calm the person down, saying he'd done all he could. Hunter had known the accusations hurled at the doctor had hurt. For a quick second she'd seen the agonized look in the doctor's eyes. And then she'd understood. The man was a doctor but he was also a human being. Just like family members grieved for their lost loved ones, doctors grieved for the patients they lost.

Tyson leaned down to pick up the folder she had dropped earlier. When he handed it to her, he said, "Look, I didn't mean to mention that. I asked you to dinner, not to attend a pity party."

"I'm glad because a pity party isn't what you're going to get. If the offer for dinner still stands, then I'll take it."

He eyed her curiously. "Why did you change your mind?"

"Because although you have the ability to irritate

me, I do need to go over these with you," she said, handing the folder back to him. "And I really should be nice to you."

At the sensual gleam that suddenly appeared in his eyes, she quickly said, "Not *that* nice."

He chuckled. "And why do you think you should be nice to me?"

"Thanks to you, I have three new clients. I appreciate the referrals."

Tyson shrugged. "No big deal."

"It's my business we're talking about, so to me it is a big deal. Thank you."

"You're welcome. But there's one thing I forgot to mention about dinner."

She looked up at him. "What?"

"It's at my place."

She frowned, not liking how he'd easily maneuvered that one. There was no way he could have forgotten to mention that earlier. "I thought you couldn't cook."

"I can't," he said, heading for the door. "But I know how to pick up takeout. I hope you like Thai food."

Hunter did, but she wasn't sure having dinner at his place was a smart idea. She was about to tell him so when he added over his shoulder, "I'll text you my address. See you in an hour."

And then he opened the door and walked out, closing it behind him.

Chapter 6

Hunter stared at the closed door and a part of her wished there was more going on between her and Tyson than physical attraction. The sexual vibes they emitted whenever they were together were so strong she bet a person walking across the street could pick up on it.

And that kiss…

Just thinking about it made her weak in the knees so she moved around her desk and sat down. The kiss had started off gentle and when she began participating, mingling her tongue with his, it had gotten downright passionate to a degree she'd never experienced before. Who kissed like that? Evidently Tyson Steele did. She didn't recall the one time they'd kissed back in high school having this type of effect on her. He had definitely gotten experience over the years. The man knew how to use his tongue in a way that could be destructive to a woman's mind. It had definitely obliterated her common sense. For a minute there she hadn't wanted him to stop and had been disappointed when he'd done so.

The kiss had evidently affected him, too. She had been able to feel the heat radiating from his body as he kissed her. And when she had wrapped her arms around his neck and pressed her body closer to his, she had felt evidence of his desire. His huge erection had pressed into her middle and all she could think about was how it would feel inside her.

Like in her dreams.

Hunter drew in a deep breath. That kiss had gotten out of hand, and on top of that, she had agreed to have dinner with him at his place. What could she have been thinking? Tyson had told her what he wanted from her and now he probably thought it was within his reach. That was the last thing she wanted him to think.

Hunter was about to pull her cell phone out of her purse to call Tyson and cancel dinner when it rang. She frowned when she recognized the ringtone. Why would Nadine Robinson be calling her? She hadn't talked to her mother-in-law in over two years. Not since Hunter had filed for a divorce. Carter's father, Lewis Robinson, had forbidden the family from having anything to do with Hunter for divorcing his son.

Curiosity got the best of her so she clicked on the phone. "Yes, Nadine?"

"Hunter? Glad I was able to reach you. I was afraid you had changed your number."

It was on the tip of Hunter's tongue to say although she hadn't changed her phone number, she had blocked certain callers from getting through, like Nadine's son. She would have blocked Nadine's number as well, but figured the older woman had no reason to ever call her.

"This is a surprise, Nadine. What can I do for you?" Hunter decided to get straight to the point. There was no reason for her and the woman to engage in friendly chitchat.

"I called to warn you. About Carter."

Hunter lifted a brow. "Why would you want to warn me about Carter?"

"His world is falling apart. He's losing clients right and left and several employees have quit."

That didn't surprise Hunter. Although Carter had underhandedly taken her clients away, she figured it was only a matter of time before he lost them. As for the employees, although Carter was a pretty good architect, he lacked people skills, so that wasn't a shocker.

"That's not my problem, Nadine."

"I know, but he intends to make it your problem."

Hunter drew in a breath. "And how does he think he can do that?"

"I overheard him and Lewis talking. They've come up with a plan for you to return to Boston and get back with Carter."

When hell freezes over. Hunter sat up straight in her chair. "What plan?"

"Carter will be in Phoenix on business in a few weeks and he plans to look you up when he gets there. He told Lewis he will apologize to you for all he's done, tell you how much he regrets losing you and that he can't live without you. The plan is to tug on your heart-strings."

"My heartstrings?"

"Yes."

Hunter raised a brow. "What does my heart have to do with it?"

"Because you're still in love with him."

Hunter shook her head. Now she had heard everything. "Nadine, why would anyone think I'm still in love with Carter?"

"Because you haven't been seriously involved with anyone since your divorce. You didn't date when you were here in Boston and from what Carter is hearing, you haven't dated anyone since you've moved back to Phoenix."

Hunter frowned. "And how can he know that?"

There was a pause on the line before Nadine said, "Carter has friends in Phoenix and they occasionally report back to him on your activities. You're not in-volved with anyone so it seems you're still carrying a torch for him."

"Well, whoever thinks that is dead wrong."

"I'm glad. I was getting worried. You did the right thing by ending your marriage to my son."

Hunter frowned. "That's not what you told me, Na-dine."

"I know. But trust me, I did you a favor. I saw what was happening and refused to let you become a mini-me. Carter had begun treating you like Lewis treated me. You had started believing the lies and accepting his behavior.

I knew you deserved better. The best thing you did was divorce my son. He's out of your life and I hope you won't let him back in."

Hunter hated admitting it, but Nadine was right. She had started letting Carter get away with murder and he knew it. Instead of divorcing him, for two years she had bought into his crap that her life would be nothing without him. She'd opted to stay married to him but moved into the guest bedroom.

It had been goodbye and good riddance to Carter Robinson. And that's the way she would keep it.

"Trust me, Nadine, there's no way I will ever get back with Carter. And if he has this bizarre delusion that I'm still in love with him then he is dead wrong."

"Good. I'm glad you moved back to Phoenix. But you need to get involved with someone. You need a life. As long as you don't have one, Carter is going to think he has a chance with you again."

As far as Hunter was concerned, Nadine had no right to tell her what she needed. And Carter could think whatever he wanted. "Let me assure you, Nadine, I do have a life."

"So you're seeing someone?"

Tyson's image suddenly came into her mind. "Yes, I am seeing someone. In fact I'll be meeting him for dinner in a couple of hours." What she'd just said hadn't been a total lie.

"I'm glad. I know you probably won't ever forgive me for siding against you during the divorce, but I did what I felt I had to do for your own good. Goodbye,

Hunter. I wish you the best and hope your young man makes you happy."

"Goodbye, Nadine."

Hunter clicked off the phone, shaking her head. Carter actually thought he could show up in Phoenix with a plan to get her back? Did he really think she was pining away for him just because she hadn't gotten seriously involved with anyone since their divorce?

At that moment her phone rang and she recognized Mo's ringtone. She was glad it wasn't Nadine calling her back. "Yes, Mo?"

"Kat called earlier. She has a date and Eric decided to come to town this weekend. Just wanted to make sure you'd be okay."

She shook her head. "You guys don't have to keep me company like I don't have a life, you know." At that moment Hunter realized she had lied to Nadine because in all honesty, she really didn't have a life.

"Mo, can I ask you something?"

"Sure."

"Do you think I'm still in love with Carter?"

There was a pause. "To be honest with you, the thought had crossed my mind a time or two. Where did that question come from?"

Hunter let out a deep sigh and told Mo about her conversation with Carter's mother. "How can you or anyone think I still care for him, Mo?"

"Well, it has been two years, Hunter, and you haven't as much as dated another man."

"The first year after my divorce I swore off men," she said, unable to keep the bitterness out of her voice.

"That's understandable."

Hunter knew that the reason Mo had divorced her ex hadn't been about another woman but about Larry's gambling addiction. When he had refused help and had sold every single item in their home to feed his habit, Mo had had enough.

"What about now since you've moved back to Phoenix?" Mo asked, interrupting Hunter's thoughts.

"I'm busy trying to start my business here."

"Then you need to learn how to multitask. And to be honest, it sounds to me like you're making excuses. Being in a relationship with someone won't consume that much of your time, Hunter. You've even got one of those Bad News Steeles hot on your tail. Do you know how many women in town would love to be in your shoes?"

"Then let them. I prefer not to do casual relationships."

"After what Carter put you through do you honestly prefer a serious one? All you'll get is nothing but heartache... unless you're entertaining the thought of marrying again."

"Never!"

"Then what's wrong with casual? I'm not saying you should start hopping from bed to bed or that you should get involved with Tyson Steele but..." Mo trailed off.

"But what?"

"If I was going to do casual after going without sex for as long as you have, Tyson would be my man. One night with him would probably make you realize what you're missing. You claim you haven't had an orgasm in so long that you've forgotten how it feels. That's sad

for any single woman to admit to…unless you're doing
the celibate thing."

"No, that's not it."

"Then what is it? I can see why Carter thinks you're
still carrying a torch for him. What you need to do is
declare your sexual independence."

"My sexual independence?"

"Yes, and I think the ideal person to start with is
Tyson. The word *serious* is not in his vocabulary so
you're safe there. And if the rumors about him are true,
he'll make you remember just how explosive an orgasm
can be and have you screaming all over the place. He
told you that he had plans to seduce you, so let him."

"If I were to do that, then I become just another
notch on his belt. I didn't want that when we were in
high school and I don't want that now."

"Then what do you want?"

Hunter should be woman enough to admit she wanted
Tyson. She couldn't help but want him after all those
erotic dreams she'd been having of him lately. But she
didn't want him on his terms and told Mo how she felt.

"In that case then why not take the initiative and seduce *him*? That way you'll maintain control."

Hunter gazed out her window and stared at the
mountains in the distance. The sun was going down
and cast a purple glow on the skyline. "Seducing a man
might be easy for you, Mo, but it wouldn't be for me."
She just could not see herself using her feminine wiles
to get a man in bed.

Mo intruded on her thoughts. "For once will you
accept that you're a woman who has needs like the

rest of us? A woman who's capable of planning her own seduction and doesn't need Tyson Steele to plan it for her?" She blew out an exasperated breath. "There's no manual detailing how to go about it. You do what comes natural."

"What comes natural?"

"Yes, and it's easier than you think. There's physical attraction between you and Tyson, as well as strong sexual chemistry. Kat and I felt it that night at the club. All you have to do is let that chemistry be your guide."

Mo's words echoed in Hunter's mind long after they ended the phone call. They haunted her as she began closing her office for the weekend, knowing she had little time to decide just how she would handle Tyson. Her conversations with Nadine and Mo had made her realize it was past time to take control of her life. For a change, she needed to do whatever pleased her.

An image of Tyson suddenly appeared in her head. The thought of sharing a bed with him sent heated shivers through her body. And if he was really a master in the bedroom, as those rumors went, then he was just what she needed. In fact, he was long overdue. However, like she'd told Mo, she had one big issue with Tyson. He'd already planned how he intended for things between them to end—with his seduction of her. He probably had a spot in his bed with her name on it—right along with all those other women he'd had sex with in that same bed.

What man targets a woman for seduction and, worse, is arrogant enough to tell her, as if it's a gift she should appreciate? Only a man with the mind-set of Tyson Steele.

She would just love to best him at his own game and still get something out of it. It was about time some woman knocked him off his high horse. It would serve him right for being so darn egotistical. Could that woman be her? It would mean her stepping into a role she'd never played before, but it would be well worth it if she got the results she wanted and on her terms.

Moments later she left her office, deciding that to-night she would not allow Tyson to seduce her. She would be seducing him.

Tyson smiled as he gazed around his kitchen and dining-room areas. His sister-in-law Brittany would be proud of him. The table was set perfectly. Brittany owned Etiquette Matters, a school that taught etiquette and manners. Tyson's mother was into all that etiquette stuff and although she'd made sure they had impeccable manners while growing up, she felt her sons needed to take a refresher course. When Brittany opened a school in Phoenix after marrying Galen, Eden Tyson Steele strongly suggested that her sons enroll in one of Brit-tany's classes. To pacify their mother, they had.

Tyson checked his watch and drew in a deep breath, not wanting to think about this being a first for him. He didn't prepare dinner for women. They prepared dinner for him. Although he hadn't actually prepared this one, he had invited her to his place and would be feeding her. He had crossed plenty of boundaries with Hunter and wasn't sure what he should do about it.

Hell, he wasn't even sure he wanted to do anything about it. And that in itself was crazy. Why was there such strong sexual chemistry between them? What exactly had brought it on and when would it end? He had tried to recall the exact moment he'd lost his head. Had it been the moment he'd seen her when she had walked into Notorious? Or had it been when he'd conversed with her while sitting at her table? Or had it been when he'd dropped in on her unexpectedly that first time at her office? Or had it been when he'd kissed her? All he knew was that if he wasn't careful, she could easily get under his skin and he refused to let that happen.

Why was she making his plan of seduction so damn difficult? She wanted him as much as he wanted her, he was sure of it. But she continued to deny what they both wanted—one night in his bed. Was that too much to ask? He didn't think so, but evidently she did.

His phone rang, nearly startling him out of his reverie. He recognized the ringtone. It was Gannon. He picked up his cell phone from the kitchen counter. "It took you long enough to call me back, Gannon."

He could hear his youngest brother's chuckle. "Now that Galen's married, am I supposed to report in with you now?"

Gannon was becoming such a smart-ass. "Wouldn't hurt."

"Don't hold your breath, Tyson. What's up?"

"I hear you're driving one of your rigs to Florida."

"That's right. Do you want to go along for the ride?"

He'd done it before and had to admit he had fun.

The women they'd met along the way had been worth it. "Wish I could but I can't."

For some reason he didn't want to leave Phoenix right now. He refused to believe Hunter McKay had anything to do with it. Hadn't he gone two weeks without seeing her? He forced the thought to the back of his mind just how miserable those days had been.

"Too much is going on at the hospital, Gannon," he added. "I was lucky to get this time off." And he was spending it with a woman who wasn't sharing his bed. How crazy was that?

"I dropped by and saw Brittany and the twins today."

"How are they?"

"Everybody's fine. Galen was changing Ethan's diaper. Can you imagine that?"

"No, but he's a father now and with it comes responsibilities. Keep that in mind if you get it into your head to invite some woman into your rig for the night."

Gannon chuckled. "Please don't cover the birds and bees with me again, Tyson. I got it the last time."

"Just make sure you remember it. And stay condom safe."

"Whatever. I'm headed out in the morning. I just left the folks' place and they're still beaming over the twins. Mom has taken over a thousand pictures already."

"Doesn't surprise me."

At that moment Tyson's doorbell sounded. "My dinner guest has arrived. I'll talk to you later."

"Dinner guest? You can't cook."

"Not trying to cook," he said, moving around the breakfast bar to head for the door.

"I can't believe you invited a woman to your place."

Tyson rolled his eyes. "Women have been to my place before, Gannon. Numerous times."

"As a bedmate. Not a dinner guest."

He didn't need his brother reminding him of his strange behavior. "Be safe on the road."

"Okay. See you in a week."

"Will do," Tyson said, clicking off the phone and sliding it into the back pocket of his jeans. He stopped in the middle of his living room and inhaled deeply, convinced he could pick up Hunter's scent through the door. He shook his head. He had to be imagining things.

He glanced around his condo again. Although he appreciated his cleaning lady, she never had a lot to do because he spent most of his time at the hospital. But still, he was glad he wasn't a slob and kept a pretty tidy place. Hunter ought to be impressed.

Tyson shuddered at where his thoughts had gone again. Who cared if she was impressed or not? A completely physical, emotion-free involvement was what he wanted with Hunter. Inviting her to dinner was a means to an end, and the end was getting her into his bed.

He walked to the door, opened it and faltered at the same time he was certain his jaw dropped. He could only stand there and stare wide-eyed. What in the world…?

"I hope I'm not late, Tyson."

He inhaled sharply as deep-seated hunger nearly took control of his senses. Hunter had changed clothes. The coral dress she was wearing now fitted her body like another layer of skin, showing every single curve.

The neckline dipped low at just the right angle to show enough of her breasts, while at the same time enticing him to want to see more. She always looked totally feminine in whatever outfit she wore, but in this particular dress she looked like sex on two legs. And speaking of legs… They looked even more gorgeous in this short dress with a pair of killer heels on her feet. The entire ensemble was meant to push a man's buttons and it was pushing his in a big way. Somehow she'd transformed her image from a good girl to a totally naughty one.

For a moment he couldn't say anything. His mind filled with thoughts of just how he would take this dress off her later. He fought the urge to do it now. He was tempted to reach out and touch her all over to see if the material of her dress felt as sensuous as it looked. Instead he stood there, leaning against the doorjamb while his gaze roamed up and down her body, appreciating every stitch, inch and curve he saw.

"Tyson, I hope I'm not late."

She repeated herself so he figured it was time to rein in his desire and respond. "You're right on time."

And with the feel of his erection pressing hard against the zipper of his jeans, he meant every single word. "Come in," he invited, moving aside.

She entered, walking past him. He appreciated the sway of her hips and how her every step placed emphasis on her delectable-looking backside, as well as those killer heels on her feet. And if that wasn't mind-boggling enough, her delicious scent almost made him moan.

"Thanks for inviting me to dinner," she said, turning around in the middle of his foyer.

Hell, he would invite her to dinner every single night if she showed up looking like this. If she bent over even just a little he was certain he would be able to see her panties. That thought made his erection even harder.

Lust began taking over his mind, drugging him, gripping him, and he hoped he could make it through dinner. After that the night would belong to him and he intended to make good use of his time. She had to have known wearing this outfit would increase his desire for her. He wanted her so badly his entire body ached.

"No need to thank me," he said, leading her to the living room. He wished they could skip dinner altogether and head straight to the bedroom.

"We're having Thai, right?"

He turned and his gaze automatically went to her legs. He could envision her doing a lot with those legs and all of them included him between them. He forced his gaze from her legs up to her face. Why did her lips look like they needed to be kissed? "Sorry. What did you ask?"

Hunter smiled at him. "I asked if we're still having Thai."

She might be having Thai but he was having her. "Yes. The table is all set and the food is ready."

"Good. I'm starving."

So was he. So were his hands. His fingers. His mouth. His shaft. All were anxious to touch her. Taste her. Get inside her.

Tyson drew in a deep breath, trying to get back the control he was quickly losing. She had a lot of guts wearing this outfit to his place tonight. Had she thought he would focus on dinner and not on her? Especially when he'd warned her of his plans to seduce her?

Wait a minute… Warning bells began going off in his head. This whole thing was too good to be true. Why did he smell a setup? Tyson crossed his arms over his chest. "Okay, Hunter. What's going on? Why are you dressed like this?"

She lifted a brow. "Dressed like what?"

"Like you'll be my dessert once we finish dinner."

Chapter 7

Hunter took a deep breath, trying to ignore the intense nervousness floating around in her stomach. What had Mo said about just doing what came naturally? If that was the case then why was she suddenly feeling like a fish out of water? Now she was wondering if she'd overdone things, especially with this outfit. She had dropped by Phase One, a boutique she'd passed several times on her way home. A twentysomething salesgirl had been more than happy to help her shop for the perfect seduction outfit.

"So, do you intend on being my dessert, Hunter?"

She licked her lips and saw his gaze follow the movement of her tongue. "Your dessert?"

"Yes." Dropping his hands, he closed the distance

separating them. "Do I need to go into details? What about a demonstration?"

She wished his eyes didn't captivate her, or that huge erection she couldn't help but notice didn't hold such promise. When he'd covered the distance separating them, he did so with the ease of a hunter stalking his prey. She had a mind to take a step back, but decided to stand her ground. "Neither is necessary, Tyson. Do you have a problem with what I'm wearing?"

A smile curved the corner of his lips. "No, I don't have a problem with it, as long as you know what it means."

"And what does it mean?"

A serious smile touched his lips. "A woman wears a dress like this to give a man a sign as to how the evening will end."

"I suggest you don't jump to conclusions. I merely decided to change into something more comfortable. But if my dress makes you uncomfortable then…"

"Doesn't bother me as long as you know I'll be trying like hell to get you out of it later."

"Do you always say whatever you want?"

"No need to play games when it comes to us. I told you my plans for you that first night. Now, let's enjoy dinner."

Hunter drew in a deep breath. Tyson Steele might think he had his own plan, but he would find out soon enough she also had hers.

As he led her over to the dining room table and pulled out a chair for her, she looked around. "You have a nice home, Tyson. It's pretty spacious for a condo. The architect in me likes the layout. I have a fondness for the open floor plan. Great for entertaining."

He shrugged. "I don't consider it as home. Since I spend a lot of time at the hospital, I think of this as the place where I eat and sleep."

Hunter figured he could have said that this was the place where he ate, slept and had sex. She figured he had a revolving door to his bedroom.

She couldn't help noticing how nice he'd set the table. Fine china and silverware, cloth napkins and crystal glasses. "Pretty fancy for takeout."

He leaned close and stared into her eyes as he poured wine into her glass. "Thought I'd impress you."

"You have."

"Good. I'll be back with everything in a second."

Hunter didn't release the breath she'd been holding until he left to go into the kitchen.

Tyson decided not to question his luck tonight. Hunter could pretend indifference all she wanted, but there had to be a reason she'd worn that dress. She was a very sensual woman and tonight he was very much aware of her body, more so than ever in that outfit.

Gathering all the dishes, he left the kitchen to re-enter the dining room and she glanced in his direction. "Need help?"

"No, I got this," he said, placing several platters and serving utensils in the middle of the table. He quickly returned to the kitchen to grab the bowl of tossed salad, the only thing he could actually claim he'd made. "I love Thai, and Latti's makes it just the way I like. Red roast duck on rice is my favorite. I think you'll enjoy it."

"I'm sure I will. It looks delicious."

"Then let's dig in," he said, taking the chair across from her.

"Umm, why don't you serve me?"

He glanced over at her. "Serve you?"

"Yes," she said, holding up her plate expectantly.

He held her gaze for a moment before picking up the serving spoon and proceeded to place several spoonfuls into her plate. What the hell was going on here? When did he serve women? He forced back his irritation and figured he would get his just reward later that night.

She took a forkful and moaned. Then she licked her lips.

Tyson felt a tightening in his groin as he watched her. He would serve her food again if she licked her lips like that one more time. It had him remembering the kisses they'd shared. Made him anticipate the ones he intended to share later.

"This is delicious, Tyson."

Why did her compliment make his chest expand? It's not like he'd cooked it himself. "Glad you think so."

For the next few minutes they ate in silence. Instead of using the quiet to his advantage to regroup and make sure he was back in control of his senses, he found himself becoming even more aware of her. Like that cute tiny mole just below her right ear. Why hadn't he noticed that before?

"I guess I really was starving."

Her words made him look at her plate. It was clean.

Mercury swore that a woman who had a healthy appetite when it came to food also had a healthy appetite in
the bedroom. Tyson never noticed a correlation, but tonight he was hoping there was one. "I guess you were.
Want seconds?"

"Don't tempt me."

He didn't see why he shouldn't when she was definitely tempting him. It wouldn't take much to clear this
table and proceed to spread her across it. "I won't tempt
you. Would you like more wine?"

"Yes."

He could have poured the wine from where he sat but
decided now was the time to make his move. He walked
around the table to stand beside her and poured the
wine into her glass. "I hope you left room for dessert."

She looked up at him and held his gaze. He could
feel her need even if she was trying to downplay it. She
wanted him as much as he wanted her. He knew the
signs. He could see it in her eyes. Desire was lining her
pupils, drenching her irises. The nipples of her breasts
had formed into tight buds and were pressing against
her dress. But the telltale sign was her feminine scent.
The aroma was getting to him and he didn't want to play
games if playing those games would delay things. He
was ready to take things from the dining room straight
into the bedroom.

He watched her tongue when she nervously licked her
top lip. "I guess this is where we need to talk, Tyson."

Talk? The only talking they needed to do was pillow talk and that would come later. "What do we need
to talk about?"

Instead of answering him, she picked up her glass and took a sip of her wine. She placed the glass back down and held his gaze once again. "About your misconception that if I sleep with you tonight it will because you seduced me into doing so."

He didn't see it as a misconception, but as a fact. "Do you have a problem with me seducing you, Hunter?"

She nodded. "Yes, I have a problem with it. I refuse to be just another one of your conquests."

Tyson hoped history wasn't repeating itself. If he recalled, she'd said something similar eighteen years ago. Back then she wanted to be his one and only girl. Surely she wasn't asking for some sort of commitment from him, because if she was she wouldn't be getting it.

He hated to ask but really needed to know. "And just what do you want to be?"

"The one doing the seducing."

"Why?"

Hunter had expected Tyson's question. "I told you. Because I refuse to be another one of your conquests. That night at Notorious you stated you plan to seduce me. If we sleep together tonight, I don't want you to think you've succeeded. I want to set the record straight that if we share a bed it will be because it was my choice and not because you've done or said anything to persuade or entice me."

"So you want to play a mind game?" Tyson asked.

"No. I don't want to play any games. I just don't want you thinking that like all those other women, I fell under your spell. I can get up and walk out the door right now if that's what I choose to do. There's no way you can touch me, kiss me or talk to me that will make me change my mind unless it's something I want to do."

An arrogant smile touched his lips. "You think not?"

"I know not."

"You wouldn't be the first woman who thought so. But fine," he said, taking a step back. "If you want to seduce me, go right ahead. Don't expect me to resist. It will be a first."

Hunter lifted a brow. "No woman has ever seduced you before?"

"No. If a woman wants me and I'm not interested in her, no amount of seduction on her part will make me change my mind. And if it's a woman I want, they usually fit into two categories. Those who are willing and those who aren't."

He paused a minute as if to make sure she was keeping up with his logic. "Now, if it's a willing woman then there's no need for seduction because getting together will be mutual."

"And if she's unwilling?" she asked.

An egotistical smile touched his lips. "Those are few, but any woman who resists my interest just needs a little coaxing. That's when my seduction comes into play. And just so you know, I'm an expert at it."

He was conceited enough to believe that, Hunter thought. She figured he classified her in the latter group, which was why he'd put his plan of seduction in place. "And you thought I needed coaxing?"

"Yes. But I can always move you to the willing category if it makes you feel better."

Hunter frowned. He just didn't get it. She wanted sleeping with him to be her choice and not his. She didn't want to be just another woman seduced by Tyson Steele. She stood and said, "I think I need to go. Dinner was great and—"

"Wait." He stared at her while he shoved his hands into the pockets of his jeans. "What's going on, Hunter? What is this about?"

"Nothing is going on. I've simply changed my mind about seducing you. I suggest you do the same."

"What are you afraid of, Hunter?"

She lifted her chin. "What makes you think I'm afraid of anything?"

"Because you're running."

He was right. She was running. "You want to seduce me and I won't let you. I want to seduce you, but you don't think I can. So what's the point?"

"I didn't say I didn't think you could seduce me. I merely stated no woman ever felt the need to try because I've always picked the women I wanted." He looked back at her, stared at her as if she was a puzzle he was trying to figure out. Then he added, "I want you, so it doesn't matter to me who seduces whom."

"It does to me."

"I see that and I'm trying to understand why."

She forced her gaze away from him and knew there was no way she could explain it to him. All this was a game to Tyson, a game he intended to win, and if he seduced her then he would be winning. It was just like with Carter. He'd played games with her for eight years. She'd been a contestant with no chance of winning, not even his heart. And God knows she'd tried. Well, those days were over and now she flat-out refused to let any man best her ever again.

But she couldn't possibly get Tyson to understand her past. "It's too complicated to explain."

"Try me," he said, reaching out and touching her arm.

She drew in a sharp breath at his touch. And held it when he slowly caressed her skin, making tingles of desire spread through her.

"And try this," he added, leaning forward and using the tip of his tongue to lick her lips. "And I would just love for you to try this," he whispered, deliberately pressing his body closer to hers so that she could feel his hard erection against the juncture of her thighs.

"You're trying to seduce me," she accused in a breathless whisper and could feel herself getting weak in the knees. Resisting him in his domain would be harder than she thought.

"I'm showing you that we want each other, Hunter. The desire is mutual. You can arouse me just as much as I can arouse you. So why does it matter who's seducing whom?"

A part of Hunter knew it shouldn't but for her it did. "It matters to me, Tyson. I refuse to be seduced by you."

He paused a moment before releasing her and taking a step back. "Fine. Since it matters so much to you, then go ahead. Seduce the hell out of me."

Tyson wasn't sure what was going on with Hunter, but he figured it had something to do with her ex. She wouldn't be the first woman who'd brought baggage into

his bedroom. And on more than one occasion he'd allowed them to do so knowing that after his first thrust
into their body, whatever issues they were dealing with
would take a backseat to the pleasures they would experience in his bed.

Hunter was being difficult and he didn't need a difficult woman. So why was he even putting up with it?
And why, even now, did he want her more than he'd
ever wanted any woman? He shook his head. Because
she was the "one who got away." All it would take was
one night of tumbling between the sheets with her to
get her out of his system. Hell, he probably didn't need
the entire night. A few hours should work just fine.

As he watched her gaze sweep him up and down, he
knew she was aware of his arousal. He refused to waste
this opportunity to get her into his bed. "Do it, Hunter,"
he whispered hoarsely. "Seduce me."

For the longest time they stared at each other and
then she took a tentative step closer, reducing the distance between them. Standing on tiptoes, she slanted
her mouth across his.

Holy hell, Tyson thought the moment she slid her
tongue inside his mouth. At that moment he wasn't sure
what was getting to him more—the way her tongue
was overpowering his mouth, or the feel of her hardened nipples pressed against his chest. He thought he
could just stand there and let her use his mouth to work
out whatever issue she was dealing with. But he soon
discovered his desire for Hunter went deeper than that.

There was no way he could ignore the erratic pounding of his heart or the insistent way his erection pressed

against his zipper. He fought back a moan and then another, and when she shifted her body to meld it even closer to his, he wrapped his arms around her waist. She continued to take his mouth in a way that rocked him to his core. He'd kissed, and been kissed, by scores of women, but it wasn't just Hunter's kiss that had him weak in the knees. It was her taste. Her personal flavor had blood rushing fast and furious through his veins even as he shivered on the inside.

Then suddenly she broke off the kiss. "I want to finish this," she said in a raspy tone, licking her lips.

His gut clenched. He wanted to finish this, as well. Tyson was about to suggest they go into his bedroom when she began moving toward his living room. "Hey, my bedroom is this way," he said.

She looked over her shoulder. "Yours may be but mine is not."

He frowned, wondering what the hell she was talking about. He got even more confused when she grabbed her purse off his sofa. She turned around and said, "I can't share a bed with you here."

"What?" he asked, mystified.

She placed the strap of her purse on her shoulder. "I can't share the bed that others have shared with you."

He stared at her and saw the seriousness in the dark eyes staring back at him. "Why?"

"This is my plan of seduction and I want to finish it at my place. In my own bed. Not one you've shared with a zillion others."

No other woman had ever made such a bold request. He would not have allowed it. So why was he allowing it now? And why was she concerned with how many women had slept in his bed? It was *his* bed and he claimed all rights to it. And for her information, not all his conquests had been brought back here. He'd taken a few to a hotel. But, he admitted only to himself, he rarely went to a woman's home. Very rarely.

Tyson knew men handled things differently when it came to having sex with women. Some didn't invite women to their home, saying it felt like the woman was invading their personal space. Galen and his cousin Donovan Steele from Charlotte had both had the same mind-set in their bachelor days. Tyson never had a problem with it because any woman that he had sex with here knew not to return without an invitation.

"I'm leaving." Hunter turned and headed for the door.

He stared as she walked away, not missing that backside he'd made plans to ride and those gorgeous legs he'd intended to slide between. What in the hell had gone wrong? One part of him wanted to think her leaving was for the best because she certainly thought a lot of herself if she assumed she could call the shots. But another part, the one determined to have sex with her regardless of whose bed he did it in, overruled his common sense, and so he asked, "What's your address?"

She rattled it off over her shoulder. When she reached his door she turned around. "I'll be waiting, Tyson."

"You won't be waiting long." He barely got the words out before she opened the door and closed it shut behind her.

Without even thinking about the craziness of what he was doing, Tyson rushed into his bedroom, grabbed an overnight bag and quickly began throwing items into it. She hadn't said anything about him being an overnight guest, but she would soon find out that he had a few conditions of his own.

Before zipping up the overnight bag he opened the drawer to his nightstand, reached inside and grabbed a handful of condoms. He was about to close the drawer, but then stopped and grabbed some more. Hell, for this little inconvenience, he intended to make tonight worth his while.

Chapter 8

Hunter glanced around her bedroom. Several candles were lit and the fragrance of vanilla floated in the air. She had changed the linens and sprayed vanilla mist over the sheets and pillows for an extra touch.

How many times had she envisioned setting up a bedroom room like this for Carter only to have him make fun of her attempt? That was after he'd accused her of trying to burn the house down with the candles and spraying stuff that he was probably allergic to. Her ex hadn't had a romantic bone in his body. Even during those times when they were trying to have a baby, he refused to let her turn their drab-looking bedroom into a romantic hot spot.

Now she had her hot spot. It was an important component in her plan of seduction. She didn't intend to start bed-hopping with men, by any means, but hopefully after this one time with Tyson, she would have the courage to at least date other men and see where it led.

She had no desire to ever get married again, nor was she interested in engaging in a serious relationship. Occasional dating would suit her just fine. If she liked the man well enough, she saw no reason why they couldn't share an intimate night once in a while. Granted, she had to feel the man was worthy of sharing her bed.

Then what was up with Tyson Steele? Was he worthy?

She wasn't sure about that, but he did know the right buttons to push to arouse her. And there was that element of sexual chemistry between them. So he might as well be her first test. Mo was right. If she was going to declare her sexual independence then it might as well be with Tyson.

At that moment the doorbell sounded. If that was Tyson, he'd arrived sooner than she'd anticipated. She figured he would at least take some time to mull over her offer. Since it appeared that he hadn't, she took it as a strong indication of just how eager he was to have sex with her.

They would have this one night together. In the end she would declare her sexual independence as well as get him out of her system. And if what everyone claimed was true, she would experience her first orgasm in years. Hopefully the dreams would stop coming and she could get a good night's sleep without waking up the next day with an ache between her legs.

Leaving her bedroom, she headed for the door. Half-

way there she paused to draw in a deep breath. There
was no need to get cold feet now, she told herself. Although she and Tyson might have different ideas regarding how to go about getting what they wanted, she was
certain they wanted the same thing. This was not the
time to question her decision to seduce him. It would be
a win-win situation for the both of them, she reminded
herself. Tyson could then move on to the next woman
and she could concentrate on building her company.

Hunter opened her front door and he stood there.
She could only stare at him, taking in all six feet and
more of him. Tyson had a way of making any woman's
body snap to salacious attention whenever she saw him.
Already the tips of her breasts were responding to his
masculine form. Sexual hunger, the likes of which she
experienced only in his company, was taking a greedy
hold on her.

She saw his overnight bag. Did he honestly assume
she would invite him to stay the night? If so, he would
be sorely disappointed later when showed him the door.
She moved aside. "It didn't take you long to get—"

That was as far as she got. Once inside, he shut the
door, dropped the overnight bag to the floor and pulled
her into his arms, slanting his mouth across hers.

Tyson hadn't meant to kiss her. This was her show
and he'd intended to let her play it out however she
chose. He had every intention of just being a willing
participant. But when she'd opened that door and he'd
gotten a glimpse of that dress again, he couldn't resist pulling her into his arms and kissing her like he'd

wanted to do at his place but hadn't gotten the chance. Now he was getting his fill of her taste.

At least she hadn't tried breaking free of his kiss. In fact she was kissing him back with a hunger that nearly matched his own. He loved the way their tongues mated, how hers mingled with his. His heart was racing. He tried to recall the last time a woman did that to him, but couldn't.

Tyson was fully aware that being here with her was overriding common sense and overlooking good sound judgment. He knew better, yet he was refusing to heed those warnings that went off in his head on the drive over here. He had called himself all kinds of fool for chasing after a woman for a one-night stand.

He would deal with the craziness of that later, once he'd gotten her out of his system. But for now all he could do was accept that there was something about Hunter McKay that had him wanting sex, sex and more sex. But only with her.

Moments later, just like he'd been the one to initiate the kiss, he was the one to end it, drawing in a deep delicious breath that included a whiff of her scent. But he was in no hurry to release her. Instead he held her in his arms while he pressed a series of kisses around the curve of her mouth and the tip of her nose. Knowing if he didn't stop touching her now that he never would, he released her and took a step back. The separation almost killed him.

He looked over at her and saw her looking at him. A part of him wanted to read her thoughts, but he figured it was probably best if he didn't know them. She didn't seem upset or annoyed, just somewhat pensive. He'd learned a woman absorbed in her own thoughts was the worst kind because he had no idea what they were thinking…or planning.

Finally, she spoke. "Now that you've gotten that out of your system, will you let me be in charge from here on out?"

Was her assumption true? Had he gotten anything out of his system? He seriously doubted it. Instead of sharing that doubt with her, he shoved his hands into the pockets of his jeans. It was either that or pull her back into his arms.

Forcing that thought from his mind, he dwelled on what she'd asked him. She wanted him to relinquish his control to a woman. To her. Under normal circumstances he would never agree to something like that. But he'd reached the conclusion while racing from his condo to here that nothing about any of this was normal.

"So, Tyson, are you going to let me handle things or not?" she asked again when he evidently hadn't responded quickly enough.

She'd asked him to let her handle *things*. As far as he was concerned, *things* didn't necessarily include him, but he wouldn't tell her that just yet. He was curious to see what she had up her sleeves. If truth be told, sleeves be damned. What he was really interested in was what was up under her dress.

"I suppose I can let you handle things," he finally said.

She raised a brow. "You 'suppose'? Need I remind

you that the moment you walked through that door you entered my territory? You came to me."

He frowned. Did she have to rub it in? "And we both know why," he said. "So why are we still talking?"

She smiled calmly. "You're trying my patience."

He chuckled. "And you've been trying mine since that night we ran into each other at Notorious."

"Would you like to sit and talk a while?"

"No. I have nothing to say and that's not why I'm here."

"I know why you're here, but first I think we need to understand each other," she said.

"Meaning?"

"For starters, I don't know what's up with that bag. Since you aren't a doctor who makes house calls, I can only assume you think you're spending the night. Well, you aren't. You will leave when we're done."

When they were done? Did she assume they would only go one round? He intended to stay the night and take her again and again, well into the morning hours.

"We can discuss that later, Hunter." He figured after he had her once, she'd beg him for more.

"No, I think we need to discuss it now."

He simply stared at her for a moment and then nodded. "Fine. I'll go along with whatever you want," he said, telling her what she wanted to hear. Evidently he'd said the magic words, if the smile that spread across her lips was anything to go by. "I guess I just made your day," he said drily.

"Yes, and I plan to make your night, Tyson Steele."

* * *

Hunter felt in control and she intended to use it to her advantage. She'd never done anything like this before, but she was ready to set the stage for what she had in store for Tyson.

"Go sit on the sofa, Tyson, and get comfortable. Make yourself at home."

A smile touched the corners of his mouth. "At home I tend to walk around in the nude. Can I do it here?"

"No." The thought of him doing such a thing made her nipples harden even more. "Would you like something to drink?"

He shook his head as he moved toward her sofa. "I had wine at dinner. I'm good."

Hunter watched how he eased his body down on her sofa, and how the denim jeans stretched across his muscled thighs. She couldn't wait to actually see those thighs in the flesh. In her dreams she had kneeled between them and—

"Nice place."

She hoped he hadn't noticed the splash of color that had appeared on her cheeks, a result of where her thoughts had been. "Thanks. Not as roomy as yours but it suits me just fine."

He stretched his arms across the back of her sofa as he leaned back in a comfortable position. Doing so brought emphasis to his chest. She looked forward to removing his shirt and was itching to rub her hand against his hard chest and flat stomach. Then she would ease her hands lower to cup him, to feel the part of him that had played a vital role in her dreams.

She could feel more heat in her cheeks. For a woman who hadn't been sexually active in four years, and who hadn't even thought much about it, her mind was having a field day.

Deciding to set the mood, she flicked off the ceiling lights so the living room could be bathed in the soft glow of the two floor lamps. She glanced over and saw him watching her, and desire rippled down her spine. She joined him on the sofa, sitting beside him but not too close. She found the distance really didn't matter. Nothing could eliminate the manly heat emanating from him. Because of it, her skin felt noticeably warm through her dress.

"So, Tyson, how was your day?" She decided a neutral topic was a perfect way to break the ice. But with all the heat surrounding them she knew anything cool didn't have much chance of survival.

A slow, sexy smile spread across his lips. "I don't recall most of it. I slept for the past forty-eight hours, remember."

"Yes. You did mention that."

"Now I'm wide-awake, full of energy and horny as hell."

The man knew just the right words to say to make every hormone in her body sizzle. "Are you?"

"Yes."

"Sleep makes you horny?" She glanced down at his thighs and saw the huge erection bulging between them, pressing against his zipper.

"Only when you occupy my dreams."

His words surprised her and she glanced up and

stared into his face. Had he been dreaming about her like she'd been doing of him? "And what were we doing in your dreams?" she asked, as if she really didn't know. It made sense that when a man like Tyson had dreams they would be nothing but erotic.

"We were making love."

She arched a brow. "For forty-eight hours?"

He chuckled softly, as if remembering. "Yes. We had a lot of ground to cover. A lot of years to make up for. A lot of positions to try."

Imagining a few of those positions had her pulse pounding. "Did we?"

He gave her a sensuous grin. "Yes, we did."

Hunter released a heated breath as his words painted an erotic picture in her mind, making shivers rush up her spine. She held his gaze, felt the stimulating attraction between them. Her face lowered again to the area between his thighs. Was she imagining it or had his erection gotten larger? Thicker? Harder?

She glanced back up at him and saw his smile had widened, as if he'd read her thoughts. But there was no way he could have, she assured herself. He was holding her gaze and sensations began pricking her skin. She didn't have to wonder what the look in his eyes meant.

"Now I know your secret weapon for seduction, Tyson," she said.

"I didn't know I had one."

"You do."

"Then tell me what it is," he said and she didn't miss how he'd spread his legs so his thigh brushed her thigh, which wasn't covered by her short dress. The contact was stimulating and she was tempted to close her eyes and moan.

"It's your eyes," she said, staring into them. "You can literally seduce a woman without opening your mouth. All you have to do is level those green eyes on her."

"You think so?"

"Aren't you trying to seduce me?"

"No. We agreed that you would seduce me. The look you see in my eyes is nothing more than an indication of just how much I want you."

If he thought his words were getting to her, then he was right. Maybe it was time she let a few of hers get next to him.

"I've turned my bedroom into a romantic hot spot just for tonight," she said softly.

She saw the desire in his eyes deepen. "Did you?"

"Yes. I think you'll like it."

"A long as you're in there with me, there's no doubt that I will."

Hunter drew in a deep breath. "It's the first time I've ever done that." She wondered why she felt the need to mention that.

"Lucky me."

Yes, lucky you, she thought. The husky tone of his voice had her easing a little closer to him. It felt like the natural thing to do. And then she reached out and placed her hand on his thigh. Doing that felt natural, as well. The muscles in his thigh tightened beneath her fingers and she heard his sharp intake of breath. She couldn't help but be pleased with his response.

"What if I told you that I've dreamed of you, as

well, Tyson?" she whispered close to his ear. He smelled good. He smelled like a man.

"Would you like to compare notes?"

His question made hot and sharp desire claw at her. Comparing notes with him *would* be interesting. "That's not necessary. I have a few good ideas of my own."

"I was hoping you did."

Considering that this was Tyson Steele, who went through women quicker than he changed his socks, Hunter wondered if what she had planned would suffice. She was a novice and he was so damn experienced. But he had agreed to let her handle things and she would, in her own way.

She felt in control. Bold. Daring. And she intended to play out her fantasies. Who said only men were allowed to have them? There were a few she hadn't shared with anyone, not even Mo or Kat. She had tried sharing them with Carter, only to get laughed at. She had a feeling Tyson wouldn't find any of them amusing. Her heart skipped a beat at the thought that with this bad boy of Phoenix she could be a bad girl. Besides, it was only for one night.

Hunter slid her hand closer to his crotch, and as she slowly stroked him there, she heard his breath hitch.

When her nerve endings began feeling somewhat edgy and the area between her legs began tingling, she decided there was no reason to waste any more time. She stood up. "Umm, it's hot in here. I think I'm wearing too many clothes."

And then, while he watched, she began removing them.

Chapter 9

Tyson leaned forward in his seat, resting his forearms on his thighs and not taking his eyes off Hunter. If a strip show was part of her seduction then she could seduce him anytime or anyplace…including here, the place she called home. His objection to spending the night in her bed instead of his own lost some of its punch. The main thing on his mind right now was seeing her naked body. The body he had dreamed about every single night since their paths had crossed.

She had kicked off those killer heels and the first thing he noticed was that her toenails were painted a fiery red. He thought she had pretty feet. Sexy feet. Tyson had never been a toe kisser, but had to admit that seeing hers was giving him some new ideas.

And then she went for her dress, that very short

dress, and began easing it down those gorgeous legs. Slowly she exposed a black lace bra and then matching panties. Seeing Hunter stand before him in just her bra and panties, he felt a slow, sensuous stirring in the pit of his stomach that made his erection even harder.

And when she reached up and released the front clasp to her bra, he almost tumbled off the sofa. Her breasts weren't just beautiful. They were absolutely, positively perfect. The nipples were dark and already hard. His tongue moved around in his mouth, in anticipation of licking them. Just staring at the twin globes made him eager for the feel of them in his hands and pressed against his bare chest.

She had a small waist and a flat stomach, and her thighs were a lover's dream. So perfect, he could imagine his body being cradled inside them.

His gaze was drawn to her fingers as she placed them beneath the waistband of her panties. From their slight tremor, it appeared she was getting somewhat nervous as a result of his intense gaze. But it couldn't be helped. He didn't intend on missing a thing. His brothers were either breast or leg men, and although he appreciated both, he was a vagina man all the way. As far as he was concerned there was no part of a woman's body that he found more fascinating than her V. So, he couldn't help it when his gaze lowered to her center in anticipation.

"I see I have your attention, Tyson," she said in a husky breath.

"You had my attention the moment you stood up, Hunter."

"Did I?"

"I wouldn't lie to you."

He wondered if the pose she was standing in—her legs braced apart and her fingers tucked into the flimsy lace material—was deliberate on her part to make him crave her even more. "After I remove my panties it will be your turn to take everything off," she declared huskily.

"It will be my pleasure."

"No, Tyson. I'm going to make sure it's *my* pleasure."

He didn't have a problem with that because he knew any pleasures that came under this roof tonight would be shared by the both of them. Tyson shifted his body somewhat to ease some of the hardness behind the zipper of his jeans, as well as to get a closer eye view of the part of her she was about to unveil. She paused a minute and held his gaze. She had to know what she was doing. All this stalling was nothing short of pure torture for him.

"You're panting, Tyson."

Was he? It wouldn't surprise him if he was.

"I'm certain you've seen this part of a woman many times," she said in a sultry tone. "And I'm also sure if you've seen one you've seen them all."

Hardly, Tyson thought, trying to retain his sanity. He had seen this part of a woman many times, but it would be his first time seeing hers and for some reason the thought had him aching. What in the hell was this woman doing to him? Never in his life had he been this desperate to see a woman totally naked.

"Since you seem to have such a high degree of interest in this, would you like to finish undressing me?" she asked him.

He swallowed a deep lump in his throat. "You trust me to do that?" he asked.

She chuckled. "It's just a pair of panties, Tyson. All you have to do is take them off me. Besides, you're here on my turf, so no matter what happens from here on out, it's still my seduction and not yours."

Why she had a problem with getting seduced, he still wasn't sure. But at the moment, he didn't care. He had a feeling that tonight would be a night that he wouldn't forget in a long time. He intended to make it so.

"Well?"

"I'd love to." Tyson eased from the sofa to stand in front of her for a second, before kneeling down on his knees. He was now on eye level with the one part of her that he wanted most. His erection throbbed, begging for release. She was sexy as hell and the man in him appreciated everything about her...especially this.

Tyson leaned forward and pressed his face against the lace. He couldn't resist nuzzling her while drawing in deep breaths, needing to absorb her intimate fragrance through his nostrils.

"What are you doing?" she asked him in a choppy voice.

"Inhaling your scent." He figured that Hunter could pretend indifference all she wanted, but this intimate act had to be doing something to her. "I love your personal fragrance, Hunter." *Maybe too much*, he thought, but pushed that reflection to the back of his mind.

"Do you?"

"Can't you tell?" Leaning back on his haunches he slowly began easing the lace panties down her legs, exposing what had to be the most beautiful V any woman could possess. She was wrong. When you saw one you hadn't seen them all. He was convinced that just like a fingerprint, a woman's feminine mound, the very essence of her being, was an exclusive part of her.

And this was hers. It belonged to Hunter McKay and it was beautiful in all its natural setting. Some men were big on the shaved or waxed look, but he wasn't one of them. This was his preference.

When she stepped out of her panties and kicked them aside, he reached up and began caressing her thighs, loving the feel of her soft skin beneath his fingertips. Then he began stroking her stomach, thinking that even her belly button was beautiful. His tongue itched to lick her, but instead he used his index finger to draw circles around her V a few times before running his fingers through the beautiful curls covering it.

"Tyson…"

His name was spoken from her lips in a sensuous whisper. He lifted his head and met her gaze. He saw all the heat flaring in the dark depths staring back at him and understood the feeling. He was there, close to the edge, right along with her. "Yes?" he answered huskily, while his fingers continued to stroke between her legs. She was wet…just the way he liked.

"I—I need f-for you to take off your clothes," she said, barely getting the words out.

He figured that might be her need, but his tongue had a different need right now. "Can I get a lick first?"

The heat he saw in her eyes flared and his fingers

could feel her get wetter. "Just one?" she asked, holding tight to his gaze.

"Possibly two. Maybe three. I'll admit that I'm one greedy ass."

Color had come into her cheeks so he could only assume her ex either hadn't gone down on her too often, or not at all. What a damn shame. Well, he intended to make up for it.

"In that case," she finally said, "help yourself."

Filled with a need he didn't understand but one he was driven to accept, Tyson spread her thighs apart and used his fingers to open her before dipping his head. The moment his tongue captured her clit he moaned deep in his throat the same time she did. He licked once, twice, three times. And when he couldn't get enough her of delicious taste, he locked his mouth to her, held tight to her thighs and drove his tongue inside her as far as it could go. She'd told him to help himself, and he intended to do just that.

The Tyson Steele way.

Hunter felt her world spinning. Weak from the feel of Tyson's tongue thrusting deep inside her, she reached out to grab hold of his shoulders for support. Nothing, and she meant nothing, could have prepared her for what she was feeling. She had no idea that something like this could bring her so much pleasure. Oral sex was something Carter had frowned upon. More than once he'd said that a man's mouth was not meant to go between a woman's legs, and he claimed most men felt that way.

Evidently Tyson had a totally different opinion about

that, judging by the way he was working his tongue inside her. The man was a master at this, an undisputed pro. She arched her back to give him further access as every nerve ending in her body threatened to explode. She'd told Mo and Kat that she hadn't had an orgasm in so long she'd forgotten how it felt to have one. Tyson was rekindling her memory in one salacious way. If he didn't release her soon, she'd climax right in his mouth.

She tightened her grip on his shoulders and in a ragged voice said, "You got to stop, Tyson. I'm about to—"

Too late. She screamed at the same time spasms speared her body, detonating in an explosive orgasm and nearly shattering her to pieces. Instead of removing his mouth, Tyson drove his tongue even deeper inside her. The lusty sounds he made pushed her over the edge again. And he still wouldn't release her.

When the last of the spasms had left her body, he freed his mouth from her and eased back on his haunches to look up at her. She moaned at the sight of him licking his lips.

He eased to his feet and said, "Now I get to take off my clothes."

Tyson couldn't resist licking his lips again. Hunter's taste was simply incredible. He was convinced it was the most delicious flavor he'd ever tasted. He figured her taste was imprinted on his tongue and would remain there forever.

Forever. He went still. Surely he didn't think that. Forever was something he could never equate with any woman. All he was feeling at the moment was some exceptional brand of passion, one so remarkable it had temporarily affected his brain cells.

The only other excuse he could come up with to explain such crazy thoughts was that he'd relinquished control to her just by showing up here. He had allowed her to seduce him and wasn't sure doing so had been the right thing. It had been seduction this time, but what if she tried making him beg for it the next? Tyson inwardly cringed at the thought and knew giving her any type of empowerment again wouldn't be happening. He had a mind to leave right now. Walk out the door and not look back.

But there was no way he could do that. He wanted her way too much and didn't plan to go anywhere. So much for taking the upper hand and putting things in perspective, he thought. But then he looked at it in another way. It was about getting Hunter out of his system and getting from her what she had refused him eighteen years ago. After tonight she would be out of sight and out of mind.

He glanced over at her, saw her studying his mouth as if she couldn't believe what he'd just used it for. *Believe it*, he wanted to say. *In fact, I plan on using it again the same way before the night is over.*

Moments later her gaze shifted from his mouth to his eyes. She looked at him with an intensity that he felt in every part of his body. She'd accused him of using his eyes to seduce her, but whether she knew it or not, at that moment she was using hers to render him totally helpless. He felt a degree of passion he'd never felt before.

The chemistry surrounding them had heightened. He was aroused to a level that at any other time—and with any other woman—he would have considered unnerving. The fact that she was standing a few feet away from him completely naked, and that he'd just gotten a damn good taste of her, had to be the reason his erection was throbbing mercilessly behind his zipper.

Breaking eye contact, Tyson eased down on the sofa to remove his shoes and socks. He then stood and his hand went to the waistband of his pants—he knew she was watching his every move.

He unsnapped his jeans, began lowering the zipper and slowly slid the jeans down his legs before stepping out of them. He had stripped down to his briefs and could feel her gaze roaming over him. His body became more heated.

Tyson was tempted to return the favor and asked if she wanted to remove his last stitch of clothing, but couldn't. If she was to touch him, he would tumble her to the floor and take her then and there. So he slowly eased his briefs down his legs, noting how her eyes widened.

"You're huge," she gasped with wonder in her voice.

His lips curved in what he knew was an arrogant smile. "You're handling things and you can handle this," he assured her. "Trust me."

Hunter stared at Tyson, finding it difficult to breathe. He was standing barely three feet away, naked as the day he was born and proudly displaying an erection so huge she figured it would put every other man to shame. Her stomach began quivering just from looking at it. The thought of it inside her filled her with a need she'd never felt before.

But that wasn't the only part of him she found impressive. Tyson Steele was beautiful from the top of his head to the soles of his feet. The man was built. Perfectly. All muscle and not an ounce of fat anywhere. He was a true work of art with firm thighs, strong masculine legs, a muscular chest and broad shoulders. At some point before the night was over, she intended to make it her business to lick every inch of him.

The very thought of doing that caused a slow stirring to erupt in the pit of her stomach. When had she become this sensuous being who suddenly needed sex like she need to take another breath? And why had it taken Tyson to make her feel this way?

Her gaze met his and she was captured by the intensity of his green eyes. He moved to retrieve something from his overnight bag and she saw it was a condom packet. As he walked back to her, his stride was slow, masculine and sexy as hell. Just watching his approach made her weak in the knees. When he came to a stop directly in front of her, he shifted his gaze from her eyes to her chest. Specifically her breasts. Her nipples automatically hardened to tight buds.

Without saying a word he lowered his mouth and took a nipple between his lips. She couldn't do anything but moan at the sensations that suddenly rammed through her. The sounds he was making while feasting on her conveyed his enjoyment, and she reached out and placed her hands on both sides of his head to hold him there. Yes, right there.

A while later he released one nipple and immediately sought out the other, and she let out another deep moan. He'd already made her come twice from his mouth between her legs and now he threatened to make her explode a third time just from having her breast in his mouth.

"Tyson, w-we need to get t-to the bedroom," she said in a heated breath, while fighting to hold back yet another moan.

Before she could take her next breath, he swept her off her feet and into his arms. "Tell me where, so I can take you there."

Chapter 10

Tyson placed Hunter on the bed then took a step back, letting his gaze roam over her from head to toe. He doubted he'd ever seen a more perfect woman. Every inch of her was flawless. He'd taken a good look at her while she'd been standing naked in her living room. But there was just something about a woman stretched out in bed, waiting to be taken, that did something to him every time.

Especially with this woman.

His gaze moved around the room. She had referred to it as a romantic hot spot and he could see why. There were candles and throw pillows situated around the room, wineglasses, a bottle of wine chilling in an ice bucket and a tray of different cheeses on a small table near the bed. Soft music was playing and the bedcovers were turned back. The ambiance was one of romance and at that moment he was looking forward to a night of passion with her.

"This room looks wonderful, Hunter. You did a great job setting the mood."

"Did I?"

He heard the surprise in her tone and glanced at her. That's when he saw the brilliance of her smile and knew his compliment had pleased her greatly. That made him wonder. Had she done a similar setup for that ass she'd been married to and the man hadn't appreciated her effort?

"Yes, you did," he assured her. "You know how to take seduction to one hell of an amazing level. Hunter McKay, you can seduce me anytime." And at that moment, he truly meant it.

He appreciated that she still lay on top of the covers, where he'd placed her, and hadn't gotten beneath them. His gaze roamed all over every inch of her body. He would enjoy making love to her, touching her, licking her all over, tasting her again, and was driven by a desire to savor every minute of doing so. Just looking at her, thinking of everything he intended to do to her and how he would do it, made his erection harder.

But first he needed to prepare himself for her. While she watched, he sheathed himself with a condom. "You just brought one?" she asked him.

He glanced up at her and smiled. "No. I brought a few." He figured it was best not to admit to having an overnight bag full. He didn't want to scare her.

Then he moved forward. He kneeled on the bed and

slowly crawled toward her. He remembered that first night at Notorious, when he'd decided he would be the hunter and she his prey. Now he wasn't sure which one of them had truly been captured.

He went straight for her mouth, needing to kiss her. The kiss was meant to arouse her, but when she began responding, he was the one getting even more aroused. Their tongues mingled, tangled madly, mated hotly, and his hands began to move, cupping those same breasts he'd sucked on earlier, loving how they fit in his hands.

Moments later he released her mouth and his lips trailed a path down to her breasts, needing to taste them again. The nipples were hard and ready for his mouth and he devoured them with a greed he only had for her.

Not able to hold off any longer, he tore his mouth away from her breasts to move up over her body. He glanced down at her. She looked beautiful, the glow from the candles dancing across her features.

He braced himself on his elbows as he continued to stare down at her. And then he sucked in a deep breath when she deliberately pushed up her breasts to rub them against his chest, as if doing so had been her fantasy. The feel of her hard nipples brushing against his chest did something to him. From the look on her face it was doing something to her as well.

"You like that?" he asked her.

"Yes. What about you?"

He didn't have to think about his answer. The feel of her nipples teasing the hair on his chest felt damn good. "Yes, I like it. Umm, what do you think of this?"

He reached down and widened her legs before lowering his body to settle his chest between them. And then he began deliberately moving his body to stroke his chest hair against the curls covering her V. He could tell from the look in her eyes that she found what he was doing stimulating.

"I like this," she said in a breathless tone.

"So do I," he said, feeling her dampen his chest. "Now for the main attraction." He eased his body back up until his erection touched the entrance to her body.

He glanced down at her and smiled. "You seduced the hell out of me tonight, Hunter. I liked it."

And with that, he thrust into her.

Hunter moaned at the feel of Tyson filling her so completely. She could actually feel his erection get harder while sliding deep inside her. He began moving, going in and then withdrawing, establishing a sensuous rhythm that had her alternating between clawing his back and gripping the bedspread. His hips and thighs jackhammered with lightning speed and when she let out one moan, she was already working on the other.

Had four years of abstinence done this to her? Make her body hungry? Greedy? Needy? She knew deep down that the length of time she'd gone without sex had nothing to do with it. It was Tyson and what he was doing to her. How he was making her feel. Whoever started the rumor that a woman hadn't truly been made love to unless it was by a Steele knew exactly what she was talking about.

Being here with Tyson was what true lovemaking was all about. The giving and sharing of pleasure was so profound she could feel it in her bones. Neither was dominant over the other; rather, they were equals. She couldn't help but let herself go and was caught up in the pounding of his body into hers.

When he threw his head back and let out a voracious growl it seemed the cords in his neck would pop. As if on cue her body detonated with his and sparks of passion began flying everywhere, igniting inside her a maelstrom of need that only Tyson could satisfy.

He bucked and then plunged downward at the same time her hips automatically lifted to receive him. He went deeper than before and she could feel every inch of him inside her.

She screamed at the same time he shouted her name while thrusting into her several more times as if he couldn't get enough. She held him tight and continued to move her body with his when she felt another delicious shiver race down her spine. And then she was screaming again, and from the way he was thrusting into her body she knew he'd had another orgasm, as well.

"Hunter…"

He said her name moments before collapsing onto her. A short while later he held up his head, eased up toward her lips and without saying anything, he kissed her again, this time with a tenderness that had a thick lump forming in her throat.

When he released her mouth she smiled up at him and he smiled back. Her heart began fluttering deep in her chest at the realization that she was the one responsible for his smile.

* * *

Hours later, Tyson eased his body off Hunter to lie beside her, flat on his back. Seeing that she had dozed off to sleep, he let out a whoosh of heated breath. How many rounds had this been so far? Five?

The two of them were mating like damn rabbits, and he still hadn't gotten enough of her. Every part of his body was sizzling for more. In the bedroom Hunter had been one of the most giving and one of the most passionate of any women he'd ever slept with, and considering his history with women that said a lot. She had totally overwhelmed him and no woman should have the ability to do that.

He would have frowned at the thought, but he couldn't help but smile as he recalled the look on her face when, after their first time, he'd dumped a handful of condoms on the table by the bed. He'd told her there was plenty more where those came from, and her eyes had gotten as big as saucers and her mouth had dropped open. "Do you really expect to use all of them?" she'd asked. Well, it was a moot point now, he thought as he looked at the handful of empty packages.

They had worked up an appetite after round three and sat naked in bed while drinking wine and eating an assortment of cheeses. They used that time to talk. He brought her up-to-date on former classmates and what they were doing now. He told her about his brother Jonas and his marriage to Nikki, Eli's marriage to Stacey and how his parents had stepped into the role of grandparents to Galen's twins with ease.

In turn, she told him about this house she'd designed

a few years ago for a well-known NBA player, and how she'd taken a Mediterranean cruise last year with some college friends. He'd noted she hadn't brought up anything about her ex and he was glad she hadn't.

Afterward, they had made love a couple more times and each had been just as intense and passionate as the other times had been. He discovered there was more passion in Hunter's pinky finger than some women had in their entire bodies. He loved the way she responded to his kisses, his touch and even the naughty, explicit words he would whisper in her ear to let her know just what he intended to do to her and how.

Jeez. When had he wanted a woman so badly, that even now he felt a surge of hot energy consume his groin? Just thinking about her, he was hard and longed to slide his erection back inside her to start round six. But he refused to wake her up. She needed her rest.

And, dammit, he needed to think.

Now was the time for logic to set in. Instead of waiting for her to wake up so he could make love to her again, he should be putting on his clothes and hauling ass, not caring if their paths ever crossed again. But logic wasn't working in his favor tonight. He didn't want to put on his clothes, and leaving was the last thing on his mind.

Why?

The question echoed in his head in the quiet room. He had gotten what she'd refused to give him eighteen years ago and he should be feeling like a score had been settled. The one who'd gotten away was now had. So why wasn't he pounding his chest with his fist, proud of himself, pleased with the way the night had turned out? Oh, he was pleased with the way the night had turned out, but it had nothing to do with him settling an old score. Far from it.

For the first time in his life he had truly enjoyed making love to a woman—every single aspect of it. The touching, tasting and thrusting had been off the charts. Mind-boggling. Super awesome. And the Mark of Tyson wasn't just on her neck, but was probably on every single part of her body. But he didn't see the mark as a sign of conquest. In his mind it had become a sign of possession.

Possession? Tyson rubbed his hand down his face as he tried to figure out how in the hell he could fix his mind to even think that way. He was a die-hard bachelor who enjoyed too many women to get hung up on just one. So there had to be a reason why he was having these possessive feelings toward Hunter.

One reason could be that for the first time in his life a woman had been a challenge. That had to be it. Other women made things easy for him, and the novelty of Hunter giving him a hard time had him thinking crazy thoughts. All it would take to clear his mind would be a few more rounds of sex with her to be assured that she was out of his system. A good night's sleep in her bed wouldn't hurt, either. When he woke up in the morning there was no doubt in his mind he would be thinking straight. When he left here it would be business as usual.

But still…

For some reason he was driven to mentally replay every single thing that had happened to him since run-

ning into Hunter more than two weeks ago. One thing
stood out: he hadn't slept with another woman since
then. Given his track record, that was odd. No, it was
downright strange. He'd gotten plenty of calls, even
one from that cute little ER nurse who was helping out
temporarily in Cardio. Her name was Macy Phillips
and she was on his "to do" list. So why hadn't he done
her? What was he waiting for? She was definitely willing. And what about Kristen Fulbright, Nancy Heart-
wood and Candace Lane? Why had he begun thinking
of them as history?

Hunter stirred beside him in bed and he glanced over
at her just as her eyes flitted open. At that moment he
thought the same thing that he had when he'd seen her
that night in Notorious. She was beautiful. She stared
back at him with a sleepy look in her eyes. For a minute it was as if she was trying to recall why he was in
her bed.

"Do I need to remind you?" he asked, seeing her di-
lemma and leaning over to kiss her on the lips.

She drew in a deep breath and shook her head. "No,
I remember now. What time is it?" she asked as she
yawned and pulled herself up in bed. The sheet covering her breast slid down and she quickly jerked it back
up. *Seriously, Hunter, don't get all modest on me now
when last night those nipples had seemed like a permanent fixture in my mouth.*

Instead of calling her out on it, he glanced over at
the digital clock on her nightstand. "It's three in the
morning."

She yawned again. "Sorry, I passed out on you."

"That's fine. You definitely needed your rest." He saw the color that flashed across her cheeks. "You're embarrassed?"

She shrugged. "Shouldn't I be? I screamed around ten times tonight. I can just imagine what my neighbors think."

"It was twelve."

She lifted a brow. "Excuse me?"

"You screamed twelve times. Not ten. And your neighbors probably thought you were having a hell of a good time and wished it was them."

The color in her cheeks deepened. "Yes, well, I was having a good time. But all good things must come to an end, including your visit to my bed."

Tyson frowned. "You're kicking me out?"

"I told you that you weren't spending the night."

Yes, she had. "But that was before the twelve screams."

She actually had the gall to look confused. "What does that have to do with anything?"

Tyson figured if she had to ask then maybe he needed to make sure she screamed twelve more times. She had seduced him earlier, so maybe it was his time to seduce her. Instead of answering her question, he asked one of his own. "Do I get a kiss for the road, since this will be our last time together like this?"

She seemed to ponder his question for a second and then nodded. "Sure. Why not? Kiss me and then I'll walk you to the door."

Tyson smiled, thinking that by the time he finished kissing her she wouldn't be walking him anywhere.

She leaned toward him, evidently expecting a peck on the lips. He leaned in as well and started off with just a light peck, but then he slid his tongue into her mouth at the same time his hand slid under the covers to settle beneath her legs.

Tyson was prepared for her reaction and deepened the kiss. He began dueling with her tongue, deliberately inflicting all kinds of sensual torment, while at the same time his fingers did the same. He loved touching her this way. She was such a passionate woman and so damn hot.

He heard the groan in her throat but she didn't pull back from his kiss. Nor did she resist moments later when he eased her down on her back and continued to kiss her, thoroughly, deeply and possessively.

Possessively...

There was that word again. Why was it determined to invade his mind when it came to Hunter? Dismissing the question since he didn't have an answer, he turned his full concentration on the seduction of Hunter McKay. His desire revved up a notch when she returned his kiss as provocatively as he was giving it. When he felt his fingers get damp from the wetness between her legs, he knew what was next.

Round six.

He pulled back from the kiss to stare down at her and saw deep-seated desire etched in her eyes. She was aroused and so was he. He leaned in and whispered against her moist lips. "I want you. Say you want me again, too, Hunter."

Chapter 11

Tyson saw the battle taking place in the eyes staring back at him. Common sense versus intense desire. He recognized it because of a similar encounter with his own emotions earlier. He still hadn't figured out what was going on with him. The only thing he knew for certain was what he'd just told Hunter. He wanted her again.

"Say it," he whispered, brushing a kiss across her forehead. "Say you want me again, too." He tried to keep the urgency out of his voice, the hunger and need. But it couldn't be helped. The bottom line was that he needed to make love to her again as much as he needed to breathe.

She hesitated a minute longer, then said, "I want you again, too, Tyson."

Tyson released the breath he'd been holding and moved aside and made quick work of putting on another condom. In no time he was back, easing in place between her legs. He leaned in and captured her mouth at the same time he slid his hard erection inside her.

Once he was deeply embedded in her, he began moving, gently at first, one long stroke after another. But when he felt her nails dig deep into his back at the same time she rolled her hips beneath him, he picked up the pace and began pounding into her, hard and fast. He broke off the kiss and continued to thrust hard, over and over again. Grazing his jaw against her ear, he growled low in his throat. "Come for me, baby."

No sooner had he made the request than her body bucked in a bow beneath him and she screamed his name. "Tyson!"

But she didn't slow down. The spasms kept coming and she continued moving frantically beneath him, keeping up with the sensuous rhythm he'd established. Tyson decided that if she wanted a multiple orgasm this round then that's what he would give her. He sank deeper and deeper inside her while thrusting harder and harder.

His stomach clenched with need every time it touched hers and the hairs on his chest stirred to life whenever they came in contact with the hard nipples of her breasts. She tightened her legs around him and screamed his name at the same time he growled hers.

Fireworks seemed to go off inside Tyson's head. His entire body ignited into one hell of a gigantic explosion. He drew in a deep breath, thinking never had an orgasm felt so good. So perfect. The impact had his entire body quivering. Leaning down, he captured Hunter's mouth in a long, drugging kiss before easing off her to lie on his side.

Tyson pulled Hunter into his arms, entwining his legs with hers, still needing the connection. From the sound of her even breathing, he knew she had drifted back to sleep and he held her closer. Glancing down, he studied her features. She was a woman who didn't go out of her way to be sexy, yet she was sexy anyway. A woman who claimed she'd never seduced a man, but she had seduced the hell out of him. A woman who'd turned her bedroom into a romantic hot spot to set the mood for seduction. And a woman who had refused his advances until she'd gotten ready to accept them.

His brain felt as if it had short-circuited and he still didn't know why. So instead of getting more confused than he already was, he followed Hunter's lead and closed his eyes to join her in sleep.

As sunlight filtered through the window in her bedroom, Hunter slowly came awake. The even breathing close to her ear let her know she wasn't alone. She hadn't meant for Tyson to spend the night and had been pretty adamant that he didn't. All it had taken was a kiss, followed by another and topped with the best lovemaking she had ever experienced in her life to make her change her mind. Although she hadn't given Tyson the okay to stay, he had known. Why wouldn't he, when all he'd had to do was slide his hands between her legs or his tongue in her mouth and she became putty in his hands?

Probably just like all those other women.

She closed her eyes, not wanting to dwell on that thought now. But she knew she had to. She had no regrets about last night. Far from it. Tyson had opened her eyes to a lot of things, such as just how much of an ass Carter had been to deny her the very things she needed, not only as a wife but also as a woman.

She thought how she hadn't experienced an orgasm in four years, even longer if she was to count the times she'd shared Carter's bed and hadn't been fulfilled. Thanks to Tyson, she'd gotten more in one night than she'd had in all her years of marriage. She didn't want to think how many times she had screamed and wouldn't be surprised if her throat was sore this morning. So regardless of anything else, she appreciated Tyson for reminding her what it felt like to be a woman again. And what it felt like to have needs and have those needs satisfied to the fullest.

Not only had he given her a chance to seduce him, but he'd also agreed that she could to do it the way she wanted. Even after she'd told him she had never seduced a man before. Yet he had allowed her to take control, to "handle things," even when he hadn't fully understood her need to do so. He had no idea that last night restored her confidence in herself as a woman. It was the confidence Carter had painstakingly stripped from her.

However, upon waking up this morning she was faced with the realization that all good things must come to an end. After today, Tyson would go his way and she would go hers. In a day or two she would only be a fleeting memory to him, if that. At least she could say she never shared Tyson Steele's bed. He'd shared hers.

"You're awake."

Before she could react to his words, Tyson surprised her by drawing her even closer into the curve of his warm body. It had been a while since she'd awakened with a man in her bed, especially one who liked to snuggle and hold her through the night. Even when she and Carter had slept together, he had stayed in his corner of the bed and she'd stayed in hers. And those times when they did have sex, afterward they returned to those corners. It had never bothered her before because she'd gotten used to it. But spending one single night with Tyson was a stark reminder of what she'd put up with in her marriage.

Hunter tilted her head to look at Tyson and wished she hadn't. He had that early morning look—sleepy eyes with dark stubble along his chin and jaw—that begged for her touch. She was tempted to reach out and run her fingers along his chin to feel it for herself. She was convinced no man should look this sexy in the morning.

Finally, she responded to him. "Yes, I'm awake."

"Good. Take a shower with me before I leave."

Why did she get the feeling he seemed rather anxious to leave? And he wanted them to shower together? She honestly didn't think that was a good idea and was about to tell him so when he added, "Just one last thing we can do together."

He'd practically said the same thing about that kiss

last night. Only problem was one thing had led to another and then another. She could see taking a shower with him that lasted for hours. She'd discovered Tyson could be very creative when it came to sex and could just imagine some of his artistic ideas for her in the bathroom.

When she hesitated he nudged her. "Are you going to deny me the chance for you to wash my back?"

She couldn't help but chuckle. "Or deny you the chance to wash mine?" she countered.

"Umm, I have no problem washing your back...or any other part of you that you'd like me to give attention to."

Yes, she bet he wouldn't have a problem with it. "I think you gave enough attention to my body parts last night. I'll be surprised if I'm able to walk today."

"Sorry about that."

She waved off his words. "Don't apologize. I needed last night. Screams and all. Trust me."

He shifted to stare into her eyes. "Why?"

He didn't need to know, she thought. The less he knew about her needs, the better. "Doesn't matter. And I'll pass on sharing that shower with you. I'm not ready to get up yet."

"You sure?"

"Positive."

He stared at her for a second and then without saying anything else, he eased away from her, got out of the bed and headed out of the bedroom. "The bathroom is that way," she said to him, trying not to notice his nakedness. He had no shame walking around naked and she had no shame getting an eyeful. He had a beautiful body, one any woman would appreciate.

"I know. I need to grab my overnight bag from the living room."

She nodded, remembering the infamous bag. The one containing all those condoms they'd nearly gone through last night.

It took him only a minute to get the bag and she watched when he walked back through the bedroom and headed for the bathroom. He stopped and glanced over at her. "You're sure you don't want to join me?"

No, she wasn't sure, but she knew it would be for the best. Too much of Tyson could become addictive. "Yes, I'm sure."

Flashing a sexy smile, one that caused her pulse to race, he entered the bathroom and closed the door behind him.

Hunter shifted in the bed when she heard the sound of the shower. She glanced around the room. The candles had burned down but the fragrance of vanilla lingered in the air, along with that of sex. She felt a tingling sensation in her stomach at the memories of their lovemaking.

Hunter felt sore between her legs but the soreness would be a reminder of all the pleasure Tyson had given her. He had made back-to-back love to her, allowing her the chance to take naps in between. He had licked her all over and she didn't have to look down at herself to know he'd probably left passion marks all over her body. Hopefully by Monday they would have faded away. At least she wouldn't have to see anyone over the weekend. Her parents had gone to a motorcycle race, and her brother and his family had taken off to Disneyland.

She would lie around and recover from Tyson's love-making, although she knew it would take more than a weekend for her to do that. He had awakened desires in her that she hadn't known existed. No wonder he was in such high demand with women.

Deciding to cover her nakedness, she reached out and pulled open the drawer to the nightstand, where she kept her oversized T-shirts. Sliding one over her head, she didn't miss the passion marks on her chest, stomach and thighs. She figured she'd find the majority of them between her legs. His mouth seemed to particularly like that area of her body.

Hunter glanced over at the closed bathroom door, tempted to go join Tyson in the shower. She knew she wasn't thinking with her head, but with overactive hormones. The only good thing was that he was now out of her system, and she was sure she was out of his.

"I'm ready to leave."

She twisted around in bed. She hadn't heard Tyson come out of the bathroom, but there he was, standing in the middle of the room, fully dressed in a pair of khakis and a polo shirt. He'd shaved but she much preferred the rugged look on him. Still, he looked good.

"I'll walk you to the door." She eased out of bed and winced, feeling a definite soreness between her legs. She grabbed her bathrobe off the chair and put it on.

"You okay?" he asked, quickly crossing the room to her with a concerned look on his face.

"Yes, I'm fine. I just need to soak in a bath today for a while."

"Do you want me to run your bathwater before I go?"

She thought it was kind for him to offer. "No, that's not necessary, Tyson. I can manage."

He searched her face. "You sure?"

"Yes, I'm sure. Don't worry about me. I'll be fine." But even as Hunter said the words, a part of her wondered if she truly would be. Unknowingly, Tyson had given her something last night that no other man had given her. A chance to be herself. To live out her fantasies. To be the sensuous and passionate woman she'd always suspected she was.

Tyson nodded and for a long moment he stood there not saying anything and just looking at her, and she could feel his stare as if it was a heated caress. Then when she was about to ask him if there was something wrong, he finally said in a deep husky voice, "I don't want you to walk me to the door, Hunter."

She arched a brow. "Why?"

"Because I want you to get back in bed. That's the memory I want to leave here with. You in that bed. Your bed. Where we spent most of the night."

She didn't understand his request. "Why?"

A seriousness she'd never seen before touched his features. "I just do. Last night was special for me." He paused a moment and then said, "And about those house plans. When I get a chance to look over them I will. After I do, I'll get back to you."

She shrugged. "You don't really have to do that. We

both know the real reason you hired me to draw up those plans."

He didn't deny it. In fact he didn't say anything for a long moment and then he leaned down and brushed his lips across hers. She figured the kiss was supposed to be short and sweet. However, the moment their lips touched, he pulled her into his arm and went after her mouth with the greed she'd grown accustomed to.

Resisting never entered her mind. Instead she returned the kiss in the same way she figured he was accustomed to her doing as well. The intensity of his tongue mating with hers nearly brought her to her knees. She moaned in pleasure not only from the kiss, but also from the feel of his masculine strength. And although she should have preferred otherwise, she liked the feel of his hard, engorged erection cradled intimately at the juncture of her thighs. It wouldn't take much to tumble back in bed and take him with her. There was no doubt in her mind if that was to happen she would eventually let out more screams.

But Tyson suddenly broke off the kiss.

He straightened and then gently brushed his knuckles across her cheek. "Go ahead and get back in the bed, Hunter."

She nodded and removed her robe. For a quick second she was tempted to remove her T-shirt as well. However, she refused to give in to temptation. The last thing she wanted was to tempt him to stay and make love to her again. They were doing the right thing by parting this way. He was who he was and she was who she was. Besides, last night had only been about sex, so there was no need to get all emotional.

She tossed her robe on the chair and slid beneath the covers. Stretching out in bed she gazed up at him. "Goodbye, Tyson."

He stared at her for a long moment before finally speaking. "Goodbye, Hunter." And with his overnight bag clutched in his hand he walked out of the bedroom.

Hunter didn't release her breath until she heard her front door open and then close behind him.

Chapter 12

"So, what's been going on with you, Tyson?"

Tyson glanced over at his brother Galen. He had stopped by to see how Brittany and the twins were doing, as well as to see how his laid-back older brother was faring. It seemed Galen had everything under control and had accepted his role as father to twins pretty easily. Almost as easily as he'd stepped into his role as husband.

To this day it still confused the hell out of Tyson. Of the six of them, Galen had been the most notorious womanizer. His reputation had extended from Phoenix all the way to the Carolinas, specifically Charlotte, North Carolina, where their Steele cousins lived. Galen was the last person Tyson thought would settle down with one woman. Yet now he was a husband and a father. Tyson shook his head. And had he heard Brittany right at dinner tonight when she mentioned them buying a van? Galen was known for his love of sports cars and as a collector of muscle cars. A van was the last vehicle Tyson would have thought his brother would be caught driving.

Deciding to answer Galen's question, he said, "Nothing's been going on with me but the usual. I've been pretty busy at the hospital." But not too busy to think about Hunter McKay, Tyson thought.

This time last week he'd been inside her. It was hard to believe a full week had passed. He thought of her often. Too damn much, in fact. The days weren't so bad, since like he told Galen he was pretty busy at the hospital. But it was at night, mainly when he went to bed, when he mostly thought about her. Not making love to her in his bed had turned out to be a good thing, otherwise he would never get any sleep.

But still…he had made love to her and that was the crux of his problem. They had shared passion, passion and more passion. And now he couldn't get all that passion out of his mind. He would get an erection just remembering their times together. And what was even worse, it seemed his desire for other women had abandoned him. Women called but he didn't call them back. How crazy was that?

"It's Friday night and you're off work," Galen pointed out. "Why aren't you hanging out at Notorious? That's usually your mode of entertainment on the weekends."

He didn't need his brother to remind him of that.

"Would you believe me if I told you I'm getting bored with the place?"

Galen stretched his legs out in front of him. "Not unless there's a reason. Scoping out the women there used to be your favorite pastime."

Tyson was tempted to remind Galen that Notorious used to be Galen's favorite hangout for that same reason before his Brittany days.

"Is there a reason, Tyson?"

Tyson shrugged. "No reason."

It got quiet and that didn't bode well for Tyson. He knew Galen. He was trying to figure out things that weren't his business. Just because he was the oldest, Galen thought he had a right to know everything about what his five brothers were doing. That assumption might have had some merit when they were kids, but now he, Eli, Jonas, Mercury and Gannon were adults and didn't need their big brother looking over their shoulders.

"What's her name?"

Tyson frowned. "Whose name?"

"The woman who left her mark on you."

Tyson almost chuckled at that. Especially when he recalled all the marks he'd left on Hunter. "No woman left her mark on me, Galen. You're imagining things."

"Am I?"

To be honest, Tyson wasn't sure. He still dreamed of Hunter and thought about her all the time. It was quite evident to him that their tumble between the sheets hadn't worked her out of his system. That annoyed the hell out of him.

"Did I tell you how I met Brittany?"

"Yes," Tyson answered, taking a sip of his wine. "The two of you met for a brief while in New York when we were there for Donovan's wedding." Donovan Steele was their cousin who'd gotten married several years ago. If everyone thought Galen falling in love was a shocker, then Donovan doing so was an even bigger one.

"True, that's when we first met. We ran into each other again six months later here in Phoenix at the auction house. To make a long story short, she had something I wanted and I had something she wanted."

Tyson nodded. "And what did you have that she wanted?"

"The title to the house she's now turned into a school."

"And what did she have that you wanted?"

"Sex."

Tyson nearly choked on his drink. And then he quickly glanced around for his sister-in-law, hoping she hadn't heard what his brother just said.

Galen smiled. "Relax. Brittany went upstairs to put Ethan and Elyse to bed. But even had she heard me, she would have backed up my story, because it's the truth."

Tyson stared at his brother. "And you're telling me this why?"

"Because I know you, Tyson. I might not know all the particulars about what's going on with you—especially why you dropped by here tonight instead of going to Notorious, where there're a slew of women just waiting for you to make an appearance. For you to deny yourself a chance to take a woman home to warm your bed can only mean one thing."

"What?"

"There's some woman you've fallen for."

Tyson frowned. "I haven't fallen for her. Not exactly. Let's just say she left a lasting impression on me."

Galen chuckled. "In other words, she was good in bed. Almost too good to be true. And you're wondering if it was great sex or something else."

Tyson's frown deepened. Was that what he was really wondering? No, he assured himself. It wasn't anything other than great sex. His problem was that he wanted more of that great sex, which meant he wanted more of Hunter. One night hadn't been enough. "You're getting carried away, Galen. It's not that serious."

"Isn't it?"

"No."

"You sure?"

He hesitated a minute, then said, "Yes. I'm sure."

"I hope you're right. Take it from a man who thought there couldn't possibly be a woman out there I'd want forever. If there's that possibility, then you owe it to yourself to find out."

"So how was your night with Tyson?" Kat asked.

"Did he remind you just how great having an orgasm can be?" Mo queried.

Hunter figured the questions would come sooner or later. In a way she was surprised they hadn't come earlier. After all, it had been a week. She couldn't believe it was Friday already. This time last week she and Tyson were engaging in what had turned into a sex marathon. She no longer had dreams to contend with. Now she had full-fledged memories, which she discovered was even worse. Now she knew how it felt to be touched by a man, tasted by a man, and all she had to do was close her eyes to remember those hard thrusts into her body.

"Well, if you're not going to tell us, then…"

Hunter rolled her eyes. "I have no problem telling you what you want to know, since it was one and done. Yes, Kat, I went out with Tyson. We had dinner at his place and later we went to mine."

Kat arched a brow. "Why?"

Hunter took a sip of her tea before continuing. "Because I knew how the night would end, and I refused to be seduced by him and share a bed that a zillion other women had shared. I told him I would be the one doing the seducing and it had to be done at my place. In my bed."

Both women stared at her with something akin to amazement on their faces. "And he actually went along with it?" Mo asked.

"Yes."

Kat and Mo stared at each other for a minute, and then they stared back at her. Kat shook her head. "I can't imagine a Steele running behind a woman."

"He didn't run behind me, Kat. He merely came to my house to be seduced."

"Okay, forget the seduction part for now," Mo said. "Did you get the big *O* at least once?"

Hunter thought it would serve no purpose confessing just how many times she had gotten it. Whenever she thought about it, she found the entire experience almost too overwhelming. Tyson had the ability to make her come with his mouth on her breasts, licking around her navel, between her legs… She shifted in her seat just thinking about it. But all she said was "Yes."

"And was it worth all the trouble?" Mo asked.

Hunter couldn't help but smile at the memory. "Definitely. I can't speak for the other Steeles, but I can say the rumors about Tyson are true."

"Hot damn," Kat said, grinning.

"This calls for a toast," Mo added. "Your dry days are over and we have Tyson Steele to thank."

"Whatever," she said, deciding it was time to change the subject. Especially since talking about Tyson was making her think of him, wonder what he was doing, who he was with.

"Do you think the two of you will get together again?"

"No," Hunter said, responding quickly to Kat's question. "There was a lot of sexual chemistry between us and we needed to work it out of our system."

"Did you?" Kat asked.

"Did I what?"

"Get Tyson Steele out of your system?"

"Yes."

Mo didn't look convinced. "Are you saying that you haven't thought of Tyson Steele—not once—since that night? That you don't dream of the two of you reliving memories of last Friday night?"

Hunter glanced around the restaurant, hoping Mo's voice hadn't carried. "I'm not saying anything."

"Umm," both Mo and Kat said simultaneously.

Hunter frowned. "And what do you guys mean by *umm*?"

Mo smiled sweetly. "Trust me. You'll find out soon enough."

Tyson entered his home and glanced around. This was a Friday night and he was away from the hospital, yet he would be going to bed alone. It was so unlike him. And he'd been acting strangely in other ways, as well. In fact, lately he had begun finding Macy Phillips's phone calls so annoying that he had removed her from his "to do" list.

Had he somehow been turned off from beautiful, sexy women? He sucked in a deep breath, knowing that wasn't true. If given the chance, he would do Hunter McKay again in a heartbeat. Even more times than he'd done her last Friday night.

He threw his car keys on the table as he thought about what Galen had said. Sometimes his older brother talked pure nonsense, but tonight Tyson couldn't help wondering if perhaps he should heed his brother's words. Should he find out if the reason he couldn't get Hunter out of his mind was because of the great sex or something else?

He pulled his phone out of his back pocket and searched his contact list for her phone number. He was a second from calling her when he regained his senses. He repocketed the phone and went into his bedroom. He would get a good night's sleep, convinced that when he woke up in the morning, his outlook on things would be different. He forced a smile. He'd even give one of the women still on his "to do" list a call.

Chapter 13

"Honestly, Mom, skateboarding?"

Hunter had rushed to the hospital after getting a call from the ER nurse that her mother had been brought to the emergency room by ambulance due to an accident on a skateboard. She hadn't known what to expect and gave a sigh of relief upon discovering there were no broken bones, just scrapes and bruises.

"I wore a helmet and knee pads, Hunter," her mother said, seemingly somewhat aggravated over all the fuss being made over her.

"And it was a good thing you did, Mrs. McKay," the ER doctor said, shaking his head. "Your injuries could have been a lot worse. You'll be sore for a couple of days, but the X-rays don't show anything broken."

"Oh, I could have told you that," Ingrid McKay said

matter-of-factly. "In fact I tried to tell you, but you wouldn't listen," she said, scolding the doctor.

"Just following procedures," the doctor said, writing information in the chart he held in his hand. "You took a nasty fall. I'm writing a prescription for any pain you might start to feel later. And I suggest you stay off the skateboard for a while."

"Whatever," her mother grumbled under her breath.

Hunter rolled her eyes, hoping her mother took the doctor's advice. "Where's Dad?"

"Today was his golf day, so I had that nice nurse call you instead of Bernie. I didn't want to upset him. And I sure wasn't going to call Bernie Junior."

Of course you wouldn't, Hunter thought. Her brother would have read their mother the riot act. Now she understood his concerns about their parents' risky playtime activities. "Can you walk out to my car or do you want me to have the nurse get you a wheelchair?" she asked.

"Why would I need a wheelchair? I can walk."

"Just asking, Mom."

She was leading her mother toward the exit door when a deep, husky voice stopped her. "Hunter?"

Hunter didn't have to turn to know who the voice belonged to. The stirrings that suddenly went off in the pit of her stomach were a dead giveaway.

She turned around and before she could regain her composure enough to answer, her mother exclaimed, "Hey, aren't you one of those Steele boys?"

Hunter fought back a smile. The male standing before them was definitely no boy. She knew for a fact he was all man. Her pulse rate escalated when she recalled just how she knew that. It had been twelve days since she'd seen Tyson last. Twelve days. Not that she was counting. He looked good, even wearing scrubs.

She studied his features, the ones that still dominated her dreams every night. Her gaze latched on to his mouth, a mouth that had sent her over the edge so many times. And as she looked at him she saw the corners of his mouth hitch up in a smile at her mother's question.

"Yes, ma'am, I am," he said respectfully, extending his hand out to her mother. "I'm Tyson Steele."

Ingrid accepted Tyson's hand. "Those green eyes gave you away." She peered over her glasses to study the name tag on his jacket. "So you're a doctor?"

"Yes, I'm a heart surgeon. Someone came through ER needing my services." Tyson's gaze left Ingrid to return to Hunter. "Is everything okay?"

She nodded, not sure she could speak at that moment. Then she found her voice. "Yes, everything is okay. Mom took a fall on a skateboard. It could have been worse."

Tyson lifted an amused brow. "A skateboard?"

"Yes. Hopefully it was her first and last time trying one out."

"Don't count on it," Ingrid muttered under her breath. Before Hunter could give her mother a scolding retort, Ingrid spoke up. "I recall when the two of you attended the same high school."

"Yes, we did," Tyson said, nodding.

Hunter hoped that was all her mother remembered. The last thing she needed was her mother bringing up

the short time she and Tyson had dated. "Well, we better get going," she said. "I want to get by the pharmacy
to pick up Mom's prescription."

"All right," Tyson said, but he didn't move away. He
held her gaze.

The sexual chemistry. The physical attraction. The
desire. They were still there. She felt it and from the
look in his eyes she knew that he felt it, too. Hadn't
they worked all that out of their systems that night at
her place?

Evidently they weren't the only ones feeling it, because at that moment Ingrid cleared her throat. When
they both glanced over at her, Ingrid asked Tyson, "Are
you the one who got expelled from high school for being
caught under the bleachers with the principal's daughter?"

"Mom!"

Ingrid shrugged. "Just asking."

Tyson chuckled. "No, that was my brother Galen."

Hunter figured she needed to get her mother out of
there before she remembered something else that was
best forgotten.

She wasn't quick enough and Ingrid asked, "What
about church?"

Tyson lifted a brow. "What about it?"

Ingrid had no problem telling him. "I see your parents on Sundays but I don't recall seeing you and your
brothers."

Tyson grinned at her mother's observation. "I haven't
been to church in a while. Usually I work on Sundays."

"Every Sunday?"

"Mom!" Hunter shook her head. "Sorry about that, Tyson."

A smile spread across his lips. "No need to apologize. And to answer your question Mrs. McKay, no, I don't work every Sunday. In fact I'm off this weekend, so you can look for me on Sunday."

"Don't think that I won't," Ingrid said in a serious tone.

Hunter thought it would be best to get her mother out to the car quickly before Ingrid invited Tyson to Sunday dinner or something. "Well, I'll be seeing you, Tyson."

"Same here."

Taking her mother's arm, Hunter led her over to the exit door. She couldn't resist looking over her shoulder. The attractive nurse who had taken care of her mother—the one whose name was Macy Phillips— had approached Tyson and was all in his face. She was touching his arm while chatting away with a huge smile on her face.

Hunter felt a pain stab her heart when she saw that Tyson was smiling back at the woman.

"Well, at least he's not the one who got caught with that girl under the bleachers."

Ingrid's words reclaimed Hunter's attention. She was still holding tight to her mother's arm as they exited the building. "Mom, that was over eighteen years ago. Galen Steele is now married with twins."

"Umm, I guess that means there's hope for those Steele boys yet. I recall they used to have quite a reputation."

Hunter was close to saying that they still did. At

least the single ones. However, she decided to keep her mouth shut.

"So what's going on with you and Dr. Steele?"

Hunter almost missed her step and glanced over at her mother. "What makes you think something is going on?"

Ingrid rolled her eyes. "I wasn't born yesterday, Hunter. I saw the way he was looking at you and the way you were looking at him."

"You're imagining things. Tyson is nothing more than a client."

"If you want me to think so."

Hunter didn't say anything to that. So what if she and Tyson were looking at each other in a way that raised eyebrows? No big deal.

As Hunter opened her car door for her mother, she truly hoped that it wasn't a big deal.

Tyson tossed and turned in the bed, finding it difficult to sleep. Each time he closed his eyes, images of Hunter and that night they spent together flooded his mind. The images were so vivid and powerful that he could lick his lips and taste her there.

Feeling frustration in every part of his body, he slid out of bed and headed for the living room. It seemed that sleep would evade him tonight, so he might as well see what was on television.

Moments later he felt even more frustrated. How could someone have over one hundred channels and not find a single thing of interest on television? He tossed the remote on the table and walked out of the living room into the kitchen, where he opened the refrigerator, needing a beer.

Something had to give, he thought, pulling a beer from the six-pack and popping the tab. Today, answering a page to the ER he had rounded the corner and seen Hunter standing there. Desire the likes of which he'd never felt before had consumed him. And when she'd turned and looked at him, their gazes had met and locked in a way that gave him sensuous shivers just thinking about it.

It didn't make sense. After all he and Hunter had done that night, how in the world could she still be in his system? Or he in hers? He knew the feelings were mutual. He had felt the chemistry, known she had felt it as well. They'd been standing there and he'd been able to actually feel her heat seep into him. It had penetrated every single pore in his body. Neither of them had said a word but their gazes had told it all.

He took a long gulp of his beer but it couldn't wash away the memories. Why was he remembering the way she would whisper his name right before she came, and the way she would scream when caught in the throes of passion? Why was he reliving in his mind all the times his body had straddled hers? Thrust into hers?

And why, considering all of that, was he beginning to believe it wasn't all just about sex? If not sex, then what? Could there be any credence to what Galen had said? That's what Tyson needed to find out before he endured any more sleepless nights.

Leaving the kitchen, he went back into his bedroom and retrieved his cell phone from his nightstand. He glanced over at the clock and saw it was after midnight. Hell, if he couldn't sleep, neither would she. He punched in Hunter's number.

A sleepy voice answered. "Hello?"

"We need to talk, Hunter."

"Tyson?"

He loved hearing her say his name. Even when it was in a lethargic voice it sounded sexy. "What other man would be calling you this time of night?"

"Why are you?"

He couldn't help but smile at her comeback. "I told you. We need to talk."

"Now?"

"No, not now. Tomorrow. I need to drop by your office."

"Fine. Call and make an appointment with Pauline."

"No. I make appointments with you personally. Expect me tomorrow. Good night."

Hunter frowned when she heard the click in her ear. *Expect me tomorrow.* Who did Tyson Steele think he was? Did she even remotely look like that young nurse who'd been all in his face today, flirting and grinning all over the place? Touching his hand? The same one he'd flirted back with? He should be making an appointment with Macy Phillips instead of with her.

And maybe you need to tone down that green streak, Hunter McKay. Jealousy doesn't become you.

She hung up her phone and then slid out of bed to glance over at the clock. Tyson had a lot of nerve calling her at this hour. But then, if there was anything she knew Tyson possessed it was nerve. Right along with an abundance of arrogance.

And what did he want to talk to her about anyway? She preferred continuing on this trend of them not having anything to do with each other. But then that hadn't stopped her from thinking of him. From remembering. From dreaming.

Sliding into her slippers, she went into the kitchen for a cup of tea. Hopefully that would help her sort out a few things in her mind. Her mother's questions hadn't ended at the hospital. Once they'd gotten on the road Ingrid McKay had been determined to uncover all the details she could. The last thing her mother needed to know was that two weekends ago she had turned her bedroom into a real live hot spot. And that Tyson had taught her sexual positions that should be outlawed. Not only that, but all those packs of condoms were also just where he'd left them on the table in her bedroom.

A short while later, as she sat down at her kitchen table sipping her tea, Hunter couldn't stop the shivers that raced through her body at the thought of seeing Tyson again.

Although she had no idea what was on his mind, she had to remember that he only wanted to talk.

Chapter 14

Hunter paced her office, calling herself all kinds of fool for being nervous about Tyson's visit. And she also tried convincing herself the dress she'd chosen to wear to work that morning had nothing to do with knowing he would be dropping by. So what if it was a tad shorter than the ones she normally wore to the office? Tyson telling her how much he liked seeing her legs had nothing to do with it. Nor was that the reason she'd replaced her comfortable pumps with a pair of high heels.

She glanced at her watch. Pauline would be leaving for the day in less than five minutes. Had Tyson deliberately timed his arrival when he figured they would be alone? She shook her head, telling herself she was jumping to conclusions. Tyson's visit to her office might just be strictly business. There was a possibility he had questions about those preliminary house plans. Yes, those same house plans she'd already dismissed as inconsequential. She knew he had no more intention of building a house in the country than she did. But she had put her time, concentration and energy into them. That was why she had billed him for them anyway. And she hadn't been cheap. He could be questioning the size of his bill, but a personal visit wasn't needed for that.

The buzzer on her desk sounded and she inhaled deeply before crossing the room to push the button. "Yes, Pauline?"

"I'm about to leave, Hunter. Do you need me to do anything before I—"

When she heard a voice in the background she knew her conversation with Pauline was being interrupted by someone. "Excuse me, Hunter. But Dr. Steele is here. He said you are expecting him."

There was no need to tell Pauline to send him in because at that moment, her office door opened and Tyson walked in. She glared at him, a little put out that he assumed he could just walk into her office whenever he felt like it. But then that thought faded from her mind when her eyes roamed over him. No man could wear a pair of jeans better.

Nor could a man remove them better, either.

She tried not to remember that night in her apartment when he had stripped out of his jeans for her. Remembering also made her recall just what he was packing behind the zipper of those jeans.

"If there's nothing else you need for me to do then I'll see you tomorrow, Hunter."

At that moment she realized she still had Pauline on the line. "That's fine, Pauline. Enjoy your evening and I'll see you tomorrow."

She clicked off the line and lifted her chin at Tyson, but before she could give him a piece of her mind, he asked, "How's your mother?"

"Mom's fine. Thanks for asking." So, okay, it was nice of him to inquire…but still. "It would have been nice if you'd given me a time as to when to expect you, Tyson."

He actually looked remorseful. "Sorry about that. It was late last night when I called you and—"

"Trust me. I know how late it was."

A small smile touched his lips as he leaned back against the closed door. "I couldn't sleep and figured if I couldn't sleep you shouldn't be able to sleep, either. Sounds pretty juvenile, doesn't it?"

"Yes, especially since I wasn't responsible for your inability to sleep."

He straightened and took a few steps into the middle of the room. Hunter's stomach immediately knotted and her breathing suddenly seemed forced. The man was testosterone personified. And why did those thighs, those hard muscular thighs that had ridden her so many times, look perfect in his jeans?

"But you are responsible, Hunter," he said, interrupting her intense appraisal of him. "That's why I'm here."

Hunter frowned. What he was saying didn't make much sense. "Okay, so you can't sleep at night and for some reason you think I'm to blame. If that's the case, what do you expect me to do about it?"

"Give me a week. I want a week in your bed since a mere night didn't do a damn thing to eradicate you from my system."

Tyson looked at the beautiful woman with the shocked look on her face. At some point he needed to stop astonishing her this way. He'd gotten the same reaction from her that night at Notorious after stating his plans to seduce her.

He shoved his hands into his pockets, readying himself for what was to come. She could get mad or glad. Either way he intended to get his week. Hell, he needed that week. When time ticked by and she didn't say anything, just sat behind her desk and gazed at him like he was stone crazy, he finally asked, "Well?"

Tyson knew he'd pushed too hard when a furious expression finally overtook her expression. She eased out of her chair to come around her desk and stand in front of him with her hands planted firmly on her hips. He could actually see fire in those gorgeous brown eyes of hers and should have had enough sense to step back, but he didn't. The way he saw it, he didn't have anything to lose at this point and he intended to stand his ground.

"You sex-crazed womanizing ass!" she said in a loud, angry voice. "What's wrong, Dr. Steele? That little nurse didn't work out for you so you thought you could just show up here demanding more sex from me because you need it? Let me tell you just where you can—"

"I don't just need sex, Hunter," he interrupted her in a voice that matched her volume. "I need *you*. And what little nurse are you talking about?"

"I'm talking about that ER nurse who was flirting with you yesterday. And I saw you flirting back."

A fierce frown covered Tyson's face when she brought up Macy Phillips. "For your information, Macy Phillips was on my 'to do' list, along with several other women," he snapped.

"Then by all means do them. What's stopping you?" she snapped back, getting in his face.

"You're stopping me, dammit, and I don't know why," he retorted, hating he had to admit such a thing. "Ever since that night I saw you at Notorious, I haven't wanted another woman. I haven't thought of anyone else. I figured that once I made love to you my life would return to normal. But things have gotten worse for me. For some reason you aren't out my system. I dream about you at night. I think about you during the day. My cleaning lady has been to my place twice since that night you were there for dinner, but I swear I can still smell your scent."

To Tyson's surprise Hunter took a step back. It was as if his words had finally gotten to her, were now sinking in. So he decided to plunge forward. "So I came up with a plan."

"Another one?" she asked flippantly.

"Yes, another one," he said, more than a little agitated. "There has to be a reason I can't get enough of you, and whether you want to admit it or not, I'm not out of your system, either. I can tell. Anyone who's within ten feet of us can pick up on the strong sexual chemistry between us. I think your mother even picked up on something."

"She did," Hunter said in a somewhat calmer tone. "I told her there was nothing going on between us but I don't think she believes me."

Then, as if she realized she'd gone soft, her spine straightened and her voice became firm. "And don't you dare stand there and tell me what I don't have out of my system. You have no way of knowing that."

He lifted his chin. "Don't I?"

She crossed her arms over her chest. "No, you don't."

"Are you saying that you don't still want me? That you don't go to bed with thoughts of me inside of you? Kissing you? Tasting you? Riding you hard?"

He saw heat flare in her eyes at his words. He also saw blatant desire that fanned the flames of what he was feeling. "Well, are you?"

She squared her shoulders and glared at him. "I'm not saying anything."

"Then it's admission by omission."

"I am *not* admitting to anything. If I'm not out of your system then that's your problem, one you need to deal with on your own. Contrary to what you seem to think, you're out of my system, Tyson. Nothing you say or do will prove otherwise," she said haughtily.

A slow smile spread across his features. "You think not?"

Hunter didn't like his tone, nor the "let me prove differently" look in Tyson's eyes. For once she felt she might have said too much, tossed out a dare she hadn't intended to make. And now he had that predatory look on his face. The one that meant he intended to prove her wrong. She took a few more steps back and came to a stop when her backside hit against her desk.

"Isn't tonight Thursday? You're having dinner with your folks, right?" she asked.

"What about it?"

During their talk over wine and cheese in her bedroom, he mentioned that over the years his mother had insisted on Thursday dinners as a way to show her six sons that married life would be wonderful. Tyson had stated that as far as he was concerned, the only thing his mother was showing him was what a great cook she continued to be. For him it was the delicious meals that were the draw.

"I wouldn't want you to be late for dinner," she told him.

A smiled curved his lips. "Are you trying to get rid of me, Hunter?"

She leaned back against her desk. "What do you think?"

"I think it's time I show you that you want me as much as I want you."

A slow stirring erupted in the pit of her stomach when Tyson began walking toward her. His expression was serious, his eyes dark and honed in on hers. Her heart pounded in her chest with every step he took. She was tempted to run, but her feet felt cemented in place. Besides, from the look on Tyson's face she knew that he wouldn't think twice about chasing after her.

Did she even want to run?

She frowned at the doubt that clouded her mind. Of course she wanted to run, to escape, to get the hell out of here. *Umm, maybe not*, she thought when Tyson stopped and kicked off his shoes and then took the time to remove his socks.

Hunter had a pretty good idea where this was going, and a part of her wanted it more than anything. She hadn't been completely honest by claiming he was out of her system. But a week-long affair wasn't necessarily the answer. It might work for him, but she ran the risk that he'd get even more under her skin.

As she continued to look at Tyson, he straightened and went for his shirt, undoing the buttons and easing it from his chest and broad muscular shoulders. Hunter tried not to remember the feel of that chest rubbing against her hardened nipples, but she failed. She heard herself moan.

"You said something, Hunter?" he asked, staring at her with a predatory look.

She swallowed and shook her head, unable to speak for a moment. When she could, she said, "No, I didn't say anything." But she knew she should. She should speak up and put an end to this madness. But a part of her was curious to see just how far he would go before she sent him packing.

And speaking of packing… He eased his jeans down his legs to reveal a pair of sexy briefs and it was obvious just what he was packing between those massive thighs.

"Is there a reason you're removing your clothes in my office?" she asked, deciding she needed to say something before he went any further.

He smiled over at her as he inserted his fingers in the waistband of his briefs. "Yes, there's a reason."

And then, without saying another word, he lowered his briefs and showed her the reason. In all its arousing and throbbing glory.

As far as Tyson was concerned, the worst thing Hunter could do at that moment was lick her lips. Major bad timing on her part. Especially when he saw the sexual hunger in her eyes.

Then she lifted her chin. "I won't be removing my clothes, Tyson."

He stood in front of her totally naked and he couldn't help noticing she had a hard time zeroing in on his face. Instead her gaze kept straying to his groin. "I don't recall asking you to take your clothes off, Hunter, mainly because I intend to take them off for you."

She narrowed her eyes at him. "You wouldn't dare."

He chuckled. "I would. And I will." He took a step toward her.

"If you come any closer, I'll scream," she threatened.

His mouth curved into a smile. "Baby, you're going to be screaming anyway, so one more scream is a moot point." He trailed a finger down her thigh. "You want to convince me you didn't wear this short dress just for me?"

"Think whatever you want."

"In that case, I think you did wear it just for me," he said, loving the feel of his fingers on her bare skin. "And I want to thank you properly for doing so." Then Tyson lowered his mouth to hers.

Hunter knew the moment Tyson's tongue touched hers there would be nothing proper about this kiss. She was proven right when he began devouring her mouth with an intensity that had her fighting back moans. Pushing him away was not even a consideration. Instead, she eased up on tiptoe and wrapped her arms around his neck to deepen the kiss.

When his hand began easing up her dress, instinctively, her legs spread apart. Just like the last time, his touch was like an aphrodisiac, making her crave things she shouldn't have but wanted anyway. And topping the list was Tyson. She wanted him doing all those naughty and sinful yet delicious things to her.

Her thoughts were suddenly snatched from her mind when Tyson's fingers settled between her legs. Oh, yes, she remembered these fingers and just what they could do to her, how they could make her feel. He knew how to work them with a skill she found astounding. The man had an uncanny ability to take her breath away.

He broke off the kiss and stared down at her, deliberately holding her gaze while his fingers worked their magic inside her, making her moan, gasp and then moan again. "You sure you want this?" he asked in a deep, husky voice. "After all, you claim I'm the only one with the problem. That I am out of your system."

Hunter knew he was toying with her, trying to make her admit something she had adamantly refuted. "You're wet, Hunter," he said, moving his fingers in slow, circular motions inside her. "I like stirring you up this way, and do you know why?"

She fought the urge to ask but failed. "No, why?"

"Because doing so escalates your scent. There is something about your scent that's powerful and intoxicating. It arouses me whenever I'm around you. Makes me want to taste you here," he said, inserting an additional finger inside her. "I miss tasting you that way."

She didn't want to admit it but that particular part of her body missed being tasted that way, too. His fingers and tongue should be considered weapons of mass seduction. He held tight to her gaze, daring her to look away, while his fingers slowly and provocatively began pushing her over the edge. "Am I out of your system, Hunter?"

Did he really need for her to answer that? Especially when her nipples had hardened and her hips moved with the rhythm of his fingers. She drew in a deep breath and shook her head.

"Not good enough. I want to hear you say it," Tyson said as he leaned down close to her lips just seconds before his tongue swiped across them. "Say it, Hunter."

There was no way she could refuse him. Not now when he'd whipped her body into a need she could not deny. "No, you're not out of my system."

Her words made an arrogant smile touch his lips. "Glad we're in agreement about that." He pulled his fingers from inside her and instantly she felt bereft. And then he was pulling her dress over her head, skillfully removing her bra in the process. His hands were there to cup her breasts the moment they were free. "Beautiful," he whispered huskily. "I missed these girls. They spoiled me."

No, in all honesty, he had spoiled them, Hunter thought. And they had definitely missed him. When he sucked a nipple into his mouth, she knew he was about to spoil them some more. She drew in a deep breath and struggled to hold herself up when she was about to slither to the floor. Tyson came to her rescue then, grabbing her by the hips to hoist her onto her desk.

"Now to get to what we both want," he said, using the tips of his fingers to trace a path toward her inner thighs. Hunter felt her heart pick up a beat when his hand closed possessively over her feminine mound through her lace panties.

"You like lace, I notice," he said throatily.

"Yes, I like lace," she responded, barely able to get the words out.

"That's good to know."

Hunter was about to ask why he thought so when he tugged on her panties and automatically she lifted her hips so he could ease them down her legs. Once that was done he captured her gaze as he gripped her hips and moved forward, leading the head of his engorged erection toward her womanly entrance.

He was almost there when common sense invaded her mind. "Stop!"

He loosened his hold on her. "Stop?" he repeated with an incredulous look on his face.

She nodded. "Condom."

The shocked look in his eyes let her know he couldn't believe he'd been less than an inch from entering her without having given any thought to protection. "Condom. Right," he said, slowly backing away to retrieve a packet from the jeans he'd tossed on the floor. "Thanks for the reminder. This has never happened to me before."

Hunter believed him and unashamedly watched as he expertly sheathed his erection. Looking back over at her, he said, "Ready to pick up where we left off?"

"Yes." She was more than ready. Shivers raced through her body at the intense desire she saw in the depths of his green eyes as he headed back toward her. And to show him just how ready she was, she boldly spread her legs. She'd never been taken on a desk before and was curious to see how they would pull it off.

When he returned, he said, "Grab my shoulders and hold on tight."

He lifted her hips, guiding his erection unerringly inside her. She threw her head back and moaned at the impact. Her inner muscles clenched, tightening around him. Tyson being back inside her felt good. Like he belonged there.

She swallowed, wondering how she could allow her mind to think that when it came to Tyson. A man whose favorite pastime was bedding women. All thoughts fled her mind when he began thrusting into her in long, hard strokes. The intensity of them shook her to the core. She understood why he told her to grab his shoulders when he began pounding into her at the same time he eased her back on the desk, nearly covering her body with his. Luckily, she had a big desk because they needed the space.

Suddenly Hunter's body jerked from what seemed like an electrical shock that traveled through her body straight to her nerve endings. It was all she needed to push her over the edge. And Tyson joined her. She released a guttural scream mere seconds before he leaned in and took her mouth with a greedy kiss that swallowed up her cry. Just when she came down to earth, he moved against her again and she was hurled into yet another orgasm. Why had she ever claimed to be over this man?

"Glad we're in agreement about that week."

Hunter glanced over at Tyson as she slid back into her dress. He had gotten dressed and was leaning against her desk watching her do the same. No, they weren't in agreement since she hadn't agreed to anything. "We had tonight, Tyson. That's the best I can do."

"I want a week."

"You got tonight."

"I want a week, Hunter."

He was persistent. After smoothing her dress down her body she stared at him. "Why, Tyson? What will a week do for you?"

"I'm convinced I'm a man possessed."

Hunter raised a brow. "Possessed?"

"Yes, possessed by passion. Yours."

Now she'd heard everything. She barely knew all the things to do in the bedroom so how could an experienced man like him get obsessed with her? It didn't make much sense. She opened her mouth to ask the question but his words stopped her.

"Please don't ask me to explain it, Hunter, because I can't. All I know is that you're the only woman I want and I need to know what we just did won't be the last time. I need that week. I'll even let you call the shots and set the grounds rules during that week if that's what it takes. But I've got to get you out of my system for good."

She hated to ask but she had to. "But what if that one week doesn't work?"

He stared at her without saying anything, and she realized that in his mind it was simply not an option. "We'll think positive. It has to work."

She didn't say anything for a minute as she remembered what they'd just done on her desk. A week of Tyson wouldn't kill her. Besides, if she was honest with herself, she would admit that a part of her wanted him just as badly. She had craved his touch, had dreamed of him inside her. However, she wouldn't go so far as to say she was possessed. She just hoped the week gave him what he wanted. Freedom from her once and for all.

"Fine. You'll get your week, Tyson, but I'm setting the ground rules. If you think you're going to keep me on my back 24/7 then you're wrong. We will do other things."

He arched his brow. "Other things like what?"

"I'll think of something."

"Yes, you do that, Hunter. In the meantime…"

He crossed the room to her, leaned forward and captured her lips with his.

Chapter 15

There had to be a reason he couldn't get enough of Hunter, Tyson thought, recalling how after making love to her on her desk, they had gotten dressed only to end up making love a second time on the sofa in her office.

And how could he have almost forgotten to use a condom that first time? That was something he'd never done before with any woman. He had truly acted like a man possessed and he needed to get his life back on track. If he didn't know better he would think Hunter was a witch. A beautiful, delicious and sensuous witch who was wreaking havoc on his brain cells to the point where he couldn't think straight. Hell, he wasn't thinking at all. When had he ever wanted to go a full week with any woman? But with him it hadn't been an option. It had been about survival. And that's what bothered him more than anything. When had he ever admitted to a woman that she was in his system like he was some kind of sex addict or something? Why hadn't he been able to let go and walk away like he'd done with all the others? For the umpteenth time he had to ask himself, what made Hunter so different?

"You're quiet tonight, Tyson."

He glanced down the dinner table. Of course it had to be Mercury who noticed. "Don't have anything to say."

He had arrived late at his parents' house for dinner. He knew his mother assumed he'd gotten detained at the hospital, but that was far from the truth. He had arrived in time to see the photos Galen and Brittany had been passing around of the twins, which had, luckily, deflected any questions about why he'd been late.

He noted these Thursday dinners were getting rather large with three of his brothers now married. And for the first time the grandkids were present, which had to be the reason his mother was smiling all over the place. Not to mention the growing family had given her an excuse to buy a new dining room table, one that seated fourteen people. Tyson could do the math. It was quite apparent that Eden Tyson Steele was counting on her three bachelor sons producing wives to fill the vacant seats at the table one day.

"Oh, you're in one of those moods," Gannon said, grinning. "That's what happens when you prepare dinner for a woman."

That got everyone's attention. "You prepared dinner?" Galen asked, surprised. Anyone who knew him knew he didn't cook for himself, much less for anyone else.

"I ordered take-out. No big deal."

"You actually fed a woman?" Jonas asked, staring at him with disbelief.

He glared at his brother. "Like I said, Jonas, no big deal." Usually he didn't get agitated easily, especially with his siblings, but for some reason tonight he was. He should be overjoyed Hunter had granted him another week, but there was that risk that it wouldn't be enough. Then where would he be?

"I ran into Ingrid McKay today at the grocery store," his mother said, eyeing him speculatively. "You didn't mention that Hunter McKay had moved back to town."

He stared at his mother, wondering why she would bring that up...especially now. And as far as mentioning it to her, he hadn't known she even knew Hunter. Had she kept a log of every girl he'd hit on in high school? "I didn't mention it because I didn't think it was a big deal. I didn't even know you knew Hunter."

"Of course I know Hunter. She was Reverend McKay's granddaughter. She sang in the choir and had an awesome voice. I also recall she was a beautiful girl with impeccable manners. How could I not know her when we attended the same church?"

But so did four hundred other people, Tyson thought, taking a sip of his iced tea.

According to his mother Hunter had a nice voice. He'd heard Hunter scream a lot of times but never sing. Nor could he recall her singing whenever he attended church back in the day. Must have been those Sundays when he'd dozed off during the service.

"Hunter McKay," Jonas said, smiling. "I remember

her from high school. We graduated together. Isn't she the one who dumped you, Tyson?"

Tyson glared at Jonas for the second time that night. "She didn't dump me."

"That's not the way I heard it," Galen said, grinning.

"Well, you heard wrong."

Brittany, who seemed to have acquired the role of peacemaker since marrying Galen, spoke up and changed the subject. "I forgot to mention that Jonas wants to use the twins in his next marketing campaign. Isn't that wonderful?"

Tyson gave Brittany an appreciative smile. Everyone at the table got so caught up with her announcement that any further conversation about Tyson and Hunter was abruptly forgotten.

He took a sip of his tea and glanced across the table at Eli, who was looking at him with a grin on his face. Eli was the only one who'd known of his plan to pursue Hunter. He was grateful Eli was the brother who knew how to keep his mouth shut, although he liked giving his opinion much too often to suit Tyson. He couldn't help wondering what Eli found amusing since he still had that silly-looking grin on his face. Then Tyson remembered. Eli had warned him about getting possessed by passion. Damn. For once he wished he'd taken his brother's warning to heart. Now he had a feeling he was way over his head where Hunter was concerned.

Hunter began drying off her body with the huge towel. She much preferred taking showers, but tonight a good hot soak had done wonders for her body, a body that had gone through intense lovemaking with Tyson Steele.

She hadn't counted on him taking her on her desk and her sofa, all in the same afternoon. In all honesty, she hadn't counted on being taken at all.

And now she had agreed to spend a week with him. Because of that decision she could see herself taking even more baths. But like she'd told him, their week would be filled with more than just lovemaking. One sure way to get her out of his system, if she was as deeply embedded into it as he claimed, was to come up with activities he didn't do with women. The thought made her smile. In the end he would thank her.

His admission still baffled her. Personally, if she felt possessed by any man he would certainly be the last one to know it. But Tyson had pretty much placed his cards on the table without any care as to how she played them. Just as long as he got his week with her. That was the craziest thing she'd ever heard.

Still, she couldn't discount the changes making love with Tyson had done to her and for her. Thanks to him she now knew firsthand just what an ass Carter had been, especially in the bedroom. And thanks to Tyson she had discovered a lot about her own sexuality. He'd opened a door to sensual exploration and adventure for her. With Tyson nothing was taboo, nothing was off-limits or forbidden. He wouldn't be the only one using this week to his advantage. She would, too, but for different reasons. For her it would be a week of sexual journeys and sensuous excursions. But the big question for her was how to keep her emotions out of the equation.

For Tyson this was about sex and nothing more and she had to remember that. More than once she'd felt a pull at her heart whenever they made love. She had to fight hard not to get lust mixed up with love.

Hunter had slid into her nightgown and was about to grab a magazine off her coffee table to read in bed when the sound of her doorbell startled her. She could think of only one person showing up at her place tonight. Hadn't they made love twice already today? He'd warned her that he was a greedy ass. Now she was beginning to believe him.

Dismissing the rush of desire moving up her spine, she put down the magazine and went to her door. A quick look out the peephole confirmed her suspicions. It was Tyson.

She fought back the sensations she felt just knowing he was on the other side of that door. The thought that she was beginning to be just as insatiable as he didn't sit well with her. Releasing a deep sigh mixed with frustration and desire, she opened the door.

He stood there and held her gaze. Although she didn't want to, her body felt heated from his deep, penetrating stare. Blood was rushing to every part of her body and she knew there was no way to stop it. Instead of saying anything, she moved aside for him to enter. And when he walked past her she inhaled his rich, masculine scent. The same one she'd washed off her skin less than an hour ago.

He paused in the middle of her living room. Hunter was surprised he hadn't just headed straight for the bedroom. Tyson was arrogant enough to do so. He turned and she felt the heat of his gaze as it moved up and down her baby-doll nightgown.

"Believe it or not, Hunter, this isn't a booty call," he finally said, breaking the silence.

She leaned back against her closed door. "Is there a new name for it now?" She wouldn't be surprised if he'd coined his own term.

"I didn't come here to make love to you…although I have no qualms about doing so if you want."

She crossed her arms over her chest and ignored how his gaze moved to her breasts. She felt her nipples harden. "Then why are you here?"

A smile touched the corners of his lips, so adorable she had to blink to make sure it was real. "I decided to drop by tonight, Hunter, because I want to hear you sing."

Tyson loved Hunter's facial expressions whenever he caught her off guard. He'd shocked her again. Without waiting for an invitation he took a seat on her sofa.

"Sing?" she asked. "What makes you think I can sing?"

"My mother. She mentioned it over dinner." At another shocked look, he smiled. They just kept on coming.

"Why would your mother bring up my name at dinner?" she asked, leaving her place at the door to sit down in the wingback chair in the living room.

"She ran into your mother at the grocery store and found out you'd moved back to town. She wanted to know why I hadn't mentioned it to her. I told her I didn't even know she knew you. That's when she said you used to be in the choir at church and had a nice voice."

Hunter smiled. "That was kind of her to think so. I'm surprised she remembered. That was years ago."

Tyson chuckled. "My mother rarely forgets anything, trust me. So are you going to sing for me?"

"No."

"Why not?"

"Other than humming occasionally when I take a shower, I haven't sung in years."

"So? I'd like to hear you sing."

"Why?"

Tyson wasn't sure. All he knew was that when he left his parents' home he had wanted to come straight here and get her to sing for him. "I just want to hear you, that's all."

She stared at him for a minute and he knew she was trying to figure him out. He wanted to tell her not to waste her time, when lately even he hadn't been able to figure out his actions, at least not when it came to her.

"Fine," she finally said. "Is there a particular song you want to hear?"

"Anything by Whitney Houston."

He saw the smile that spread across her lips and it stirred his insides. "Throw me a real challenge, will you? But okay, I got this. Lucky for you I happen to love all her songs." Easing from her chair, she grinned. "I really feel silly doing this, but you asked for it. Here goes."

And then while he watched she threw her head back, closed her eyes and began belting out "The Greatest Love of All."

Tyson sat there spellbound, mesmerized and totally captivated. His mother was right. Hunter had an awesome voice and listening to her sing touched him deeply. There were so many facets of Hunter McKay and he wondered if her husband had appreciated every single one. Apparently not.

He couldn't take his eyes off her, standing there in the middle of her living room, singing for him and him alone. She appeared shrouded in sensuality and his pulse throbbed at the effect she was having on him. It was crazy. It didn't make much sense. Yet it was happening. Hunter McKay was drawing everything out of him and without very much effort.

Moments later when she finished and opened her eyes, she stared across the room at him, a tentative smile touching her lips. "Okay. I'm done."

Tyson knew in all honesty, so was he. Hunter had done him in. He felt his heart pounding in his chest. She looked beautiful standing there in her short lacy nightgown that showed off a pair of beautiful legs. It sounded crazy but he was beginning to think this entire thing with Hunter was more than her being deeply embedded in his system. It was more than him being possessed by her passion. And he needed this week to figure it out.

Standing, he clapped his hands. "Bravo. You were excellent. Superb. If you ever quit your day job you can—"

"Become a backup singer for Prince? That was my childhood dream for the longest time."

He chuckled. "Was it?"

"Yes."

"If you didn't make it, then it was his loss." He crossed the room to her. "Thanks for singing for me. Mom was right. I had no idea. You have a beautiful voice."

She shrugged. "Carter never thought so. He claimed I always sang off-key."

Tyson shook his head. "The more I hear about your ex-husband, the more I believe you were right."

She raised a brow. "About what?"

"About him being a bastard." He then leaned down and placed a light kiss on her lips. "Walk me to the door."

Another shocked look appeared on her face. "You're leaving?"

"Yes." He took her hand as he headed toward the door. "I have surgeries in the morning, but call me tomorrow afternoon to let me know of your plans for our weekend. I have the entire weekend off."

"All right."

Before he opened the door he couldn't resist taking her into his arms and devouring her mouth. He knew leaving her alone tonight would be hard but it was something he had to do. Hunter was a puzzle he had to piece together for his peace of mind.

When he released her mouth, he whispered against her moist lips. "Good night."

"Good night, Tyson."

And then he opened the door and walked out.

Chapter 16

"This is Dr. Steele. May I help you?"

Hunter loved the sexy sound of Tyson's voice. "Yes, Dr. Steele, this is Hunter and you can definitely help me."

She heard the richness of his chuckle and wished it didn't make her pulse rate increase. "And what can I do for you, Ms. McKay?"

"I thought we'd take in a movie tonight. Anything you prefer seeing?"

There was silence on his end and Hunter knew why. Rumor had it that if Tyson Steele took a woman out, his bedroom was as far as they got. This week wouldn't be status quo for him. He'd said she could set the ground rules and she had.

"Doesn't matter," he finally said. "Anything you

want to see will be fine with me. I'll pick you up at seven. Is that a good time for dinner and a movie?"

She was surprised at his suggestion of dinner. "Yes, seven is fine. I'll see you then."

"And, Hunter?"

"Yes?"

"Bring your dancing shoes. I want to take you dancing after the movie."

He wanted to take her dancing? "Okay." After ending her call with Tyson, Hunter leaned back in her office chair as she remembered his visit to her apartment last night. No booty call, he'd just wanted to hear her sing. How strange was that? Had he asked to spend the night she probably would have let him. But he hadn't asked.

She hated admitting it, but Tyson Steele was beginning to confuse her. Like his suggestion of dinner, dancing and him picking her up. She'd honestly assumed that he would ask what time the movie started and say he would meet her there. Anything else would constitute a real date, and Tyson Steele didn't do real dates. He'd told her that himself during their little bedroom talk that night over wine and cheese. He claimed dating would encourage women to get the wrong ideas regarding the nature of his intent.

So why this sudden change of behavior? She could only assume that he figured she knew the score so she wasn't anyone he had to worry about. He was trying to work her out of his system and nothing more.

She looked at her watch. If Tyson was going to take her to dinner, a movie and dancing, she needed to make a few shopping stops before going home. Her goal was to make this a week neither of them would forget. And tonight was the kickoff.

"You dance as well as you sing," Tyson whispered to Hunter hours later when he led her to the center of the floor for another dance. This one was a slow number. About time, he thought, as he pulled her into his arms. He was beginning to think line dancing was all they'd be doing tonight.

"Thanks. I love to dance."

Tyson could tell. Even when they'd sat out a few she had moved from side to side in her chair, keeping time with the music.

He had picked her up promptly at seven and when she opened the door he had to stand there for a moment to get his bearings. From head to toe, she looked fabulous. And he had told her so many more times than he probably should have tonight. He totally liked her short, tight-fitting dress and killer heels.

They had dined at Toni's, an Italian restaurant located in the heart of the city. Over dinner she had told him about the additional clients she had acquired and again thanked him for the three he had referred. He was glad everything seemed to be working out for her.

Tyson wrapped his arms around her, loving the feel of holding her as they moved slowly around the dance floor. Tonight had been great and he had enjoyed her company. He'd even enjoyed the movie she'd chosen for them to see. He was surprised to discover that, like him, she liked Westerns. This one had been one of the good ones and had held his attention most of the time.

Hunter held it all the other times. He had to admit he'd enjoyed sitting beside her in the theater, sharing popcorn with her. Holding her hand.

She pressed her cheek against his chest as they slowly swayed to the music. Their movements were so slow that at times it appeared neither of them was moving. And their bodies were so close he could feel her every curve. He was getting sexually charged just thinking about tonight and how it would end. Again, she'd made it clear that she would not spend a single night this week in his bed, and he had no problem wearing out the mattress at her place if that's what she preferred.

Resting his cheek against the top of her head, he couldn't help but think there was more to his relationship with Hunter than just great sex. Dinner and the movie had proven that and he looked forward to spending more time with her outside the bedroom this week.

When he felt her stiffen in his arms, he glanced down at her. "You all right?"

She glanced up and met his gaze. "My ex is here."

Tyson lifted a brow. "Your ex? Here?"

"Yes. I heard he might be coming to Phoenix on business, and I can only assume that's why he's here. He just walked in with a group of men."

Tyson nodded. "If his presence makes you uncomfortable, we can leave."

She shook her head. "No. He's seen us and maybe that's good thing."

"Why?"

"My mother-in-law overheard Carter's plan to contact me while he's here and play on my heartstrings."

"Your heartstrings?"

"Yes. He has this crazy notion that since I hadn't dated since our divorce that I'm still in love with him and would take him back, even after all he's done."

Tyson didn't know what all the man had done, but just from the time he had spent with Hunter he knew she felt only loathing for her ex. "You say he's seen us?"

"Yes. In fact he's sitting at the table, staring at us now."

"Good."

Tyson pulled Hunter closer into his arms, leaned down and covered her mouth with his.

Hunter suddenly sat straight up in bed. When she saw a naked Tyson sleeping beside her, she realized it hadn't been a dream at all. They'd gone to dinner, a movie and dancing. The evening had gone great. Not even seeing Carter had put a damper on things, because Tyson had refused to let it.

Although it had been pretense, he had gone out of his way to give the impression that the two of them were a hot item. In addition to kissing her in the middle of the dance floor, when they had returned to their table Tyson had taken her in his lap and hand-fed her the chips and dip they'd ordered. She couldn't help but enjoy Tyson's attentiveness, even if it was playacting. He had lavished her with attention and affection. Tonight Tyson had made her feel significant, appreciated and desired right before Carter's eyes.

From the angry look she'd seen on her ex's face, he'd gotten the message Tyson had intended. The message

that she belonged to Tyson. And in a way she did…
even if it was for just a week. They had left the nightclub only after Carter had done so, satisfied their mis-
sion had been accomplished.

The moment they had entered her apartment Tyson
had swept her off her feet and carried her into the bedroom. There he had undressed her and his skilled body
had taken her over the edge. Not once. Or twice. Three
times before they'd finally drifted off to sleep.

Smiling now, she settled back down in bed and snuggled her body deeper into his. Why was she allowing
herself to get wrapped up in the moment?

And why tonight, when she had seen Carter again
after all this time, had she felt nothing…absolutely nothing? It seemed her mind, body and soul refused to waste
any more emotions—loathing or otherwise—on the
man she'd spent eight years trying and failing to satisfy. But now, thanks to Tyson, she knew the failures
weren't her fault, but were Carter's.

She drew in a deep breath. In Tyson's mind, he had
wanted another week with her because he believed he
was possessed by passion. And she would admit the
two of them could generate a lot of that. But now she
could finally admit to herself the reason she'd agreed
to a week with him. She had fallen in love with him.

It really didn't matter how it happened or when but
she knew it had. She wanted to believe it happened the
first time they'd made love. He had treated her like a
woman who deserved to be treated with dignity and respect. But he'd gone even further by treating her like a
woman who deserved to be appreciated. Each and every

time they made love he'd made her feel special, like a woman worth having, even in the bedroom.

It didn't bother her that he didn't return her love or that he would never know her true feelings for him. Loving him was her secret. After this week was over and he returned to his world—the one filled with all those other women—she would always have these precious memories.

"You okay?"

She glanced over at Tyson. She hadn't meant to awaken him. "Yes, I'm fine."

"Baby, I know you're fine. That dress you wore tonight showed just how fine you are."

She chuckled. "You liked my dress?"

"I told you I did. A number of times. I like every outfit you put on your body. And I like your body, as well."

"Do you?"

"Yes, I do."

She eased out of his arms to straddle him. "Your erection is rock-hard. I definitely want to put something like that to good use."

"And your girls wants my attention," he said, reaching upward to cup the twin mounds in his hands. "I plan to put them to good use, as well."

"Not before I give you a little attention, Mr. Steele."

And then she eased down in bed and took his shaft into her mouth. He grabbed hold of her shoulders to pull her back up, but she figured the feel of her lips and tongue pleasuring him enticed him to change his mind. Instead he let his fingers tunnel through the curls on her head as he began groaning deep in his throat.

"Hunter! You got to stop. I'm about to come."

She recalled giving him a similar warning one night that he'd ignored just like she intended to do. Instead of stopping, she took him deeper and suckled him right into an orgasm.

"Hunter!"

A short while later she lifted her head and looked up at him and smiled. In her heart she knew she loved him but he would never know.

"You, Hunter McKay, are a naughty girl," he said throatily.

"And you, Tyson Steele," she said, licking her lips, "are one delicious man."

"Tell me about your ex-husband," Tyson said, holding Hunter in his arms. It had taken him a minute to recover from the orgasm she'd given him. It had been explosive and left his entire body reeling.

Hunter lifted her head and he could see the surprise in her eyes. If she found his request odd, then she wasn't alone. He'd never asked a woman about her ex. Usually her past didn't matter. It certainly didn't have any bearing on the present. But with Hunter it mattered. He'd seen Carter Robinson tonight and other than what Eli had told him, Tyson didn't know everything the man had done.

She didn't say anything for a long moment, and then she finally spoke. "I guess after tonight I owe you an explanation."

"No explanation needed. You told me why you needed him to see us together. The heartstrings thing.

But I want to know about him. I'm having a hard time understanding what man in his right mind would let such a passionate woman like you get away."

She snuggled deeper in his arms, as if she needed his closeness to tell him what he wanted to know. "That's just it. Carter never thought of me as passionate." She paused a moment. "We met at a party a couple of years after I finished grad school. We dated for a year and he asked me to marry him. I thought we were perfect together. We shared the same profession and the same dreams and goals. Three years after we were married I discovered he was having an affair with a former client. He asked for my forgiveness, said it wouldn't happen again. But it did. By then he didn't care that I knew and said if I left him I would have more to lose than he did. I believed him, so I stayed, although we didn't share a bed. I moved into the guest room."

She drew in a deep breath. "Things continued that way for two years until I hired a private investigator who uncovered a number of things, including the fact that while I slept in the guest room upstairs, Carter would on occasion sneak his mistress into the house to spend the night with her in our bed."

Anger flared through Tyson at the thought of any man disrespecting his wife that way. No wonder she had a problem with sharing a bed with him where she'd known other women had been before her. "Did you confront him about it?"

"Yes, and I told him I was divorcing him. He laughed, and said I didn't have the backbone to do such a thing. He saw how wrong he was the day he was served the divorce papers. Everyone turned against me for divorcing him. His family. People I thought were our friends. And then on top of all that, he set out to hurt me by taking my clients and making things difficult for me in Boston." She drew in a deep breath. "In a way my brother's request that I come home to help with our parents gave me the perfect excuse to return to Phoenix to start over."

While he listened, Hunter also told him how during her marriage her ex had tried eroding what little self-confidence she had. How he had tried making it seem that his involvement with other women was her fault and how he'd tried controlling her. "And to think Carter actually believed I could still love him and he could get me back after all he did." He could hear the sadness in her voice as she spoke.

Tyson didn't say anything as he continued to hold her in his arms. He felt a huge sense of protectiveness swell inside him where Hunter was concerned, and knew at that moment he would never give any man the chance to hurt her ever again.

Chapter 17

"What's this I hear about you making a fool of yourself with a woman, Tyson? You've been seen around town on several occasions, taking her to dinner, movies, dancing and concerts. I even heard you attended church with her one Sunday."

Tyson had known when he'd opened the door to find Mercury standing there that there had to be a reason for his visit. "And what of it?"

"Acting all infatuated with a woman is not like you."

Yes, Tyson agreed. Mercury was right, it wasn't like him. But he had discovered his interest in Hunter had gone beyond just the physical. It was a lot more than being possessed by the passion they could generate, as he'd assumed. What was supposed to last only one week was now going into its third week. Neither he nor

Hunter had brought up the fact that the one-week time limit had expired. They both seemed to be intentionally overlooking it.

Because of the ground rules she'd established, all their time together hadn't been in the bedroom. They were doing other things, activities he would not have bothered doing with a woman. In addition to movies, dinner and dancing, they'd taken walks in the park, gone to the zoo, tried mountain climbing…and he'd even made an appearance at church. During the course of that time he had gotten to know Hunter in ways he hadn't thought possible. He knew her likes, her dislikes, things she tolerated and things she considered not up for negotiation. Likewise, he'd opened himself up to her as well. He felt comfortable telling her about his days at the hospital, and he even let her in on the Steele brothers' early plans for their parents' fortieth wedding anniversary.

This morning before leaving her bed he had been able to put the final piece of the puzzle in place. Now he knew why she had gotten under his skin, why he'd let her stay there and why he hadn't been able to get her out of his system. And why with her he felt possessed by passion. Bottom line was that he had fallen in love with her.

He'd tried convincing himself it was only lust, but he knew that wasn't the case each and every time they made love. Now he fully understood how Galen, Eli and Jonas felt about the women they'd fallen in love with and married. And as hard as it was to believe, he had no problem being included in that group, mainly because he couldn't consider his life without Hunter as a part of it.

"Tyson, are you listening to me?"

He really hadn't been. "Sorry, what did you say?"

"I asked who she is."

Tyson had no problem giving his brother a name. "Hunter McKay."

Mercury lifted a brow. Tyson could tell from his brother's expression he was recalling the time Hunter's name had come up during one of their parents' Thursday night dinners.

"Well, I hope you have a good reason for what you're doing."

He met his brother's stare. "Trust me. I do."

After Mercury left, Tyson knew exactly what he needed to do. He pulled out his cell phone to place a call. "Hi, Mom. Would it be a problem to set out an extra place setting for dinner tonight? You will be happy to know I've found the woman who will be permanently filling one of those three empty spots at the table."

"The flowers are beautiful."

Hunter had to agree with Pauline. The huge bouquet of red roses that had been delivered to her that morning was simply beautiful. She didn't have to read the card to know that Tyson had sent them. They had gone over their one-week agreement and were now into a third. She figured their time together had come to an end and the flowers were his parting gift to her.

Before leaving her apartment this morning he'd asked if he could decide where they would go tonight.

She didn't have a problem with his request. He hadn't said where they would be going. All he'd said was to dress casual and be ready at six.

Then she had arrived at work to see the flowers sitting on her desk. It had been years since she'd received flowers and like she told Pauline they were simply beautiful, although their suspected meaning caused a pain in her heart.

After Pauline left Hunter's office she sat behind her desk and drew in a deep breath. She'd been hoping…

What? That like her, Tyson would continue to ignore that they'd gone beyond the week they were to spend together? That he would claim she still wasn't out of his system, that he still felt possessed by passion and wanted more time together? Maybe that's what she was hoping, but unfortunately, the flowers were a clear indication that he had gotten over her and was now ready to move on.

Once again she had fallen in love with a man who would never truly love her in return. Story of her life, it seemed. But she would get over it because whether Tyson realized it or not, these past three weeks had meant everything to her. They had reinforced her belief in herself and she owed that to him.

He had made every single day with him special. Instead of protesting about anything she'd had on their list for them to do, he had readily embraced every activity. Whether it was going out to dinner, movies, concerts or dancing, he didn't seem to have a problem being seen with her. He'd even kept his word to her mother and gone to church with her. And because they had sat together, more than one pair of curious eyes had been on them.

The buzzer on her desk sounded. "Yes, Pauline?"

"Dr. Steele is on the line."

"Thanks." Was he calling to cancel tonight? Had he figured there was no need to wait until later to end things between them?

"Yes, Tyson?"

"Have you had lunch yet?"

"No."

"Good. I'll pick you up in a few minutes. There's something I want you to see."

He sounded rather mysterious but she went along with him. "Okay."

She hung up her phone, wondering what Tyson wanted her to see.

"Where are we going?"

Tyson smiled over at Hunter. He figured she would be curious since he hadn't given her much information. They had left the Phoenix city limits and were now headed toward the outskirts of town. "I think I've mentioned my cousin Morgan Steele to you before."

"He's the one who's the mayor of Charlotte, right?"

"Yes. His wife, Lena, owns a real estate company that has expanded into several states, including this one. I hired her to find some property in the country for me."

Hunter raised a brow. "Why?"

"To build that house you designed for me."

She frowned. "Tyson, we both know why you had me draw up those plans."

"Do we?" He knew Hunter thought she had things figured out.

"Of course. That was just a part of your plan to seduce me."

"Was it?"

Her frown deepened. "Okay, Tyson. What kind of game are you playing?"

A smile touched his lips. "No game. What if I told you I was dead serious about those house plans?"

"That would be news to me. Until today you haven't mentioned those plans since I gave them to you over a month ago."

Tyson brought his car to a stop in front of a wooded piece of property. He looked over at her. "I guess you can say I was waiting for a good time to do so."

The male in him appreciated her outfit. Today she was wearing another dress and although it wasn't as short as he'd like, it still showed off her gorgeous legs.

He glanced out the car window. "This is the property Lena found for me. What do you think?"

Hunter glanced around. She thought the land was pretty nice and told him so. Even from the car she could see a view of the mountains. The drive hadn't been too far from town, which wouldn't make his commute to the hospital too much of a hassle. Once he got on the interstate it would be a straight shot and he could get to work probably within twenty minutes.

"It's twenty-five acres on a private road," he said, intruding into her thoughts. "Not another house around for at least ten miles, and I think I'll like the seclusion. There's a huge lake on the property and plenty of trees."

"I think you'll like the seclusion, too," she said, not missing the excitement in his voice.

He pushed the button to extend his seat back to stretch out his legs. "Any ideas how the house will fit on it?"

Hunter shrugged as she glanced out the window again. "It shouldn't be a problem if you face the front of your house to the east. That way your bedrooms can take advantage of the view of the lake and mountains from any window."

He nodded. "I'm thinking of increasing the square footage to add a few more bedrooms. When I marry and have children I want to make sure they have plenty of space."

Personally, Hunter thought the house she'd designed had more than enough space already. However, if he thought he needed more than that, it was his business. She tried dismissing from her mind that this was the first time he'd ever mentioned a wife and children. He'd claimed he had no interest in ever getting married. Even when he'd given her specifics for what he wanted in a home, the subject of a wife and children had never entered the equation. "You're the client," she said. "I can modify the plans any way you want."

"I hope I'm more than just a client to you, Hunter."

Hunter nibbled on her bottom lip, not sure how to address that comment. She couldn't help but remember the roses sitting on her desk and what they probably meant.

"Thanks for the roses, by the way."

"You're welcome. Glad you liked them."

She drew in a deep breath. Even now while sitting in a parked car in a secluded area she could feel the chemistry between them. It seemed over the past few weeks, instead of diminishing, their physical attraction had gotten stronger. That would probably account for why their lovemaking was even more intense every night.

Tyson claimed he wasn't playing games, but for some reason she felt that he was. She was about to tell him so when he said, "You didn't respond to what I said about me being more than a client to you."

She studied him and then decided to turn the tables on him. "My response depends on whether I'm more than an architect to you."

Tyson knew he could put her mind to rest about that and intended to do so. He wasn't sure how she felt about him, but he figured any woman who'd given him as much of herself as she had during the time they'd spent together had to feel something for him.

He reached out and took her hand. "Hunter, there's something I need to say."

She pulled her hand away from him. "You don't have to say anything. I got the message with the roses."

He raised a brow. "And just what message did you get?"

"That you want us to end things."

He didn't say anything for a minute, and then he asked, "And you got that message from me sending you roses?"

"I had an employee back in Boston years ago. When

her boyfriend broke up with her, instead of sending her a 'Dear Jane' letter, he sent her a dozen 'Dear Jane' roses."

"And you figured that's what I did?"

"Isn't it?"

"No. You're right about me wanting us to end things…at least, wanting to end this phase of our relationship. But only for a new beginning."

She nodded. "I get it. You want another week."

He chuckled. "No, Hunter. I want forever." Tyson watched her face and wasn't surprised when shock spread across her features. He was tempted to lean over and kiss it right off her face.

"Forever?"

He nodded, watching her closely. "Yes, forever."

She evidently wasn't sure they were on the same page, because she asked, "You mean forever as in till death do us part?"

He chuckled. "Yes, that pretty much sums it up."

She stared at him like he had suddenly developed some kind of mental problem. "Why?"

"That's easy to answer. Because I've fallen in love with you."

She continued to stare at him for a long moment and then she shook her head. "That's impossible."

"And why is it impossible?"

"B-because you're Tyson Steele."

"I know who I am."

She glared at him. "Need I remind you that you're a man who goes through women quicker than you change your socks?"

"Last time I looked you're the only woman I've been with in well over a month now. I told you that I hadn't desired another woman since that night I ran into you at Notorious."

"But our relationship has been only physical."

"I beg to differ. Think about what we've been doing for the past few weeks. What we've shared. I've enjoyed spending time with you and doing things that had nothing to do with the bedroom."

When she didn't say anything he added, "I appreciate the time that we've gotten to know each other. Now more than ever I know you're the woman I want in my life."

When she didn't say anything but continued to stare at him, he pressed on. "I know I've laid a lot on the table and you need time to take it all in. I also know you probably don't reciprocate my feelings but I feel strongly that one day you will."

Hunter could not believe the words Tyson had spoken. He loved her? Really loved her as much as she loved him? She tried hard to fight back tears. "But I already do," she said, swiping the tears that were determined to fall anyway.

"You do what?"

"Reciprocate your feelings. I love you, too, Tyson. I think I fell in love with you the first time we made love. You made me feel so special. Like a woman who was truly appreciated. But not in a million years did I think you would, or could, love me back. You have... shall we say, a history with women."

"Yes, I do. But you effectively destroyed that history. You're the only woman I want. The only woman I could and will ever love."

More than anything she wanted to believe him, but hadn't Carter told her that same thing? But then, hadn't she discovered that Tyson wasn't anything like Carter?

"Hunter, will you marry me?"

She blinked. "Marry you?"

He nodded. "Yes."

"But how can you be sure that I'm the woman you want to spend your life with?"

He smiled. "I'm sure. Trust me, I fought it. Marrying anyone was the last thing on my mind, but my dad was right."

"About what?"

"Jonas said Dad once told him that a smart man knows there's nothing wrong with falling in love if it's a woman you can't live your life without. And I can't live my life without you, Hunter."

She wanted so much to believe him. "But what about those other women?"

"They don't matter. Not one of them had me possessed by passion. But you do, Hunter. I believe a man knows he's run his course with other women when they no longer interest him and none of them is more important to him than the one he wants to wake up with every morning and make memories with forever. And that's you."

He paused a moment to clear his throat. "So, I'm asking again. Hunter McKay, will you marry me? Will you be the only woman in my life? The one to share this

house I'm building for us here on this property? The
only one I want to be the mother of my children? The
only one I want to wear the name of Mrs. Tyson Steele?"

At that moment, numerous emotions ran through
Hunter and she knew what her answer to him would
be. He was the only man she wanted in her life as well.
"Yes, Tyson. I will marry you."

A huge smile curved Tyson's lips and he leaned
over and captured her mouth with his. Shivers raced
all through her body from the way his mouth was devouring hers. He was building passion neither of them
could contain. And when he slid his arms around her
waist to pull her over the console and into his lap, she
followed his lead and returned the kiss with the same
sexual hunger. Their tongues mated hotly, greedily. The
degree of her desire for Tyson always astounded her,
made her appreciate that she was a woman who wanted
this man. And just to know he loved her as much as she
loved him sent her soaring to the moon.

Moments later when the need to breathe overrode everything else, she pulled back from the kiss. He reached
up and traced his finger across her moist lips. "I can sit
here and kiss you all day," he said huskily.

"Umm, I prefer we do something else," she said leaning in to trail feathery kisses along the corners of his
lips and chin.

"Something like what?"

"This," she said, climbing over his seat into the back
and grabbing his hand to entice him to follow. He did.
And then she shoved him on his back and straddled him.

"We can start here. We never got around to doing it in the backseat of your car eighteen years ago."

He chuckled softly as his hands grabbed hold of her thighs, easing her dress up nearly to her waist. "Back then you were a good girl."

"Now I'm bad," she said, pulling his zipper down. "Tyson's naughty girl."

"Soon to be his naughty wife," he said and then sucked in a deep breath when she reached inside his pants and took the solid thickness of his erection in her hand. When she began stroking him he released a guttural moan.

"You did say this is a private road, right?" she asked.

"Yes, it's very private."

"Good."

She opened her legs to cradle him and then remembered something. "Condom."

"Here," he said after working a packet out of his back pocket.

She took her time to sheathe him the way she'd seen him do many times. When he eased her panties aside she slid down, releasing a deep moan when the head of his erection touched her center just seconds before he tightened his hold on her hips and slowly entered her.

It was as if he was savoring the moment, though for her it was pure torture. She needed all of him now. She leaned in and bit him gently on the lips. In retaliation he thrust hard into her, melding their bodies.

"I thought that would get you going," she said, licking the mark her teeth had made on his lips.

Instead of responding he began moving, stroking her

insides, thrusting in and out, over and over again. Never had she felt so thoroughly made love to except for with Tyson. He had the ability to make her purr, yearn and become obsessed with everything he was doing to her.

"Hunter!"

When he screamed her name, she knew his world had tipped over the edge and hers would soon follow. He continued to stroke her while groaning out his pleasure. And she moaned, saying his name on a breathless groan, as the two of them were tossed into waves of pure ecstasy.

When Hunter found the energy to lift her head from his chest, she met his gaze. Their bodies were still intimately connected, and sexual chemistry, as explosive as it could get, still flowed between them the way it always did. A flirty smile touched her lips. "Let's do it again, Tyson," she said, leaning in close to lick the underside of his neck.

He smiled at her. "Yes, let's do it again. And then we'll go to the jewelry store for your engagement ring."

Epilogue

A beautiful day in August

Hunter couldn't stop looking down at the wedding ring Tyson had slid on her finger. It was beautiful. And then she glanced up at him. He was beautiful, as well.

"Tyson, will you repeat after me," the pastor said, reclaiming her attention. "With this ring, I thee wed."

Tyson held her gaze as he repeated the pastor's words loud and clear. She couldn't stop the tears from rolling down her cheeks. Mo and Kat would kill her for messing up a perfectly made-up face, but she couldn't help it. It was her wedding day and she could cry if she wanted to.

"By the power vested in me by this great state of Arizona, I now pronounce you husband and wife. Tyson, you may kiss your bride."

She smiled as he pulled her into his arms, sealing their vows with a kiss. When he released her he swept her off her feet as the pastor introduced them. "Dr. and Mrs. Tyson Steele."

As he carried her out the church while holding her in his arms, somewhere in the audience Hunter heard a voice say, "Another Bad News Steele bites the dust."

She tightened her arm around Tyson's neck, grateful that this particular Steele was hers.

Tyson tried to keep the smile off his face as he spoke with his brothers. "We're happy for you, man," Gannon said. "Hunter is wonderful."

"I think she's wonderful, too." He glanced over at Mercury. "Sorry, but the heat is going to be on you two guys. Maybe it won't be so bad since Eli and Stacey announced they are having a baby. That might keep Mom occupied for a while."

Mercury chuckled. "We can only hope. And I agree with Gannon. Hunter is great for you. She makes you happy and we can see it."

"Yes, I'm a very happy man." Tyson took a sip of his wine while glancing around Hunter's parents' beautifully decorated backyard. He and Hunter had decided on an outdoor wedding with only family and close friends. He saw his wife of one hour standing in a group talking to the wives of his cousins from Charlotte.

It was time for their first dance together as husband and wife. "Excuse me, guys."

He headed across the patio and as if she sensed his approach, Hunter glanced up and met his gaze. She smiled, excused herself from the group and met him halfway.

"Dr. Steele."

"Mrs. Steele. Ready for our first dance together?" he asked, taking her hand in his.

"Yes, I am ready."

"The sooner we can start our honeymoon the better," he said. They would be flying to Aruba, where they would spend the next two weeks.

"You sound rather anxious."

"I'll show you how anxious I am once I strip you naked," he said, leading her to the area designated for the dance floor.

Hunter lifted her head from Tyson's chest as they shared their first dance as husband and wife. "I never wanted to marry again, Tyson, but you made me change my mind about that."

He smiled down at her. "And I didn't want to ever marry but I was a man possessed and I couldn't do anything about it, sweetheart. You stole my heart before I knew what was happening."

She couldn't help but be filled with love for this man, who continued to show her what true love was about. He was the one who went out of his way to make her feel that she was everything a woman should be. Worthy of his love. Hunter couldn't help but remember that day they'd made love in the backseat of his car. Afterward, he had taken her to Lola's, one of the most exclusive jewelers in Phoenix. Together they had selected her engagement ring—a beautiful four-carat cushion diamond with a halo setting—as well as their diamond band wedding rings.

That evening he had surprised her by taking her to his parents' home to take part in the family's Thursday night dinner. Tyson's parents and the rest of the family had congratulated them, and of course the women had fallen in love with her engagement ring. Dinner had been special and since that night she'd been included in the Steeles' Thursday night dinners. She loved his parents and loved getting to know all of Tyson's brothers, as well as their wives.

"What are you thinking about, sweetheart?" Tyson asked, leaning down to whisper close to her ear.

"I was thinking just what a lucky woman I am."

"I feel lucky as well. You are everything I could ever want, Hunter."

He pulled her closer into his arms. He couldn't wait to be in their new home, dancing in their own backyard. Already the property had been cleared and construction had begun. According to the builder, they should be ready to move into their dream home in about six months.

"There are only two single Steeles now," Hunter observed, seeing Mercury and Gannon standing in a group talking with their cousins from Charlotte.

"I know, and I can't wait to meet the women who make them believe in a forever kind of love," Tyson said. "They're going to find out the same thing I did. You can't run from love."

Then he leaned down and captured her mouth with his, ignoring the claps and catcalls from their audience. When he released her mouth, she pulled in a deep breath. "What was that for?"

He chuckled. "Don't you know, baby? I am a man possessed. Not only am I possessed by your passion, I'm also possessed by your love."

Hunter sank closer into her husband's embrace and smiled up at him. "And I'm possessed by yours."

* * * * *

LET'S TALK

Romance

For exclusive extracts, competitions
and special offers, find us online:

- facebook.com/millsandboon
- @MillsandBoon
- @MillsandBoonUK

Get in touch on 01413 063232

For all the latest titles coming soon, visit
millsandboon.co.uk/nextmonth

MILLS & BOON

THE HEART OF ROMANCE

A ROMANCE FOR EVERY READER

MODERN

Prepare to be swept off your feet by sophisticated, sexy and seductive heroes, in some of the world's most glamourous and romantic locations, where power and passion collide.

HISTORICAL

Escape with historical heroes from time gone by. Whether your passion is for wicked Regency Rakes, muscled Vikings or rugged Highlanders, awak the romance of the past.

MEDICAL

Set your pulse racing with dedicated, delectable doctors in the high-pres-sure world of medicine, where emotions run high and passion, comfort an love are the best medicine.

True Love

Celebrate true love with tender stories of heartfelt romance, from the rush of falling in love to the joy a new baby can bring, and a focus on the emotional heart of a relationship.

Desire

Indulge in secrets and scandal, intense drama and plenty of sizzling hot action with powerful and passionate heroes who have it all: wealth, status, good looks…everything but the right woman.

HEROES

Experience all the excitement of a gripping thriller, with an intense ro-mance at its heart. Resourceful, true-to-life women and strong, fearless me face danger and desire - a killer combination!

To see which titles are coming soon, please visit

millsandboon.co.uk/nextmonth

JOIN US ON SOCIAL MEDIA!

Stay up to date with our latest releases, author news and gossip, special offers and discounts, and all the behind-the-scenes action from Mills & Boon...

 millsandboon

 millsandboonuk

 millsandboon

It might just be true love...

MILLS & BOON

MODERN

Power and Passion

Prepare to be swept off your feet by sophisticated, sexy and seductive heroes, in some of the world's most glamourous and romantic locations, where power and passion collide.